Praise for

Farrell Covington

and the

Limits of Style

"Dazzling and funny . . . [Rudnick] proves himself to be in top form, and each page is loaded with quippy dialogue and winning character work. This is a roaring good time."

—*Publishers Weekly* (starred review)

"I loved *Farrell Covington and the Limits of Style*. Just ate up every word; it will make a Rudnick fan out of every reader. No funnier, wiser, or more charming book will come out this year, I guarantee. So what are you waiting for? Get it!"

—Andrew Sean Greer, Pulitzer Prize–winning author of
Less and *Less Is Lost*

"This is precisely the novel I've been dying for this year, a case study in elegant, honest tragicomedy. And it's also by the genuinely hilarious Paul Rudnick, so you know at least every other sentence is going to lay you out on your side, gasping for air, or at least another martini."

—Gary Shteyngart, *New York Times* bestselling author of
Our Country Friends

"Rudnick writes with such engaging wit, side-eyed perceptiveness, and barbed élan, with such irrepressible life, that before you quite notice the shadings of loss, mortality and poignant retrospection in his new novel, they have already touched you with their power."

—Michael Chabon, *New York Times* bestselling author of
Moonglow and *The Amazing Adventures of Kavalier & Clay*

"If you believe that there should be more pleasure, more style (high and low), and more genuine wit in this world, then read *Farrell Covington and the Limits of Style*. If you don't, I am sorry for you and if anyone cares for you, even a little, they will run out and get you this joyful and snarky, life-affirming, love-celebrating novel."

—Amy Bloom, *New York Times* bestselling author of *In Love*

ALSO BY PAUL RUDNICK

Fiction

Playing the Palace

I'll Take It

Social Disease

Nonfiction

I Shudder

If You Ask Me (as Libby Gelman-Waxner)

Farrell Covington
and the
Limits of Style

A NOVEL

Paul Rudnick

WASHINGTON
SQUARE PRESS

ATRIA

New York   London   Toronto   Sydney   New Delhi

WASHINGTON
SQUARE PRESS

ATRIA

An Imprint of Simon & Schuster, LLC
1230 Avenue of the Americas
New York, NY 10020

First Washington Square Press/Atria Paperback edition April 2024

WASHINGTON SQUARE PRESS / ATRIA PAPERBACK and colophon are trademarks of Simon & Schuster, LLC

Simon & Schuster: Celebrating 100 Years of Publishing in 2024

For information about special discounts for bulk purchases, please contact Simon & Schuster Special Sales at 1-866-506-1949 or business@simonandschuster.com.

The Simon & Schuster Speakers Bureau can bring authors to your live event. For more information or to book an event, contact the Simon & Schuster Speakers Bureau at 1-866-248-3049 or visit our website at www.simonspeakers.com.

Interior design by Jill Putorti

Manufactured in the United States of America

1 3 5 7 9 10 8 6 4 2

Library of Congress Cataloging-in-Publication Data is available.

ISBN 978-1-6680-0467-8
ISBN 978-1-6680-0473-9 (pbk)
ISBN 978-1-6680-0468-5 (ebook)

I assume this book is dedicated to me.

—FARRELL COVINGTON

1

When I arrived at Yale, I had no idea who Farrell Covington was. In 1973, as a middle-class kid from the New Jersey suburbs, I had no idea who anyone was.

As the child of an office manager mom and a physicist dad, I'd been encouraged to apply to Ivy League schools but with Jewish fears attached. I should strive to succeed but expect obstacles. As a gay kid, my image of Yale was based on Cole Porter songs, satiric novels with upper-crust characters named Tad and Muffie, and photos of any university, from Oxford to Harvard, with stalwart brick buildings surrounding leafy, sun-dappled courtyards strolled by students wearing button-downs with Shetland sweaters knotted around their hips, along with news footage of fist-pumping, shaggy-haired undergraduates of the sixties staging die-ins atop the steps of the law schools they were attending.

I was installed in a dormitory suite shared by Breen, a tall, scowling über-Republican who'd already draped an American flag outside our window, and Walt, an affable and outgoing guy from Connecticut who, while sheepishly enjoying golf, also played bass in a band called the Wild Stockbrokers. I'd never lived with anyone but my family, and I was dimly aware of my freakishness, from wearing thrift store gabardine shirts to sporting the blow-dried, feathered mall hair of my Jersey heritage.

My exposure to gay life consisted of the following artifacts: best-selling Gordon Merrick paperback novels, where dashing, strong-bodied men, often surgeons and senators, would rut lustily with each other in penthouses on champagne-colored silk sheets; *After Dark* magazine, which, while not officially gay (so it could be sold on newsstands), detailed every aspect of show business with an eye to placing seminude male ballet and Broadway dancers on the cover, shielding their crotches with, say, a straw boater or a violin; and porn magazines called *Inches* or *Blueboy* or *David's Thing*, which I'd buy at fluorescent-lit Times Square smut shops and tuck into the lining of my fake-fur parka for the train ride back to Piscataway, a town named for the Piscataqua River in New Hampshire. Not making sense doesn't bother anyone in New Jersey.

I never felt guilty about my reading habits. I adored these varied publications and took them as proof that glamorous, sexual gay lives existed. Gorgeously lit black-and-white photography, along with stapled pages of raunchier, hard-core doggy-style couplings, were delicious promises.

I was a virgin in so many ways, innocent of physical sex (except for constant masturbation), Brooks Brothers madras patchwork blazers, natural blonds, and, especially, the seriously wealthy. The richest person in Piscataway was a contractor and low-level mobster who'd built his own stucco-drenched, faux Mediterranean compound with an in-ground pool and a three-car garage to hold the van enameled with flames, the Chevy station wagon, and a few mammoth Harley-Davidsons. In New Jersey, money meant not taste but more stuff. For my family, money was something to be strenuously fretted over, encompassing mortgages, used cars, and two August weeks at a beach house far from an actual beach; none of this could be debated in front of me and my older brother. I was the recipient of student loans, which I had no real grasp of. I knew we weren't rich, but I'd never lacked for anything except a Barbie doll, which a well-timed tantrum eventually achieved.

Glossing over things, and hurriedly ending adult conversations when a child wandered in, was my family's rule for anything monetary, sexual, or grim (for example, illnesses and deaths). This agonizing politeness and denial could be suffocating, but weirdly helpful for a gay teenager: no one was asking me any squirm-inducing questions.

Knowing no one, I spent my first weeks at Yale investigating the campus, walking everywhere and wondering if I'd ever make any friends. I had vague theatrical ambitions, as an actor or playwright or simply someone who'd call other people "darling," so I pushed myself to attend a freshman orientation at the Yale Dramat, the largest and most well-funded drama club, which availed itself of a gloomy but full-sized theater ordinarily the province of the illustrious graduate drama school. (Meryl Streep and Sigourney Weaver were enrolled at the time, and yes, just from watching them in misbegotten Chekhov and midnight cabarets, everyone predicted where they were headed. People who'd never met them, and never would, were already referring to these performers as "Meryl" and "Siggy.")

As I perched on the arm of a battered leather greenroom couch, two seniors introduced thirty assembled wannabes to the joys of painting scenery, taking box office ticket requests, hand-laundering costumes, and other forms of grunt work. "We have a proud history here at the Dramat," chirped the female senior, a perky administrative type in a Fair Isle cardigan, kilt, and knee socks. "And we also have a heckuva lot of fun," added her more bohemian male counterpart, wearing white Levi's and a stretched-out black cotton turtleneck, aiming for James Dean in moody rehearsal wear and landing as a preppie who dared to smoke pot in his parents' finished basement.

"Oh my," said a voice that had the oddest and most elegant calibration of Midwestern graciousness and crisp New England diction. It was a voice that could only be classified as mid-Atlantic, that invented MGM mode of sounding unplaceably fancy, as if the person was forever flinging open the double doors to a well-appointed drawing room. The voice was maddeningly but somehow naturally affected, as if the person had been raised by a bottle of good whiskey and a crystal chandelier.

"Look at all of you," the voice continued, and the crowd swiveled to see someone vanish from the greenroom doorway, a WASPy blur in khakis, a navy blazer, something hot pink, and something Kelly green, like a well-bred magic trick.

A week later I was splayed across an armchair at the cross-campus library, pretending to read Aeschylus, when the same person materialized from the stacks, like a ghost in a cornfield, coming off as disoriented yet regal, a pedigreed hound sniffing the breeze for a hint of fox or hare. He stared at me and flung himself onto an adjoining armchair.

"You must save me," he said, in a lower, raspy octave of his impeccably modulated voice.

"From what?"

"From myself, of course."

For the first time in my life, I felt like I might have a life. No one in Piscataway talked like this. Or took my hand like this. Or lowered his chin like this and gazed directly into my eyes.

"I saw you," he said, "at that theatrical organization, at whatever that was. I was intrigued yet afraid, of all that yearning for aesthetic grandeur and all that bad skin."

"Who are you?"

"Farrell Covington. And I may very well be in love with you. Madly in love. Hopelessly in love. Whom would you like me to kill?"

I didn't know how to take any of this: Was he joking? Was he mocking me, or fabricating a conversation because someone else was following him? His gaze held and he seemed sincere or deranged or both, all of which struck me as seriously sexy. Although at a virginal eighteen, the touch of anyone not related to me could become instantly arousing.

"We need to have sex," he said.

Oh my God. Was I hallucinating, from loneliness and porn and those soft-core paperback romances, had I manifested this guy from so many nights of jerking off into an old pair of Jockey shorts, which had become my encrusted teenage equivalent of a toddler's beloved blankie?

I called upon whatever courage I could fake and looked back at him. Looking Farrell in the eye became my first adult act, as if I was leaping the threshold from cosseted Jersey safety into adult desire. Farrell was ridiculously stunning; he was the male model whose photo comes with the sterling silver frame. He was a golden age movie idol who'd never made a film, an Arrow shirt collar ad come heartbreakingly to life.

He was too much, a luxurious prototype never meant to be manufactured, only dreamt of by collectors. His lush, dewy handsomeness disconcerted everyone, even himself. I've since noticed this effect in the truly beautiful, in men and women distressed by their own good luck, as if, through no fault of their own, they'd inherited billions and aren't sure how to spend it.

To be more specific: Farrell wasn't simply my cultural opposite, a blinding sun god to counter my pale, Jewish, brown-haired, generous-nosed eagerness. He was a genetic accident, a green-eyed, six-foot-three-inch, broad-shouldered gift, and yes, there were dimples when he smiled, something that, I later discovered, was an effective means of dealing with law enforcement. He didn't own that blank, lacrosse-ready dopiness of a New England jock; he was something more sensual, alert, and generous. He was a dangerously friendly oil portrait of some blond Venetian prince, the picture everyone at the museum wants to date, or at least buy a postcard of.

"I must go," he said, withdrawing his hand, as if it were dawn and we'd already had sex multiple times and his wife and children were waiting at their restored colonial in Greenwich.

He stood and left without another word, with the quick, shambling stride of someone still navigating a fabulous growth spurt. As I watched him go I registered his white polo shirt, with the collar carelessly and unevenly raised (a gesture that had undoubtedly taken many generations of Covingtons to perfect), his rumpled cream-colored cotton pants with rolled-up cuffs, and his exquisitely thin, perfectly battered, sockless, ivory-toned kidskin loafers, the sort called driving shoes, with pebbled soles—these are shoes for people who don't partake of any blue-collar walking, shoes for people with a shoe wardrobe, and shoes for people who break their shoes in privately, to deflect being caught wearing anything crudely brand-new. These were, in short, the shoes of the rich and the damned. Just from Farrell stalking away I was absorbing so much, including the fact that at any given moment in history, and excluding nurses and brides, there are only at most three people on the planet who can get away with wearing all white, and Farrell was at least two of them.

I didn't see him again until a month later when he pounded on the door of my suite at 2 a.m., waking everyone—the suite had two tiny bedrooms, and I'd moved my narrow metal bed into a corner of the communal sitting room rather than bunk with Breen. He and I were cordial but wary, and Walt had told me Breen was pretty sure I was at least a socialist, because I read *People* magazine.

I opened the front door and Farrell plummeted in. He might've been drunk, but as in our earlier encounters, Farrell was always wrestling with unseen forces, or maybe dancing with them. He stretched full out on my disheveled bed and freshman-fragrant sheets.

"I'm trying to get some shut-eye," said Breen, at his doorway in a junior version of his dad's freshly laundered and starched Christmas morning tartan pajamas.

"Everything okay?" asked Walt, bleary-eyed at his own door, in a limp prep school T-shirt and boxers.

"Are these your male lovers?" Farrell demanded, as I stood in between everyone, in my Piscataway High black-and-gold T-shirt and matching gym shorts; I hadn't yet caught on to how such garments could be fetishized by gay men in their thirties, who often dress as their favorite porn archetypes. As a rule, the boys who despised gym class and intramural soccer will later prize and pay dearly for athletic wear, as if it was a more rugged, locker room–seduction Chanel.

"What did he just say? Are we your lovers?" asked Breen, offended by Farrell's question on so many Christian levels.

"Guys? What's going on?" asked a fellow freshman who lived across the hall, clustered with his own two roommates, all in the sagging terrycloth, acne medication–stained bathrobes their parents had supplied. For many guys, freshman year is the last time they'll ever wear a bathrobe, or underwear, or anything their mom sewed a name tag into.

"Is this a forbidden homosexual orgy in progress?" Farrell wondered. "Was there a sign-up sheet?"

"Everyone, it's okay, go back to bed," I said, and then, hearing my mom's good manners in my head, "this is Farrell, he's a friend, sort of."

"Farrell Covington?" asked Breen, wide awake and galvanized. "Of the Wichita Covingtons and Covington Industries?"

"You may fondle me, gently," Farrell told Breen, extending his arm, highlighting his undoubtedly real, substantial gold ring set with a chunky, elevator button–sized emerald. As Breen wavered between shaking or kissing Farrell's hand, he held back, asking me, "How do you know him?"

"We're about to sodomize one another," Farrell confided, to the room. "Does anyone have a manual, or perhaps a brief educational film, with puppets, to help us go about this?"

The assembled straight boys had no idea how to respond, until Walt smiled and said, "Do you have a napkin and a crayon?"

This earned Farrell's grin. He loved it when someone returned a volley. He stood and told me, "Get dressed. I've spent the past month summoning my courage, so we musn't falter."

I pulled on my jeans and a sweater, and soon we were hiking across campus. It wasn't easy keeping up with the long-legged, determined Farrell.

"Are you drunk?" I asked.

"Never. But everyone in my family, going back eighteen generations, has consumed so much gin that I was most likely born pickled; my mother's amniotic fluid was floating with an olive and a silver Cartier toothpick. So I may very well suffer from fetal alcohol syndrome, or to use the proper Latin terminology, inherited wealth."

We left the campus, halting at a pale yellow brick townhouse in the wide-avenued, fussily landscaped neighborhood reserved for tenured faculty—had Farrell borrowed a room in a professor's home? Were we shattering undergraduate bylaws? Were we really about to have sex, or was this all some elaborate prank or fraternity hazing—would I be spotted hours later, shivering naked and duct-taped at a downtown public park? I was torn between anxiety and adventure. Had my grandparents trekked through Poland and crossed the Atlantic in steerage so I could be degraded by some Mayflower pretty boy?

I'd always had a bubbling imagination, concocting the most extreme and malevolent scenarios in milliseconds. In my brain, I was forever being cornered at gunpoint, shoved flailing out skyscraper windows, and hounded into explaining the meaning of Chanukah onstage in a junior high school auditorium to three hundred gentile cub scouts (this last nightmare had come true).

But I was young, and I'd read somewhere that if anything scares you, the optimum solution is to tackle it head-on and grow stronger from the experience.

The townhouse's carved oak door was opened by a youngish man in a dove-gray three-piece suit and white cotton gloves.

"Mr. Covington," he said, in a decent English accent. He was, I came to know, a third-year acting student in the drama school, making ends meet and building a nest egg before hitting the audition circuit in New York.

"Bates," said Farrell, nodding solemnly. Farrell's essential morality was becoming evident. He later told me, "Respect all staff members. They're usually the only halfway decent human beings in the house."

The townhouse was surprisingly airy, with limewashed antique Swedish furniture and a gallery's worth of modern art, including a wall-sized Hockney of a trim young guy diving into a Malibu swimming pool, with a lovingly rendered splash. I froze, because unlike the Chagall prints and Ben Shahn exhibition posters in my family's tract home, this painting was real and valuable. This was the first time I'd encountered an A-list artwork outside of a museum, and it terrified me, because chances were I'd destroy it. I'd trip and knock the painting off the wall and the canvas would be sliced open by a lamp, or I'd dare myself to touch the painting's surface with a forefinger and unfixably smear a brushstroke. Rich people, and certainly Farrell, could be comfortable with their vaults of irreplaceable goodies, with their heavily insured versions of teen bedroom pop star pinups; but like Farrell himself, the Hockney made me light-headed and ready to flee. But no, I told myself: Face your fear of luxury investments. You can do this. Bring on the Vermeers.

"Where exactly are we?" I asked.

"My home. Darling, you can't possibly imagine that I'd live in one of those, what are they called, dormitory cells? Those undergraduate hellholes? With other people, carrying their sad little mesh bags bulging with drugstore grooming products into some hideously mildewed petri dish of a shower?"

"But . . ."

"Bates?" Farrell called out, and Bates returned with a brass-handled mahogany tray set with a crystal pitcher of orange juice, slim cans of imported sodas, and small, crackled Japanese ceramic bowls of cashews. It was now almost 3 a.m., but no one appeared sleepy. I was wired by the situation so far, I wasn't sure if Farrell ever slept, and Bates was either incapable of fatigue or a really good actor.

After depositing the tray on a molded bronze coffee table/award-winning sculpture, Bates withdrew and Farrell motioned for me to sit beside him on a modular Italian leather sofa facing a Lichtenstein, a benday-dot comic strip of a heartsick secretary whose thought bubble read, "If I can't have him, I'll die! I'll just die!"

"When I pictured you," Farrell told me, "trapped in that squalid freshman abattoir, engulfed by those hormonally deformed boys—I thought only of rescue. I couldn't leave you there."

Freshmen were required to live in the dorms, to ram them into social collisions with a range of fellow students. Undergrads could only choose their roommates, or move off campus, as sophomores, and this rule was absolute. As Breen had stoically related, "Everyone needs to live with someone they hate."

"Of course I've been assigned to some reeking, fetid attic," Farrell went on. "But I've never been there. And this building is in my father's name, so even if some, I don't know, snitty little freshman advisor reports my absence, Yale has no interest in losing the Covington Rare Book Library, the Covington Contemplation Courtyard at the divinity school, or the under-construction Covington Center for the Study of Global Economic Theory, which, according to my father, boils down to 'tipping 5 percent is far more than enough.'"

"So you live in this whole house by yourself? With your—staff?"

"Why are you looking at me like that? As if this is any sort of choice? I need cedar closets, a butler's pantry, and a billiards room. The basics. Believe me, I'm roughing it."

"You're roughing it?"

He steeled himself, raised his palms, and with difficulty, admitted, "No gift-wrapping room. None. Unless I convert the solarium."

On some level Farrell was always kidding, but not deliberately. This was how he talked, in a glittering tumult of satire tinged with social history and cocktail chatter. He relished conversation; he celebrated and savored anointing a shimmeringly pleasing word or phrase, treating the English language as a treasure trove to be plundered. Or more plainly: he loved to talk, and made sure he was good at it. Talking, he'd later inform me, "isn't just my career—I've been called to it. The Lord spoke unto me, and I interrupted Him."

I was undone, by the house, the presence of Bates, and Farrell's swirling attention. To anchor myself, I asked, "What are we doing here?"

"Eek. No. I can't. I'm . . . all right. Don't you understand? All of this, my home, my chitchat, the artful swoop of my hair—it's all subterfuge. Avoidance. An immaculate cover for blind, shrieking alarm. Have you ever had sexual intercourse?"

"You mean, am I a virgin?"

I deliberated, should I do what most virgins do and mumble, "Define sex" or "Not totally" or "That's really personal," which are synonyms for "Of course I'm a virgin. Look at me." But Farrell, for all his expensive exuberance, was being direct, or as direct as he was capable of being. And I didn't want to continue being a virgin. And my brain was pounding, "Now. Now. NOW."

"Yes. I'm a virgin. But not by choice."

"Exactly. Me too. Which is ideal, because we'll have no basis for hurtful comparisons. We won't be thinking, well, he's not Sam or Roger or the Carlsberry twins. Good. Yes. So—how shall we do this?"

"Is there a bedroom?"

"There are five."

"Your bedroom?"

"Yes. Of course. Spot-on. But first—just one thing. Because I want to get this right. Shall we kiss?"

"Yes."

Farrell was flustered, which lent me an unexpected confidence, as if we were collaborating on a science project. As if I had input.

I'd never kissed anyone romantically. I'd nurtured the standard crushes, on clueless swimmers and hunky young English teachers with acoustic guitars and rolled-up sleeves (to show off their nicely muscled forearms), and a tattooed, rawboned ex–heroin addict who'd lectured a bored high school assembly on getting clean, while I fixated on the sinewy thighs barely constrained by his upright-citizen beige polyester pants. I was so young that I didn't have a type, not yet. That's the real gift of being young: You have no taste. You're indiscriminately horny. You want to fuck everything.

But I'd never kissed anybody, not out of timidity, but from a sheer lack of prospects. I'd had no interest in dating, let alone kissing, even the most appealing, most willing, and most understanding girls. This would have been not just deceptive but exhausting. But try as I might, I couldn't locate any other gay people (this was long before hookup apps or even single earrings on men). Years later, via Facebook, I unearthed similarly disgruntled gay classmates, some now married to each other, but in high school we were isolated and unaware of secluded corners of public parks or tribal original cast albums. We were New Jersey teenagers before the advent of volcanically publicized gay everything. We were huddled in our bedrooms, in the murk, before the invention of gay electricity. It hadn't been agonizing, just frustrating, puzzling, and lonely, which are common symptoms of teenagehood.

So I'd gone unkissed. Until now. And this heartbeat of hesitation, of preamble, was delectably maddening. Farrell and I were preparing to kiss, moistening our mouths, but it hadn't quite happened. We stood hunched on our starting blocks, goggles and swim caps in place, ready to race.

As Farrell moved toward me, his face blurred, in the most wonderful way, as if pre-kissing was warping our senses. He put his arm around me. He smelled so great, from either soap hand-milled by nuns in a Florentine abbey, or one of those light, dry, fresh-washed-linen colognes, or more likely, just from being Farrell Covington.

He smelled like beauty and money and youth; he was every high-end marketing goal in one, but beyond that, he smelled like someone I really wanted to kiss.

Then Farrell did something heart-stoppingly clunky. He shut his eyes and puckered his lips, in the modest manner of a pinafored, sausage-curled girl on a vintage "Be Mine" valentine. I thought about pursing my lips and having them brush against his, so we'd be like two of those tiny plastic Scottie dogs you can buy from boardwalk vending machines, who rush toward each other, due to magnets encased in their doggie snouts.

Farrell opened his eyes, conscious of a roadblock. He smiled and put his hand on my neck and we both stopped thinking so much and we kissed. Our lips met, which was really nice, and then they opened, which was even nicer. As our tongues collided I thought, I'm kissing someone, I'm joining an ancient, ongoing, boundless yet still exclusive club, of people who kiss. I'm no longer a kissing virgin. And best of all, I'm kissing Farrell Covington, who, for some reason, even in my thoughts, I referred to by both names, maybe to antagonize Breen. I was figuring out that sex includes both the physical event and the story you're telling yourself; kissing Farrell wasn't only mindless euphoria, but added a potential love interest and a plot twist to the page-turning yet critically acclaimed novel I desperately needed my life to become. My brain didn't die when my hard-on ached. They worked together.

Farrell pulled away and we considered each other, as if we were strangers accidentally entwined on a swaying subway, and then we lunged back into kissing, because now we were experts. The heat rose from Farrell's body, and as I unbuttoned his white oxford-cloth shirt he said, "Upstairs." Passing a hall mirror, he grabbed me for another kiss, so we could witness ourselves kissing. This turned me on even more, because I was costarring in a movie about two guys kissing on a townhouse landing, but Farrell had already taken my hand and was yanking me up to his bedroom, which occupied the entire third floor.

2

Here's how excited I was: as we kept kissing and tugging at each other's clothes, I only subliminally took note of the bedroom's quarter-sawn golden oak paneling, high mullioned windows, the pair of classic Italian tubular chrome chairs, and the window seat with a cushion stitched from an oriental rug—but as even an inexperienced gay man, I inventoried everything for later, because details are sex, too.

Farrell pulled my sweater and T-shirt over my head. Because I was so young and it was the seventies, I hadn't started working out. I was skinny, and because I hated gym class so devoutly, I hadn't made the logical joining of exercise and vanity. Back then, I had free time, no plastic jugs of muscle-building protein powder, and no sense of what it meant to be appraised on my deltoids or glutes; I'd never heard of either. I hadn't become an object to be found wanting, then refined and improved. I was only flesh panting to be touched.

Farrell shrugged off his already unbuttoned shirt and contrived to fling it suavely across the room, but it caught on one of his wrists, so he held up a forefinger as he freed himself and repeated his flinging, with success. When I saw Farrell's princely shoulders, hardened chest, naturally defined abs, and absurdly narrow waist, my brain and every other part of me lurched. In that pre-obsessive period, guys in porn weren't chiseled or steroid-bloated, so they weren't my point of reference. There were well-built guys I'd avoided gaping at in the showers, but Farrell was right here, and looking at him wasn't merely allowed, it was the whole idea. I reacted as if he were another Hockney or Cadmus or marble-sculpted Vatican Jesus: I backed away, unwilling to blunder.

Farrell's chest was heaving as he unzipped his jeans and stepped out of them. He wasn't wearing underwear and of course I became my mother and mentally demanded, Did he run out of clean underwear? Another neuron babbled, Oh my God, there are guys who don't wear underwear! That is the most offhand and hot and unhygienic thing I've ever heard of! I compelled myself, I gave myself permission: I couldn't stop staring at Farrell's cock.

It was hard, which was thrilling because it was gorgeous and because I had to assume I was making it hard. Gay men have a specific rapport with hard cocks: They validate us. They tell us, yes, as you've suspected, being gay is a fantastic idea. And with no insult to vaginas, for gay men, a hard cock on someone who looked like Farrell was so beautiful it made me want to suck it and shove it up my ass, featuring it in some lurid version of a baby book or a yearbook photo, captioned "My First Cock."

"I'm quite something, aren't I?" said Farrell, not bragging but participating in my heavy-breathing delight. Farrell had the ability to appreciate himself, to stand at a remove and make an unbiased judgment. He didn't have a crush on himself; he was a fair-minded critic reviewing his own work.

"Oh my God."

"Take off your pants."

Because I was in a pre-competitive state, I wasn't intimidated by Farrell but by nudity itself. I was scared of being fully exposed, but couldn't wait. I'd been naked in the bathroom at home, and briefly in the locker room, as I swapped my towel for my Mom-purchased briefs, but in those instances, my being naked was strictly functional and rushed. With Farrell I was getting naked for the best reason; I was getting naked to be seen. I was getting naked to fathom what being naked was really like. I slid off my jeans and tighty-whities (which I unthinkingly wore before such garments became a signifier and prior to the advent of boxer briefs) and stood there, not sure what to do with my hands, slouching then admonishing myself, Posture. The air acknowledged my skin, making me more naked. I was in a police lineup, only hoping to be chosen. My cock wasn't quite Farrell's cock, but it was hard and it was pointing at Farrell; it was like a puppy straining at its leash, although I hate using metaphors for sex organs. It was my cock, responding and ready, the final, irrefutable proof of being naked.

"Oh my Lord," said Farrell, "we're both naked."

It was time to stop talking. We moved toward each other and kissed, running our hands over each other's bodies, our cocks getting to know each other. I was doing what guys did in porn, but in three dimensions or maybe more, and most significantly, I was doing everything a nice boy from New Jersey shouldn't be doing. I wasn't ashamed but victorious; I was verifying that I was seriously, sweatily, joyously, slurpingly gay.

The rest of the sex wasn't ferocious or even memorable. We weren't falling in love, not yet, and not in the way we catastrophically would. We were de-virginizing each other and getting the job done. We were ascertaining what we liked, what would take some getting used to, what hurt, what felt incredible, and what would be filed under "further research." Farrell, or maybe Bates, had provided a small bedside wicker basket of lubricants, as if they were guest soaps or hotel shampoo. This was the detective-show evidence of Farrell's and my erotic checklist: we made an ungodly, sticky, feverishly damp mess, of the sheets and our bodies and our hair and, inventively, the window seat cushion.

Afterward we lay on our backs; neither of us smoked, so we pretended to, passing an imaginary cigarette between us.

"Okay," I began, "I know why I never did this before. It was because I couldn't find anyone. But what about you?"

Farrell took a long drag on our invisible Marlboro or Parliament and exhaled, studying the nonexistent smoke as it drifted in the air above us.

"I've had offers. So many girls, a boy at school, one of the teachers, oh, and the father of a friend, who exposed himself to me in a cabana, and didn't seem to comprehend precisely how much his seersucker robe and flip-flops repulsed me. Can you imagine?"

I shut my eyes in horror: "Stop."

"But I was afraid, of course, of everything being ordinary. Expected. Of it being everyone's, anyone's, disappointing first lay. Which I couldn't abide. Nate, you understand, don't you? You must."

Hearing Farrell say my name gave me a fresh sexual shudder. We'd just had our cocks in each other's mouth and everywhere else. I'd actually, definitively had sex. With someone who was touching my cheek and saying my name, which might've been the greatest seduction, as if my name, short for Nathaniel, had become what I'd always dreamed it could be: my name said by another guy in bed.

"But there are tons of guys here," I said. "At least some of them must be gay. Why me?"

That's how obliviously young I was. I'd just done something that I'd grasp, through the most gut-wrenching trial and error, to never, ever do: Don't ask a question you don't want the answer to. Don't leave yourself wide open to the ugliest or, even worse, the most casual truth.

Farrell spared me. He smiled.

"First of all—the coat."

"My coat?"

"You know just what I'm talking about."

I did. Back in Piscataway I'd worked at a community theater, ushering, playing intensely minor roles, assisting the lighting guy, and flicking cockroaches off the pastries in the snack bar. Since I hadn't been paid, I'd pilfered items from the costume storage, including a neglected, shin-length, wide-lapeled bearskin coat from the 1920s (the grizzly in question was long gone and fur was not yet ethically taboo). I'd been wearing this massive garment around campus, hoping for a vintage swagger, or at least an Edward Gorey–esque hauteur.

"When I saw you, I thought, that's courage. Everyone else is demurely camouflaged by their baggy corduroys and Levi's jackets, to blend in. You weren't having it. And then, at the Dramat, your knapsack was open, and I noticed a copy of the new Dorothy Parker biography, the latest issue of *Interview* magazine, and a canister of Pringles, those potato chip–like products that inexplicably stack. I was beguiled. And then you smiled and looked away, ducking your chin. But then you glanced back, and I saw that your hair was thick and dark, much like your coat. I thought, I need to know him. I couldn't stop staring, which was rude, so I ran out. But I kept searching for you everywhere and trying to compose some bright opening remark. Except when I approached you at the library, I spewed everything I'd been obsessing over and made a hopeless ninny of myself. I had no idea how to repair the damage, so I fled, again. I was certain that you loathed me. That I'd hurled my personality in your face and you'd recoiled. But I allotted myself one final opportunity, tonight. I couldn't sleep, I haven't slept in days, so I went to your room. I would make this happen, or perish. And here you are, in my bed. And you're convinced that I'm mad. And I most likely should apologize for all of this, for my pursuit and my lunacy, but I won't, because may I be honest? None of your facial features belong together, it's as if they were ordered from separate catalogues, yet they've formed the most marvelous peace treaty. And in your own oddly cubist way, you're quite sexy."

As with my body, I'd never inspected my face that closely. In New Jersey, beauty is a matter of not leaving food on your chin. Farrell's description was such a specific neo-compliment that I trusted it. All I'd really heard was the word "sexy." And he was gazing at me, unguardedly. Being physically wanted was dizzying.

"Really? You think I'm . . . sexy?"

At eighteen, for a gay boy, this was the dream. I hadn't picked a persona yet, as, say, a Levi's-and-Lacoste clone, or a tight-khaki'd would-be Exeter grad, or a glowering late-night leatherman in a studded vest, bared biceps, and assless chaps. I wasn't any of the Village People, that disco-fied paper doll book. I hadn't been handed a menu, by some omniscient, eyebrow-arching maître'd, policing the velvet rope to gaydom.

But I'd gathered that an elite were ranked as desirable. These gifted few didn't need to present their SAT scores or driver's licenses; such natural insiders were thirsted for by strangers. Being sexy wasn't exclusively the realm of the beautiful. Less conventional specimens could spark mass lust. But the indisputably sexy were often movie stars or someone you'd glimpse from a bus window, washing his car and scratching his flawless, shirtless stomach. Sexy wasn't something you could fake or study for, although so many of us try. People hoping to become sexy are the basis of almost every American industry, from unaffordable sports cars to wraparound sunglasses to icy hot sugarless gum.

I'd never wondered if I was sexy. It would be like asking if I could perform open-heart surgery or fix a carburetor, something light-years beyond me.

But of course, being sexy, along with being praised and applauded and nabbing a rent-controlled one-bedroom apartment in New York, was the reason I pined for adulthood or at least independence. I wanted to establish, the only way a person can, which is through the eyes and kisses of someone else: Could Nate Reminger be at least lied to as sexy?

"I think you're incredibly sexy," said Farrell, kissing my nose. "I mean, you're not me, but you're really sexy."

Farrell's words were more than enough, because I'd memorize them, I'd tuck them into my emotional back pocket, to be cross-referenced (topic: Nate Reminger—sexy?) and freshly exulted over and maybe tattooed.

Which led to a much more focused second round of sucking and fucking, now that we'd confirmed our mutual, if unequal, sexiness. We had to have more sex. I mean, look at us!

3

Now that I was sexy, and now that I'd had sex, I climbed an even higher rung for a gay guy: I was just about convinced I was starting to have a boyfriend. Farrell and I began hanging out. We'd leave messages for each other, with my roommates and Bates: this was a steam-powered epoch before answering machines, cellphones, or texts, a hardscrabble frontier of indecipherable names and phone numbers scrawled on torn scraps of notebook paper and, using Bic pens, on people's hands. I'd race to my dorm room between classes, to scan the felt-tipped notes on a laminated message board Velcroed to the hallway door, to see if Farrell had called, or just my parents again. I'd lie on my bed on my stomach, wrapping the curled phone cord around my wrist, rechecking the dial tone like a petulant small-town prom queen, cursing quarterback Brad for his overtime at the hardware store.

Even sexier than sex was walking beside Farrell across the leaf-strewn November campus to the library or the Durfee snack bar for brown paper bags of almonds and chocolate-covered raisins, with me in my bearskin and Farrell in what at first could be taken for a more conventional pea-coat, except it was Italian cashmere. We looked like a rough-hewn Montana trapper and a dandy from back East, or a fur haystack and a fountain pen from a Fifth Avenue shop.

"Farrell," I asked, during one of these strolls, "I know we don't have to declare anything until the end of the year, but what are you going to major in?"

"Hold on."

Farrell took me behind an oak and kissed me. We were barely hidden, but the modified secrecy was everything. Farrell would do this as the mood struck him, to keep me off-kilter and enslaved. He'd kiss me, murmur, "Mmmm . . . ," and then continue walking, resuming our conversation as if nothing had happened.

"Well, I suppose what I'd really like," he said, "is to major in connoisseurship, perhaps the History of Taste. The comprehensive study of the world's most perfectly achieved flourishes and deadpan, devastating remarks. The sculpting of time and space through excess or refusal. And the Aristotelian debate over off-center vase placement on a hall table. But because this school is so limited, I'll probably end up in Art History or English Literature. And you?"

I'd been dwelling on this. Being away from home, coupled with Farrell's kisses, had emboldened me. College is about defining yourself, not just in particulars of career or even sexuality, but point of view. What was I going to value, how did I long to be regarded? If I was hit by a truck, what betrayed youthful promise would I seek to have wept over by as many desolate mourners as could be jammed into the synagogue or arena?

"Drama," I said. "I'm going to be a Drama major."

I love that back then, the program wasn't called Theater Arts or Performance Studies or some other doctoral-thesis, high-minded blather, anything to disguise the trashiest, least responsible truth: I wanted to major in Being Gay. I wanted to fulfill a dream, and a certainty, that I'd always hungered for. While I knew that many gay people were tormented by self-loathing or family oppression (often enforced by religious hogwash), I shared none of this. Being gay isn't merely a simple fact of nature. I hate it when conservative gay activists remark, "It's like having blue eyes or brown hair." Being gay should never be minimized, as a throwaway footnote, especially in hopes of currying "tolerance" from nervous straight people, as a means of soothing a Republican evangelist, "Don't worry. It's nothing. You won't even notice that we're gay."

I don't believe that being gay is a matter of equality. Being gay is better. This is, of course, morally and scientifically insupportable. I don't care. For me, and I'd wager, for many gay people, it's my truth. And I didn't arrive at this lunatic conclusion after careful, exhaustive study. It's an innate and utterly sublime prejudice.

Conversely, are straight people convinced of their own superiority? Please. Just consult pretty much every Great Work of Fiction, Film Classic, or election result. Heterosexuality is the world's default setting, it's humanity's go-to correct answer. I'm not worried about straight people; as Farrell once said, "I maintain a royal pity for them."

For me, being gay meant being instantly and gratifyingly different. I gained an outsider's perspective. I'd take nothing for granted. Being gay meant I'd already demolished a cardinal rule of social acceptance, so why not pulverize, or at least splinter, as many as I'd like? Being gay meant membership, in a tradition of culture and style and outrage—I'm not claiming that gay people are always, or even often, gifted at these things, but I longed to be. A Gay Pride parade may be garish and clichéd, clattering along for wearisome miles, but it's still designed for pleasure rather than a meek show of acceptability.

Everything I loved and sought out was gay: the heightened reality of theater, the *Vogue* coverage of St. Laurent's legendary Russian collection, and imitating Andy Warhol by covering the walls of my boyhood bedroom with aluminum foil, adhered with double-sided tape, even if this facsimile of Warhol's glittering Factory headquarters ended up resembling an enormous Reynolds-Wrapped baked potato. I gravitated toward Oscar Wilde, James Baldwin, and the snarling wisecracks of Paul Lynde without a second thought. These unconventional heroes were smart and witty, making their audiences uncomfortable and deliriously happy. Is it conceivable to be heterosexual, male, and fabulous? Maybe, but the research has never been done, because those guys don't need to be fabulous. Which is either their enviable strength or their infinite tragedy. Which is a very gay thing to say.

Also: Are there gay men who in no way subscribe to, or have any interest in, my Caravaggio-and-Noël-Coward-infused brunch-warrior outlook on gayness? Of course, and I respect their ordinariness. But I've found that even these undetectables often wield a secret command of the gay vernacular, as a second language. These helplessly Average Joes, in their windbreakers and pocket protectors, can murmur, "Oh, honey," when needed. And as for those craven few, who purport they've "changed" from homosexuality, via coercive therapy or, more likely, lying about it, Farrell would later ask, upon hearing testimony from a stalwart Christian, "You've changed? Really? For dinner?"

I knew I was a Drama major, which didn't necessarily entail being a drama queen. Drama majors reserve their most appallingly neurotic behavior for the stage. But here's when I knew I was card-carryingly, achingly gay: I was maybe twelve years old and watching an afternoon talk and variety program called *The Mike Douglas Show*. Mike was a square-headed, gushing, blazer-clad host. This meant that when he sang, it was tuneful but uninteresting, and when he told hackneyed jokes, he'd be indulged like a drunken uncle at a wedding, and while he had nothing of value to say, he was adept at presenting the more talented and asking them basic, so-when-does-your-holiday-special-air-right-here-on-CBS questions.

This specific afternoon he introduced "someone very special," a "new discovery," and "the toast of Manhattan": a woman named Bette Midler.

Female performers at that time were most often honey-voiced hostesses, like Dinah Shore, or platinum-beehived, thickly mascaraed vixens go-go bopping in sequined op-art minidresses and white patent leather boots; the age of the Peruvian ponchoed, Malibu-morose singer-songwriter was just gaining acoustic traction. Bette Midler sampled all these ladies, and exploded them. To my twelve-year-old eyes and libido, she was a jolt of pure, irrepressible, unstoppable happiness.

She shimmied across the TV screen, her lush, iodine-red hair flying, her breasts skimpily contained by little more than a silk scarf worn as a halter, her platform heels skittering beneath billowing, thirties-chorus-girl satin trousers. She couldn't keep still. The music, a propulsive reworking of the Andrews Sisters' "Boogie Woogie Bugle Boy," kept her scarcely tethered. She beamed with the most wickedly irreverent joy and an irony-laced invitation I couldn't begin to decipher, but knew was targeted directly at me.

Bette Midler, in between commercials for compact sedans and vacation getaways in the Poconos, let me know that a stylized bliss had been prepared for me, if I could hoard her albums and track her every appearance via *TV Guide*. She wasn't gay, but she embodied all the most kinetic, worldly, subversive aspects of the life I wanted. If gay men were her most passionate fan base, sign me up.

Scholars argue: Why are certain gay men so mesmerized by outsize female icons, by single names like Cher, Judy, and Bette? Theories abound: these chanteuses channel the soapy anguish of queer lives, or they borrow the loving mockery of drag. No other performers are asked to diagnose their ardent followings, as if their talent is a pathology. So if anyone needs to know why gay guys were among Bette Midler's first and most vocal fans, the only accurate answer is this: Why wasn't everyone? Because eventually, the world caught on.

So that's what I wanted to major in: Bette Midler, musical comedy, Hockney, cashews, and Farrell Covington.

"Farrell," I said, "do you like Bette Midler?"

"When my father saw her," Farrell replied, "on Johnny Carson, he was horrified. He said she was unpleasant, undignified, unattractive, and everything he despised about Jewish show business."

"What do you think?"

"I worship her."

4

I began spending almost every night at Farrell's townhouse, much to Breen's consternation. "But I don't understand how that's permissible," he told me. "I know that the Covingtons are one of this country's finest families, but it still seems a bit much. Do you sleep in a guest bedroom?"

"No."

"SHUT UP! SHUT UP!"

Whenever Breen imagined that I was about to get more explicit, he'd run back into his room and furiously immerse himself in very thick books on constitutional fundamentalism, tomes he'd ostentatiously leave atop my stacks of play collections, Ronald Firbank novels, and issues of magazines like *Show* and *Rolling Stone*, which Breen would circle, open gingerly, inspect a page of, and then slam back down in disgust, as if he were a Puritan minister happening upon a sepia postcard of a music hall hussy.

Because I'd never had a boyfriend before, I wasn't sure how to wrangle it. Should I wait for Farrell to call me, should I hang on his every word, how often should I wash my hair? I did what would become a pattern: I let the stronger personality take the lead. As a freshman I had the excuse of innocence, which later in my life would become cowardice or, at best, indecision.

For much of that year, Farrell and I were cocooned. We both left for the holidays. I spent those weeks being insufferable in New Jersey, refusing to offer my parents any tidbits of the education they'd made possible. When my mom asked about a backup plan for my theatrical ambitions, I sighed heavily and excruciatingly mumbled, "Why?" When my dad asked if I liked school, I barely managed, "It's great," and he was too nice and too timid to press further.

I languished in my childhood bedroom, which I'd decorated years earlier (following my Warhol phase) with glossy, oversize houndstooth-checked yellow-and-orange wallpaper, with a coordinated yellow-and-orange accent mural depicting either silhouetted protestors or the cast of *Hair*, and yes, there was yellow-and-orange shag carpeting. My dad, God bless him, had carpentered a wall of shelving and drawers, so I holed up in my yellow-and-orange how-could-even-a-dead-person-not-know-I-was-gay module. I talked to Farrell late at night, on my orange push-button phone. He was at one of his family's many homes, this one in Wichita. When I asked him to describe the house, and the city, his voice developed a strangled sob, as he whispered, "I can't. I just can't."

Farrell whispered throughout our conversations, as if a vicious warden stood nearby tossing inmate body parts to snarling dogs. "I can't stand this," he told me, "you have no idea, and I can't really explain. Someday you'll see. But I can't be myself and I'd rather die than please these people, so I spend most of my time on a sun porch, fondling an unopened paperback of Proust and thinking about you. They all assume I'm headed for law school or some other hellish Republican planetoid. If you hear a gunshot, either tell the police I was murdered or that my service revolver went off and accidentally slaughtered four people, right between the eyes."

Each night Farrell requested a New Jersey travelogue, as a bedtime story:

"Tell me about the mall again. Are there really cement planters filled with plastic ivy and rhododendrons year-round? Is there a kiosk selling those gold electroplate necklaces with names like Debbie-Arlene-Andrea and Michelle-Amber-Nicole?"

"And today I went to Chess King," I told him, "which sells men's high fashion for less. I bought plaid mini-wale corduroy high-waisted David Bowie pants and these bright blue-and-yellow shoes that look like taxis, but my mom made me return everything because she says she didn't raise a pimp."

"Tell me about Carvel."

"There's one downtown in New Haven, I'll take you. But Carvel is New Jersey at our best, even in winter. I came up with my own treat and I beg them to make it. They take one of those flat-bottomed wafer cones and fill it with rainbow sprinkles. Then they swirl on soft chocolate ice cream, which they roll in more sprinkles. Then they dip the whole thing in melted chocolate, which hardens. It's called a brown bonnet. The final product weighs fifteen pounds; it's like diabetic cement."

"What about Fudgie?"

"Fudgie is an ice cream cake made in a whale-shaped pan. And at Christmas they turn the pan vertically and Fudgie turns into Santa's head. On Father's Day the founder, Tom Carvel, does radio ads telling everyone to buy Fudgie as a gift, 'for a whale of a dad.' I once asked my dad if he wanted Fudgie and he looked both ways, to make sure my mom didn't hear him, and said, 'More than anything.'"

"Your life is so deliriously exotic! How I envy you!"

"Don't they have ice cream in Wichita?"

"How would I know? Where would I find it? I'm a prisoner."

"You're a prisoner?"

"Of expectations."

On our last night apart, which was the evening of New Year's Day, Farrell was weirdly reticent. When I asked him if everything was okay, he said, "Yes. But I've been anticipating this call, because I have to tell you something and I'm not sure exactly how to phrase it, or how you'll receive it."

My mouth went dry because Farrell was breaking up with me. I'd never had this happen, because I'd never been with anyone, but I'd sat through enough divorce-themed movies of the week to recognize Farrell's tone. He was about to say, "We both know this isn't working" or

"We've grown apart" or "I've been seeing someone. Her name doesn't matter, it's about the way she makes me feel, when we're together. Allison, please stop crying."

"Nate?"

"What?" I rocked on the wooden frame of my trundle bed, beside the window which overlooked our January-shrouded aboveground backyard pool.

"I love you."

The phone went dead. When I called back, an older woman's voice answered and said, "I'm so sorry, but Farrell isn't available, we're sitting down to dinner, but I'll tell him you called." Then she hung up, without asking my name.

5

The phone was ringing when I got back to campus. Breen had answered it: "Yes . . . yes . . . I'll tell him. Are you sure?"

"What? Who was it? Was it Farrell?"

"It was someone named Bates, he sounded British. He said, and I'm quoting him, he said that 'His Lordship wishes to see you, and that there isn't much time. He wants you to bring morphine, absinthe, and a ceremonial sword.' Nate, what's going on? Have the Covingtons been informed of their son's condition?"

"The Covingtons probably caused their son's condition," I said, my coat already on.

"I have weed, if that helps," volunteered Walt, who was, as always, sweetly generous.

"You have an illegal substance on these premises?" I heard Breen thunder, as I took the stairs two at a time.

"It's not illegal in a dorm," Walt said reasonably, and I prayed that Breen wouldn't call the campus police, the way he had when he'd come upon what he deduced might be a vial of opium in the communal shower, but was of course an amber bottle of bespoke conditioner, mixed by a chemist in Berlin from botanicals, gold leaf, and bee pollen, which Farrell had given me for our three-month anniversary. The officers still hadn't returned it.

Bates let me in and brought me to the third floor, where Farrell was lying in his darkened bedroom, completely still beneath a sheet and a sable throw, with his eyes shut and a bedside humidifier wheezing a healing mist.

"Farrell?" I said, in a hushed voice.

"Is . . . is someone there?" he answered, not opening his eyes.

"It's Nate."

"Nate," he murmured, "Nate. Yes, of course. I know you. Come, be with me." His eyes resolutely shut, he extended a languid arm, straight up into the air.

"Are you okay?"

"Do I look like I'm okay?" he retorted, opening his eyes briefly and then gasping in horror and clenching them shut again.

"What? What is it? What did you see?"

"I saw—those people. No, they're not people, I saw those antediluvian homunculi, they were half wild pigs, half crocodiles, with five horns and faces ripped from open graves and nailed into place. When I open my eyes they're still here, in burgundy cable-knit cardigans and tweed Norfolk jackets and plaid hostess skirts with velvet sashes and enameled Christmas tree brooches, holding snifters of brandy and jabbering about unspeakable crimes like 'the game' or 'the club' or 'the Wydenhams' Chrysler Imperial.' They are the blood moon apocalypse!"

"So we're talking about your family. What happened?"

"I . . . I got there and it was a two-week interrogation. My parents and my brothers, they tag-teamed me, poisoning me at breakfast with dry toast, forcing me to play squash at gunpoint, and then all of them, the entire Covington elite ground force, they'd assault me over dinner, wielding forks with slices of glazed ham! With cloves! They're stipulating law school, so I can eventually join the investment branch of the firm and grapple my way towards product development and then global oil. Not one of them has ever read a book that isn't set during the Civil War, or seen a film that isn't a western, a biblical epic, or the heart-tugging saga of a devoted hound, and when I mentioned that new Jerome Robbins piece at City Ballet, I could swear my mother started fingering a syringe, a rosary, and a straitjacket. I kept them at bay as long as I could until . . . until . . ."

"Until what?"

Farrell opened his eyes, genuinely forlorn, as if he couldn't retrieve the desired words, some sparkling carnival of adjectives and curlicued assessments, which would transform his sorrow and protect him. Farrell without language was heartbreaking. It was as if he'd been in a twelve-vehicle highway pileup, and lost his power of theatrical exaggeration.

He lifted the sheet for me to join him. He was wearing a linen night-shirt with a heart-shaped bloodstain on his chest, produced, as far as I could tell, by a scarlet Magic Marker. He was going for "extremely hand-some, woefully forgotten rag doll."

I snuggled beside him and he put his arm around me. As he spoke, he stayed on his back, addressing the ceiling.

"When I was on the phone with you, I'd foolishly forgotten that I was under constant surveillance. And when I said . . . what I said, I heard a gasp, and my mother strode into the room, grabbed the phone, hung it up, and ordered me downstairs. Where a court-martial was convened in the front parlor, which is reserved for visits from senators, ambassadors, and only the most odious white-collar felons, along with family conclaves. The last time everyone occupied the parlor was following my twenty-three-year-old brother Wainwright's arrest for drunk driving, after he'd seriously injured a young mother and her toddler. The entire conversation had revolved around whether we should countersue the woman for damaging the headlight of Wainwright's Lincoln Continental, and the phrasing of Father Densmore's letter to the judge, attesting to Wainwright's piety and reverence for human life. Something I assume he'd been expressing at the hotel bar where he'd acquired the two prostitutes who were with him, and fellating him, in the car."

"But why were they angry at you?"

"After my mother overheard . . . all I'd said, she turned keening harpy. She kept half screaming and half sobbing, 'Who is she?' My father asked if I'd gotten involved with, as he put it, some 'godforsaken New Haven strumpet,' and Wainwright and Bolt, my other brother, he's five years older, they sat beside each other and positively throbbed with juvenile vengeance. Wainwright said, 'Yale isn't Harvard. It's a glorified whorehouse'—after he'd barely crawled his way through Notre Dame, in five years! And Bolt kept shaking his head like some village elder and muttering that I'd probably taken up with some little actress, concluding, 'At least I hope she's white.' "

"He really said that?"

"And worse. My mother composed herself, smoothed her skirt, and asked, 'Farrell, whatever sorry mess you've gotten yourself mired in, we will extricate you. Is she . . . with child?' "

"Oh my God."

"I know. I wanted to hurl myself at her feet and cry out to the Lord, 'With triplets! And at least one of them is Cantonese!' But I didn't, I couldn't, because, I can't really explain it, but Nate, when I'm with them, and I'm outnumbered, and there's all of this hideous brown furniture rumbling towards me, I . . . I stop being myself. I vanish. I'm no one."

He paused, choking back sobs, which unnerved me, because beneath his exuberance and occasional tap routines, Farrell was a very tough cookie. That's part of why I was so attracted to him. Over the years I've been drawn to not just outsize personalities with arsenals of self-confidence, but people of strength, people who can endure even the most painful events and remain clear-eyed and strategic.

Farrell in tears was shocking, because he was at a loss.

"When I was twelve," he said, "I gratefully fled to boarding school, because I expected I'd be free from my family's gothic oppression. But everyone there, they were spies, rich, officious little spiders intent on aping their parents and gauging which classmates were the richest, the most well connected, and the most likely to provide an invitation to the largest possible summer place on Nantucket or the Vineyard or in the most desirable Hampton. It was a trust-funded launching pad for twitching social skyrockets, who clamored to meet my father, or ask my father for investment advice, or become my father. And I'd been so afraid that Yale would be more of the same, another training camp for future Caucasian autocrats yowling at their estate managers to fire the entire grounds crew because the pea gravel in the drive leading to the stables hadn't been properly raked. Which admittedly, can be disheartening.

"So when I settled in here, I'd made a vow, to remain alone. To entomb myself in a library carrel, studying Persian enamels and the letters of Evelyn Waugh to his tailor. But of course that was inexpressibly lonely, especially after almost an hour, with only five vending machine breaks, so I wandered into that theatrical organization, and there you were, straddling the arm of that couch and wearing those fascinating sneakers. And since we've been together I keep thinking—this is new. This isn't my family. This is—salvation."

Which sounded like a sizeable responsibility. Was I really supposed to save Farrell? Did he need rescuing, or was he handing himself an Oscar, for Most Over-the-Top Weeping by a Silent Film Heroine?

"I'm sorry, I'm sure this all sounds ridiculous, as if I'm imploring you to carry me in your arms from the most luxurious battlefield, or an especially barbarous sale in the shoe salon at Bergdorf's, bandaging me with Hermés scarves and dabbing my brow with eau de parfum and Pellegrino. But Nate . . ."

He was staring at me. When Farrell did this, when he abandoned any hint of performance, I didn't just melt, I wanted to stay with him, in bed, forever, with Bates bringing us cashews and chocolate (the only essential food groups). I didn't only aim to help Farrell feel better but to prove that our fucking could defeat his family. To believe that our being gay, that the fact of us could outweigh everything; that my kissing Farrell was an antidote, a miraculous vaccine for ignorance and toxic parental game plans, and a means of warding off sneering older brothers.

"I know it's appalling, after just these few months, to say what I said to you. And after we've only had sex with each other. But when I was there, among them, in that monstrous house, in Kansas, I needed to say it. I needed to claim you. Which isn't fair at all. So I won't say it again, not yet, and if you try to say it, out of some misguided sense of obligation, I'll do something awful. I'll get some grotesque haircut and tell everyone you like it. But Nate, I meant what I said."

"I know."

I was, of course, bursting with happiness, which Farrell's agony only amplified. I was here, with this wondrously bizarre guy, who'd told me he loved me. And not as an imitation of adult behavior, or a bribe to get my pants off—they were already on the floor. Ever since Farrell had said "I love you" on the phone, I'd been stunned and elated and desperate to tell someone, to ask, "Do I look different?," but there wasn't anyone I trusted, and my family was out of the question.

And yes, Farrell had been proclaiming his love practically since the day we met. But this had an authenticity; this was life versus art. When a gay man says "I love you," it's often an ironic salute to your ski sweater and matching headband and muffler. The gay "I love you" is linked to "I love it!" and "I love that!" as expressions of camp esteem. Farrell's "I love you" was so sincere it was almost heterosexual. Farrell wasn't voicing a penchant but a need. And he was teaching me the difference.

But for right now, Farrell's love was a secret, between the two of us. And because we couldn't talk about it, I was in a holding pattern, call it emotional blue balls, from knowing but having to stay silent, from both my brain and my crotch wanting to sing one of those musical numbers in which our leading man or lady is alone onstage, exulting in whichever cowboy or perfume store clerk or Austrian Count has just pledged his devotion, one of those songs that would send me cartwheeling across the set to swing around a lamppost, and then I'd leap onto a park bench with my arms open wide to embrace all the joy in the universe, as the first act curtain fell and a lady in the front row turned to her sister from Long Island and declared, "Tony award! You heard it here first!"

Yes, I'm that gay.

Because love is gay. Farrell and I were inventing love. We were the Thomas Edisons, the Henry Fords, the da Vincis of love; I'm convinced that da Vinci's Vitruvian Man, his 1490 proportional sketch of a naked hunk, was the first valentine. Let me rephrase: when a gay person falls in love, it makes them more gay.

6

Farrell reassured his family that the "I love you" his mother had over-heard was a figure of speech, and that he'd been talking to a female classmate who'd been aiding his research on advances in strip-mining. "It was perfect," Farrell told me, "because my family can only accept the word 'love' if it's applied to ravaging a small Kentucky town and its picturesque forest in pursuit of making a profit. My father would only say 'I love you' to my mother if she was holding a picture of his current mistress in front of her face, or the deed to a diamond mine with child laborers."

"So they still don't know, about me. Or you."

"No. And yes, I should—express that, and tell them everything, be-cause hopefully it will kill all of them at the same time, like the Ro-manovs. But not yet."

I got it, although in retrospect, that exchange, and Farrell's reluctance, would be the seed of so much that happened later, and everything that would separate us. I wanted being gay to be purely celebratory, I insisted on it, but I was eighteen, and the only real obstacles I'd faced denoted bus travel to New Haven, Breen's father asking me if theater was an actual profession, and the occasional stranger shouting "Faggot!" on the street. While this could be scary, especially if the stranger wasn't alone, I always had the urge to yell, "Thank you!"

Farrell and I agreed on exploring a larger world. Especially for first-time couples, infatuation can become claustrophobic, and one day in February, Farrell showed me a creamy parchment card, with the most elaborate, disjointed Indian ink calligraphy, inviting "Messrs. Covington & Reminger" to attend "An elegant soirette chez His Excellency Mr. Jackson Bell Rains." The envelope was loaded with multicolored sequins and feathers, and the script was so fanciful that we borrowed a magnifying glass from a librarian to puzzle out the address.

The invitation had been slipped inside Farrell's superbly battered leather backpack (he'd leave it outside during snowstorms to hasten its decay) one morning after we'd had breakfast at the largest student dining hall, an echoing, quasi-Tudor barn. Our host, we unearthed, was a man we'd seen there often, seated with a group of friends. They were in their late twenties or early thirties, and when Farrell and I passed by, we'd received comments like "Oh my," "The blond is rich," "I'm loving the almost matching soiled T-shirts," and "Ladies and gentlemen, I give you—young love. Brava!"

Jackson Bell Rains was a graduate student in costume design, and he lived three flights up in a tenement building a few blocks from campus. On the specified night, we were greeted by a batch of gold and red helium balloons tied with silver ribbon to the rusting, cast-iron railing out front, and there was glitter strewn on the steps leading to the building's front door. As Farrell pressed the buzzer, we heard, from the intercom, in a syrupy, giddy Dixie accent, "Third floor, my darlings! Only stairs, I'm afraid! What are we to do?" And we were buzzed in.

Jackson opened the door breathlessly, because he did everything breathlessly. He was continually knocked for a loop and delighted by life itself, with the rosy cheeks of an ageless cherub, round gold wire–rimmed eyeglasses, and a mop of blond curls. In his navy blazer, starched white shirt, rep tie, and khakis, he was a cross between a pixilated headmaster and a capering Roman emperor passing hors d'oeuvres at a spur-of-the-moment Colosseum orgy.

"You're here! You came!" he cried out. "I can't believe it! I'm thrilled, I'm staggered, I wasn't sure if you'd be tickled or insulted, so I told myself, why not both! Everyone look, it's, let me be certain I'm pronouncing everything correctly—it's Farrell and Nate! From the dining hall! *Les gentilshommes du* cornflakes!"

Farrell nudged me. What were we in for? But before we could confer, Jackson was sweeping us into the apartment, which was a shabby railroad flat that he'd beribboned. Every hard surface had been painted with fresh white enamel, and the secondhand armchairs had been slip-covered with bold cabbage-rose chintz. There was a psychiatrist's couch, in painted canvas, rescued from the street, and an inviting circle of mismatched ottomans, benches, and folding chairs. There were empty, ornate gold frames on the walls, along with thumbtacked watercolor costume sketches. Drapes had been improvised with yards of striped silk, and the lamps were swathed with tissue-thin scarves hand-dipped in tea, for a flattering glow. The place was half–opium den, half–New Orleans bordello, and altogether genteel slapdash madness.

"I like it," Farrell whispered to me. "It's like a consignment shop after a hurricane. No, during a hurricane."

"What can I get you fine young fellows?" asked Jackson, guiding us toward a bar set out atop a bookcase heaped with oversize art books. "We have champagne and lemonade and beer for me, because I'm trash, just sad dirty Carolina trash."

Farrell and I accepted lemonade, served in frosty, mismatched stemware with Murano glass swizzle sticks. There were two other people present, and Jackson ushered us onto central seating and proclaimed, "All right, everyone, hush! Because I have terribly important and instructive things to say!"

He opened his arms to the group, as a born host. "Look at you! I know we're all wondering why we're here, and if there's going to be a murder. Well, I say, surprise me! Now, I know some of you all too well, but there are new faces. And what I'm doing, what I'm attempting to initiate, is a salon, in the footsteps of Marie Antoinette, the Mitford sisters, and Mr. Cecil Beaton. We need a gathering of minds and spirits, and an exchange of ideas, and I suppose what I'm really saying is, we're in New Haven, we're all in one school or another, we're on the cusp, we're in despair, so let's make magic!"

The room was wary but willing, as Jackson continued: "So let's go around the circle and introduce ourselves, and as an added bonus, I'd like each of us to reveal our most terrible secret, the one truth with the power to absolutely destroy us for all eternity. As an icebreaker. Sally, will you be so kind as to start us off?"

He indicated the most improbably pretty girl I'd ever seen. Her features weren't classically ideal in any way, but she was style itself. Her skin, makeup-free, had the poreless glow of a newborn. Her soft, gleamingly unassisted blond hair was cut in an easy pageboy, with a tortoiseshell headband, but rather than coming off as prissy or preppie, she was winningly fresh, a daisy from the most carefree meadow. She was wearing a pleated navy-blue skirt and a striped French sailor's shirt, with pearls. She was the Platonic ideal of a certain type of American pink-and-gold shampoo-ad loveliness. That was the only accurate word for Sally: she was lovely. And when she smiled, Farrell and I both made tiny whimpering sounds, as if we'd just lifted a towel from a basket of laundry to find a kitten.

"Good Lord, Jackson," she said, with a slightly husky laugh. Her low-slung speaking voice only enhanced her charm. She didn't sound tinkly or simpering, but amused. "I'm Sally Mayhew and I'm a sophomore, and I met Jackson when he zeroed in on me at a concert of sacred music and asked if he could study my pearls; he said he was researching the accessories for a thirties comedy and needed to know what the real thing looked like."

"I did!" Jackson admitted merrily. "And do you know what I discovered? It's all about luster. Real pearls are lit from within. Even the finest cultured variety can't quite keep up. Cultured pearls try so hard, which makes them a little bit sad, doesn't it?"

Farrell was nodding, in rueful agreement.

"And I'm not quite sure what I'm doing here," Sally continued. "At this party or Yale or anywhere else. But I'd like to meet God, only without dying just yet. I want to become the first saint on the best-dressed list."

She smiled, because despite the oddness of this quest, she was completely serious. "And my deepest secret," Sally said, "which I've never told anyone, and which I'm trusting all of you with . . . No, I can't say it. It's too ghastly. You'll hate me. You'll shun me."

"Let us decide," advised Jackson. "Tell us."

"All right," Sally said, with no small difficulty. "Here it is. I'm just going to put this out there. I'm a natural blonde."

"No!" Jackson gasped.

"Isn't it hell?" Farrell asked Sally, who held out a slim hand to him, as if saying, "Only you can understand."

"Ariadne?" said Jackson, to the most simmeringly angry person on earth. Her name felt off and not of her choosing. She was more of a Killer or Smasher or Destructo.

Ariadne was small and wiry, but in her steel-toed boots, her mountainous, heavy green wool, double-breasted, calf-length military overcoat, with a thick iron chain slung diagonally from her neck to her waist, she was stern and monumental, a Rodin bronze or a brutalist statue of Lenin presiding over an Olympic stadium in Moscow. The chain was ordinarily used to secure her bicycle, which Jackson had prompted her to park in his kitchen.

"Jesus fuck," she growled; Ariadne's voice matched her presentation, basso but with deliberate, don't-mess-with-me diction. "I don't fucking know why I'm here or if I'm staying, but I met Jackson at the Hadassah thrift store and we talked about monogrammed dress shirts and he knows his shit. I'm Ariadne Glatt and I'm a junior and I'm here because my dad went here for Engineering, but I'm fucking with him because I'm a Religious Studies major. I told him, Fine, I'll go to Yale but I'm never gonna make a fucking penny."

Ariadne was fascinating; so much about her was a contradiction. She was a menacing, potentially violent chain-smoker who, I would gradually come to see, was the most deeply moral person I'd ever met.

"And your secret?" asked Jackson, bravely.

"My secret is that I don't take speed to stay up late and study, or to keep my weight down. I use speed because I fucking love it."

Everyone in the room quickly and silently assimilated this and conspired to never provoke Ariadne. Rage was her resting pulse rate, and I had this image of her taking a slow drag on an unfiltered Marlboro, while seated atop a pile of freshly chainsawed, dismembered professors.

"What have I missed?" asked a tall, cheerful girl, a gung-ho figure in a macraméd leather skirt, a cowl-necked sweater, and at least one cape, hurling herself into the room.

"Jess!" said Jackson, scooping her into a hug. "You're here! We're all just introducing ourselves and trading secrets and confessing illegal activities! It's a party!"

"That sounds like fun!" said Jess, who was beautiful in a sturdy, athletic, strong-jawed mode; she'd been a dance student for years, until her parents' disapproval, injuries, and her height had stopped her. She removed many items of clothing and pulled up a chair, with whirlwind ease. "I'm Jess Janeway, which I know sounds like a fake name but it's real, and I'm an actress, or I'd like to be an actress, so it's really sort of handy. And I met Jackson when, even though I'm a freshman, I was playing a tiny part in *Midsummer Night's Dream* at the grad school, as a member of Hippolyta's royal entourage, and he put me in this divine sort of silver cobweb with a headdress, and I knew we'd be friends. Can I get a drink? Is there vodka?"

As Jackson brought the bottle, Jess continued. She had a gift for taking a roomful of strangers into her instantaneous confidence, with very little filter: "And I need a secret, is that right? Oh, dear. Are we looking for trauma or divorce or anorexia, because all of the above. All right, here's something totally bonkers: I'm an Honorable. Technically. One of my mother's several husbands was a Duke, and even though the marriage only lasted two years, I'm Lady Jessica of West 81st Street. Bow down!"

For most people, this might have been boasting or a self-aggrandizing lie, but with Jess it was matter-of-fact, as if she were reporting a sprained ankle or a missed train. Jess had a directness I liked, and Farrell touched my knee and mouthed the word "Later," which meant there was gossip in store.

"Gentlemen?" said Jackson, to Farrell and me. I was getting a twinge, which would become more familiar as the years went by, from the tension of meeting groups of new people all at once, and grappling to measure up;

this was why'd I'd gone to college, to test myself against the world. I was glad to be with Farrell, because being his boyfriend was a sort of armor, but I didn't want to be like one of those girls at my high school, clinging to, and entirely defined by, her junior varsity swain. I'd been thrust on-stage, without a script or direction: Who should I be?

"I'm Nate Reminger, and Jackson invited Farrell and me to come by, and I'm . . . I'm . . ."

Recognizing that everyone here was far more interesting than me, I was hit with a rare and helpful instinct: don't lie. I won't get away with it, I'll need to remember the lie, and everyone will see right through me and, at best, feel sorry for me. I'd unreel more than my share of lies in the future, but not today.

"I'm feeling very intimidated and dumb, because I'm from the New Jersey suburbs and I'm a freshman and I'm very impressed with all of you. I have no reason to be here, except I think Yale has a certain quota of students from New Jersey, so I snuck in under the wire. I'm going to be a Drama major, so I someday hope to develop a personality. And my secret is . . . I'm from Piscataway."

After a nervous-making silence, the room burst into applause, as if encouraging a child who'd stumbled through reciting his first three-line poem. I basked in the ovation, as Jackson cried "Huzzah!" and placed a crown of origami flowers on my head. Jackson always had an array of crowns, jeweled masks, wands, and derbies on hand.

"Well, I certainly can't top that," said Farrell. "So I'll just say that I'm Farrell Covington, and I'm here with Nate."

I blushed as deeply as I ever had in my life, as the room took this in, with interest and approval. This was the first time my being gay was considered a public advantage, like a knack for the piccolo or walking on my hands. Also, being attached to Farrell was its own social bliss, and I utterly became that corsaged Piscataway teen on her Corvette-owning stud's arm, as they were elected Prom King and Queen and led to crepe paper–wrapped thrones donated by a local furniture outlet.

"Wait," said Ariadne, holding Farrell to account. "What's your secret that can destroy you?"

"That would also be Nate," said Farrell. "This morning he was standing at my bedside with this twisted look on his face and a revolver, and he said, 'There are no more clean washcloths.' "

"Nate," said Sally. "You had every right."

"My father is gay," said Jess, both to make Farrell and me comfortable and score a bohemian brownie point or two.

"And I think this apartment is enchanting," Farrell went on, "especially that oil portrait. Jackson, is that your great-great-great-whoever?"

Farrell was evaluating a dour, heavily sideburned man in a high collar, against a dusty black background.

"I found him at the Hadassah thrift store for two dollars," said Jackson, "but I'm sure he's someone's great-great-great-whoever, and I like to think that he died while this was being painted."

"Yes," Farrell concurred. "And I have a thought—has anyone ever been to a bar downtown called Ryders? I think there's a dance floor, and Nate and I have been dying to go."

This was true. There hadn't been much nightlife in Piscataway, and heading out unchaperoned would be another milestone. Jackson distributed everyone's belongings, and we walked twelve blocks to a (deliberately) nondescript place on a side street, with a sputtering neon sign. Ariadne informed me, "This is a gay bar, you know. Have you ever been to a gay bar?"

I hadn't. I'm sure there were gay bars in towns near Piscataway, but I didn't drive and I couldn't have leaned on my parents for a lift. I had only the haziest notion of what such a bar might contain, based on "searingly raw" movies where hardened detectives in trench coats flashed their badges as they infiltrated windowless basements with lurid red lightbulbs and the disgraced patrons turned their faces away from the camera. Gay bars also suggested the Weimar era, like the Kit Kat Club in *Cabaret*; maybe Ryders would have an epicene MC and marcelled lesbians in tweed suits with monocles.

"I've never been to a gay bar per se," Farrell told Ariadne, "but I'd like to think that once we show up, even a McDonald's would become a gay bar."

Ariadne stared at him with what was either titanic disgust or clinical appreciation. Ariadne's stare was every bit as potent as Farrell's chatter.

"Do they allow women?" Jess speculated, which brought up another aspect of gay life. I wasn't sure how subdivided the gay world was, and until Ariadne, I'd never met a lesbian. Ariadne would later identify as a stone butch top, which also sounds like a rustic kitchen counter in an updated New England farmhouse, which is the sort of thing I'd never say to Ariadne.

"You'll be fine," Ariadne told Jess, "you're with me."

"Jackson?" asked Sally. "Is this the best idea?"

"We'll find out," Jackson said agreeably; he and Sally had already bonded over vintage-sterling-silver-napkin-rings-and-tea-towels decorum. Sally hung back for a second, then lifted her chin and smiled, like a missionary approaching a cannibal village, bringing Jesus and holiday aprons embroidered with poinsettias.

I was glad to be with Farrell, and part of a group, because a gay bar was a major step. We left our outerwear at the coat check (while hefting my bearskin, the fellow hanging things up commented, "I'm gonna marry this"). The lighting was dim but cheery, with strands of primary-colored Christmas lights stapled to the ceiling. Music throbbed; dance music is any decent gay bar's plasma. Farrell took my hand. We were Hansel and Hansel, braving the woods together. There was a rough wooden bar stretching one full side of the room, manned by two good-looking, jovial guys, one bare-chested with an emblematic mustache, and the other in a shredded T-shirt, as if his bodybuilder's torso was uncontainable. There were guys, some college age but mostly older, some alone, nursing mugs of beer, and others in clusters, commenting on the video screens, which were alternating between edits of hard-core gay porn and musical numbers from canonical films of the last four decades.

A fundamental of this era's gay life: Marilyn Monroe cooing "Diamonds Are a Girl's Best Friend" in a pink satin gown was on equal footing with a grunting, naked porn star getting fisted in a leather sling (when you Cuisinart these two genres, you get Madonna). Sally was eyeing the monitors intently and said to me: "They're both very good at what they do."

Farrell bought us two Cokes, as if we'd wandered into a malt shop after school, and just about everyone in the bar was checking him out. Farrell was the only event capable of competing with a young Judy Garland, in bangs and a striped Victorian shirtwaist, warbling "The Boy Next Door" and five guys forming an anal daisy chain in the foyer of some Beverly Hills interpretation of a Tuscan villa.

At least two guys glanced at me as well, cuing a revelation: even Farrell wasn't everyone's type. Cruising was an unruly beast. Before that night I'd cruised unconsciously, gawking at someone and then sinking into the earth from embarrassment when they asked, "Is there something in my teeth?" But cruising is why gay bars came into being. These men had gathered to inspect one another, like picky housewives in a produce aisle, and make an educated or hazardously last-call selection. It lent the place a pulsingly carnal vibe, as if the air were equal parts stale cigarette smoke, generously applied cologne, sweat from the crush of bodies, loneliness from the lack of anything beyond basic conversation, and seething desire.

"All right," Farrell suggested, "we'll each make one circuit."

Farrell was way ahead of me. He was more accustomed to being cruised, and he was nudging me to get the hang of things. We traveled in opposite directions, intuitively practicing the first rule of cruising: feigning to look for an imaginary friend while scoping out everyone. Some guys add a fingertip to their lips and a puzzled expression, as if the imaginary friend was here a moment ago and where could he have gotten to?

I let my eyes rest fleetingly on one guy after another, and then away, to lessen the sting of rejection. Most of the men did the same, erasing me from any potential dance cards, a few with a flash of "In your dreams, asshole." Three guys held my gaze as a vibrating question mark, transmitting "maybe"; "if I get a little more drunk"; "at first I was interested, but it passed"; and once, with a bona fide smile, an invitation to—what? As a rookie, I had no follow-up ploy, and because I was with Farrell, I was off the market. But as with Farrell, I tingled from—being wanted. Found worthy. Becoming inexplicably lusted after. And as with Farrell, this was unsettling and heady, especially because I was young, which is a brief yet valuable card to play. You can be rich or clever or a Nobel Prize winner in neuroscience until the day you die, but you're only eighteen for a year.

Farrell veered toward me, as Jess leaned in, remarking, "I love it here. No one's paying any attention to me, and I don't mind a bit. But I loved watching whatever you guys were just doing—you're fresh meat."

"It's fascinating," said Farrell. "This place is like an open wound with an attitude. And I saw my Pre-Columbian Art professor, without his wife."

"Did you say hi?" asked Ariadne.

"I wasn't sure what to do," Farrell admitted. "So I saluted."

"I've been to these places, but only down South," said Jackson, who'd been making his own rounds, "where it's more of a roadhouse setup, lots of good old boys pretending they're drunker than they are, with their tractors parked out front. There's an unspoken agreement, that no one's gay and everyone's available."

"This one fellow just asked me if I was a drag queen," said Sally, perturbed. "I'm not sure if I should take that as a compliment."

"But you must!" insisted Jackson. "Imagine a drag queen so refined he's wearing pearls and ballet flats. You're a pioneer! You're a drag debutante!"

Sally remained doubtful, so Farrell proposed, "I think we should dance."

I'd danced to liberating pop hits on 8-track tapes, and original cast albums spun on my boxy woodgrain record player, alone in my childhood bedroom, with great bravura and Broadway precision, according to me. And I'd danced in the chorus of a high school production of an Andrew Lloyd Webber musical; drama club choreography is calisthenics without the flair. I'd never attended any school dances, because everything about them seemed like a bad musical. I'd spent prom night on a hillside with stoner friends who'd just gotten into a wish-fulfillment offshoot of Buddhism. As one of them had outlined, "It's so cool, it's like, if I want my own car instead of driving my mom's Rambler, I can just chant for one!"

The dance floor was a square of battered parquet with the low ceiling common to gay bars, which are often converted warehouses or storefronts. There was a rotating disco ball, small enough so that dancers wouldn't bump their heads, along with minor-league theatrical lights, which could spin and change color, with an after-hours blue deepening into a hellish red replaced by a sunshiny gold. Gay bar dance floors, as opposed to cavernous dance clubs', have a rec room friendliness, but like the other dancers, I'd be on display.

Jess, because of her outgoing nature and dance training, twirled onto the floor, with only a hint of that operatic-soprano-singing-Gershwin stiffness. Jackson floated beside her, with a courtier's grace; he was comfortable in any social situation. He beckoned to Sally, who gave a why-the-hell-not grin and struck a few mild modern dance poses. Sally would've preferred a waltz or gavotte. Ariadne put out her cigarette and kept to a corner, chugging away, like a super-practical piston, her arms and legs repeating polished rhythms. She was already a good, focused dancer, but not the flag-swirling mascot she'd become.

Farrell held out his hand and I followed him. Stepping onto a dance floor, even in this limited venue, panicked me, like testing an icy lake to see if I'd glide or drown beneath the ice. I lived in my head, but Farrell was activating my body below the neck, in sex and now here. The dance floor was even more daunting than Farrell's bedroom, because people were watching.

Then, bless the gay gods, it happened: the DJ, tucked away behind the bar, played a truly incredible song. These were the fledgling days of disco, that reviled and thoroughly glorious form. This was when disco still belonged to Black, Latin, and gay people (with plenty of overlap). This was before disco had infected aerobics classes, elevators, and wedding receptions. I'd never heard a song like this: the beat was insistent and predatory, coursing through my arms and legs. At its best, disco turned everyone into a dancer, into someone howling with joy at the miracle of music.

Farrell and I, along with everyone else on the floor, screamed, because the song was so good, and we started gyrating, helplessly enthralled.

To my amazement and relief, I wasn't a washout. I didn't prance or audition high-degree-of-difficulty spins, but I matched Farrell's full-body brio. I'd wondered if Farrell was a good dancer, or if his wealth and private schooling might keep him tense or polite, shuffling his feet and almost dancing, disdaining such a plebian pastime. But I'd underestimated him, because he possessed the most essential qualification for any great dancer: he loved to dance.

Dancing unleashed Farrell, and incited his dreams of freedom. Sometimes we locked eyes and sometimes we shut them. Sometimes we held each other, and during the slower, more sultry songs, we'd grind our pelvises together, hoping to infuriate our parents. I loved to see Farrell dancing: when a boy that beautiful could really move, it became the most heavenly injustice. Above everything else, I loved seeing Farrell so happy.

That first night, our group persisted on the dance floor until 1 a.m., because we had stamina, there were more great songs, and the crowd was congenial. Even Sally resolved not to worry about sweating in public. Just as a song was peaking, Farrell kissed me, to complete the moment, and include me in everything he was feeling. If I had to choose, that would be the exact second at which Farrell and I began to fall dangerously and truly in love (which sounds like an overheated song title, which is what I'd ached for love to be). The kiss ended with certainty and fear. Something had happened, something that we could never deny, and something that was launching us toward a shared future.

Falling in love at eighteen isn't uncommon, but it's suspect. Farrell and I were both, if not innocent, untried. But holding back, sensibly awaiting maturity, would've been foolish. Because after that kiss and that night, being in love was no longer a decision. I'd made the leap, from musical comedy to grand opera. I was on the poster, over the title. Being in love is a means of starring in your own life. It's why, when teenagers smirk that a person or vulnerability is "so gay," I want to respond, "You wish."

"That was fabulous," said Jackson, "but I have a class in Jacobean undergarments tomorrow at 8 a.m., so I'll need to head back."

"I feel so much better," said Jess.

"About what?" I asked.

"Oh, you know, the zit on my chin and my mother and the scene from *Streetcar* I have to do in class tomorrow. All the usual nightmares. But dancing always helps."

"If anyone asks," said Sally, "I was never here. My grandparents would be extremely concerned."

"There's a women's bar downstairs," Ariadne suggested. "We could tie you up and leave you there."

"I'll think about that," Sally replied, entertained by Ariadne. And if the truth were told, Ariadne hailed from a more prominent, if disgraced, family (Dad's binge drinking and uncanny knack for bad investments) and had gone to a more esteemed prep school than Sally. While in many ways opposed, they were both well-brought-up young ladies.

"We shall return!" Farrell called out to the crowd, which had dwindled. He'd also been careful to fill the bartenders' tip jars with bills.

Once outside, the air was chillier and there weren't many working streetlights. New Haven side streets can get very deserted, but our group had become friends, and we staggered back toward campus, huddling together, with Farrell as our intrepid guide. For such an independent figure, he took care of people, he tended to them, and of course, when such a radiant being did this, we became a chosen flock, as if we must have something to offer, because Farrell liked us.

"New Haven in February!" Farrell decreed. "It's a Dickensian fantasyland!"

A car barreled down the street, packed with young men yelling something rancid, and one of them leaned out a window and pitched an unopened glass bottle of beer, which slammed Farrell on the side of his head, propelling him face-forward onto the street, blood spurting, as the young men barked with laughter and sped away.

7

Ariadne ran back into the bar to call an ambulance. I rode with Farrell to the emergency room, and everyone else would meet us there. The paramedics began cleaning his head with alcohol and applying compression to stop the bleeding. There was so much blood that I couldn't estimate how badly Farrell had been hurt. He tried to talk, to reassert his Farrell-ness, as I told him that he was going to see a doctor. I'm usually pretty good under pressure; when I'd broken my arm in three places, while clumsily executing a high jump over a metal bar in a seventh-grade gym class, I'd walked myself to the nurse's office alone, the misshapen limb dangling. But this was Farrell, so I willed the ambulance to go faster and held his hand, which the gay paramedic approved of, while telling me, "You guys gotta be careful."

As a nurse wheeled him out of the hospital's waiting area and into an examination cubicle, Farrell forbid anyone from notifying the police or his family: "They don't need to hear that I was attacked outside a gay bar. I won't give them that."

"How can people be such pigs?" Jess wondered, as the group sat together beneath generic, manufactured landscape paintings. I swore that once he was on the mend, I'd ask Farrell to analyze hospital art.

"People are idiots," said Ariadne, "and I bet that's not the first time those morons have done this. They know where the bar is and they know it stays open late."

"I've had experience with such creatures," said Jackson. "I grew up around them. It's their idea of a great high time."

"We shouldn't have been there," said Sally. "We turned Farrell into a target."

I got why Sally said that, and she was as shaken as the rest of us, but I hated the idea of making this the group's fault, and even more, I hated that the paramedic was right, and that going forward, we'd have to be watchful. College, I'd thought naively, would be a refuge from this degree of hatred; I'd worked hard to dismiss the uglier precincts of reality. I'd theorized that Farrell and I would be insulated by how we felt about each other, by a force field of affection, but the opposite was true. The more gay people loved each other, and the greater openness we represented, the more beer bottles would become weapons. Those thugs were exactly the sort of people who, a few years later, would chant "Disco sucks!" and "Rock and roll!" while torching bonfires of 12-inch dance singles at football stadiums.

The strange thing was, back in Piscataway, I'd never been physically attacked or even taunted, at least not to my face. Granted, I wasn't out to almost anyone, but I was recognizably, as my mom might say, creative. The lack of harassment was most likely due to my fellow New Jerseyans' I-don't-give-a-fuck jauntiness, along with their belief that gay people didn't exist. Prejudice was stockpiled for Black people or, in some parts of town, Italians. My being gay and Jewish didn't enter most of the town's field of consciousness. Piscataway natives had blind spots, along with an often stoned absence of snobbery. When I'd been accepted at Yale and told a few people, the school's prestige had meant nothing, so I was congratulated with a puzzled, egalitarian warmth. My classmates were off to the Air Force Academy or prison.

"I'm fine, really," Farrell reiterated, once he was released from the hospital four hours later, with eighteen stitches in his scalp. He had a black eye, his head was bandaged, and he was holding a plastic bottle of prescription painkillers; Ariadne scrutinized the label with a professional's finesse, concluding, "Yeah, this is decent stuff, unless Farrell's driving or operating heavy machinery. Once you take these, you can basically chop your arm off and not notice. And Farrell, if you don't finish the bottle, just let me know."

At the townhouse, Bates and I got Farrell undressed and into bed, where he sat up, resembling a post-bout prizefighter.

"Are you sure you don't want me to call anyone?" I asked. "A lawyer or somebody about insurance?"

Farrell smiled then winced, as his head throbbed. I was clueless, about how personal injury attorneys or insurance agents functioned.

"Money is not an issue," he said quietly. "But if my family, if my brothers or my parents hear about any of this, they'll have questions and accusations; they'll have a lip-smacking triumph. Oh, Nate."

"What?"

"I hate this. Not so much for me, I'll recover, and I'll tell people I was in a bar fight on the waterfront, with a drunken sailor. I'll say I killed him and refuse to talk about it. But Nate, you're not really built for this, are you? What's the worst thing that's ever happened to you?"

I was torn, between cooking up a gunslinging roster of tough-guy credentials, and the truth. As a child of the suburbs, I'd been coddled; aside from why-is-my-bedtime-so-early frustrations, any real suffering had been more observed than experienced. My older brother, Max, had flaunted unkempt hair to his shoulders, sold marijuana, dropped out of high school, and most damning of all, had once, while our parents were at a restaurant, wheeled his motorcycle into the living room and Polaroided it, parked atop my mother's esteemed wall-to-wall olive wool carpeting, in front of the lamps and end tables that had taken her years to settle on, returning rejects to furniture stores across the tristate area.

There hadn't been a stain or tread mark, but Max had strewn the photos in plain sight, and warfare had ensued. My parents, like many first-generation Jews, badgered their kids to advance as conventionally as possible. Their face-offs with Max had been savage, and one evening my dad wrestled him to the ground, planning to hack off his hair with the scissors my mother had handed him. I'd begged everyone to stop and I'd run up to my room. That night had exposed my parents' violent compulsion for the worst brand of normalcy, but I'd been only a quivering witness.

Such nights also accounted for my desire to please, to become the polished, chronically well-prepared, straight-A alternative child, with everyone relieved and proud. I'd respected my brother, who wasn't especially rebellious, just stubborn and set on listening to Jethro Tull at an ear-splitting volume. Once Max left home for good, at seventeen, to crash on friends' couches and make his own, far more agreeable way, my parents had given me free rein, as long as a façade of achievement and handwritten bar mitzvah thank-you notes was bolted in place. I'd even kept my hair longer, in my brother's honor, but my parents hadn't been troubled by this, especially once I'd been accepted at Yale.

And to their credit, my parents had also supported my gay habits, under the guise of cultural appreciation. I was taken to the theater and museums, with wardrobe leeway. They'd questioned my bearskin, but it was suitably warm for the winter. As an outwardly good boy, I could let my thoughts roam, and slide my porn into an underwear drawer. I wasn't exactly closeted, because I didn't pretend to pursue girls, I was more—non-straight.

And now, tonight, I'd continued to stand right beside a painful event, without becoming its victim. Was I lucky or a coward?

"Nothing bad has happened to me," I admitted. "Except once my record player broke and I had to wait until my dad fixed it before I could listen to *Funny Girl* again. So I could finish writing down the lyrics."

"My darling," Farrell said, taking my hand, his eyes brimming with tears, "I had no idea."

"Shut up! But Farrell—are you going to be okay? I mean, how can we make sure this never happens again?"

"We can't. And this is only the beginning."

"What do you mean?"

"Bates?" Farrell called out, and the bedroom door instantly cracked open.

"Yes, Mr. Covington?" said Bates; he maintained this formality, to stay "in character."

"Bates, do we have any of those sublime milk chocolate nonpareils, with the rainbow sprinkles?" asked Farrell.

"I'm afraid not, sir. I'll pick some up first thing tomorrow."

"Get out," Farrell hissed, as Bates, suitably shamefaced, withdrew.

"You see what I mean, about tragedy?" Farrell told me. "Life is an unending, toxic hellscape. And do you know why we don't have any nonpareils left?"

"Why not?"

Farrell whispered bitterly, "Because we're gay."

Now I loved him even more, even though saying it was off-limits. His head had been sliced open by cackling assholes, but he was Farrell, and he refused to stop being gay, at least with me. I wanted to get into bed with him, but he should rest. As I stood up to go, he opened the covers and said, "Come on. You've been through something, too. Neither of us should be alone. But if you touch my head I'll scream."

As I took off my clothes and was three yards from the bed, he yelped in bloodcurdling distress. Then he smiled and said, "Just practicing."

I crawled into bed beside him, carefully. I'd only begun to process the full evening, with my maiden visit to a gay bar, my debut on the dance floor, a soul-shaking kiss, and an assault.

"I know," said Farrell, kissing my ear.

8

Over the next weeks, Farrell's stitches dissolved and the section of his hair that had been shaved grew back, although he'd trace the scar with a fingertip. That night made Farrell and me more serious, about each other and our classes. We'd hold symposium-intense conversations about the state of the world, including the final gasp of the Vietnam War, whether Pat Nixon drank, and Faye Dunaway's work in *The Towering Inferno*, where Faye escapes a burning skyscraper wearing low-cut beige chiffon. As Farrell said, "You can tell that San Francisco is about to be engulfed in flames, because Faye's hair flutters as she slightly widens her eyes."

When we studied together at Farrell's townhouse, we'd end up snacking, having sex, or listening to Bates rehearse a Shakespearean monologue for an upcoming national competition, so we switched to the library. We'd sit across from each other at one of the long oak tables, with piles of books, and one afternoon, when I'd finished highlighting a chapter with a neon-lime marker, I glanced up at Farrell, who'd given himself a hot-pink marker mustache. We had prearranged rendezvous zones deep in the stacks, in the unpopular and therefore less inhabited sections like Particle Physics and Native Grasses of the Outer Mongolian Tundra. We once choose Byzantine Monasteries of the 14th Century, forgetting Ariadne was a Religious Studies major, and during our make-out session a husky voice intoned, "Really?"

There was a contrast, between that initial, only-two-people-on-earth isolation with Farrell, and my days brimming with essays to be researched on feminist prototypes in Willa Cather, painting plastic bricks for a harshly Brechtian production of *Pal Joey* at the Dramat, and loafing around Jackson's apartment with everyone, griping about our course loads, our professors' critiques, and everyone's collective crush on Woodward and Bernstein, who were young, belligerent, and unkempt enough to qualify as undergraduate heroes.

I'd had friends before, but mostly kids my age who'd lived on our block. We'd ride our bikes to smoke dope on the picnic tables at the playground, and set off firecrackers in people's mailboxes, but there hadn't been much back-and-forth about Sondheim versus Kander and Ebb. My college friendships were blooming from mutual interests and group lunges at sophistication. We'd speculate about movie stars' sexuality (based entirely on rumors) while attending screenings of John Waters movies at the student film society, or we'd amble through an art show of feminist oil paintings where the artist depicted herself nude and sullen with chipped black nail polish, having sex with the dean of the art school atop his desk (the dean denied everything). I pursued my social education, as Jackson charted the important gradations between a classmate whose flashy gold wristwatch marked him as "deeply nouveau," a shabbily dressed guy whose frayed cuffs indicated "Old Money up the wazoo," and a lanky, possibly heroin-addicted Italian who was "dreamy but doomed Euro-rich."

As an outlier, I could ask questions directly and have Farrell dispense corollary insights later. Farrell was up on everything and noted, "It's not gossip if you care about the person." While I was getting filled in about imprisoned celebrity uncles and hushed-up campus suicides and untrustworthy twin sisters at Harvard, the school year ended. Farrell became a Death Row inmate, since "I'm going to be submerged in Wichita all summer, because my father says it's high time I interfaced with the Covington Industries personnel department, from the ground up. He's assigning me to shadow some junior executive and report back every evening. So you may get a call to identify my body."

I'd stick around New Haven through August, toiling as a waiter/janitor and costume assistant to Jackson at the Summer Cabaret, which produced themed musical revues and abbreviated versions of famous plays for a local audience, with a new show every week. Farrell moped. "You'll be having fun," he said, to which I replied, "I'll be scrubbing toilets." "But in the theater!" Farrell moaned jealously, and then, "But the worst part is, we won't be able to see each other for months. And even our phone calls will be limited, because nefarious Covingtons will be lurking and listening in on the extensions. My father keeps threatening to install recording devices, which means he's already done it. When I yelped about privacy, he said, 'Farrell, if you're not doing anything to be ashamed of, you have nothing to worry about.'"

After farewell sex, and Farrell hugging his favorite pieces of furniture ("Neo-Bauhaus credenza, I think I'll miss you most of all"), a car came to fetch him; he'd be flying west on a corporate jet. I was equally spoiled because while I was making well below the minimum wage, Farrell was letting me stay in his townhouse all summer with Bates, who, it turned out, would be a member of the Summer Cabaret acting company. There was something queasily sinful about having my rich boyfriend loan me an entire building. I should've repurposed the premises as a free clinic or a hostel, but it wasn't my house.

"Listen to me," said Jackson, on my first day at the mildewed costume shop, in the basement of the Summer Cabaret's postage stamp–sized theater. "When a rich person offers you something, take it. It's most likely not costing them a penny, and it makes them happy. So if you think you're selling your soul, don't worry. That won't happen until, I'd say, the first semester of your junior year."

In his private life, Jackson was nothing but caring and effervescent, but as a boss, there were timetables and taskmaster lectures.

"All right, I need you to take these fifteen yards of corduroy and cut them into three-foot squares, which we'll use for tunics in the forty-five-minute *Romeo and Juliet*. Can you sew?"

Another instance when I almost lied but caught myself: "No, I'm so sorry . . ."

"You can't sew? Who are you? Why weren't you taught the basic masculine arts? Fine, just section the corduroy and I'll do the real work."

Jackson passed me a hefty pair of gleaming silver shears, and as I began to slice into the corduroy I heard the bone-rattling shriek of a mother as her infant crawls beneath the wheels of an idling garbage truck. An especially traumatized mother. An especially traumatized mother from South Carolina.

"WHAT ARE YOU DOING? ARE YOU MAD?"

"Um, I was cutting the squares . . ."

"You were cutting HORIZONTALLY, which destroys the fabric and renders it worthless! Give me those shears!"

Jackson strove to harness his trembling wrath: "I understand, you are not a professional seamstress, and perhaps you've been raised in a home without corduroy or shears or common sense. So I am not blaming you. For murdering fabric. Pay attention, are you paying attention, sit up straight, because I will demonstrate the correct method for sectioning corduroy and then I will supervise as you follow my example."

He faced away, too bereft to function. He stroked a few yards of corduroy and murmured to it, "He doesn't know any better, he's just some common ham-fisted underling boy from New Jersey, I am so very sorry."

After a massive time-out, Jackson tried to look at me, couldn't, lifted the shears, and expertly cut a flawless vertical square: "Did you see? Were you watching? Now the fabric is usable, now it remains alive and has value. Unlike . . ."

He indicated my unfortunate, dead square, and was able to instruct, "You're learning. And here is all I shall say: I have the most wonderful, mentally challenged sister, who was raised with self-esteem and charm and excellent table manners. She's learned to read, she can sing beautifully, and she works two afternoons per week as a greeter at our local waffle house. So if Miss Narelle Calypso Rains can comport herself with poise and efficiency, so can you."

So far, my yearning for a theatrical career had been only that: a heart-felt, fingers-crossed wish. For many people, theater promises glamour (whether old-school or revolutionary), an acquired family (to replace or enhance your biological bunch), and a flashbulb-lit array of pivotal opening nights, eighty-three standing ovations, bouquet-stuffed dressing rooms, rapturous reviews the next morning, sold-out runs, and access to champagne-drenched cast parties at producers' penthouses, rife with scampering chorus boys. I coveted these perks, based on repeated viewings of *All About Eve*, reference books covering every decade of musical theater ("*Song of Norway* was a last vestige of operetta"), unpaid labor in community theaters where the performers, often real estate agents and probate attorneys, referred to Broadway stars by their first names, and countless trips into Manhattan for matinees with *Playbills* to hoard and brownies à la mode at Midtown restaurants afterward.

I was tiptoeing toward that crossroads where theater can be overthrown, as a wistful phase, a childhood mirage like becoming an astronaut, a ballerina, or any career draped in a distinctive uniform that Barbie might wear. It's that rude yet helpful awakening when people accept that they'd rather go to the theater than work in it. But for me, the hermetic, life-only-better dream, however vague and unrealized, refused to evaporate. Many theater artists begin as actors, greedy for the emotional highs and stage-door acclaim. I'd acted in school shows and played waiters and bellmen in summer stock comedies. But real actors, like Jess, were another breed entirely, possessing a talent and discipline far beyond my reach. Until Jackson, I'd never met anyone professionally set on a life in the theater, and even more, he was training for that life and how to finance it.

"Oh, I tried to resist," Jackson told me, over a takeout lunch at our worktable; as soon as we were off the clock, Jackson resumed being outgoing and confessional. "My family still works in a pageant drama down South, it's called the Carolina Cavalcade."

"A pageant drama?" I asked.

The next day he pulled, from one of his trademark white canvas tote bags, a souvenir program with photos of an outdoor amphitheater, its wide stage bustling with a scene of pilgrim-hatted settlers being solemnly gifted with papier-mâché pumpkins and ears of corn by white actors in loincloths, slathered with brown "Texas dirt" makeup, as Native Americans. This was followed by a Caucasian family, their once fine garments in tatters, reuniting amid the embers of their plantation after the Civil War. Next up were brave Carolina soldiers enlisting in both world wars, and finally, a full-skirted mom, slacks-clad dad, and baseball-capped, snub-nosed children seated around a campfire beside their Ford station wagon, beneath a banner painted with "The Carolina of Today!" or at least, say, 1951. There were over one hundred actors, along with an orchestra, a choir, and effects duplicating a sunrise, torrential rain, and lightning igniting a faux log cabin (the flames being red-and-orange silk banners shot skyward by hidden electric fans).

"And yes, I know it's racist and historically demented," Jackson told me, "but it's where I grew up. My father was the technical director and my mother, Miss Mabel Doralee Rains, well, she was . . ."

He opened the program to a full-page portrait of a tiny, sweet-faced woman dressed as Queen Elizabeth I, in a stiff lace ruff, an elaborately coiled wig studded with pearls, and a brocade gown the size of a Volkswagen Beetle. The woman's demeanor was oddly right at home in this finery, while teenage interns dressed as caped and tricorned nobles bowed low before her.

"She's been Queen Elizabeth for over thirty years and she sends Sir Walter Raleigh to the New World, and she also runs the theater's Christmas shop during the day, where customers can buy candy cane ornaments and snowball-shaped mugs in July. When I was five years old they put me to work in the props department, and I adored it."

"But you said you tried to resist."

"Of course. I'm older than you and your Mr. Covington, and this was the South, so things were, shall we say, prehistoric. My family loved the Cavalcade, but I was expected to pursue something far less frivolous. After college I enrolled at Chapel Hill, where I was dead set on getting my doctorate as a professor of French History, specializing in the sixteenth to eighteenth centuries. And I was engaged to be married, to the sweetest girl, Miss Martha Shay Barrington, and everything was full speed ahead."

I was amazed. Jackson was so deeply gay, in the most hall-of-fame manner, that I couldn't place him anywhere but backstage, with a mouthful of pins, hand-stitching lace onto petticoats, or serving fleur-de-lis gingerbread cookies and plum brandy to guests at his salon evenings. I considered him a beacon of frisky candor and baroque high style.

"What happened?" I asked.

"I will tell you, as we staple these paper camellias to Juliet's gown." The gown was a thrift shop find, a $14 wedding dress that Jackson had altered, adding flowing trumpet sleeves, velvet panels, and the origami flowers that he was pinning in place for me to very carefully attach; Jackson was a wizard at micro-budget miracles.

"Remember to hide your staples in the petals so the dress doesn't look like it's been shot with a BB gun. Very good, you see, you're applying yourself. Where was I? Oh that's right, my life. So I was just two credits short of my degree, and five months away from my wedding, when I took a trip, alone, through Europe, which I claimed was for final bits of research on my thesis. But I was really going to, I don't know, escape from all worldly matters and quite possibly kill myself."

"Jackson?"

"Hush, I'm telling you everything, so you'll know what you're getting into, with a life in the theater. Because I see myself in you, you're right at the precipice, and you're trying to decide if you really have the nerve. Because you and I, we don't have the economic cushion of your Mr. Covington, who can fill his townhouse with signed Warhols and vicuña topcoats and Wedgwood soup tureens brimming with rubies."

Jackson liked Farrell and probably harbored a crush on him, but he'd been cagey. He always referred to him as Mr. Covington or His Royal Blondness. Jackson was a barometer of social boundaries and class distinctions; he was jealous of Farrell's cultivated dash, and didn't trust it.

"So I got one of those student rail passes and traveled through the French countryside and the Italian hill towns and German villages, visiting every Renaissance chapel and crumbling fresco I'd ever seen in my books. And on the last day of my trip I took a room in this tiny Swiss inn, and I went to a bar and met some almost-handsome but adorably jug-eared farm boy, who brought me back to his barn and fucked me silly. Oh, I'd had sex with boys before, it's quite common down South, everyone fools around with their Marine Corps buddy and then everyone gets married, it's a tradition. But I thought of being gay as, well, perhaps something between a hobby and an extracurricular activity, but hardly a main event, and never my life, because in my family, well, it just isn't done. Not among decent folk."

Which brought up what might happen if I told my family I was gay, at our Passover seder or when answering the question, "How are you?" Being a Drama major was a prelude, or at least a vague wave from a distant shore, but saying it out loud, and forcing the issue, was something I'd postponed. What was I waiting for? Would I dent my Ivy League, favored child, tell-Aunt-Yetta-about-your-prize-winning-book-report veneer?

"So the next morning, I climbed some sort of alp, by myself; I was wearing the silliest little green felt Tyrolean hat, with a turkey feather, which I'd bought in a tourist shop at the train station, as if I was about to yodel or clog dance. And I stood at the edge of a cliff, because of course I did, but once I got up there I knew: I couldn't do it. I couldn't get married and live in some even halfway acceptable ranch house with a carport and indoor-outdoor carpeting and teach French History. And I'd been fully prepared to toss myself right off that cliff, because I couldn't imagine a way out. But then, well, and you're going to laugh at me, and go right ahead, but I had this bird's-eye view of myself, this tragic police detective photo of my crumpled, broken dead body, deep in a crevasse, being pecked at by Swiss vultures. And I'd still be wearing that absurd little Tyrolean von Trapp hat. Which made me giggle."

I could see it, Jackson's painfully hilarious tableau. Jackson was piercingly smart, with a streak of Carolina lunacy. His personality echoed his boldly florid watercolor costume sketches, with slashes of ink and rivulets of jewel-toned color, everything fluid, impressionistic, and circus-like.

"And once I laughed, well, it was all over. I told myself, Jackson Bell Rains, you're a big nelly queen and you want to design costumes and you belong in the theater, and if you don't at least try, well, that will be a far worse death than some Alpine suicide. Nate, do you understand what I'm saying to you? You're not a child, not anymore, and you've fallen under the bespoke suited sway of our dear Mr. Covington, who I can tell from his lack of undershorts is a fellow of multiple gifts. But he's rich and he'll need to make his own decisions and you'll need to make yours. And oh my dear Lord, you have stapled that lovely camellia directly to your blue jeans!"

That night, as I lay half-awake in Farrell's bed, I remembered Jackson's directive and thought: Where am I headed? Would Farrell continue to subsidize me and was it in any way healthy to let him? He'd said he loved me, but was that romantic hypnotism? I talked a good game, but how gay was I willing to be? Should I sprint headlong toward the theater, expecting a victory, or at least a participation medal? I had three years of college left, but was that anywhere near enough time to revamp myself into someone worth introducing to New York? I was Joan Crawford, her fists at her temples, amid a tempestuous black-and-white nervous breakdown. I yawned and stretched, luxuriating in the 600-thread-count Egyptian cotton sheets, telling myself, Nate Reminger, you're a New Haven whore. Why wasn't I wearing too much rouge and a sleazy kimono hanging off one shoulder, with a single fishnet stocking, rolled to the knee? But I slept like a baby, because there's nothing more therapeutic than fine linens, which are God's way of saying hope exists.

Two weeks later I got a call at the costume shop, and I caught on that someone was eavesdropping because Farrell spoke in code: "Bates, it's Mr. Covington. I'll be sending a car tomorrow at eleven, I need you to help me with a real estate matter in Rhode Island. Please bring a change of clothes, as things may get dusty. The driver will have the address, and I'll see you by 1 p.m."

He hung up. Jackson was adjusting a bias-cut satin gown on a stained dress form, for a reduced or, more accurately, starved production of *Anything Goes* (with a cast of six).

He said knowingly, "What does Farrell want you to do? Is it illegal? Remember, rich people never leave their fingerprints. Only yours."

"I'm not sure what he wants, and I already have tomorrow off, but I may need an extra day, is that okay?"

"Nathaniel, you have responsibilities, you can't just go gallivanting off when your well-endowed male lover crooks his little finger or other portions of his anatomy. I'll only allow it on one condition."

"What?"

"That afterwards, you tell me everything. You're not the only person who needs to masturbate."

9

By 11 a.m. the next day, a car was parked outside the townhouse, as the driver, in a dark suit and chauffeur's cap, stood obediently by the open rear door. I'd never used a car service before, which skewed distinctly un-American: Should I chat with the driver? Would that annoy him? Should I have sat up front beside him, as a show of workers' solidarity? Farrell was comfortable with being waited on, but I was conflicted, although never enough to deny myself a single indulgence. I asked the driver if he belonged to a union and if he owned the car, and he said an untroubled no to both. Later, when I was about to tip him, he murmured, "It's been taken care of."

The drive to Newport, Rhode Island, lasted just under two hours, and if I'd been conscience-stricken by taking a car, I was now gasping at one of America's greatest robber baron spectacles. During the previous century, New York's most appallingly prosperous manufacturers had bought up miles of the pre-income-tax ocean frontage for "summer cottages." I'd ogled these estates in the luscious pages of *National Geographic*, but on a clear, sunny August day they were, if anything, even more overweening and photogenic.

We passed a piss-elegant Lombardy château, and a colonnaded Greek pavilion, beside a Regency limestone hulk. Newport was less a town than an architectural history slideshow. Many of these homes remained in private hands, but some were open to the public for a few hours each week, to middle-class mortals pushing strollers and wearing tube socks and cut-off shorts.

The car passed through the gates of a remote cliffside edifice, distanced from its braggart neighbors. This "cottage" appeared as large as, and even more elaborate than, the others, designed in the Gothic Revival style, which I'd admired in everything from the House of Lords to the Woolworth Building in lower Manhattan. Following Gothic Revival precepts, this residence merged the stature of a soaring cathedral with toy box eccentricity, with the painted spires and gingerbread trim of a fairy tale retreat, or, under gloomier weather, a haunted manor from a Vincent Price horror movie, with circling bats and yapping werewolves.

As with everything associated with Farrell, my first reaction was: I don't belong here. I'm trespassing. I should purchase a day pass and a booklet of postcards while renting an audio-guide headset. Had this place already become a museum-piece attraction, was it a Catholic school, or did someone Farrell was chummy with, or related to, get to live here? And was there a doorbell?

I climbed the front steps, my sporting-goods store nylon knapsack over my shoulder, but when I went to knock on the high, curved wooden front door, with its curlicued metalwork, it swung open. Was the place abandoned? Weren't the owners careful about thieves and partying teenagers and me? I stepped inside, to be swamped by not just dome-like ceilings with gilded tracery, but a wide, forced-perspective central hallway, open to room after room but sun-soaked by far-off, open doors, leading to a rear lawn and, finally, the Atlantic Ocean. The sunlight bounced off every mirror and mirror-bright polished floor and expanse of pale pink, heraldic crested wallpaper, blinding me, but as I squinted, the silhouette of someone swooped toward me: it was Farrell on roller skates treating so much extravagance as a rink.

"Do you like it?" he asked, coming to a gracefully angled halt. "Is it too cramped, you know, for us and the dogs?"

Then he grinned and rolled into my arms and kissed me. "Oh my

God," he said, "I can't tell you how much I've missed that. Wait, let me make sure."

We kissed again, but I was too discombobulated to really go for it.

"Farrell—where are we?"

I'd asked him this before, at the townhouse. Maybe rich people get bored and seek to keep topping every vista, making sure their slack-jawed fans stay dazzled. Would I always be so many steps behind, pleading with Farrell to demystify his universe? And where should I put my knapsack?

"I'll take that," Farrell said, dropping the knapsack onto a round marble-topped table. "Come along and I'll explain."

Stepping out of his roller skates, Farrell took my hand and padded into a parlor, seating us on a high-backed, tufted sofa.

"Okay, first we drink it in," he said, letting me inhabit the room, where every piece of furniture was hand-carved with gothic trefoils and linen-fold paneling; where the wooden heads of tonsured monks, armored knights, and mane-tossing unicorns jutted from armoires and chimney-pieces. Every chair was a throne, and the sunlight flooding through the stained glass windows made vibrant puddles on the rugs, all woven in repeated, geometric gothic patterns.

"Do you know about Mad Ludwig, the King of Bavaria?" Farrell asked. "He built all of these storybook castles, like stage sets you could walk around in. This has Ludwig written all over it."

I'd studied Ludwig, who was born in 1845. In thrall to Wagnerian operas, he'd commissioned hunting lodges, palaces, and grottos based on his fantasies. He'd ride in a swan boat across an artificial indoor lake and dress as mythic heroes, in velvet and ermine. He'd invited a tenor to dine, but had been sorely disappointed when the guy didn't speak with Wagnerian pomp. His brief reign had been scuttled by reportedly manic flights of dining atop a snowbank in January and waltzing with phantoms, and his parliament had him declared insane. Soon after this degradation he drowned in a lake, either by suicide, as a failed escape, or from a government plot.

Ludwig may have been certifiable, or merely a Spielberg or De-Mille ahead of his time. Above all else, he struck me as epically gay, and reminiscent of Farrell. Ludwig was handsome, rich enough to subsidize every whim, and constrained by his less imaginative handlers and by his ordained role in society. But was Farrell crazy and gayness unbound? Was his Ludwigness part of his appeal? Were we sitting inside one of his manias?

"But who built this place?" I asked. "And do they still live here?"

"It was built by my great-aunt Mirielle in 1927," Farrell began. "I only met her once, when I was five, so all I remember is a frail, distracted woman, but tall, with very soft hands. She was my father's aunt, but he almost never talked about her, and whenever I asked my mother, she'd just shake her head and say it was all too sad, and poor Mirielle, and that the life of an invalid is never easy."

"So was she sick? While she lived here?"

"I'm not sure, I have no details. All I know is she died last month, at seventy-one, and that my father of course wants to sell this place. My brothers are crunching the numbers, to see if they can make more money from a single buyer, or from donating the property to Rhode Island and getting some obscene tax break, or by tearing the place down and selling the land in parcels. So I've been sent to inspect everything and write up a full report, although I don't think I'll have any say in the final decision. But the minute I received my assignment I decided, Bates should assist me, or at least that's what my darling family thinks is going on. I'm sorry I couldn't be more coherent over the phone. Do you hate me?"

I hadn't seen Farrell in months, let alone touched him. I could tell he'd been around his family; he was downtrodden, as if he'd gone without nourishing food or fresh air. Which of course made me hug him, so our bodies could breathe together, and he could start to feel not just better, but more completely himself. That's when it struck me, that one of the reasons I was put on this earth, my responsibility, was to embolden the people I cared about, to let the divine oddness of their personalities flower. I wanted Farrell to glean, without my saying it, not yet, that I loved him for exactly who he wanted to be.

"Thank you," he said, as we ended the hug, having begun our reconnection. We'd been separated for an extended period. There was a strangeness; we couldn't just pick up where we'd left off. If you love someone, you need to keep getting to know them, especially after being apart. While this was disconcerting, it was also sexy, as if we'd just spotted each other across a hotel lobby and begun to envision each other naked.

"Are you hungry or thirsty? I've got a car so we can grab something later although I'm sure there's a kitchen. Or should we just get started? And crack the wall safe and abscond with Great-Aunt Mirielle's tiara collection?"

"Let's do it!"

I'd never been inside a house this large or this ornate, and Farrell was right: we'd become cat burglars, as if we'd crowbarred a basement window and crept in while Mirielle was away, maybe during December, although as Farrell mentioned, while these places were only occupied during the scant summer months, they were fully staffed and heated year-round, so the pipes wouldn't freeze and dust wouldn't accumulate.

We ventured into a baronial dining room, with a formal table set for thirty guests, the sterling silver centerpiece burgeoning with fresh blue and pink hydrangeas. Farrell pushed open a door embedded in the Chinese mural lining a breakfast room, which connected to a vast white-tiled kitchen, where hundreds of different-sized copper pots dangled above pristine metal prep tables.

There was an elevator, but we bounded up the circular stairway to a second floor, to find a surprisingly meager number of bedrooms. Farrell told me that during the Golden Age, guests were expected to have their own cottages nearby. A master bedroom boasted a matched suite of gothic furniture in mahogany, including an emperor-sized, canopied bed. Rather than disturbing the immaculate sheets, pillows, and duvet, we chose to invade the bathroom, which was far more erotic. It had the square footage of a three-bedroom apartment, with a fireplace, a quarry's worth of veined Carrara marble, gleaming nickel-plated hardware, and mirrored walls. Farrell yanked off my shirt, and we had preliminary sex on the black onyx floor, cushioning ourselves with the thickest white towels I'd ever known, embroidered with Mirielle's gothic monogram.

"Look at us," Farrell said, as we lay on our backs, our naked bodies reflected in the mirrored ceiling. Embarrassed, I moved to cover myself with a towel, but Farrell wouldn't let me. "We're making the world's first Gothic Revival gay porn movie," he declared, straddling me. I'd never watched myself having sex before, and I have to admit, it was incredibly satisfying, because it was, literally, hard evidence that Farrell and I could make each other so happy, and that I was vanquishing every suburban inhibition.

We scrubbed off together in what was too spacious for a broker to call a walk-in shower; it was a live-in shower. After depleting another stack of towels, we dressed and came across a third-floor mini Venetian opera house, a gymnasium with medicine balls and leather pommel horses, and finally, and most entrancingly, we entered a music room.

"Mirielle must've lived for music," Farrell said, because the walls were hand-painted with scenes of lute-playing troubadours and cavorting nymphs brandishing tambourines. There was a small stage, and instruments were leaned against the walls, including a cello, a bass, and assorted oboes and trombones. I managed a few scales on the grand piano, a gothic achievement where the legs were carved with figures of Beethoven, Brahms, and Liszt, all wearing wizardly robes and squashed velvet hats. I'd taken childhood piano lessons, but as with so much else, I wasn't good enough. I'd spy on student musicians during the rehearsals for drama club shows: their hands had a more natural agility over the keyboard, and they weren't working way too hard, the way I would, like a klutzy dancer anxiously counting steps and lifting his cement feet.

"I didn't know you played," said Farrell, and I wished I could nonchalantly unfurl some intricate, towering sonata, and then mutter, "I'm so rusty."

"A tiny bit. My parents bought me a used piano as a bar mitzvah present."

"I'm so obtuse. Is that a traditional bar mitzvah gift?"

"Yes, because after I stopped practicing, I could feel guilty."

"What songs do you know?"

I had a few perennials, mostly Jerome Kern and Harold Arlen. Like many theater brats, I revered songbooks composed long before I was born. I loved these songs, and deemed them markers of superior taste. Farrell and I had disco hits that we'd cheer for a DJ to spin, from Donna Summer, the Emotions, and Thelma Houston, but we still hadn't compared deeper dives into our record collections. Because what if, despite our lust for each other, one of us couldn't get past Captain & Tennille?

I had a lasting yen for Chet Baker, the ill-fated, drug-addled dreamboat who, while primarily a trumpet player, sang in a broken, whispered croon that destroyed me. He was my haunted crush; I was at that age of nurturing lonely, late-night passions. I noodled my all-time #1 Baker ballad, the plaintive anthem titled "I Never." During the years when I didn't have a boyfriend, meaning most of my life, I savored a private sorrow, as if my bedroom were a smoky, word-of-mouth jazz club.

As I played the first notes of the introduction, Farrell began to hum, and then sing softly, with perfect pitch. This was another trait we hadn't revealed to each other: if either of us could carry a tune. In a way, singing is more intimate than sex, maybe because to a certain extent, everyone can have sex. But so few people can really sing.

I wasn't one of those few people, and I'd certified this the hard way. In junior high school, I'd fancied myself a rising pop star, and had my parents buy me a cheap guitar and pay for a cycle of lessons in a local pothead's garage. I'd sing in talent shows, where anyone could clamber onstage and screech numbers with a minimal vocal range, like Leonard Cohen's "Suzanne" and Joni Mitchell's "Both Sides Now." I'd thought I was melodic and a shoo-in for a recording contract, until I made the greatest and most necessary mistake in borrowing my dad's valise-like, reel-to-reel tape recorder. Listening to the playback, I was not only devastated by my own nasal tonelessness, but crazed that someone, maybe a kindly schoolteacher, hadn't shot me in the face with a sawed-off shotgun to end the embarrassment.

After that I never sang again, not even in my room with the windows sealed and the curtains drawn, while everyone was at the mall; I knew better. I still credit my complete inability to sing as the central horror of my life, the dark not-so-secret that explains everything else. The rest of my days would be a who-cares second choice, a make-do settling for crap, because I can't sing. A substantial part of me still believes this, because it's a very gay metaphysical observation.

Farrell, on the other hand, could sing. It shouldn't have surprised me, since he had a gift for just about everything. But like a cackling troll, I'd hankered for a single flaw, to gloat over in my dank cavern. As I continued to play, Farrell's voice didn't grow louder or more substantial, but he was delivering the song with pathos and unmistakable beauty:

I never knew what I needed
Until one day you were there
I never thought, I always fought
the slightest desire to care
I never knew what I wanted
I thought that the songs weren't true
I never believed, I never conceived
that Cupid would ever come through
Now I do
I never thought I'd discover
What so many babble about
I thought I was smart so I didn't start
I'd scoff and I'd laugh and I'd doubt
I never thought I'd know real passion
I'd swear that it's all just a sham
That I wasn't the type to put up with such tripe
But I am

His smile was a signal, so I kept playing. He was singing right to me, which was captivating and unsettling, because of the song's mournful lyrics:

I'm sad and I'm scared
Someone stop me from falling
Before I am far too far gone

Please can't you see that this just isn't me
It's a trap, it's a dream, it's a con

I could only guess at the source of Farrell's lightly held but gorgeous despair. He wasn't singing to wow me, but because he loved to sing, and because it released something in him, something more straightforward or sentimental than he'd ever admit to, emotion without irony.

I had two choices: I could hate Farrell, for being so adroit at everything, and now this, or I could love him even more. Best of all, even with my marginal proficiency, I could accompany him, I could make his song possible. As he sang, he was watching me with gratitude and a regret we'd never talk about, not until far later. We were collaborating on something unexpected and perishable, a moment of harmony and the very best sort of art, because it was bubbling up and elating both of us. Music can be style incarnate; it isn't necessary, like food or shelter, yet it sustains life, or turns life more bearable:

I never thought I'd be drowning
In moonbeams and kisses and more
I'd had so much at stake so I'd stayed wide awake
In case there was heartbreak in store
I never thought there'd be someone
Who'd make me become someone new
I never thought I'd wish on a star
I always assumed that I'd watch from afar
I never dreamed you'd be here in my arms
But you are

As the song peaked, rather than bursting into tears, we held the emotion in reserve, and silently agreed that we were in a movie, at a Casablanca café or beneath a tacky chandelier in a tawdry casino lounge. I plinked a final note, which Farrell held for exactly the right span of big-screen luster. Then we did what we had to do: Farrell leaned over and kissed me, and while I kept commanding myself, as harshly as possible, Don't cry, I was about to.

A woman's voice asked, "May I help you, gentlemen?"

She was standing in the doorway, wearing a starched uniform in the home's signature pink and gold. She was in her sixties, although back then I estimated anyone over thirty to be in their sixties. She had a care-worn face, her hair in a neat bun, and an astringently professional manner, as if she'd had quite enough of rich people's whimpering complaints and soiled laundry.

"I'm so sorry," said Farrell, as we moved apart. "We didn't know there was anyone here."

"I'm Mrs. Wainlett," the woman said, "and you must be the youngest Mr. Covington, and this is . . . ?"

"Bates," I said, "his associate."

"Assistant," Farrell said, demoting me.

"I'm the housekeeper here at Lionheart House," she said. "And I apologize for any disarray, we're ordinarily fully staffed, but Mr. Covington—your father—has asked that we cut back, to a maintenance crew."

"Of course he has," said Farrell, "but thank you so much for staying on. How long have you worked here?"

"Forty-two years in September," said Mrs. Wainlett, with a sliver of pride that she promptly smothered. "And I've already attended to your debris in the master bath."

Oh my God. What had we left in our wake? And why was this place called Lionheart House?

"Forty-two years!" Farrell exclaimed. "That's marvelous! So you must've known my great-aunt Mirielle very well. I can barely remember her, so please, what can you tell us?"

"I'm sorry, but sad to say, I never met her. Mirielle Covington only resided here for three months, just after the house was built. That was before my time, but my predecessor, Mrs. Draxton, was in service then."

"Mrs. Draxton?" asked Farrell.

"Who remained, and took me under her wing. Until her death, this past year. The kindest and most devoted woman."

"Wait," said Farrell. "I didn't know any of this. Why did Mirielle only last three months? And where did she go? And who's been living here?"

"Just the staff. We were instructed to keep the home in spotless condition, in anticipation of Miss Mirielle's return, or that of another family member. We've done our best."

"So no one's lived here except for those few months?" I blurted out. "Since 1927?"

It made an eerie sense. The house sparkled, but nothing felt handled or worn. The premises were frozen in readiness, the dining room table set for a banquet that would never be served. Even the piano had been kept in tune. I hoped that Mrs. Wainlett, or some butler or handyman, had taken advantage for an afternoon's show tune or concerto, but I doubted it. Had the staff ever ceased trusting that a Covington, any Covington, would reappear? Or had they become cemetery keepers, forever tidying and polishing for the dead and the unaccounted for?

"Mrs. Wainlett," said Farrell, "I don't want to seem rude, and if you'd rather that your memories stay private, we completely understand. But, as you're obviously aware, my family is extremely secretive. And deranged. Is there anything else you can tell us about Mirielle?"

"By no means," she replied curtly. "I have my pension to think of, which specifies discretion. As soon as the house is sold, I'll retire."

"Will you miss it?" I asked.

She took in the music room, a place she'd vacuumed and scrubbed and kept just so, for absolutely no reason. But it was a beautiful room and an extraordinary house. Did that make preserving it a satisfying duty, or a spectral nightmare? Did Mrs. Wainlett permit herself an opinion?

"I love this house," she said, in a small, restricted voice, to the college boys who'd trespassed on her domain, abusing the towels and tracking gravel onto the rugs, showing no respect.

"Come with me," she said, leaving.

Mrs. Wainlett, with her martinet stride, took us through the kitchen and down a flight of concrete stairs, to the basement servants' quarters. There was a shadowy hallway painted an institutional mint green, and then Mrs. Wainlett opened an anonymous door. "My rooms," she said. "And I've been grateful."

We weren't in some wretched cell. There was a suite, with a bedroom, a bath, a kitchenette, and a windowless living room, with a slipcovered couch, a floor lamp, a coffee table, and a small TV on a stand. It was adequate, until I thought about the huge, unoccupied house upstairs. Mrs. Wainlett was condemned to economy, despite an empty first class cabin.

"I wish I'd been onto all this," said Farrell. "You deserve much better accommodations, for all you've done, and I'll make sure your pension is increased."

"That's not why we're here," said Mrs. Wainlett, cutting him off, flicking her hand toward the sofa. She disappeared into the bedroom and returned holding a cardboard shoebox close to her uniformed bosom.

"First of all," she said, "we're striking a bargain. You must never breathe a word of what I'm about to show you, especially not to the Covingtons or anyone else. I know your family, and if you betray me, I'll be only too willing to remember everything I've seen and heard, since the two of you barged into Lionheart House. I don't suppose that your father, in particular, would be especially pleased."

"I'm with you," said Farrell. "Fair enough."

"But Mrs. Wainlett," I asked, "if you're so nervous about this, whatever it is, why are you telling us? At all?"

Her lips got tighter and her eyes more clouded.

"Because," she said, measuring her words, "because there hasn't been a note of music, let alone a song, from that room, in all the decades I've been here. Oh, I've got a little transistor radio, and sometimes I'll drop by my sister's; she lives in town over her husband's butcher shop, and he's very keen on that stereophonic what-have-you, with a system set up, and I'll admit, his recordings sound very nice, and it's certainly better than listening to him berate my sister, but out here, with that music room just sitting there—it's a crime. I once dared to suggest that it might be used for lessons, for local children, but your father told me they'd only break the instruments or smear them, and I'm quoting his own words, with 'their grimy little paw prints.' So when I heard someone singing, at first I thought we had a ghost or an interloper. And I went to phone for the police, but I couldn't stop . . . listening. It was a lovely song, and Farrell, you have a sweet voice. And I told myself, Fancy that, a Covington who sings. I'd ask if you were adopted, but I can tell that you're not. There's a bit of Mirielle in your face, so you deserve to, well, you'll never really know her, but I can provide—a remembrance."

She opened the shoebox, which was piled with yellowed press clippings and sepia photographs, along with souvenir trinkets. "Mirielle was a great beauty, and quite the girl about town, before coming here."

She picked out a fragile rectangle of newsprint, dated 1923, headlined "Mirielle on the Move!" There was a central image of a very attractive twenty-one-year-old girl, with a Dutch bob, in a spangled flapper dress. Other photos circled this one, with Mirielle on horseback, touring the World's Fair, on skis, and in a novelty shot, about to topple the Leaning Tower of Pisa with a fingertip.

"She was gorgeous," said Farrell, and Mrs. Wainlett was right, he had his great-aunt's amused eyes and faultless cheekbones.

"She even appeared in a silent movie."

Mrs. Wainlett passed us a still, in which Mirielle, in a waist-length, curled dark wig, sat alone on a granite bench in the moonlight. "The film was called *Juliet of Manhattan*," said Mrs. Wainlett. "It did well, and Mirielle had offers, but she was restless, she wanted to try everything. She took flying lessons and acrobatics and she became obsessed with Gothic Revival architecture—she said it was solemn and outrageous at the same time, just like her. She apprenticed herself to Julia Morgan, who designed San Simeon and many of William Randolph Hearst's other homes. Julia took her to Europe, where Hearst would buy up historic Tudor rectories and Spanish haciendas, and have them taken apart, with the components carefully numbered, and then incorporate them into his California estates. Mirielle couldn't get enough; she said it was much more fun than just paging through books."

"But Mrs. Wainlett," Farrell asked, "I love hearing about this, but since you never met Mirielle, how do you know so much? And who saved all these clippings?"

"Mrs. Draxton. She was devoted to Mirielle; she thought she was a New Woman, so spirited, although she could be headstrong and even lean towards hysteria. But Mrs. Draxton said she was the only rich person she'd ever known who didn't waste her days consumed with suspicions of other people taking advantage of her."

Farrell and I pored over another set of photos, where the young Mirielle was less expertly lit and groomed. There were shots of her meditating beside a cactus in Santa Fe, skinny-dipping in a Montana river, and riding a camel loping toward the pyramids.

"So what happened to her?" I asked. "Why didn't she become an actress or a senator or an architect?"

Mrs. Wainlett stared at me, because I'd made these lives sound so attainable. "Young man," she said, "while the Covingtons tolerated what they called Mirielle's antics, they dismissed them as a juvenile prelude, a blowing off of steam, before an appropriate marriage and childbearing. She had several suitors, nice-looking men, an archduke, and the heir to a department store dynasty, and a railroad tycoon, with a cottage just a few doors down. And she made at least a token effort."

There was another clipping, of Mirielle with a guy her age in a tuxedo, on a New Year's Eve rooftop with an ostentatiously well-to-do crowd. Mirielle was clutching a noisemaker and a glass of champagne, but seemed listless and longing to be anywhere else.

"And she might have finally settled on someone and made a go of it, and had a family, except then she met Stella Arngrim."

Mrs. Wainlett silently held up a formally posed photo, of a young woman with a prominent nose and her hair in looped braids, in a glinting matador's suit, with a cape. It was an incongruous portrait, of someone who'd only consented to have her picture taken if she could dictate every aspect.

"She was an artist, wasn't she?" said Farrell. "I've seen her work, mostly cubist ceramics, some vases and bowls, but there were also these enormous statues of women, sort of pre-Columbian meets Easter Island. And I think—didn't she kill herself?"

Mrs. Wainlett resolved to complete her story: "She may have killed herself, by leaping from the terrace of the Cloud Club, a nightclub near the pinnacle of the Chrysler Building. There were rumors of drug addiction, and even foul play. But Mrs. Draxton believed—Stella was utterly heartbroken."

"Mrs. Wainlett?" said Farrell.

"After Mirielle met Stella, in Santa Fe, they were inseparable. They would dress alike, in theatrical costumes and sometimes workingman's clothes, in rough woolen trousers and canvas vests and even denim overalls. They traveled together, and those sculptures, the ones you've referred to—those were of Mirielle. Stella wanted to show Mirielle, to convince her, of how strong she could be. And again, the Covingtons went along with all this . . ."

"Up to a point," said Farrell.

"Yes. Until Mirielle announced her intention of living with Stella, romantically. There was a vogue for such things at the time, but it was viewed as a bohemian fad, and the women were called overage tomboys. But Mirielle wanted to support Stella and open an art school, to champion young women, and then finally, Angus Covington . . ."

"My great-great grandfather," said Farrell, "the one who made all the money . . ."

"He sat Mirielle down and gave her no alternative: she had to stop seeing Stella, and cease all contact. And she needed to reconcile herself to one of the eligible bachelors whom the family had vetted, and marry him. And at first Mirielle laughed and said she'd live as she pleased. Which was when Angus threatened to cut her off without a penny. And even then, Mirielle stood her ground, asserting she'd still be happy, that she'd get a job with Julia Morgan, or as a waitress. Which would have been unheard of but conceivable, and a solution, until Angus announced his quite serious intention to have Stella arrested and jailed."

"For what?" I demanded, set on somehow interrupting the story and saving the lovers.

"A morals charge," said Mrs. Wainlett. "Corrupting a female. There were so many laws back then promoting a father's total jurisdiction over even his adult daughters. Women couldn't own property, or open a business, or a bank account, without a man's consent. And Angus's ultimatum infuriated Mirielle, because she couldn't bear the thought of seeing Stella hurt in any way. Angus encouraged a final meeting between the two women, to terminate what he described as 'a coercive illness'—he stipulated that Mirielle end things in person, to verify her cooperation. There was a cocktail party at the Cloud Club, celebrating a museum's acquisition of one of Stella's pieces. Mirielle was by her side, and from what bystanders recalled, there was an argument. No one knows if Mirielle was doing as her father asked, or if the women were plotting to flee the country forever, or if anyone else was implicated. Angus was notorious for hiring brutes, right off the Bowery, to, as he put it, 'get the job done.' So it's unclear what truthfully happened, if Stella leapt or was pushed from an open area without a railing. But a coroner's report stated her blood alcohol was abnormally high, and there were traces of cocaine in her body. Although the document might've been falsified at the behest of Angus Covington."

"Oh my God," said Farrell.

"Did Mirielle talk to anyone?" I asked. "Did she ever give her version?"

"Mirielle was destroyed," said Mrs. Wainlett. "Near catatonic. The Covingtons had her bundled onto a ship and delivered to a Swiss sanitarium, where none of the treatments for nervous disorders, often quite barbaric, had the slightest effect. The only thing that helped even mildly was a stay in Rome, where she began to paint, mostly tourist fodder, the Pantheon and the Spanish Steps."

Mrs. Wainlett pointed to a small oil painting that I hadn't noticed, on a wall near the kitchenette. It was a competent but uninteresting Roman scene, of the Trevi Fountain at dusk. It was signed with the initials MC.

"And of course Mirielle knew that Stella had been the true artist, but the family was impatient to get Mirielle, as Angus said, 'back in the fold.' And because Mirielle loved Gothic Revival, Angus built her this house. He may have thought himself at least partially responsible for Mirielle's condition, and she was persuaded to spend a few weeks here, in early June. According to Mrs. Draxton, she appeared almost pleased; she'd wander from room to room, marveling at things, but spent most of the day standing out by the ocean, smoking a cigarette. Until one morning Mrs. Draxton detected someone on the roof, and there was Mirielle, sobbing uncontrollably and rocking back and forth. Mrs. Draxton tried to console her, or at least get her to come downstairs, but Mirielle was convinced that her father was trying to murder her, and that she could fly away."

"I don't blame her," said Farrell, quietly.

"She said she couldn't abide being here, that the house was a prison, and she began carrying a pistol and a hunting knife. Angus had her committed to a well-thought-of asylum in Connecticut, for the mentally ill or otherwise disagreeable children of the very richest families; these offspring would be marooned there indefinitely, most often under assumed names, to avoid further scandal. Mirielle was diagnosed with acute paranoid schizophrenia, and she was calmed by living in a small room at the asylum, with guards and round-the-clock sedation and nursing care. The Covingtons still believed that someday she'd be restored to sanity, and come back here. Angus named it Lionheart House, because he thought it would give her strength. And while Angus and other family members would speak to Mirielle's doctors, and skim their monthly write-ups, I'm not sure that any of the Covingtons ever made arrangements to see her, not once. But that may very well have been by Mirielle's choice."

"So she lived in that asylum, in that room, alone, for over forty years?" I said, stunned.

"What did Mrs. Draxton make of all this?" asked Farrell.

"Mrs. Draxton," said Mrs. Wainlett, "was a sympathetic yet practical-minded person. After entrusting me with this memorabilia, she said it was a cautionary tale, to never envy the rich, and to remain on our guard."

"On your guard?" I wondered. "About what? Getting rich?"

"About everything. Because Mrs. Draxton and I were, well . . ."

She held off, but then lifted her chin with a tiny but hard-won fervor.

"Mrs. Draxton and I pursued a friendship perhaps something like your own. But we'd had the example of Mirielle and Stella. And even as staff, if we were exposed, there'd be consequences. It's not just that we'd be fired; our reputations would follow us. The Covingtons were already exceedingly powerful people, and they continued to blame Stella for being what Angus called 'an unnatural influence' and an enemy."

"But you and Mrs. Draxton had husbands and families, I imagine," said Farrell. "Wasn't that a kind of protection?"

"Of course," said Mrs. Wainlett, smiling. "But sadly, neither of us had children, just many years of spinsterly companionship. We were both widows."

It dawned on me: Mr. Wainlett and Mr. Draxton had never existed, except potentially in a few grainy, falsified photographs. Mrs. Draxton wasn't merely practical-minded; she was ingenious.

"I appreciate certain goings-on," Mrs. Wainlett said, restacking the photos and clippings in the shoebox and closing the lid. "I know why you were singing."

10

Farrell would drop me off in New Haven on his way to JFK, where he'd catch a commercial flight back to Wichita. We drove in silence, until I said, "Poor Great-Aunt Mirielle."

"I know," Farrell said, "but did you believe all that?"

"I . . . I think so. Why would Mrs. Wainlett lie?"

"I don't think she's lying," said Farrell, "it's just, we've only heard one side of the story, the version Mrs. Draxton pieced together."

"What do you think really happened?"

"I'm not sure," Farrell admitted. "Maybe it was exactly as Mrs. Wainlett extrapolated, and I know what my family is capable of. But the details. She said that Mirielle was given to hysteria. And she was exactly the age when symptoms of schizophrenia begin to manifest. And Stella may have been an addict and unstable in her own way. I'm just saying that it may very well be a tragic love story, or it could be something else, about two damaged people making a terrible mess."

I was shocked by Farrell's cynicism, because I was after the most star-crossed tale, of doomed gay victims, set against a wondrously cinematic Jazz Age backdrop. But as with Jackson's history, gay lives are more complicated than that. But most of all, I was hungering for any gay stories whatsoever, especially love stories, and I wouldn't be denied. Rather than argue with Farrell I asked him, "What are you going to tell your family, about Lionheart House? What will you recommend?"

"Before I say anything, I'll work around them, and check on whether the whole place is landmarked on some Registry of Historic Homes, so it can't be torn down or tampered with. And if that's the case, I'll tell them to either open it to the public or turn it into a shelter for wayward lesbian heiresses. But they won't be paying the slightest bit of attention; once I've told them how superb the house is, they'll burn it to the ground to collect the insurance."

Farrell grinned, as a retort to his family's villainy. He'd often mock the Covingtons and distance himself, but for how long would this be enough?

Our sophomore year opened with a tantalizing proposition: Farrell suggested that, rather than my moving into one of the residential colleges with more roommates, I live full-time with him at the townhouse. But were we ready for nonstop coupledom? What if we irritated each other; what if I left empty cereal boxes on the kitchen counter, or Farrell hogged the imported Irish marmalade, and Bates couldn't keep up? What if the second I was a permanent fixture, everything went to shit and neither of us could work up the nerve for a confrontation? What if our love nest became a shrill, undergraduate, all-male production of *Who's Afraid of Virginia Woolf?*

Jackson, a cooler head, instructed, "Darling, when someone asks if you'd like to live rent-free in a townhouse with a manservant, here's what you do: You say yes. You find out what happens. You move in so fast you leave clouds of dust and skid marks. And you steal things."

"Or," Ariadne chimed in, "you can tell people that you turned the whole thing down, and we can nickname you the Biggest Fucking Idiot Who Ever Lived. Of course you say yes, and you let me smoke in the backyard."

"I think it sounds heavenly," said Jess, "like you'll have matching silk dressing gowns and velvet slippers embroidered with your combined initials. No, on second thought, that sounds disgusting."

"It's a very big step," Sally cautioned. "You'll be living in sin." Sally laughed when she said this, but she was thinking about it.

"But we're gay," I told her, "so we're already going to burn in hell."

The clarity of this satisfied her: "Then go right ahead!"

There were caveats. Bates had to answer the phone, in case outlying Covingtons were calling. I'd be officially ensconced in one of the spare bedrooms, in case a Covington dropped by. Farrell and I couldn't swap clothing because it would be a gateway drug to reprehensibly adorable matching outfits. And I would do my own laundry (I was adamant about this, because having Bates enzyme prewash and fabric soften my high school underwear was a line I couldn't cross. I was like a doctrinaire Marxist who'd select his own amethyst bracelets at Bulgari in the name of the people.)

I told my family I was living off-campus with a roommate, which was technically true, and the September day I stepped over the threshold, with my knapsack and duffel bag, was strange and titillating. I loitered in the front hallway like Annie or Paddington Bear or some other orphaned creature adopted by a cushy benefactor. Most of me loved it, but a contradictory voice taunted, "You greedy amoral little gold-digging bitch," an epithet that might also look nice in sapphires on my tombstone. Farrell descended the central staircase, grandly inquiring, "Yes? Did the agency send you?"

The next few months were our most idyllic time together, lacking only a lazy rowboat ride with parasols, limpid hands trailing in the Thames, and recitations of Walt Whitman, in French. I loved waking up beside Farrell and whining about which of us should drag himself out of bed and shower first; I loved having Farrell tell me why he'd chosen each particular artwork and then refuse to divulge what any of the pieces cost. ("Don't be crass. Twelve thousand dollars.") I loved that when I got home, from rehearsals or a meeting with a faculty advisor, he'd be there to take my side or murmur, "You might want to rethink your infantile overreaction." I loved having sex whenever we wanted to, and Farrell standing naked, picking today's specimen from a drawer of thirty identically bleached and ironed white T-shirts. ("A perfect white T-shirt," he said, "should make you weep.") We were playing house and banishing any premonitions of collapse, because that's what love, especially first love, should be: blissful, willful ignorance.

We accumulated more friends to round out the core gang. There was Justine, the daughter of Manhattan surgeons, who drove a tank-like gold

Lincoln Continental, owned cashmere sweaters in twenty-four colors, and deconstructed foreign films without being an asshole. ("I really like Truffaut and Godard, but Ingmar Bergman reminds me way too much of my parents.")

There was Dean, a human exclamation point, who entered even a convenience store majestically and issued pronouncements with a masterful hyperbole: "Today I saw the most, I'm not kidding, the absolutely most stunning suede jacket I've ever seen in my entire life, in anyone's entire life. It's the only suede jacket I could ever possibly own, that anyone should ever dare own. When I see any other suede jackets, I avert my eyes."

There was Louis, compact and fretful and aristocratic, who'd squint at Farrell and mutter, "If I looked like that I wouldn't care if I was happy or not"; Patricia, whose sense of humor was so dry people placed bets on her being a serial killer; and Terrence, with enough elegant tenaciousness to become the first Black gay member of the Whiffenpoofs (Yale's most prestigious a cappella singing group).

But through it all, there was Farrell. There was a precision to him, as if once he'd rolled his sleeves to the exact unforced midpoint of his forearms, read and notated two chapters of a monograph on Giacometti, swept the leaves from an elderly neighbor's front walkway, and one by one sucked the three red Lifesavers lined up on his desk, as if compassionately sending them to their deaths, and then waggled his reddened tongue at me, he was invulnerable. Style was his armor. Style, he once told me, is "a form of protest, against gross inhumanity or inclement weather. Without style I'm shivering and miserable. But equipped with a proper umbrella, and not one of those malevolent folding contraptions, I'm crusade-ready, especially if I turn my face towards the heavens and inquire, 'Must we?' "

From our excursion to Newport, and the strained deliberations I overheard with his family, I suspected a cloudburst or tornado was brewing, and had been since Farrell was born. He'd been girding himself, and there were mornings when he'd ask to be alone. He'd seem very far away, and I taught myself not to prattle or moronically inveigle him to "cheer up."

We both went home for Thanksgiving, and when my parents asked after my roommate I said he was pre-med and always studying, so I never crossed paths with him, and that we lived in a grungy two-bedroom apartment on a barren block. As an American teenager, I was an accomplished strategist, conveying enthusiasm for the paper I was writing, on Joseph Urban, a scenic designer from the twenties, and the play I was rehearsing and designing the poster for, an absurdist Belgian farce called *Pantagleize*. My parents were conflict-avoidant enough not to ask, "And why are we paying for this?"

Once we were back in New Haven, Farrell recounted an unnaturally peaceful weekend, "because almost all of them were gone. It was just me and my brother Wainwright, who was pretending to like me. He's a decent man, but he's imbedded in the Covington cult, so it's hard. He patted me on the shoulder, but when I went to hug him he said, 'Hold on there, cowboy.'"

We'd both be leaving for Christmas as well, but not before a treat: our group had been invited to a holiday party, on December 23, at the apartment of Jess's mother, the renowned actress Rebekah Tanner.

While Manhattan was my soul's destination, I'd never been to a private home, and as we gave the doorman our names, Farrell said the building was "a pre-war gem." The lobby had the musty, old-world gloom of a deserted Viennese café, with terrazzo, tarnished sconces, and a cramped accordion-gated elevator with a uniformed attendant. Farrell and I were jittery, because while we'd never met her, we were Rebekah Tanner devotees, and the party, Jess had mentioned, was "show-bizzy but down-home, all the people my mom's known for eons, from before they all got annoyingly famous."

There was a wheeled coatrack in the hall, and hired, good-looking, helpful young people took our things (only urbanites refer to their coats and bags as "their things," because these things might be from Bergdorf's) and ushered us into the apartment, which was already emitting that very specific clamor of New Yorkers all talking at once, along with a cocktail pianist and the muted sounds of traffic (we were on the twenty-third floor—"above the treeline," Farrell observed, meaning the view of Central Park would be unobstructed).

There was a raised area with a railing just inside the front door, for an overview of the living room, in all its cultured, resplendent, Upper West Side comfort. The apartment was large (eight rooms) but not garish; professionally decorated, in shades of Dutch blue and a buttery yellow, but not prohibitively don't-touch; and there was plenty of cozy-looking seating, upholstered in what Jackson later confided was "a very exclusive Scalamandré regimental stripe." There were crowded rows of silver-framed photos on a sideboard, featuring many of the party's guests on crucial opening nights, receiving Pulitzers, and lounging by swimming pools, in summery straw hats, as they leafed through the *Times*. Farrell touched my hand, because while he was far more worldly than me, there were a lot of people here, most of them legendary.

I'd already spotted a genius-level Broadway composer/lyricist at an early spike in his once-in-a-generation rise; a director I recognized from his many Hirschfeld caricatures, with his trademark eyeglasses perched atop his tanned dome; a quirkily sexy male movie star who I'd always presumed was gay; a world-class photographer with his hair still luxuriant in a Swinging Sixties pageboy; a witty female essayist Oscar-nominated for her first screenplay; an elfin, notoriously unpleasant choreographer in a black turtleneck, honored for both his theatrical dazzle and more high-minded ballets; and a buzzing assortment of invaluable best supporting theater actors, schmoozing for future employment.

"Is that . . . ?" I whispered to Farrell, with the most imperceptible nod toward someone who just might be a braying, seminal TV star about to top-line a Broadway rom-com, her mere presence rendering the stock vehicle what was termed "critic-proof."

"Yes," Farrell murmured back. "The sunglasses mean she's just had her eyes done."

"Farrell! Nate!" Jess called out from across the room, as if stamping our social passports, for proof we'd been invited.

Farrell and I waded into the mob. Jess met us halfway for darling-you're-here kisses and introductions to elbow-close celebrities, trilling, "You know Steve, Steve, this is Nate and Farrell, you'll love them," and "Jerry, the tall one is Farrell, oh no, Nate, it's not that you're not perfectly tall as well, oh, and here's Madeline, whom we adore . . ." I was deeply thankful for the crush and the decibels, because I wasn't sure if I should gush at my heroes, or if that would be juvenile, because famous people most likely came to these parties to escape from gawkers like me, from autograph hounds and slobbering fans (I'd soon suss out that even the most deliriously rewarded titans never tire of praise—it's their primary antidepressant).

"Mom!" Jess shouted. "Come meet Nate and Farrell!"

There she was, fluttering from the kitchen, never an especially grand room in these apartments: Rebekah Tanner. Rebekah had been discovered minutes out of the North Carolina School of the Arts, when her saucer-eyed, brashly flirtatious talent and messy blond tousle won her a coveted ingénue role in an unlikely Broadway smash—she'd played a klutzy con artist masquerading as a nurse to a momentarily stricken businessman. Her character triumphed by marrying his handsome chemist son, and bringing a pseudo-criminal larkiness into everyone's lives.

Rebekah had won a Tony and repeated her role in the movie version, nabbing an Oscar, and her ascent became global. She was that quixotic hummingbird, a movie star who'd flit back to the theater; she'd just finished a sold-out limited run as Beatrice in *Much Ado About Nothing*, set onboard a cruise ship. Her last movie had been a middling repeat of her previous megahits, in which she'd play an adorably frazzled surgeon or nervously sensual bookkeeper or disgruntled fashion model who meets an everyday guy in an elevator or while asking directions, and well, audiences swarmed to sigh and dream as Rebekah fell in love, and cavorted in the latest peasant dress or matching polka-dotted newsboy cap and bell-bottomed pantsuit combination, while shoving her hands into her hair when the suave playboy proposed but her heart had been hijacked by the dogwalker/saxophonist.

Our group hadn't relentlessly quizzed Jess about her mom, because while we cherished our link to Rebekah Tanner's daughter, we didn't want to come off as climbers. "The rule," Farrell had told me, "is to identify the offspring of the famous, pretend to bump into them, and take it from there."

But we loved Jess, for her own oddball nature, and now Rebekah was rhapsodizing, "My darling Jess keeps going on and on, she just adores both of you, which is good enough for me! Now, you must be Nate, and you're a Drama major like Jess, so you're . . . an actor?"

"I'm a playwright," I said, which was news to me and everybody else, but I just couldn't pretend to Rebekah Tanner that I was an actor, the fraudulence would be unspeakable, and "playwright" sounded weighty and Rebekah-adjacent. "A playwright!" she purred, in her wickedly husky vibrato, a key to her fabled charm, and much imitated, including by Farrell. "And you're Farrell," Rebekah declared, "and you're drop-dead gorgeous so you don't need to be anything."

"Except right here," said Farrell, with only me and possibly Jess catching his flawless Rebekah impression. "And thank you so much for having us. Jess is a dream."

"Isn't she?" said Rebekah, sweeping Jess into a full-body theatrical assault. "She's so lovely, especially once she finally bids farewell to those pesky last five pounds and stops mooning about how I made her stop dancing. She's going to be an exquisite actress, miles better than me, and someday—Jess, I don't think I've told you this—but I'm going to find exactly the right vehicle for the two of us! Can you imagine? The Tanner girls together? We could print money!" Her attention tilted toward someone nearby, and she cried, "Hal, I must speak to you! Jess, your friends are sublime, and all of you need champagne! Wait, you're not minors, are you?"

"I'm nineteen, Mom," said Jess, rolling her eyes at Farrell and me, as Rebekah swanned off, hugging and smooching her way into the room, because everyone had something shocking and confidential to tell her.

Half an hour later, Farrell and I had reconnoitered with our friends in a side room, which was less packed. There were framed posters from Rebekah's successes and waiters veered toward us with lacquered trays of hors d'oeuvres, which Jackson rolled up in paper napkins and stashed in his pockets. "These tiny salmon pizza things are scrumptious," he told us, "and I don't want them to go to waste."

"Jess's mother is terribly sweet," said Sally. "Although she asked if I was studying at a convent." Sally was wearing a cream-colored silk dress with black velvet ribbon accents; not everyone recognized her under-stated, near-Parisian chic.

"Do you know any of these people?" Ariadne asked me, munching a bowl of smoked pecans.

"I know who they are," I said. "I think I saw Maggie Smith and three cast members from *Chorus Line*. I want to be all of them and also be their friend and also kill myself."

"That guy who just starred in what was it, that secret agent thing, he just cruised me," said Farrell. He was right, and I'd caught many of the guests, both men and women, appraising Farrell, as if calculating, Okay, who is that person and who does he belong to?—and ultimately, How much does he cost?

There were raised voices from the living room, dwarfing the gossipy din. A man yelled, "You're being ridiculous!"

Rebekah replied, "Oh, am I? Well, I know what I saw, and yes it was ridiculous! Especially for a man your age!"

The party went silent, and everyone from the side room clustered in the archway to see what was happening. Rebekah was by the bar, harangu-ing a soap opera–craggy guy with a not-roguish-enough beard, in a bottle-green velvet blazer and an open-necked black shirt; it was the seventies.

"Nothing happened!" the man contended, offended and pleading. "You're letting your imagination run wild! You always do this! You're beautiful and I love you, but your jealousy is mind-boggling!"

This was either exactly the wrong thing to tell Rebekah, or exactly the right thing, if the crowd wanted another Tony-winning performance, for Best Actress in Her Own Home.

"Jealous?" growled Rebekah, in a low, menacing, don't-fuck-with-me-because-you-will-regret-it rumble. "*Jealous?* Why in God's name would I ever be jealous of you, some half-baked never-was who can barely get a three-week stint in summer stock, and who took advantage of my ro-mantic goodwill, and now of my very own daughter! You . . . you . . . you pedophile!"

Jess had entered from a hallway to a bedroom, straightening her skirt: "Mom, stop it. First of all, we were just talking, and second of all, I'm not a child so he's not a pedophile. And Gerry just wanted a younger person's take on his work as Benedick."

"A younger person? Oh, Jess. Oh, my poor innocent idiot daughter. I can tell Gerald, or Gerry, as you call him, exactly what people think of his Benedick. He was barely adequate on his best night, and he was damn lucky to be appearing opposite me, because no one was even watching him! But he's going to pay, for trying to desecrate our family and laughably attempting to simulate chest hair!"

Rebekah reached into the pocket of her black sequined jacket, worn over a wantonly unbuttoned blouse, and yanked out a revolver, which she pointed at Gerald or Gerry or as I'll always think of him, the guy who augmented his sparse chest hair with a ballpoint pen.

"I loathe you! I despise you! And I'm going to keep my daughter pure!"

As Rebekah cocked the trigger and the crowd somehow managed to leap backward for safety and lean forward for a better look, Farrell nudged me aside and walked toward Rebekah.

"Ms. Tanner," he said, "Rebekah. That was superlative, and I think you'll refine everything with future rehearsal, and we're all at your feet, but please, give me the gun."

"Why? How dare you! How can you possibly comprehend what I'm—undergoing? The unholy savaging of my heart? You're nothing but a simpering if marvelously tall college boy!"

"I can comprehend that you're tempestuously lovely and of course, Academy Award–winning and nominated in two additional years," said Farrell. "And I can also see that you're clutching a starter's pistol, which might singe your sequins and blow out a few eardrums, but it won't slaughter a mouse. Darling?"

Farrell reached out his hand, in a kind but insistent manner. Rebekah shuddered, debating between a headfirst swoon onto a chaiseful of guests or catapulting herself through the plate-glass windows onto Central Park West, but she snorted and gave Farrell the gun.

"Ladies and gentlemen," Farrell told the room, "Ms. Rebekah Tanner."

As everyone burst into applause, Farrell gently led Rebekah down the hall to the bedrooms. Rebekah glanced over her shoulder, basking in the ovation, but then remembered how distraught she was supposed to be. She raised her hands in picturesque defeat and let Farrell gallantly escort her.

"How did you know it was a starter's pistol?" I asked Farrell, once our group had left the party and hiked to an all-night diner near the West Side Highway, a hangout for long-haul truckers, transgender sex workers, freelance drag queens, and college kids feeling edgy.

"Because I know guns," Farrell explained. "Most of my family hunts, and it was a very basic revolver, a prop, really. And I remembered that in her last movie, Rebekah had shot up her fiancé's tires after he cheated on her, with most likely the same gun."

"Sherlock Covington," said Jackson, admiringly.

"I was scared to death," admitted Sally. "I thought Farrell was so brave."

"I wanted her to kill that guy," said Ariadne, "because he seems like such an asshole dick."

"He is and he isn't," said Jess, whom we'd kidnapped from her mother's place. "I mean, he was fine in *Much Ado*, and he had to put up with an awful lot from my mom, who kept upstaging him and giving him notes, while she had her back to the audience. I love her, but she hates sharing the stage with anyone—no, I take that back, she hates sharing anything, period."

"But why did she think you were fucking him?" asked Ariadne.

"Oh, probably because I am," said Jess, matter-of-factly. Then she giggled. This was why the group loved Jess, for her moonbeam directness. Jess wasn't tactful, but she was honest, and didn't spare herself. In an upbeat, benevolent manner, she'd tell people exactly what she thought of their one-act play, their recent face-lift, or their newborn baby. ("No, it's fine, really, I'm sure that in a few weeks she'll be cute.") It was impossible to get angry at Jess (unless you were Rebekah). She was too straightforward and analytical.

"It was a few weeks ago," Jess said. "I'd just seen *Much Ado* for like the fifteenth time, and I'd slobbered all over my mother about how amazing her performance was, and I wasn't lying, but she kept pestering me to tell her what she could do better. She acted like she really wanted to know, emphasis on the word 'acted.' So I finally told her, that while I worshipped what she was doing in one of her second-act speeches, she should stop fussing with the flowers she was holding, because it was distracting. And she ripped into me and accused me of trying to sabotage her entire performance. And she wouldn't stop; she told me I was an ungrateful brat and that the only reason I'd ever get work would be because I was her daughter. And I started crying and then she started crying and hugging me and she told me her big brainstorm. She wants to do a production of *The Seagull*, the Chekhov, with me in it, too. And I was thrilled because I've been studying Nina, the teenage ingénue, for class, and my mom would be superb as Nina's actress mother. But when I said that, my mom got this look of like, Norma Desmond horror on her face, and said that I was sorely mistaken, because she was going to play Nina and I'd be the maid, who doesn't even get a name, but my mom said it would look good on my résumé."

"Jesus," said Ariadne.

"You could play the maid and keep spilling drinks on your mom," suggested Farrell.

"But look," said Jess, "my mom just hit forty—well, off the record, forty-two—and I know that isn't easy, especially for an actress, and that someday, God willing, I'll know what that's like. But meanwhile, I was really pissed at her, and so was Gerry, so he and I went out for a drink on Tuesday to commiserate, and one thing led to another, it's no big deal, unless we're going to get all Freudian about it. And tonight, in my childhood bedroom, Gerry was asking about my scene work, and he kissed me, which was nice enough, but then my mom stormed in like the wrath of at least twelve martini-enhanced gods, and decided to go for another Oscar. So there you have it."

The group was united in sympathy for Jess, but we were also bursting with insider exaltation. We'd had orchestra seats for a prime Rebekah Tanner meltdown, at her Central Park West spread where a Broadway prodigy had premiered fragments of the score from his upcoming, sure to be acclaimed and controversial new project.

We were in college, but inching ever closer to adulthood and, best of all, New York City. The diner's plate-glass windows overlooked the New Jersey coastline, the Hudson River, and the West Side Highway: a map of my progress. I took Farrell's hand under the table, and a drag queen seated in a nearby booth saw this, tapped her drag queen friend on the shoulder with a three-inch-long leopard-skin press-on nail, and they both smiled at us, their glossy red lipstick a benediction, and said, "Awww."

Farrell and I spent the night at a Midtown hotel, like grown-ups or petty thieves who'd lifted a credit card and hit the town. As we lay in bed naked, I asked Farrell, "What do you think our lives will be like?"

"We're already living our lives," Farrell said.

"No, I mean, I don't really know what I mean, I just—I keep trying to picture us, in two years or ten years, and I can't figure out what we'll look like, or what we'll be doing, or what the world will be doing. It's scary."

"Don't be scared," Farrell said, kissing my cheek. "Whenever I start to think about the future, it's like I'm standing on some sort of train tracks, as this shrieking, nuclear-powered bullet train is bearing down on me. And I can laugh and let it hit me, or slap myself and jump out of the way, or test whether I've developed superpowers which will upend the train. But I'm not fond of any of those options, so instead of thinking about scary things, I think about you."

"I'm not scary?" I sulked. I coveted a modicum of threat, some bad-boy homicidal irrationality.

"No, you're not scary, even when you write 'Disagree strongly!' in the margin of a textbook, in pencil. You're like . . . a much better version of that train. You're the person I didn't see coming. And if I don't start sucking your dick within the next five seconds I will die."

So I sighed and let him, just to save his life. It's who I am.

The next morning, after we'd taken a normal, non-nuclear train back to New Haven, and Bates unlocked the front door of the townhouse, Farrell's father, Harwell Covington, was seated on the couch, inspecting the Hockney.

11

"Gentlemen," said Mr. Covington, not standing up, or even turning his head to regard us.

"What are you doing here?" Farrell asked.

"This is an odd painting," said Mr. Covington, still appraising the artwork. "Farrell, if this was purchased as an investment, it wasn't a particularly wise decision. But you've never specialized in wise decisions."

"Why didn't you tell me you were coming?" said Farrell. He was straining to be nonconfrontational, with effort.

Mr. Covington made a small throat-clearing noise, and rotated his steady, unblinking gaze toward us. "This must be Mr. Reminger," he said. "Your acquaintance."

"Nate," I said, extending my hand, which wasn't accepted.

"Yes," Mr. Covington said, "I'm aware of your existence. I'm aware of a great many things."

He did something with his face that might've been his version of a smile, a miniscule movement of his lips indicating that smiling was a waste of time. His gaze narrowed as he asked me, "Why are you wearing that—costume?"

He was referring to my bearskin, which became not boldly theatrical but embarrassing, as if I were wearing full clown regalia, or a lacy evening gown. I hesitated about removing it, but Bates had sidled into the room, tugging the coat off my shoulders. I had an instinct to cover myself, as if I were naked, but instead I assumed a neutral pose, taking my first real look at Farrell's near-mythic father.

Farrell had no family photos on display and I hadn't asked; even at the library I'd been unable to dig up images out of curiosity. The Covingtons shunned the press at all costs, having their attorneys issue only the most terse and uninformative statements at periods of crisis, meaning lawsuits brought by unions or the families of deceased employees. These filings were invariably scorned as "baseless and unwarranted."

I'd expected Mr. Covington to be imposing and tyrannical, a rigid Captain of Industry, a less animated oil portrait from the cover of an annual report. But instead he was mild-looking, like the irked head of a small-town school board, or a mid-level administrator at a company that manufactures car seat covers or oil cans. There wasn't a breath of Farrell in his face or body. He wasn't fat or thin, but assiduously middle-of-the-road, and I didn't initially glean that he was wearing an expensive, custom-made navy-blue suit, a cream-colored dress shirt, and a necktie chosen for its burgundy nothingness. Mr. Covington had spent many thousands of dollars to come across as imposingly anonymous.

"Sit," he said, not raising his voice.

"Why?" said Farrell. "You're not staying."

"Farrell, may I remind you of something? This building and this uncomfortable sofa and this mindlessly colorful painting were all financed by me. I own them. And we have much to address."

"Farrell, it's okay . . . ," I said, to de-escalate the encounter.

"No, it's not," said Farrell. "Father, just say whatever you've come here to say, and then leave."

Farrell and his father were both deliberately spurning the word "please."

"Very well," said Mr. Covington, as Farrell and I continued to stand; I was taking my cues from Farrell.

"I've been apprised of precisely what's been occurring, in this building and in my son's life," said Mr. Covington, not ominously but with a reasonable, nearly affable air, which was more disconcerting.

"Farrell has a sad history," he went on, "of eccentricity and defiance. Which I more than empathize with. My own father was unappeasably strict, and I deemed him a monster, incapable of change or affection. But as I grew older and forged my path, I came to be exceedingly grateful, for his obstinance and his disinclination to . . . defer to, or be cowed by, my adolescent rage."

"Rage over what?" Farrell asked. "When did you ever resist Grandfather, for even a heartbeat?"

"You see?" said Mr. Covington, to me. "That knee-jerk, cocksure sneering, it's almost admirable. Almost."

"What are you doing here?" Farrell repeated, his anger brimming.

"All right," said Mr. Covington, raising his chin, as if any preliminary charm or social foreplay had been completed, or swept aside. "Mr. Reminger, as Farrell may have told you, or you've researched, my grandfather founded a corporation, based in the mining of coal and the manufacture of steel, which now encompasses over thirty-five separate divisions, in transportation, agriculture, pharmacology, and real estate, among many fields of endeavor. We are in fact the third-largest corporate entity in the continental United States today, and we'd be the first should I be inclined to disclose overall assets more publicly. But my grandfather, who was even more brutal and dictatorial than my father, believed, without question or regret, in three entwined principles: profit, family, and God. And please don't bother asking me in what order, as these factors are equal and inarguable."

"Great-Grandfather also believed that women and Black people didn't deserve the right to vote," said Farrell.

"As a man of his generation," said Mr. Covington, as if that settled the matter amicably. "My father, and now myself and my sons, have been entrusted with a profound legacy, and with the financial well-being of many thousands of employees, the satisfaction of millions of customers, and in a very real way, the character of this nation."

"Oh my God," said Farrell, almost leaving the room.

"Sit down and be quiet," said Mr. Covington, and while Farrell didn't sit, he also didn't interrupt or exit.

"Farrell's mother, my wife, Ingrid, is, like myself, a devout Catholic, Ingrid even more so. Which brings us to this room, and this artistic affront . . ."

He motioned to the Hockney, as if there were a stench.

"And to Farrell's behavior. Farrell's mother and I have long been familiar with Farrell's emotional turmoil. And his pattern of perversion and deceit."

Would Farrell allow this? He was staring at the Hockney, as if he could bring it to life, like a pastel Frankenstein, to pummel his father.

"When I received word of Farrell's current regression, I discussed it with his mother, but we held off, hoping he'd exhaust a youthful, if misguided and abhorrent, fling. We spoke with our minister, Father Densmore, who underlined that Farrell's proclivities are far from uncommon, treatable, yet ultimately, not to be legitimized. And so I evaluated this, what shall we call it? This episode? This wandering? This descent? And I waited, with no small measure of patience, for it to end, of its own accord. From Farrell's self-disgust or boredom. But this hasn't transpired."

"Father . . . ," said Farrell.

"I am speaking," said Mr. Covington. "It's been reported that Farrell's sexual ambivalence has endured for well over a year, and that the two of you have traveled together, and that Mr. Reminger, to all intents and purposes, resides here and shares your bed. And Farrell, I'm more than willing to give you the benefit of the doubt, and conclude that this repellent young man, upon taking note of your background and generosity, has misled you, and seduced you, into an unnatural way of life."

"That's not true!" said Farrell. "I went after Nate! This is my life!"

"Then let's ask him. Mr. Reminger, do you live here, in quite luxurious surroundings, entirely rent free?"

"Yes," I admitted.

"Because I insisted!" said Farrell.

"And Mr. Reminger, have you advised your family of your, what are they calling it, in the *New York Times*? Your homosexuality? Do they approve? Don't bother to respond, because I've made inquiries, through private detectives, and I've confirmed that your parents and your brother remain oblivious to your unsavory activities. Shall I tell them? I have your family's home phone number and I'm happy to make the call. Shouldn't they be told?"

"Please don't," I said, as he reached for the phone.

"So here we are," said Mr. Covington, withdrawing his hand. "Amid a situation that only seems to metastasize. A disease that continues to rampage. And that is unacceptable."

"To whom?" said Farrell, his voice quavering.

"To any decent human being," said Mr. Covington. "And most especially, to your mother, your brothers, and myself. And critically, to the public, which provides the economic stability of our corporation. You've uncovered the lamentable tale of your great-aunt Mirielle, a woman who sought to demolish everything our family holds dear. This can't, and won't, happen again. So let me ask a few simple questions, so that we might resolve all of this, as quickly and discreetly as possible. Obviously, Mr. Reminger can no longer stay here, and your relationship must be dissolved, completely, and shall never be spoken of again. Mr. Reminger, would a payment of twenty thousand dollars be sufficient?"

My knees buckled, not at the figure he'd proposed, but at everything that was happening. Just a few hours earlier, Farrell and I had been naked, making love and gabbing about the future. How could we have been so stupid, and so careless?

"No," I said, with all the authority I could muster. "Absolutely not."

Mr. Covington's micro-smile increased by a flicker, as he asked, "Are we negotiating?"

"No," I said. "I'm not taking your money."

I heard myself sounding shaky yet firm, as if I were on a witness stand or confronting a schoolyard bully. But I'd meant what I'd said. I wasn't even thinking of Farrell, not yet. It was the insult, the idea that I could be paid off, that scorched. It was Mr. Covington's perfunctory evaluation of me, as a minor player, a gold digger and a cheat. Of course, it's easier to reject any bribe, and to cast yourself as an audacious Joan of Arc, when you're nineteen years old, and have very little to lose. But I maintained one unswervingly vehement conviction: I hated Mr. Covington's guts and I'd do anything to piss him off.

"As you wish. Farrell, your . . . companion, or your coconspirator, is positioning himself as a valiant defender, of heavily underwritten depravity. So let's turn to you. Let's say, for the sake of argument, that you and Mr. Reminger resume your disgrace. And let's say that with a few phone calls and a sheaf of swiftly drafted documents, I cut you off without a penny. I invalidate your trust fund, I discontinue your more than generous monthly allowance, and I expunge you entirely, from the corporation's future and from my will. The spigot goes dry. Are you equipped to leave not just this townhouse, and all of its decoratively appalling artwork, but this university as well? Can you so casually renounce the chauffeur-driven limousines and the private air travel and the imported clothing and fine restaurants and untrammeled credit cards? Let me ask you the most difficult question for someone of your profligate nature: Farrell, could you ever find, let alone hold, a job?"

I'd never seen Farrell trembling like this, and at such a complete divide. His father's interrogation was borderline comic, but not his smirking condescension. I remembered Farrell telling me about how his family could erase him, and now he was shrinking and mute, not out of weakness, but self-doubt. I wanted to speak for him, to shout his father down, but that would be a terrible mistake, and Farrell was pulling himself together.

"Father," said Farrell, "I know that you, and everyone else in that frightened, slavish, deadly dull Wichita coven we call a family, you've all dismissed me, as not just a lost cause, but a mistake in every respect. And you may very well be right, because in so many ways your low opinion of me can never match my own. But I won't give you the satisfaction. So yes, if you disinherit me, I'll most likely fail more quickly and pathetically than even you could predict, but maybe not. I might surprise myself. Which could also be the most ludicrous wishful thinking. But by all means, go right ahead. Convene your festering legal minions, make my brothers euphorically pleased with their larger inherited slices of the Covington corporate pie. In our family we never give each other gifts because, as you've so often told me, you're opposed to unearned rewards. So let me break precedent and for once in our lives, celebrate the holiday. Cut me off. Merry Christmas."

I was stunned and silently cheering; Farrell was back. He'd regained his superpowers, meaning his vocabulary and personality, and I was so proud of him. Mr. Covington had been knocked off his game. Today wasn't going as he'd planned. His aberrant college boy son had neglected to surrender.

"Thank you," said Mr. Covington. "So, Farrell, let me gift-wrap something in return, with a festive Yuletide bow and a steaming mug of eggnog. You've reviewed at least a partial history of our family, and our track record with obstacles. You might also inquire after your second cousin Frederick, who embezzled funds, a minor amount really, but that wasn't the point. He'd betrayed the Covingtons' ethical code. And he died tragically young, in a car accident on an especially clear night, on an otherwise deserted stretch of highway. There's also your mother's brother, who'd discouraged her from marrying me, because, to his mind, I wasn't entirely human. An advocacy he clung to, until I proved my solicitude, by paying for a new house, after an unexpected electrical fire reduced his beloved childhood bungalow to ashes. And let's not even list the string of whistleblowers, seeking to slice our factories' profit margins and alienate their fellow employees. The smart ones took buyouts and left the country, with the shreds of their families, and the more stubborn, well, who knows where they are now?"

Was any of this true? Was he bluffing? Farrell had said he knew what his father was capable of, but this wasn't even a veiled threat. This was the ugliest, proudest declaration of vicious intent.

"Bottom line, Farrell, my last and final offer. You must immediately eject Mr. Reminger from the premises, and from our lives, and you must never see him, speak to him, or attempt any contact with him whatsoever, not today, not in the near future, but forever. He must cease to exist. And if you don't comply, if you can't make that happen, a campaign will begin, and it won't be pleasant. Mr. Reminger's future at Yale, his family's livelihood and well-being, and his physical health are all on the table. And your responsibility."

I couldn't look at Farrell. I'd been wishing for a more eventful life, but I got why Farrell had cherished me, because I'd seemed immune from havoc like this.

"Mr. Reminger," said Mr. Covington, "I expect that you think me an ogre and a murderer and a plethora of the most vile accusations, many, even most, of which may be accurate, at one time or another. But none of that matters when set beside one immutable fact. I'm a father who loves his son. And I want him back."

He stood up, placidly, as if the three of us had exchanged nothing more than a morning's chitchat. He had the air of someone who wasn't only accustomed to winning, in every aspect of life, but addicted to it.

"Gentlemen," he concluded, "out of an indulgent parental leniency, I'll give you a minute alone, to make your goodbyes. I'll be outside in the car, awaiting Mr. Reminger's departure. Mr. Reminger, I can't say it's been a pleasure, but as I'm sure you'll agree, we've had a most productive morning."

He left.

As the front door clicked shut, Farrell faced me and said, in the most urgent voice imaginable: "Go."

"But . . . ," I sputtered.

"He's not joking. I've seen what he can do. This is all my fault, and now it's a grudge match. You need to go, now."

"But Farrell, can't we call the police . . ."

"And tell them what? That one of the most powerful men in America just threatened his faggot son's boyfriend? Not only would no one believe us, but if they did, they'd take my father's side. This is the world, Nate. This is how my father operates. I didn't believe he'd go this far, but he won't back down. Get out of here."

"For how long? Are we just going to do everything he said? Am I never going to see you again?"

"I don't know, it's possible, but for right now, and probably for a very long time, he'll be watching both of us, every second. We can't fuck up."

"But how did he know everything? Did Mrs. Wainlett report us? Who else knew about everywhere we went and everything we did?"

Bates came down the staircase, hoisting my bearskin, knapsack, and duffel bag, haphazardly jammed with my books and other clothing. He was trying not to snicker, but not very hard.

"Fuck you, Bates," said Farrell. "And you're fired."

"Let's ask your father about that," said Bates, and it was the first time I'd heard his real, Ohio-flat speaking voice. Mr. Covington's payoff would cover at least his first year in New York.

"Don't pay any attention to that shithead," Farrell told me. "He's an extremely limited actor and all my father's money can't change that. And there's something that a greedy bastard like him, and like my father, will never understand."

"What?" I asked, unable to keep up.

Farrell grabbed me by the shoulders and said, "I love you," not romantically, but to make sure I heard him, and that what he'd said would last. He wanted not just to incinerate his father, but to defeat everything he stood for, with those three words.

From Farrell's eyes, I could tell: He was distancing himself from the world. He was barricading himself. He wasn't just leaving me but any thought of escape. I couldn't let him retreat so completely.

"I love you," I said, for the first time. I'd never dreamed of these circumstances, when the phrase would become a battle cry from a member of the resistance. My words were most likely feeble, a pitiful gay nineteen-year-old's stab at significance, but they were all I had. Farrell wasn't just a mad crush or a first boyfriend, to be hazily recalled in a year or two, superseded by far more complex relationships. Meeting Farrell had been lucky and maybe random. I had no idea if I believed in fate, but I needed to believe that love had value and weight and even power. Hating Farrell's father was necessary, but my loving Mr. Covington's son was stronger. It had to be.

Or was I making Harwell's point, about the worthlessness of gay people? Were Farrell and I negligible errors, sidebars to the more honorable business of heterosexual progress? Was style the most inconsequential defense against unmitigated authority? Did being gay, in the march of less trivial undertakings, even matter?

We kissed, a kiss that could never do what we were asking of it, which was to change everything, or to engrave a memory for however long we'd be apart. Kisses are wonderful, but this was war. And for once I wasn't exaggerating, to inflate commonplace events to theatrical or wide-screen dimensions. Harwell Covington wasn't a mustache-twirling Saturday morning cartoon villain, a harmless, brightly colored approximation of evil. He was the real thing: a man without scruples or boundaries, a sociopath, meaning someone who might recognize decency as an abstract concept, but practiced a far more grounded and efficient self-interest. A criminal is a pig with a baseball bat, lurking in an alley at midnight; a monster has an untraceable chain of command, hiring the pig to solve, or eliminate, a nagging hindrance.

"Go," Farrell repeated, yanking my belongings from Bates and shoving me toward the door.

As I went out, I planned for one last exchange with Farrell, maybe a glance, but the door was closing; Farrell was refusing to credit his father's malice, by acceding in any way that we might never see each other again.

Mr. Covington's sleek black sedan was parked out front, and I intended to shit on it, or vomit; my idiot brain wanted to kick the door. I didn't do any of these things, or peer into the tinted windows and spit. Instead, I began walking. Mr. Covington, I was sure, had broken into his fullest, most corpse-like grin yet. It might even turn sexual, since punishing his son, and me, was his orgasm. For men like that, scheming or lying or torture were the most visceral satisfactions.

My vision of Mr. Covington's satanic excess was most likely wrong. Having accomplished his task, he wasn't jerking off or chanting auxiliary curses over a bubbling backseat cauldron. He'd be scanning a contract or dictating a letter. He'd have moved on seamlessly to the next item on his agenda.

But something had finally happened to me, and all I wanted, even if it took a lifetime, was to fight back.

12

I sat in the student housing office that afternoon, filling out forms for a mid-semester dorm assignment. I couldn't organize my thoughts, between total disbelief at Mr. Covington's tactics, wondering how and if I should tell our friends about what had happened, and blocking any acceptance of Farrell disappearing from my life.

This wasn't a breakup or a spat that could be solved by a cooling-off period or couples counseling. This was careening and unstoppable.

As I told the administrator about a roommate who'd returned to Venezuela and a broken lease, I knew what I had to do, before making any more decisions. There was a bus to New Jersey that dropped me a mile from my family's house, and I strode and then jogged, picking up speed from sheer fortitude. It was early evening, and my mother and father had finished dinner and settled in for the nightly news in our TV room.

"Sweetheart?" said my mom. "What are you doing here?"

"Why didn't you call us from the station?" asked my dad. "We could've picked you up."

As my dad switched off the set, I said, "Okay, here it is. I'm gay."

I'm not sure what I'd foreseen—Explosive sobs? Red-faced protests? Biblical fury? Entreaties for psychiatry and dates with nice girls, or even not-so-nice girls? Getting kicked out of my second home of the day? They'd had so many altercations with my older brother, over much tamer offenses. I'd been the honor roll alternative, but that was now exposed as devious scrubbed-little-face propaganda. My parents would wail their crushing disappointment, and adopt a third child, as a grief-stricken last chance.

Instead, my mother said, "And?"

What? Excuse me?

"If you're happy then we're happy," said my dad, "and we love you very much."

I was dumbfounded and a bit miffed at the lack of parental breast-beating and garment-rending denouncements.

"So—you already knew?" I asked.

"Nathaniel," said my mom. "We've seen your room. And your under-wear drawer."

"And of course, we've had conversations, between ourselves," said my dad. "We didn't know for sure, so we read some books, and we talked to other parents."

"My friend Sheila Rosenbaum's son Josh is gay," said my mom. "And at first she had a real problem with it. And I watched her, crying and yelling at him and blaming herself, and it just seemed so—unnecessary. I finally told her, Sheila, I've read that Michelangelo was gay and Leonardo da Vinci, and I saw those men on the David Susskind talk show who said it's perfectly normal and all they want is to love someone and not be condemned for it."

"Although Susskind got confused, and he kept asking this one couple which of them was the wife," said my dad. "But Susskind's always con-fused."

"But we didn't want to confront you," said my mom. "Especially not after everything we went through with your brother. I told your father, let's leave it up to Nate. He'll tell us when he's ready."

"But—Josh Rosenbaum?" I said, referring to a chubby boy I'd gone to Hebrew school with, who was so spellbound by his new pocket calcula-tor that I'd never thought of him as having any sexuality at all.

"I was surprised, too," confessed my mom. "But he showed Sheila a newspaper article about gay liberation, and he told her, 'That's me.' And at work, remember my helper, from Rutgers, Joan Nebley? She was dating that good-looking guy . . ."

"Danny," said my dad.

"And he proposed, and I was so happy for her. And not just because Danny's about to graduate from medical school and specialize in dermatology, although I'm not holding that against him. But Joan told him no, that's not what she wants, and I thought, I'm not going to say a word, it's her life, and then one day, a year ago, she introduced me to this very pretty girl named Kathy, and she said, 'This is my lady friend.' "

"You could've knocked me over with a feather," said my dad.

"And Kathy is just lovely," my mom continued, "even if I don't understand her poetry, it keeps referring to the intestinal problems of sparrows, and I'm more of an Elizabeth Bishop person, but I thought, good for Joan. She found someone. Although I'll admit it, and I'd never say this to Joan, but I did ask myself, Couldn't she be a lesbian and still marry a rich man?"

Okay. Okay. I sank to the sofa, heaping my belongings on the floor. My parents had reacted with only the most placid common sense. I'd benefited from a generational shift. My brother was a ponytailed, bandana-headbanded, Harley-gunning child of the sixties, which had been all about peace signs at the Pentagon and torching draft notices and choosing a side, and a hash pipe. The seventies embodied a no-fault relaxation of social strictures, and even my parents, most likely from exhaustion, had signed on. Because unlike Harwell Covington, they read the *New York Review of Books* and weren't policing a dynasty.

"But why did you come all the way out here to tell us?" said my dad. "Even though it's great that you did."

"Do you have a person?" asked my mom. "Is there someone waiting outside?"

I could detect the matchmaking maternal spark in her voice, and my optimism vanished. Why couldn't I be Josh Rosenbaum or Joan Nebley? Why was this newfound acceptance so badly timed? Only a day ago, I could've brought Farrell to Piscataway, to be pinched and kvelled over, even if I might've had to translate the word "kvell." But after this morning, how should I describe our months together, and their result? If I told my parents about Mr. Covington's gentile Armageddon, they'd be protective and livid on my behalf, but he hadn't just gone after me—they were targets as well. He had limitless resources and he'd compiled dossiers about me and my family. How could I expose my parents to such sadistic worry about our combined physical safety? Should I leave a note on the fridge, "You might want to check under the car, before turning on the ignition"?

"I . . . I had a kind-of boyfriend," I ventured, "but we broke up. It's no big deal."

"Oh, sweetheart," said my mom, hugging me, to flex her freshly tolerant parenting skills. I'd never needed a hug this badly and I collapsed in her arms.

"Was he a nice boy?" asked my dad.

Was Farrell a nice boy? He was the nicest boy I'd ever met and the most unknowable and troubled and dreamy and surprising and, of course, rich. Was his money the key to so much of this, had it poisoned our lives? Money had fueled Farrell, as he cultivated his personality. He'd purchased a world. Being rich suited him. It was his medium, his palette, his sumptuous box of crayons. But that same money stoked his father's hatefulness, and his prowess at manipulation, of his son, and me, and as he'd boasted, Covington Industries' loyal consumer base, millions of acolytes all over the world.

"He was really nice," I told my parents.

"So what happened?" asked my mom. "You don't have to tell us, it's your business, but if you need someone to listen . . ."

Oh my God. My mom wasn't just transforming herself into a model of gay cheerleading, she wanted details, as if they were grandchildren. No, that wasn't fair. My mom had never pressed either my brother or me to reproduce, and while she'd burble at infants in elevators, slung over their parents' shoulders, she rarely babysat for the offspring of nieces and nephews. My mom pined for romance and youthful passion and maybe a few edited sexual tidbits. But wasn't it too late?

"In the morning," I promised, when I'd concoct some bland, PG-rated version of the truth. I craved sleep, in my childhood bedroom, where my gay life had been an Ethel Merman–accompanied, magazine-prompted fantasy, and didn't spotlight death threats or forced goodbyes.

The next day I went back to campus and my single room in the basement of a residential college (there were twelve, in a menu of architectural motifs, from Hobbit whimsy to corrugated sixties cement boxes). The room was an undistinguished, cinderblock-walled hideout, as if I'd just entered a witness protection program after offending the Mob, which on a more Midwestern, corporate level, I had. The group called a summit, sitting cross-legged on my new-but-already-fraying sisal rug and perched on the flimsy Indian-print fabric covering my rickety twin bed. That's how depressed and cut-off I was: without even thinking about it, I'd bought an Indian-print bedspread, the IKEA bookcase of the seventies.

"Farrell told us everything," said Ariadne. "And we think his father is the über-fascist fuckhead of all time."

"But I still don't understand how he can get away with this," said Jess. "I mean, how can he do this to his own child? And to you? Or to anyone?"

"Because he has pots of money," countered Jackson, "and platoons of lawyers, and these things happen all the time. It's Romeo and Romeo. Which is no consolation."

"But what if we went to him, all of us?" asked Sally. "And spoke calmly, and didn't turn everything into a fight. And what if we told him about how happy you and Farrell were. And how normal. Maybe we could change his mind."

Sally meant well, but normalcy, or its even more humdrum cousin, conformity, wouldn't interest Farrell. "Nothing will ever change Mr. Covington's mind," I said. "He wants to demolish Farrell. I'm just collateral damage. A bug on the windshield of his Bentley."

"Okay, and I'm just spitballing," said Jess. "But what if we killed him—Farrell's dad? What if we followed him, and bought a gun, and one of us, maybe Sally, because she's so sweet, she could just stroll up behind him and shoot him in the back of the head."

"I couldn't do that," Sally protested, as we all pivoted to her. "I'm sorry, I know we hate him, but that isn't the answer."

Ariadne pretended to cough, rasping the word "pussy" under her breath.

"So when did you see Farrell?" I asked. "Since I'm guessing that unlike me, you're allowed to."

There was a pause until Sally spoke for the group: "Last night. He came over to Jackson's. He said we had to impress upon you that his father is serious about this, so you can't contact Farrell in any way."

"But what if I see him on campus?" I asked. "Because I'm going to run into him, so what am I supposed to do? Ignore him? Run? Change my name?"

"You won't have to do any of that," Jackson said softly.

"Why not?"

"Oh, sweetie," said Jess. "None of us wanted to tell you this, but in the most repulsive way, it's for the best. Farrell isn't here. He's transferred to Amherst, up near fucking Northampton, Massachusetts. His father made a few calls and it was done. The townhouse is empty and it's up for sale. Farrell's gone."

This wasn't just another cannonball blasted into my chest. Somewhere Mr. Covington was laughing, which would be a dry, wheezing bark. Out of some imbecilic faith, I'd been plotting to leave encrypted notes for Farrell in a hymnal at a church, so we could steal unobserved moments together in the campus bell tower, with the pealing bells frustrating audio surveillance. This was ludicrous, but I'd seen way too many implausible spy movies. Farrell had been rapidly and heartlessly removed from my life, or airlifted out and spirited to another planet, where, from what I knew about Amherst, people brought their skis to class.

"We're so sorry," said Sally, taking my hand.

"Amherst," said Jackson. "Can you imagine? It's like Siberia, with L.L.Bean duck boots and hot toddies."

"But couldn't I . . . ?" I began.

"No, sweetie," Jess said emphatically. "You can't go up there. It's actually better, because this way you'll never cross paths."

"And his asswipe father won't have you strangled by a goon with piano wire," said Ariadne. When Sally looked at her, Ariadne said, "I'm trying to stay fucking positive."

"We're not going to tell you that you'll meet someone else," Jess said. "Because we're not total idiots. But whatever you need, except for, you know, personal happiness, we're here for you."

"And you're all going to mock me," said Sally, "but I've been meditating at this local ashram, I'm the only person there with a decent handbag. But the guru is a very interesting person, and it's uplifting. So if you'd like, I can bring you with me. It's not a cult and you don't have to participate if you don't want to."

Sally's spirituality was sincere, and as always, never interfered with her skincare routine. But I couldn't see myself at an ashram, because I knew I'd end up choosing "Farrell" as my mantra, although I appreciated Sally's intent.

"And I made this for you," said Jackson, handing me a black cardboard portfolio. "It was the only thing I could think of. And I recommend you keep it well hidden, for obvious reasons."

I undid the ribbon closure and opened the portfolio, to find Jackson's portrait of Farrell, in India ink on the creamiest vellum. Jackson had selected the most luscious, translucent colors, lemon yellow and malachite green and cobalt blue, along with a dusting of clear glitter and a peacock feather, to create a surreal yet supremely accurate study of Farrell, with a nod to Hockney, but wholly in Jackson's fanciful hand. The portrait looked dashed off, as if Jackson had chanced upon Farrell lost in thought, on a window seat at the townhouse. The sketch was a sequined emanation, capturing his subject's tumultuous hairstyle, carelessly but precisely rolled cuffs, glinting green eyes, lightly freckled nose, and soul. This was the closest I'd get to holding Farrell, to being with him, and while it wouldn't be enough, it gave me faith he still existed, the way I wanted to think of him, the way his father despised.

"Thank you," I told Jackson, closing the portfolio, because the portrait was luminously radioactive. I'd study it later, for far too many hours.

"You poor baby," said Jess, and the hugs commenced. I'm not a huggy person, but this was an emergency.

The rest of my years at Yale were buoyed by plays, deepening friend-ships, and show business–centered coursework ("Shakespeare on Film," "From Kern to Sondheim: Emerging American Melodies," "Global Media at a Crossroads"). I marked off a full year before walking briskly past the townhouse, which had been sold and was now the Center for Etruscan Studies, according to a bronze plaque out front. I didn't linger for even a second, predicting a tiny circle of red light on my forehead, from the laser sight of a sniper's rifle. I never heard from Mr. Covington or anyone as-sociated with him, which was more harrowing than direct contact. He'd calculated that my paranoia would flourish on its own.

I resisted phoning or writing to Farrell, in care of Amherst College, because any communication could be intercepted. Farrell didn't stay in touch with anyone, and I didn't know if he was keeping us safe, or dis-ciplining himself to forget us, and I couldn't blame him. I didn't have sex or go dancing, but I still managed pockets of happiness, especially while painting scenery beside a chain-smoking, cursing, drug-crazed Ari-adne. Simple tasks could make a speed freak even more loopy fun, as she blamed her brush, the paint, and "fucking Reagan" for mushing the painted window into the painted wallpaper.

Because I packed my empty hours with classwork, I graduated early, in December. On the night before I vacated the campus for good, I came across a small, deserted courtyard within, of all things, the divinity school. I liked the silence, the juniper trees, and the seclusion, away from not just undergraduate hubbub but civilization itself. It was a refuge for the most elevated thoughts, the moral harangues and self-judgments that were too pretentious, and heartfelt, for anywhere else.

It was snowing lightly, but not too cold, and I brushed off a wooden bench and sat in the moonlight. I guessed at Farrell's whereabouts: Had his father paid for some New England-y clapboard carriage house, or a porticoed Victorian, where Farrell was lounging on his low Italian leather couch before a roaring fire? Was he alone or nuzzling some local Aryan specimen? I wished him well and hated him and missed him. I'd started to question our history, as if I'd hallucinated him, and were strapped to a bed in a gruesomely medieval ward, feverishly clinging to my delusion.

But I'd trained myself, not to forget Farrell but to file him away, like an unsolved murder. Because tonight I was counting down the ominous final minutes of my collegiate life, of a period when personal fumbles and misshapen facial hair were rampant and forgiven, when everything was introductory, still malleable and taking shape.

Tomorrow I'd be headed back to Piscataway, temporarily, while I stalked my first apartment in New York, and scrambled to pay the rent. I couldn't abide the thought of more schooling. I wanted the cascading terror of a highest-possible-stakes entry into Manhattan. I was so scared that I didn't notice the snow mounding on my head and eyebrows. I was wearing an army/navy parka; my bearskin had begun to smell, perhaps seeking hibernation, and it reminded me too much of Farrell. Through Jackson, I'd donated it to the wardrobe stock at the drama school.

Then someone or something rushed past the arched entrance to the courtyard and fled. Was it Farrell, risking everything to signal that he still existed? Was he leaving a bread crumb?

I stood, sweeping the snow from my sleeves. As I departed, I caught sight of a small rectangle of carved limestone on a wall. The Roman letters read "Covington Contemplation Courtyard, Gift of the Covington Family." I'd been sitting in one of the donations that had assured Farrell's acceptance at Yale. I shivered, for so many reasons.

NEW YORK

13

My new home was a one-room, fifth-floor walk-up on Charles Street, at $135 per month, payable in cash to a landlord with office hours at a nearby luncheonette. I'd procured this cubbyhole-sized studio, with a bulging, water-stained ceiling, as one did, through a listing in the *Village Voice*. I'd beelined for the West Village because of the area's literary bona fides and walkable streets, and most desirably, because it's the cradle of gayness.

I stepped out of the Seventh Avenue subway in February, but I date my true Village citizenship to April, when thanks to an unseasonably warm Saturday, the centrally located Sheridan Square burst into homosexual pageantry, because everyone decided it was tank top weather. There was no exact holiday or even a tribute to the Stonewall riots of 1969, eight years earlier. Men had been cooped up for too many radiator-hissing winter months and were compelled to do the following: wear as little clothing as possible and jam the streets, lolling atop parked cars as they gossiped with drag queens, one of whom carried a white patent leather purse to match her Boca Raton strappy sandals. A shirtless guy roller-skated past me with suspenders clipped to his barely existent cutoffs, as a quartet of burly porn stars strolled side by side (they were royalty below 14th Street), while a stud with a barbed wire tattoo around his bicep used the pay phone and I heard him tell a friend, "Get down here and bring weed." Disco blasted from the open doors of the bars, which functioned as stalls of a bustling sex market. I'd never seen so many well-built, swashbucklingly mustached, busily happy men. The scene surpassed any lives-of-the-subculture brochure. The day became a street festival, welcoming queer boys from all over the world to a sharply coded but expansive homeland. There were lesbians as well, in tube tops, satin track shorts, and spike heels, waging furious, often violent spats outside a Seventh Avenue bar called the Duchess, where women clustered to feud over each other and yell that Nadine should choose between Shannon and Diane, *right now, bitch*!

I was in the right place, but on the periphery. One night I lay in bed beside a pickup, a Cuban ex-priest who'd encircled us with candles, for a mood of human sacrifice. This guy ran his finger along my unremarkable chest and told me, pointedly, "You could have a nice body if you tried." This wasn't idle chatter; he was speaking on behalf of a community and briefing me on my prospects. I was stung and attentive. I'd been ranked hovering near undateable, with a catechism for self-improvement. Being gay in New York meant joining a monastic order, and it followed that a former clergyman had lent wise counsel: he knew his way around enclosed societies of his kind.

My first gym was primal, on the second floor of a building at the hub of Christopher and West 4th Streets. I climbed a steep flight of stairs to a shabby, fluorescent-lit, near-dystopian room, with muscular men heaving and grunting and arguing venomously about opera. There was a glorious disconnect between the mountainous, hairy bodies in sweat-stained rags and the yummily exchanged dish (the topics ranging from a soap star's cosmetic surgery to what objects someone across the room was willing to shove up his ass, including shampoo bottles and highway safety cones). If a silent film were being made, this would be a Soviet work camp or a brawny Alaskan outpost awaiting mail-order brides. Turn up the volume, and the pitch rose, as a brute would decree, "Leontyne Price is the only Aida—period," while another six-foot-five stud, monitoring an equally chiseled workout partner on the bench press, said,

"Two more reps. And you need to see Liza in *The Act*; it's a terrible show but she's fabulous."

I'd surreptitiously copy exercises from other guys, who were gracious enough to adjust my atrocious stabs at "correct form" when hoisting iron kettlebells over my head or grasping a torturous pulley system to nurture my nonexistent pectorals. "You're using too much weight," one man said. "You'll hurt yourself, honey. Here, I'll show you." While cruising was rife, it receded beside the more crucial business of developing triceps and deltoids worthy of being cruised. The gym was a dedicated warm-up for the street and the night, and one afternoon a regulation policeman's uniform, in a dry-cleaning bag, was stretched carefully across a locker-room bench. It belonged to an airline ticket agent who donned it when moonlighting as an escort; "Abusive Cop" was a commonly requested subheading, along with "Leather Daddy," "Toys and Watersports," and appointments during which the escort assumed bodybuilder poses while demeaning his client as "a worthless little pussy boy" and standing on the pussy boy's balls. The pussy boy, I was told, was in charge of this exchange, as a power bottom, which differed from a messy bottom or a lazy bottom. And don't get me started on the lexicon of bandanas (light blue for oral only, black for bondage) and key rings (worn on the right if you were a top, or was it the left?), which sprouted from the rear pockets or belt loops of a guy's Levi 501s, the surpassing choice for gay men of quality, who'd highlight their asses and groins through sandpapering and wearing the jeans in the shower, then sitting atop a towel as the garment dried and molded clammily to their crotches.

My body began to respond. Ariadne, who was bunking with her alcoholic mom in a rambling, Grey Gardens–like apartment on West End Avenue, glowered at my newly defined bicep and asked, as if it might be a tumor, "What is that?" I'd scrutinize myself in the mirror, any mirror, seeking shoulder caps and a six-pack, but as I chugged protein shakes and filled out my T-shirts, I deliberated: What would Farrell think? Would he applaud, or think I was wasting valuable hours, or be jealous?

During a still unthinkable meet-up, would he comment, "You look great" or "Have you been working out?" or "You look like every other gay guy in New York." This last critique I might take as a compliment, because New York was becoming a gym-induced beauty capital, the template for a body-consciousness that would infiltrate the three-story Calvin Klein underwear ads looming over Times Square, the compulsory bare-chestedness of action movie heroes, and every small-town gym franchise for decades to come. In twenty years' time, a fag-baiting Jet Ski salesman in East Douchebag, Ohio, would owe his upper torso (everyone neglected their legs) to the diligent gay men of the late 1970s.

I had sex, to verify my progress, but I was handicapped, because while I met some staggeringly attractive, or at least voracious, or sometimes unconventionally hot, men, none of them was Farrell. This wasn't a barrier to pleasure, but it did lead to distraction; even with a far more massive cock in my mouth, it wasn't Farrell's.

Was I cheating on Farrell? I'd asked myself this, during that first night with the ex-priest. Farrell and I had never set parameters. We hadn't bothered to, because as young lovers, we were the only two people on earth. But since Harwell Covington's edict, Farrell was out of reach, for an indeterminate period and potentially forever. Would he have asked me to stay celibate? I didn't think so, or was I acting in my own best, and horniest, interests? I quizzed Ariadne and she scoffed: "Of course Farrell would want you to get laid. What do you think he's doing?"

Over the next year I eked out a subsistence living by assisting Jackson as he gained a foothold in regional theater and off-Broadway—he was making next to nothing but paid me off the books, keeping me in subway fare and Cheerios. I also cater-waitered, in a white polyester jacket, clip-on bow tie, and black pants. I worked everything from fundraising galas ("A Winter Wonderland for Juvenile Diabetes") to the bar mitzvah of a thirteen-year-old whose mega-wealthy parents rented Madison Square Garden and hired Olivia Newton-John to serenade the guests. I wore a neckerchief and cowboy hat to pass canapés at a rodeo-themed wedding in a hotel ballroom, and squeezed my way in between the tables at a Phoenix House event, where the ex–drug addicts being honored were outnumbered by the rich cokeheads in the crowd.

I'd get home after 2 a.m., smelling of chicken Kiev, industrial cleaning products, and the secondhand cigarette smoke that permeated my clothes and hair. I was a subterranean shadow, fortifying the city's economy by slinging my garment bag across my back, smiling mechanically, and pulling a double shift when a coworker had booked an audition for a laxative commercial. I became stooped from bussing aluminum trays stacked with dirty dishes, but I'd swipe a leftover helping of crème brûlée, sleep in, and get a call the next day, to circulate with flutes of cheap champagne at a Wall Street law firm's Christmas party (in my Santa hat, because I refused to wear the headband with reindeer antlers).

I delivered gift baskets to real estate brokers who'd just made record sales, and was placed on a dolly and slid beneath the stage at the Metropolitan Opera to paint the substructure with toxic fire-retardant black paint (the odor made people move away from me on the subway afterward). As my literary debut, I composed dust jacket copy for a small, undistinguished publishing house, where I made the rookie mistake of reading the books I was assigned and tailoring my descriptions to their contents, until a veteran editor clued me in: "Call every first-time writer 'the voice of a generation.' Call every mid-list nonfiction writer 'a national treasure' and every romance novelist, who are the only ones that sell, the 'high priestess of love.' Use the term 'roller coaster thrill ride' for everything and you'll be fine."

Farrell, I assumed, had graduated, but I had no idea of his whereabouts until, as my second October rolled around, I was skimming the Sunday *New York Times* social pages and happened upon an announcement, beside a black-and-white photo of Farrell and Sally, who were engaged to be married. It could've been captioned "Unattainable Blonds to Wed."

My first thought was: I've entered a parallel universe, in which this was the expected and even happy outcome if Farrell was straight. My second thought: I didn't have one, because I was so hurt and stymied, so unable to have seen this coming. How could this be Farrell's doing, or Sally's? What had Farrell's father manipulated them into? Or, worst of all, was this a heartfelt union, which vaporized everything Farrell and I had claimed to feel for each other? Did I have any right to my corrosive resentment, given that I'd just been fucked by a bank teller who dabbled as a weekend go-go boy? Who should I hate? Who should I want dead, other than myself?

I called Jackson: "Have you seen this? Did you know about this? Why haven't you told me?"

"You'll need to come up here."

I stormed up the twenty or so blocks from my place to the Chelsea Hotel, that immortal redbrick pile, home to maverick celebrities from Auden to Jagger to every rakish heroin addict/abstract expressionist/ dissolute heiress who was anyone. That day, as I fumed through the lobby, the elevator doors parted and a gurney was pushed forward, bearing the body of Nancy Spungen, the sloppily peroxided girlfriend of punk rocker Sid Vicious, who'd stabbed her to death minutes before.

Here's all you need to know about the Chelsea Hotel: as Nancy's body was wheeled through the lobby, past artworks (dour Rothko-like canvases and coat-hanger-y mobiles) bartered by tenants in lieu of rent, no one batted an eye, or even glanced up from their stupors. At the Chelsea, a ravaged dead body with smeared black lipstick constituted décor.

Jackson's third-floor apartment was compact but high-ceilinged, and benefited from his trademark teetering white enameled bookcases and gardenia-heavy chintz slipcovers. There were French doors leading to a balcony, with a railing of wrought iron sunflowers, overlooking 23rd Street. I had a key, and I confronted Jackson, as he was boiling his collection of dildos in a battered stewpot on the stove of his galley kitchen. Jackson was conscientious, and a boiled pink latex dildo was a clean dildo.

"Tell me," I ranted, waving the social pages of the *Times*.

"Calm down and I'll explain everything."

Jackson wiped his hands on a dish towel, having set the dildos on a paper towel beside the sink to dry, like durable cucumbers.

"I knew about it," Jackson began, sitting in a bulbous armchair and pouring himself tea. I paced, until he instructed, "Sit down or you'll have a stroke, which you'll probably have anyway, which is why I haven't told you. And I wasn't sure if they were really going to go ahead with things, but now they have."

Jackson was close to Sally, in their fondness for starched Irish linen handkerchiefs, and a spirituality that led them to both Episcopal chapels and exhibits at the Metropolitan Museum's Costume Institute devoted to the silk hosiery of Louis XIV's court.

"So," said Jackson, "are you ready to hear this without having a breakdown, although I won't blame you if you do. But first of all, Sally has sworn me to secrecy, but I suppose that cat's out of the bag. For the last year or so, Sally's been living in Boston."

"She was working as an au pair, right?" I said. "And a social secretary, to the mayor's wife?"

"Correct."

I hadn't spoken to Sally in months. Jackson was more Sally's breed of gay, a confirmed bachelor who'd stow his library of VHS porn tapes in wicker sewing baskets beneath his bed. I was more down-market. Sally worried that I might be prone to naked Polaroids or novels written in the last thirty years. But up until this morning I'd liked Sally; there's a comradeship in mutual disapproval.

"Farrell reached out to Sally," Jackson told me. "Six months ago. She says that after Amherst he'd gone home to Wichita, but that things had gotten very bad. She's not sure of the details, or if Farrell's father had caught him with someone, with another young man, at college, or if Farrell had challenged his father in some other way and made him more than routinely unglued, but Farrell told her he'd tried to kill himself."

I gasped, out of instantaneous heartache for Farrell, and from a selfish indignance, that he'd contacted Sally instead of me. But calling me, especially if his father was in the vicinity, would only have made things worse.

"How?" I asked. "How did he try to kill himself?"

"Pills. He said that he'd made a terrible mistake, not in wanting to die, but in not being sure he was alone for the weekend. His parents came home early, from some business conference, and his mother found him, unconscious on the floor of his bedroom. The family of course brought in a private doctor so Farrell wouldn't be hospitalized and there'd be no record of the whole thing. He said that within forty-eight hours he was physically fine, but hideously embarrassed. He said there was nothing worse than an amateur suicide attempt, and that it's like entering the Miss USA contest and dropping your baton during the talent segment."

We smiled, because that sounded like Farrell, but this wisp of his style made me want to scream or sob or mount a lawsuit, all inadequate responses that would bring me no closer to Farrell.

"His father sat him down and was remarkably concerned and sympathetic, because he'd assumed Farrell had tried to kill himself because he was gay."

Of course. My hatred for Mr. Covington, which I'd kept at a low boil, so it wouldn't contaminate every second of every day, flared into a bloodlust, a choking zeal for the most medieval vengeance. I'd hated people before, but more from irritation at a political figure's stupidity; this was something else, like clawing at the cement walls of a pit, far from where anyone might find me. To this day, I have no idea how higher-functioning people cope with the worst forms of injustice.

"Mr. Covington brought in a quack therapist, who'd had great success with, as he put it, restoring homosexuals to healthy and productive lives. Farrell said that the prospect of listening to this idiot, let alone any extended interaction, made him want to buy a gun and do the job right. But instead, he told his father that he'd only swallowed those pills because he was in love. With a woman."

"Oh my God."

"I know!"

"It's . . . diabolical." I marveled at Farrell's lifesaving ingenuity and shook my head, at whatever deceit would follow. Jackson and I were open-mouthed.

"And Farrell said that his father not only bought this, but sat beside him, practically with tears in his eyes. He said he was so grateful. Wait, wait, it gets better. Mr. Covington told him there were other fish in the sea, and that he'd find the right girl, and that he was so proud of him. And then Farrell being Farrell, he went with it, and told Mr. Covington that after he'd recovered from the pills, the woman he loved had called him, and told him how much she returned his love, and how madly she wanted them to be together. Wait, wait. Because then Mr. Covington asked for her name."

"Jesus!"

"And Farrell said his mind became this spinning Rolodex of every woman he'd ever met, prep school teachers and dental hygienists and daughters of his parents' friends. He said in that instant, he narrowed the field. He eliminated Jess, because she was an actress, which would seriously displease his father, and that even Mr. Covington would spot Ariadne as a lesbian, especially after she punched him in the face. Which left Sally. Farrell didn't give his father her name, not yet, because he wanted to check with her first."

"Which he did," said Sally, walking in from Jackson's bedroom, in a crisp white blouse, pearls, and the neatly pressed jeans she favored on rare occasions. Sally in denim was the equivalent of a Supreme Court justice flashing fishnet tights beneath his or her robe. She looked grave and apprehensive, but of course, immaculately fresh-faced and composed, still Sally.

"I begged Jackson to fill you in," Sally told me. "So you wouldn't throttle me or toss me off the balcony. But I should tell you the rest myself."

She sat on an ottoman across from me but stood back up.

"Farrell called me and asked if we could have lunch. I haven't spoken to him in years, but his voice was trembling so of course I said yes. He flew to Boston and we met in the Oak Room at the Fairmont, which is a bit dowdy but that's why I like it."

"How does he look?" I blurted. I wasn't anticipating signs of decay. I wanted to see Farrell again, even through Sally's eyes.

"He looked gorgeous," she said. "Not that much older, and even, in a way, frozen. As if his life was on hold so he was refusing to age. But he also looked terrible, like those hostages who've been held captive for years, and even when they finally get off a plane at JFK, they're starved and jumpy."

"What was he wearing?" asked Jackson, adding, "For research purposes."

"A blazer and flannels. Horn-rims. Very swank but again, cautious. And he told me about his suicide attempt, which he tried to pass off as a lark, some sort of momentary fist-shaking at the cosmos. But his voice cracked, and he was just so deeply unhappy. So I asked him, 'Farrell, why can't you leave? Get as far away from your family as you can? How can we help you?' "

Sally was being honest. She touched her pearls, as a talisman, a means of centering herself in a capricious and vulgar universe.

"But he said he didn't want to run away," she continued, "which would be cowardly. He said he wanted to beat his family, and especially his father, at their own game. And he wants their money. He said it's rightfully his, not because he deserves it in any way, but because he'll put it to much better use."

Farrell had told me about the struggling dance companies and offbeat, mom-and-pop opera houses and free clinics (in Mexico and Ethiopia) he'd already donated to, with the limited funds his father made available, and he'd shown me photos of an earthquake-ravaged Tibetan temple and a tumbledown Milanese palazzo that he yearned to restore. He kept a billionaire's scrapbook, marking coffee table books and real estate catalogues with Post-its, with fields of fluttering adhesive yellow promises. I was never sure how committed he was to these grails, because the economics and legal issues were beyond me. I'd listened to his plans as if they were bedtime stories, or postcards to himself.

"He told me he needed access," said Sally, "to the Covington line of inheritance, and that he wanted to become a corporate trustee, like his brothers. He said, and I would never use this phrase, and I don't want to repeat it, but he said you must tell Nate, because he'll get it, he said he wants to become a powerful faggot."

I sensed what Farrell was up to, although I had no idea how he'd get there. But he was fighting back.

"And then," said Sally, "he asked me to marry him."

"Personally," said Jackson, "I find it highly romantic. Because it was in a hotel restaurant in Boston and I'm picturing the October light flooding in, and a regatta on the Charles River, with those Harvard boys on crew teams. Did you know, the losing team strips off their shirts and tosses them to the winners?"

Jackson wouldn't be shamed: "Well, it's true! I'm providing local color."

"Okay," I told Sally, "I'm almost with you. But what's his endgame? How would the whole thing work? And why did you say yes?"

Sally turned away. She valued serenity, but today was the opposite. She sat, and leaned slightly forward; this deviation from her ordinarily ramrod posture was shocking, and quickly corrected.

"Farrell said," she went on, "that his family has to accept that he's ditched his actual personality and gone Wichita. So he needs to not just be heterosexual, but to prove it, by getting married to someone the Covingtons will rate as a prize. And of course I'm utterly penniless, but my mother is a Peabody and my father was a Hawthorne, and my great-great-uncle signed the Declaration of Independence. I've got something a family like the Covingtons itches for: the most arbitrary social brownie points."

"Exactly," agreed Jackson. "It would be like Farrell marrying the Liberty Bell, if the Liberty Bell had gone to prep school with a descendant of John Quincy Adams's niece."

"And at first I laughed," said Sally. "Because it was the most preposterous idea. But Farrell wasn't joking. He said we wouldn't need to have sex, or produce an heir, at least not right away. He said he'd always admired me, for not being the least bit frivolous. And he said if we were married, we'd establish our own charitable foundation. Which I could guide."

She reckoned with herself: "I've been working for Mayor Branley's family, and with his wife, Martha, for two years. And they're wonderful people, and I've watched them navigate a public life, and barter political expedience for good works. I've seen Martha smile at the most vile Back Bay political hacks, and chuckle at their jokes and bring them into the dining room, so her husband can trade personal favors for affordable housing and bridges and playgrounds. And I hate it. Every second of it."

"Why?" I asked.

"Because of the backroom dealmaking and the lying and the compromises. But of course if I married Farrell, it would be a deal and a lie and the most massive compromise ever. But there's more: Since we graduated, I've had three proposals of marriage, all from perfectly sweet, handsome, wealthy men. A stockbroker, an Olympic water polo player, and the Business Affairs editor at the *Globe*."

"I've got photos," Jackson murmured to me. "Picture it. Perfect white teeth. Riding boots. Tennis shorts."

"And I genuinely liked all of them," Sally said, ignoring Jackson. "They could hold a conversation about something other than property taxes or imported beer, they had decent work ethics, and in each case, I could guarantee my future: the duplex in town, the house in the country with the split-rail fence, the towheaded children, the squadrons of nannies, the Christmases in Maine with his folks in their zillion-dollar farmhouse. And it might be cushy and secure and Lord knows my mother would be ecstatic, but it comes off like a prison sentence with a five-thousand-bottle wine cellar and a golden retriever named Brandy or Laddie or Tucker. Because I know myself, and I don't want to be married."

"Ever?" I said.

"Never. I know you've always thought I was precisely that sort of person, redoing the first-floor powder room for the umpteenth time to forget about my husband's latest affair, when the cooking sherry's no longer doing the trick. But I want to be better than that, although I don't have the slightest interest in a career. I want to create pen-and-ink notecards, for my own satisfaction, and I want to make the world a far more coherent and spiritual destination, for as many people as I can."

"The first saint on the best-dressed list," Jackson echoed.

"I'm serious about that," said Sally. "And it struck me, if I married Farrell, I wouldn't really be married, not in the conventional, suffocating sense. And Farrell and I were of one mind about spending his money, which would accrue in increasingly helpful amounts, to do some actual good. I once saw a photo of Audrey Hepburn chatting with Eleanor Roosevelt, and they're both so elegant and so . . . I'm not sure what the word would be—decent. Or charmingly but unequivocally intent. When I saw that picture I had one thought: I want to be their child."

"I'm picturing Eleanor in Givenchy," said Jackson.

I was astonished, because Sally's logic was sound. She and Farrell might make a superb team of gilded benefactors. She'd breezed past the sexual, or nonsexual, aspect of the bargain, but fucking wasn't high on Sally's to-do list. She wasn't keen on any activity that caused perspiration, creases, or unpleasant sounds. I wasn't judging her; there's a sliding scale of sexual fervor, and Sally leaned toward the no-thank-you-I'm-fine end of things. Farrell, however, was another story, which at one time had been my story.

"It's nuts, but I think I'm almost there," I told Sally. "But—has Farrell said anything about me?"

"Yes," said Sally. "And he made me repeat it, so I'd remember every word. He said you'd know why he's never contacted you, and that his father alludes to you, including your address in the Village and the fact that you've become, in his father's words, 'a devout homosexual.'"

Devout? Who was the saint now? The saint with biceps?

"But Farrell said to tell you that everything he ever said to you is still true. And that if we get married, the rest of his life might become feasible. And that you were part of the plan."

"Did he say exactly how?" I asked.

"No," Sally replied, "and I didn't press him. I've been caught up in the insanity of all this. I've flown to Wichita, and sat beside Farrell and met his family. In a way, it's what I've been trained for. Farrell and I held hands, and since we truly like each other, we've pleased the Covingtons no end. Have you met Farrell's mother, Ingrid?"

I nodded no—Farrell rarely spoke of her, except as a more reserved version of his father.

"She seems, I'm not sure, tranquilized or depressed, sort of unreachable. But she likes me and we're masterminding the wedding, at a church in Wichita. Everything's been falling into place, along the lines of whatever ceremonies Farrell's older brothers had. As far as I can tell, they're both married to the same woman, one is Annabeth and the other is Lindsay, and they both like to ride and fire housekeepers and host holiday cookie swaps. But here's the kicker: Farrell wants to see you. He says New York is too suspect, but you can rendezvous in Boston, at my apartment.

Because even if his father is having him followed, there's a plausibility. He says the two of you won't have much time together, but it's absolutely vital, and worth the risk."

I couldn't handle anything else, so I thanked Sally for her honesty, and told her I'd be in touch.

When I'm in mind-bending trouble, I never take the subway, because I'll just sit and stew; I walk. I strode the many blocks to my apartment, with my oversize thrift store Harris Tweed coat flapping. The city was deep into a years-long financial slump, with boarded-up storefronts, plastic bags spilling garbage onto the curbs, and a page of the *New York Post* blowing against my leg. This was a New York without brands or franchises. I passed an abandoned donut shop, a photographer's studio displaying an oversize portrait of a formally posed, somber-eyed teenager on her confirmation, and one bodega after another, the shelves jammed with long-expired products and candles in glass jars with labels pledging money, love, and "medical issue healing" to the user.

What did I expect from Farrell? What future had I ever sketched out? This was long before gay marriage was anything beyond a theoretical footnote, and while I was meeting gay couples, and entering New York's bar-and-club scene, I wasn't sure where Farrell and I might place ourselves. And soon he was getting married, sort of.

Was this a temporary stopgap, a cunning subterfuge, or a cruel prank that would only irreparably damage everyone involved?

I didn't blame Sally for accepting a conceivably life-enhancing bargain. I was long past envisioning Farrell thwarting his family and living in whatever his concept of poverty might be, with me: a destitute Farrell was inconceivable. If money was Farrell's curse, it was also his art. Farrell poor would be Farrell diminished in every way; he'd congratulate himself on taking public transportation, he'd entertain the other passengers, and then he'd murmur, "You can be killed by a crosstown bus. If you have to ride it every day."

Did I want money, to a Farrell-esque degree? My parents emphasized security and budgeting, and I was squeaking by on a precarious, cobbled-together assortment of menial jobs. But Farrell had been raised with wealth, which alters a person's biology. After breathing money for so many years, mere oxygen can't sustain life.

As Farrell had once told me, while contemplating a floridly pastel Renoir in a gallery, "I'd buy this, but only as a hostess gift for someone with no taste."

By the time I got home, past a pre-Starbucks coffee house with mismatched chairs, and the dry cleaner run by an elderly, combative couple, and the all-night head shop stocked with bongs, skull-shaped cigarette lighters, and racks of very targeted porn in cellophane wrappers (*Busty Babes Over Forty*, *Barely Legal Farmboys*), I hadn't decided anything because I had no choice. I had to see Farrell.

14

A week later I met Sally at Boston's South Station, and as we hugged, she slipped a set of her apartment keys into my pocket. I wasn't sure if we were being shadowed; in this cavernous, commuter-thronged citadel, Mr. Covington's spies could've been anywhere, scoping us out from behind their newspapers and speaking into their wristwatches to engineer our, or at least my, doom.

"Good luck," Sally whispered in my ear. "You have two hours."

I wasn't familiar with Boston, so I splurged on a cab. Sally lived in a pretty white brick wedding cake of a building, and as I fumbled with the front door I thought: it's said that people look like their dogs, but they also resemble their apartment buildings. I climbed four flights of marble steps and midway down the hall, there was Apartment 4G. I almost rang the bell, to alert Farrell, but didn't. I could leave, in order to stop my heart from pounding; this wasn't a metaphor—the anticipation had become a medical condition. I could say no, not again. What if I opened the door to find Farrell pointing a loaded shotgun at me? I touched my hair and straightened my jacket, improving nothing. I hadn't seen Farrell in over three years. I was a soldier shipped back from an extended overseas deployment, to greet a spouse who might dimly remember me, and after an awkward hug and some disjointed reminiscing, we'd pray for death.

I opened the door, to a light-filled apartment where everything was white, pale blue, or a sunshiny yellow. Farrell wasn't there. Of course not. His father had intervened, or Farrell had been struck by second thoughts or an asteroid or a pickup truck.

Farrell entered from what was most likely a bedroom. He stopped.

"Oh my dear Lord," he said, and we were in each other's arms, not kissing, not yet, but renewing everything about ourselves, asserting the reality of our bodies, having our bodies say everything.

"You are so gay," said Farrell, squeezing my enhanced forearms. "I like it."

"You are . . . ," I began, as I searched Farrell's face. Sally was right; he appeared exhausted but unable to sleep, as handsome as ever, but in limbo.

"I love you so much," I said, without thinking about it, which is the best way.

"Everyone does," he replied, and his grin was even better than hearing that he loved me back. He hadn't grinned for a long time, so I'd done my job.

We kissed, with passion but, even more, conviction, as an act of defiance, as if we'd met behind enemy lines. We laughed, out of manic relief, and Farrell brought me to the couch, which, because this was Sally's place, was upholstered in cream-colored linen without any signs of wear. It was like resting on a cloud, with pale blue raw silk throw pillows hand-painted with an exclamation point and a question mark.

"Before I fuck your brains out," Farrell said, taking my hand, "are you okay with this? With Sally and me?"

"Are you . . . are you asking for my blessing?"

"Yes. Or at least your incredibly dubious, justifiably appalled, forced-to-at-gunpoint consent. Because I won't do this without you. I need you on board."

"The *Titanic*?"

"Not everyone died. Some passengers muscled their way onto lifeboats with their diamond bracelets in the pockets of their furs."

"But—what exactly will happen? You'll get married and . . . ?"

"And we'll need to stay in Wichita for an as yet unknown amount of time, to establish our obedience. Our matrimonial bliss. Which shouldn't be difficult, because while my family's been devastatingly charmed by Sally, they're also scared of her. Of her graciousness, and the fact that she hasn't shrieked obscenities at them."

"Of course. You chose well. But—will we ever get to see each other? Or even communicate?"

"Not for a bit. No red flags. My father's hypervigilant. But I'm after legal advances and binding agreements. Like any blushing bridegroom, I've hired my own attorneys. Everyone in my family has their team, to do the dirty work. It takes a village to destroy a nation."

"Will you ever be in New York?"

"Yes. That's the dream. But for right now, I'm feeling my way. I'm stepping up. For too long I was this passive, whimpering flower, reclining on my divan with a hand flung across my forehead. But after . . . my little escapade, with a cocktail of barbiturates and chocolate milk—I know, it was moronic, but I'd read somewhere that dairy products can increase the drugs' effectiveness, and I had this image, of a lethal dosage left by the chimney for Santa."

"Farrell . . ."

"No. Let's not. Yes, I was adamant, not so much about dying, but about doing something my family would have to explain to themselves and lie about to everyone else, and avoid at every meal and meeting and church service, like with Great-Aunt Mirielle. I'd type my name in the Covingtons' deviant debit column. But when I came to, with the family quack beside me, it occurred to me that if I'd really meant to finish myself off, I wouldn't have been so half-assed. Of course I'd be discovered. I'd made sure I wouldn't die, because I had to see you. And I need my revenge. No, that's too small and mean—I need my triumph. Which will be our triumph, because of what Harwell's put you through. So I'm sorry I can't furnish a timeline or a secure phone number. I'm making this up as I go along, but I'm getting stronger. Which was monumentally overdue, and which you were far too polite to mention. But I need you in my corner—see, I'm already using a sports metaphor. Très butch. But Nate, if you say no, I'll stop."

This wasn't fair. Farrell was asking me to solve his future for him. But he was also trusting me: he wouldn't grant anyone else this authority. He was calling for, maybe not deafening, full-diva applause, but confirmation, that we were in this together. That I'd be waiting.

"Do it. It's beyond dangerous and could go nightmarishly wrong, and I can't believe I'm saying this, but yes. Get married. Be good to Sally." I clutched a blue silk throw pillow to my chest, adding, "They grow up so fast."

Another grin. We were leaping from a cliff, hand in hand, and praying for either deep water or a freeze-frame.

"Thank you," said Farrell. "And now I'd like to see whatever is going on beneath your artfully taut and streamlined T-shirt, and inside those— what are they called? 747s?"

"501s. I was issued them, by the gay police at my gym. You're not the only one getting hitched. I married New York."

The bedroom was a sophisticated dollhouse, with a maple dresser, framed Jackson Bell Rains costume sketches, and a bed layered with sinless white Swiss eyelet, chenille, and an heirloom quilt in blue-and-yellow seersucker. How could we deface such purity? Had Sally made sure we couldn't have sex?

"Wait," said Farrell, as he pulled back the outer coverings, to reveal a brand-new set of the cheapest available flimsy, somewhat cotton sheets, in one of those memorably 1970s geometric patterns of turquoise and orange stripes against a headachy beige backdrop. Such designs graced the opening credits of drive-in movies about illegal cross-country car races, and the album covers of the very worst disco acts. There was a pristine piece of Sally's stationery centered on this horror, with the directive, in her most fastidious script, "Burn these sheets afterwards."

This was why I loved Sally. When it came to a diamond-sharp irony practiced with white-gloved finesse, Sally could vanquish any gay man on earth.

The sex was greedy and relentless, as if Farrell were being launched into space the next morning and might never return. Farrell's body was everything I remembered, but he was less carefree. I didn't ask him which, or how many, men he'd been with during our years apart. I didn't care. He was here, and I was taking every chance to showboat my recently attained muscles and pickup-honed techniques, until Farrell said, with the most satisfying awe: "You are such a whore."

We had a checkout time. As we pulled on a sock or shirt, we reached for each other, to delay the rest of our lives, but unavoidably we were dressed and lingering near the front door. We'd stripped the bed, and Farrell had tucked our grotesque and abused sheets into a brown paper shopping bag, from a tidy stack in Sally's pantry.

"Um, so . . . ," I began, "mazel tov?"

"That's one of your Jewish folk expressions, correct? What does it mean?"

"Congratulations on entering into a loveless marriage to punish your family."

"L'chaim!"

I adored Farrell using Yiddish expressions, because it was the one thing he wasn't good at. He'd sound too careful and overstress the *ch* sounds, as if he were speaking with a deaf Jew.

"Seeing you here," Farrell said, "isn't enough. But I'll keep these repulsive sheets and inhale them. Would that sound better in Hebrew?"

"If you get wobbly," I said, "or everything blows up in your face, Sally has my address and phone number. Just find me before your father has all of us killed."

"I love you. And I'm promising this will work out. I can do this. The crime of the century."

"Oh my God."

"Oy vey."

Pronounced as if it was the name of his Connecticut boarding school horse.

He kissed me and shoved me out the door, before we could lose ourselves in a more extended and definitive farewell. Farrell wouldn't allow that, because with Farrell, nothing was ever over.

15

Farrell and Sally were married three months later, at the All Souls Catholic Church in Wichita. Only Jackson was invited, but not as a guest. He'd designed Sally's gown and had it custom-stitched at a Manhattan costume shop. He'd chaperoned the finished product on a flight to Kansas (the dress, swathed in acid-free tissue paper in a huge cardboard box, had its own seat), helped Sally assemble herself, and taken up a position in a rear pew. Back at the Chelsea he pored over local and national press coverage with Jess, Ariadne, and me.

"It was a lovely ceremony," Jackson said, smoothing a two-page spread in the Sunday edition of the *Wichita Eagle*. There were photos of the happy, or at least conspiratorial, couple at the altar, arm in arm before a floral arch at the reception, and with Sally feeding Farrell a slice of wedding cake. Farrell wore a dark suit, and Sally's dress was refined, in a white satin shirtwaist style with pearl buttons and an almost nonexistent veil. "I'm sure the Covingtons were dying for something more ribbons-and-bows and all-stops-out," said Jackson, "but Sally was strict."

"She looks perfect," said Jess, "as if she's also the clerk who issued their wedding license."

"It's so beyond creepy," said Ariadne, who didn't approve of the marriage. "And I hate weddings in general. They always feel like funerals with bridesmaids instead of pallbearers. At every wedding I go to, I want to stand up and scream, 'Are you people out of your fucking minds?'"

The photos were eerie, and the flawless newlyweds could've existed during any time period. They were a junior version of the Duke and Duchess of Windsor, or a swellegant Fred and Ginger about to hoof through a matrimonial finale. My superstitious nature surfaced. Were Farrell and Sally taunting the Almighty and would they be punished? And would I, for being a party to their blasphemy? Only Jews get this Catholic.

"These are the brothers," said Jackson, pointing to a pair of stolid, young-ish guys in another paper. "Wainwright and Bolt, which sounds like a hardware store, or an English paint company where every color is gray. I'm sure they were ultra-hunks in high school, and they still have shoulders and jawlines, but they're getting thick-waisted and fleshy."

"Did you talk to them?" I asked. "Or to Farrell's parents?"

"That was verboten. I was a servant. I caught Mr. Covington glaring at me, as I was adjusting the hem of Sally's gown. And the mother was zonked and clutching her rosary. And we won't talk about her hair, but it reminded me of the Sydney Opera House. You know, like billowing sails except they don't move."

"So the whole thing," I said, "was it depressing or weird or just corporate Christian Midwestern, which would be both?"

"Well, I'll tell you," said Jackson, thoughtfully. "I've been to many weddings, especially in the South, where the husband was obviously gay, or the bride was pregnant with the best man's child, or the mother of the bride staggered into the center aisle and fainted, so things would be all about her. And I approve, of all of it. Because weddings are theater. They're one of the few days when straight people get to dress up and be in a show; it's almost never about some grand, enduring love, it's about look at us, in the spotlight. And human beings need ritual and music and flowers, so why not? And Sally and Farrell were, as you'd imagine, stunningly beautiful and poised and effortless; they were stars. And there's this."

Jackson held up the program for the country club reception. Sally had drawn a Covington family tree on the cover, with her own face on a freshly sprouted branch.

"I'm using this as my Christmas card," said Jackson.

Later, curled up on the narrow bed that occupied my entire apartment, I thought about what Jackson had said. Is viewing the world as theater, as a weightless yet diverting spectacle, the essence of camp, that gayest of perspectives? Does it banish sincerity and belittle suffering? Or is affectionate mockery the only supportable response to human behavior? Is it a glittering shield against randomness and evil?

And is "evil" the most purely camp designation of all, crying out for a crashing soap opera organ chord and a scarlet-lined cape? Were Farrell and Sally now touring in a pre-Broadway tryout of their own marriage? And where did that leave me—hawking refreshments and vacuuming the aisles?

The answer was enmeshed in the duality of closeted lives. Farrell was consciously disguising his sexuality, as many are forced to do. If all the world's a stage, gay people are often expected to understudy themselves, reinterpreting the truth of their performances, depending on who's out front, and who's paying their salary. This can't be healthy, and the more polished Farrell and Sally's deceit became, the more it could become a long-running prison.

For the next two years as I patched together my rent, I did two other things. First, I wrote one terrible, or at the very best unworkable, play after another. I imitated, or outright plagiarized, my heroes. I sampled absurdism, satire, living room shouting matches, lyrical front porch pathos, every tired form. What I liked about being a writer was the semblance of control. I could scribble at 4 a.m., on a yellow legal pad, once I'd exhausted the *I Dream of Jeannie* reruns on my tiny TV, which teetered on an upended crate at the foot of my bed. What I didn't like was the bipolar frenzy. A first act would be soaring, my Pulitzer was a given, and then I'd inadvertently reread the pages, and be pummeled with the truth: I couldn't sing and I couldn't write.

As a painfully aspiring writer, my second task was to obsess over everything that didn't matter in the slightest. After I'd scan a rave review of someone else's work, I'd do research, by reading subsequent interviews with this lucky competitor. Was the writer younger than me? If they were, fuck them. What famous person were they related to? How rich were their parents? How could I attribute their out-of-the-blue, overnight success to anything other than talent?

This is a small-minded and petty response, shared by every writer who's ever lived.

A bonus tip: a carrot-and-stick approach is a workable substitute for blinding inspiration. Tell yourself, If I finish two more pages, I can have a Mallomar. Proust, I'm told, weighed over twelve thousand pounds.

Bonus freakout: I was already twenty-five, edging toward being too old to die young. And yes, twenty-five-year-olds think twenty-six is old.

After years of abject mediocrity, and a smattering of readings in off-off-Broadway basements, I happened across an actual idea. I'd tricked with a graphic designer living in an enticingly decrepit apartment just off Washington Square. It had once been the home of none other than the exalted nineteenth-century actress Sarah Bernhardt, who'd rented the place during one of her American tours, when she'd cross-dressed and played the title role in *Hamlet*.

The sex had been only okay, because we'd kept taking breaks to debate whether *Brigadoon* could be successfully revived. But while on my back, I noticed a faded fresco on the ceiling, of the masks of comedy and tragedy, which the trick bragged had been painted at the behest of the Divine Sarah herself. For the uninitiated: tricking was the 1980s equivalent of hooking up, or any activity that is bookended by stumbling back to your own place after 3 a.m. and realizing you've left your underwear behind, and not as an excuse to call the guy (a ruse that entails "forgotten" eyeglasses).

The Bernhardt apartment nagged at me, as a theatrical location, and I noodled with a drawing room comedy, the story of a young actress, in the present day, cast as Hamlet. Her fears and reluctance could conjure the ghost of Sarah, who'd coach her as a protégée. I'd explore the mystique of a legendary performer, along with the daunting Everest of playing Hamlet. A stage picture lodged in my brain, of two actresses, both dressed in Hamlet's black velvet tunic and tights, facing off, with rapiers. The initial draft was titled *Dueling Hamlets*, a heavy-handed dud, exchanged for *Player Queens* and, finally, *Enter Hamlet*.

This play was an improvement over my stack of discarded fizzles, more substantial. I sent a Xeroxed draft to Florence Gruber, who was toying with becoming my agent. Florence was in her sixties; a brusque silver haircut and decades of chain-smoking unfiltered Camels had lent her the weathered stature of Isak Dinesen's mug shot. She'd been an American citizen for over forty years, but her German accent had only thickened, especially when haggling over the phone. Her *w*'s became *v*'s, her *r*'s became *w*'s, so I remained, or wemained, Nate Weminger.

After Florence had read *Enter Hamlet*, a meeting was set at her ground-floor Chelsea office, which had curtains made from the linked pop-tops of thousands of cans of Diet Coke, a Florence dietary staple, along with Reese's peanut butter cups. She took a drag on her Camel and scowled at me, asking, "So do you like zis play?"

"I think so. It's got two great leading roles, a decent structure, and it's solid."

"Weally."

"Did you like it?"

"I thought . . . ," she drawled, taking her time, "that it is . . . commercial."

"Is that a good thing?"

"Possibly. You might finally make some money, so I vill be less ashamed of you. I have shown the play to a pwoducer."

She named a successful Broadway team, responsible for many hits.

"And?"

"They liked it. They vant to option it."

"Oh my God."

This was the first glimmer I'd had, of not just potential success, but being able to legitimately call myself a playwright.

Florence smiled, ghoulishly, which was her equivalent of rapture. Her voice went even more gutturally Teutonic: "I vill make zem pay."

Once I'd almost kissed Florence (who'd never countenance such a display), floated out of her office, and was on the street in the brisk October air, I yearned to be wearing Mary Tyler Moore's beret from the opening credits of her TV show, so I could toss it madly into the sky. This was a New York catharsis, when the Gershwin soars, the pavement seems danceable, and the Empire State Building glows that much brighter, because the city was meeting me halfway, or more. Someone had read my work and liked it. Someone with money. This might seem crass, but opinions are cheap and money is proof. Money doesn't say, "We enjoyed your work"; money says, "We mean it" and "Maybe someday you won't be wearing those cheap black dress shoes to work every night."

I longed to tell Farrell. Sally had sent updates, through Jackson: the Covingtons had bought the not-so-newlyweds a house in Wichita. There'd been family Thanksgivings and Christmases (an exceptionally harrowing thought). Farrell had been made a junior trustee, a definite if still frustratingly tenuous boost up the corporate ladder. Farrell and Sally were learning French and playing badminton and serving on the boards of a Wichita cultural center, an orchestra, and a children's hospital. As an antidote to the Covingtons, they'd flee to a secluded cabin on a lake in Wisconsin.

But I couldn't call Farrell or write to him or have him give me a congratulatory bear hug. I couldn't scream and jump around and then remind myself that the play had only been optioned, not produced, and then jump around some more, while Farrell laughed.

The initial payment would be minimal, so I still had to work. I was notified of a last-minute gig at a Waldorf banquet. I entered through the hotel's kitchen and got changed in a cramped locker room. I was joined by Terry Whitby, a friend from Yale and an aspiring singer. We'd done many events together and would report to each other on a cute guy at Table #3 or a party of drunken assholes at Table #12. Tonight Terry had a major bulletin: "Have you seen who's right down front?"

"Who? This is some sort of magazine thing, right?"

"*Forbes*. They're honoring Heroes of the American Marketplace. And first on the list is Harwell Covington. He's sitting with Farrell and Sally."

"What?"

Terry had heard that Farrell and Sally were married, but I'd never shared any background; the story was too complicated and potentially life-threatening. He assumed that Farrell and I had split up long ago, and that I most likely resented Sally. He asked, "Do you want the table? So you can spill things on them, or spit in the entrée?"

My terror and curiosity were in pitched combat. I hadn't seen Farrell or Sally since Boston, three years earlier, and I hadn't laid eyes on Harwell after that day in New Haven. A direct confrontation would be far too risky, but I was desperate for any contact with Farrell, even from a distance.

"Terry, I can't . . . It's not a good idea for me to get within range. Can I stick to the balcony?"

The Waldorf ballroom had a second level, with seating overlooking the main floor. Terry asked our service captain if we could switch assignments, and I volunteered overtime, at no additional salary, to seal the deal. I made my way upstairs, and as I handed out menus and took drink orders, I stayed in the shadows, but I was able to tuck myself into a corner behind a column, with a decent view of the goings-on below. There were twenty round tables, all active with honorees being stroked by family and staff members. The evening was black tie, and Terry and a handful of other cater-waiters were the only visible people of color outside the kitchen.

Harwell was seated dead center, in easy proximity to the small stage and podium. Farrell and Sally were to his right. In their formal wear and success, the group exuded a public superiority, a sense of rightful placement. I wished I had binoculars, to more accurately parse Farrell's behavior, but as I watched him I could tell: he was constrained. He was listening to his father attentively, as Sally smiled and rested a hand on Farrell's shoulder. I knew instantly: her hand was a reminder, to stick with the plan. I could see Farrell keeping his breathing even and his facial expression careful and subdued. I wanted to scream or grab the chandelier and crash onto the table, either rescuing Farrell or causing as much chaos as possible.

"He looks good," Terry whispered in my ear; I'd been so riveted by the scene downstairs that I hadn't felt him sneak up behind me. "I eavesdropped. The dad was telling Farrell about some report he expected on his desk by tomorrow. Very vomit-y, but Farrell said he was on top of things and Sally urged everyone to just enjoy tonight."

"Did Farrell and Sally see you?"

"Yes. They both said hi, which made Harwell suspicious: What were they doing talking to a Black waiter? Sally murmured, 'A friend from school,' and that seemed to satisfy Harwell, because I'm sure he thinks cater-waitering at the Waldorf is a real career peak for a Black Yalie. Do you want me to tell Farrell you're here?"

Did I? What would happen? Could we meet in the men's room, or on the street outside? Of course not. Even if Harwell didn't notice, his executives occupied two additional tables. I'd promised Farrell to let him proceed with his manipulations. But I was keen to deliver my update, about *Enter Hamlet*, to prove I was making progress as well. And now Farrell was standing and excusing himself.

"What do you think?" asked Terry, but I was already headed downstairs, certain I shouldn't be doing this, that I was inviting catastrophe, but I couldn't be this close to Farrell without touching him or at least prompting a flash of mutual awareness. As I hit the last step into the lobby, a guard was holding the ballroom door open and Farrell was only yards away, stiff and angry, as if he couldn't behave appropriately one second longer. I was just smart enough not to rush toward him, as he saw me and stopped moving.

In his tux, with his hair shorn and tamed, Farrell could've been just what he was masquerading as: an obediently corporate husband, in town on business with his family, avoiding the more decadent or tempting blocks of the city. In my ill-fitting polyester I was, at best, his temporary lackey. He stared at me and mouthed the word "no," as his brothers entered from the ballroom. I recognized Bolt and Wainwright from the wedding coverage. They pounded Farrell on the back and he joined them, for semi-boisterous man-talk about wearing monkey suits and how proud they were of the Old Man.

The longer I hesitated, not leaving the staircase, the more betrayal and threat I represented. I couldn't do that to Farrell. I acted as if I'd just remembered a task left undone and trotted back upstairs, wondering if Farrell would try to find me and knowing he couldn't. As I reached the balcony, Terry asked, "So? Did you see him? Did you congratulate him, on his dad's award?"

"I . . . I saw him. But—Terry, I can't go anywhere near him."

"Got it. Just stay up here. Everyone's almost done with their salads. You okay?"

I nodded and all but ran past Terry, as if those salad plates were forcibly beckoning. Terry was a good guy and I wished I could confide in him, but the potential for even innocent gossip was too great. I spent the rest of the dinner imitating a robotic cater-waiter of the future, materializing silently at guests' elbows, refilling water glasses, faultlessly removing half-nibbled Steak Dianes and retrieving napkins and cutlery that had fallen onto the carpet. I forbid myself from any further spycraft. I didn't even approach the balcony railing, until Harwell was being praised and introduced by Malcolm Forbes, the magazine's gregarious, silver-haired publisher, a Manhattan celebrity, due to his family's wealth and sway, and a right-wing power broker with a 162-foot yacht in the harbor, furnished with Chippendale and Gainsboroughs.

As Harwell neared the podium, I took my earlier place by a column, trying not to imagine myself hoisting a crossbow. I studied him, to dispel his lasting, corrupt hold on my life and Farrell's. In his tux, he remained self-satisfied yet nondescript, as if he'd sent a reasonably accurate body double in his place.

"Thank you, Malcolm," he began, "for this generous, wholly unnecessary but welcome tribute, which I accept not on my own behalf, but as merely the current caretaker of Covington Industries."

He'd received many such honors and had probably adapted this speech from earlier ceremonies, which meant he could entertain himself by taking stock of the room and calculating who was properly worshipful and who might be dozing. He glanced upward, at the tables where guests had paid slightly less money, and he caught sight of me. I tried to duck behind the column but I was too late. There'd been a split second of absolute recognition, accompanied by the grisly half smile I remembered, that faint glare of dissatisfaction and punishment.

I almost left the hotel, but that would cause more unwanted fuss. Instead I finished my duties quickly and with my head down, hoping to become as unmemorable as possible. I stashed myself in a corner until the entire lower level had cleared out, after which I took a rear staircase to the locker room. As Terry and I, along with our peers, were changing into street clothes, the door swung open and Malcolm Forbes leaned in, tan and grinning, with those oversize, thickly framed black eyeglasses only the wealthiest men favor, as if daring the lesser world to comment on their cartoonishness.

"Good job, gentlemen," Mr. Forbes told us. "Just wanted to say thanks."

He paused a beat too long, as I recalled Terry dishing that Forbes, while married, was gay, and our all-male cater-waiter crew, heavy on the gym bunnies, was in various states of undress. Malcolm took a good long gander, saluted, and left.

"Maybe we'll get invited onto his yacht," Terry commented. "I read somewhere that it has a full-size helicopter."

As I lugged my garment bag onto the subway, I recovered, telling myself that everything was fine, Harwell most likely didn't remember me, I hadn't spoken with Farrell, so no harm, no foul. The overall duplicity was intact. But I hadn't felt this degree of buzzing apprehension since my first hostilities with Mr. Covington. The dread and resentment were back, as if even his snide glance from across a ballroom could level me.

I'm okay, I assured myself. The Covingtons were passed out in their hotel suites or already speeding back to Wichita on their private jet. I was no one, so I didn't matter. I hadn't damaged Farrell or Sally.

The door to my apartment was open; the lock had been jimmied. I could alert the police station a few blocks over, but I didn't hear any movement from within. I switched on the light. The place was so small that it was readily apparent: I was alone. Had I forgotten to lock the door? Had my landlord been by? The single, coffin-sized closet was as I'd left it, hanging with my more than limited wardrobe. The bathroom, barely able to accommodate one tenant, was as stained and drab as ever. If only someone had broken in with paint and cleanser.

I went to wash my face with the coldest water the uncooperative plumbing could manage, but there was debris in the sink, shards of recently burned paper, blackened at the torn edges. It was Jackson's portrait of Farrell, which I'd kept in the portfolio under my bed. It had been ripped to pieces and incinerated, as what—a second warning? A further demonstration of Harwell's calculated disgust?

I sat on the bed, wondering if Harwell could murder me with his thoughts. But in a way, he'd done something worse. He'd stolen not just my privacy but my only remaining artifact of his son, my proof that I loved Farrell, and that Jackson, through his artistry, had captured everything I felt.

The next day, when I told Ariadne, Jackson, and Jess about the evening, and what I'd come home to, there was an outcry.

"Harwell should be arrested!" Jess proclaimed.

"How dare he!" Jackson added.

"That malevolent fuckheaded fucker," said Ariadne. "But he knows there's nothing you can do; you can't tell the cops, 'I think my boyfriend's repulsive father had someone invade my apartment and charbroil a picture.' They'd laugh."

"Jackson," I said, "I'm so sorry about the portrait."

"Well," he decided, "this means we'll need to create a second portrait, only from life. When Farrell returns to us."

"So what should I do?" I asked the group.

We were sitting in a bagel hangout on Christopher Street that had replaced the Stonewall Inn, where the gay civil rights movement had been kickstarted. It was now a bland, fern-filled, mirrored place to snag a cheap breakfast.

"At least you got to see Farrell and Sally," said Jess. "Or did that make things worse?"

"No," I said. "It was like an espionage mission. As if they were working undercover as a carefree couple, and I was disguised as a cater-waiter."

"At the Waldorf," said Jackson. "With Terry Whitby, who's so dreamy."

"Here's what you do," counseled Ariadne. "And it's the only thing you can do. It's what you've committed to."

"What?"

Ariadne pointed out the hideous fact of the matter: "You wait."

16

Ariadne was only partially right. I couldn't just sit around, with my life on trembling hold. I would match Farrell's audacity, and become exactly what would unhinge his father: a powerful faggot. To Harwell I was still a piddling annoyance and swiftly intimidated. I was lower than gay, I was insignificant. So I'd develop my own visibility and strength. Becoming a produced playwright would be my birthright, something Harwell couldn't touch. *Enter Hamlet* would be not merely a calling card, but my own Covington Industries—a faggot's domain.

A director was hired, a guy my age who believed the play had merit and oversaw my rewriting. Together we hatched a casting coup, which had been gnawing at my filthy Broadway-bound soul. What if we offered the role of Sarah Bernhardt to Rebekah Tanner? I told Jonathan, the director, about meeting Rebekah at that holiday party, as she'd brainstormed a project for Jess and herself. Jess would be ideal as Maggie, the young actress. She'd highlight the character's charm, her gauche impulsiveness and her mistrust of tackling Hamlet and coping with the inexplicable ghost of Sarah Bernhardt prowling irritably around her apartment.

Jonathan brought this notion to the producers, who were all in. Jess was an unknown, but that would become a selling point: Rebekah Tanner and her gifted young daughter, arm in arm onstage. A torch would be passed, a legacy burnished. The press releases would write themselves. Eat shit, Harwell Covington. A script was messengered to Rebekah, and the next day I was summoned to her apartment.

A uniformed maid opened the door. For a star of Rebekah's eminence, employing only a maid and a cook was a modest indulgence. Without partygoers, the apartment was even more of a stage set, for a frothy, matinee-friendly romp about a beloved actress with multiple suitors. Rebekah's many Tonys were grouped on a bookshelf, while her Oscar towered over them, as their Hollywood scoutmaster. I thought, She's got almost enough awards for a really special menorah.

Rebekah made her entrance, in pants, a loosely knotted scarf, and a deceptively simple hand-knitted sweater, blurring into a graceful flurry of expensive at-home chic.

"Ned!" she cried, opening her arms, and I had no idea what to do: Correct her? Unobtrusively mention my actual name later? Change my name?

After an airborne embrace, as if a delirium of butterflies had swirled past, Rebekah said, "Please! Sit!" and curled up in the corner of a couch, gesturing toward an ottoman, because she couldn't quite ask me to crouch at her feet. She executed a trademark tousle of her expertly highlighted mane, which delighted both of us. She brandished her copy of my play, from a nearby pile of manuscripts.

"Ned! Your play!"

My name was on the cover. I bit the bullet. "It's Nate, I'm so sorry."

"Nate! Of course it's Nate! What is wrong with me! Maybe it's because until yesterday, I'd thought of you as one of Jess's little friends, whom I adore. But now I know—you're a playwright! The most marvelous playwright!"

I didn't care what she called me. Rebekah Tanner had praised me and I was hers; I could hear Farrell snorting but conceding, "She's heaven!"

"So . . . ," I began, totally fishing, "you liked it?"

"Liked it? I . . ."

She leaned back, nestling the script to her bosom, searching her thoughts, as if with a flashlight. "It's superb. I mean, where did this come from? Sarah Bernhardt and Hamlet? And yet you've brought her into the modern age! It's brilliant!"

"I've been in her apartment," I said, editing the sluttier particulars. "And I couldn't stop thinking about it. She's so iconic, and for a woman to play Hamlet is still a huge statement, but I didn't want it to be just a biographical piece, so I added Maggie. I want the play to be a love letter to actors and Shakespeare and the theater."

This was true, yet also schmooze. As with that dust jacket copy, I was packaging myself and my work. I wasn't lying or exaggerating, but I was, I suppose, writing myself, and pitching my personality, for an optimum result. I was Farrell-ing.

"I love all of that," said Rebekah. "And Maggie—what a marvelous role. She's just starting out, unsure yet headstrong, with a fire in her belly yet emotionally fragile—she's asking herself, Am I good enough? Dare I heed the distant trumpets, and reach high, for the golden crown? And I could see myself, instantly, maybe in jeans and a T-shirt, with the perfect little jacket, just throwing myself around the stage, like a frisky colt taking her first steps."

Oh no. Oh my God. Did she think we were offering her—Maggie? Who's twenty-one years old? This was worse than Rebekah not remembering my name, much worse—should I say what the hell, just to keep the project churning forward? Who'd play Sarah? An eighty-year-old? But Rebekah was way ahead of me. She was posed by the bookcase, her hand resting on her Oscar's polished golden head.

"But no," she said, with downcast eyes. "I can't fool myself. I'm no longer an ingénue. Oh, I could play Maggie, I could play the shit out of Maggie, but do you know what? I've done that. I've played Maggie a thousand times, to thunderous acclaim, and that's why I need a damned change! A perilous challenge! Sarah Bernhardt! The Divine Sarah!"

"And you'd be incredible!" I gushed, again utterly honest, but grateful for Rebekah's self-correction. "Because we need a star to play a star. Someone with that total command. With you in the part, it makes so much sense, and the audience will go berserk!"

"It's a grueling task," said Rebekah, "and of course I'd read up on her, every word I can get my hands on, and we'd need historic yet flattering costuming, and when Sarah first materializes, from the great beyond, it wants ethereal music and billowing fog and otherworldly magic, and perhaps I'd hold for a moment, as I return to human form, and let the audience join in my tremulous wonder, I'm back, it's me, Sarah, oh, but I'm getting ahead of myself. We're only just talking. Nattering up a storm!"

What did that mean? A second ago she was all but pawing the ground to start rehearsals, but had I misread everything? What cues had I blanked on?

"So tell me," said Rebekah, a drink in her hand, sitting down, touching my knee and leaning back into her couch, "Maggie. Who are you thinking of?"

The director and producers had urged that I bring up the idea of Jess, since I was Jess's friend and fan, and Rebekah had told me of her fervent hunt for a mother/daughter vehicle. Farrell would love this. "Go for it," he whispered in my ear. "Make every gay man in New York thank you."

"Well," I proposed, "I've been thinking. Because when we first met, at your wonderful party, I remembered something you said. You said that you'd love to find a play, for you and Jess."

"Ahhh . . . ," she said, sipping her blended whiskey. "And what play are you thinking of?"

How was this happening? Why did Rebekah keep drawing me in, and then tossing out detours or oil slicks, as if I were driving a very used car down an unlit back road, during an earthquake?

"*Enter Hamlet*," I said. "With you as Sarah, and Jess as Maggie. She'd be amazing, and people would love it. To see the divine Rebekah Tanner and her . . . her . . ."

I was grappling for an adjective that would praise Jess without insulting Rebekah.

"Rebekah Tanner," I said, "and her feisty daughter."

Feisty? Feisty? Had I suddenly written a Wyoming western, where Maggie would gallop out onto the prairie in calico, cussing people as dadgum varmints?

"Jess," said Rebekah, as if she'd just heard the name for the first time in her life. "Jess. My Jess. My little Jess. As Maggie."

A lifetime passed, and another, as Rebekah squinted into some middle distance, toward the faraway, inscrutable home of her ego, her volatile relationship with her daughter, and my opening-night gift to her, which I'd already planned to be a leather-bound copy of the play, inscribed "With so much love, from Nate Shakespeare." She sailed back to her living room and took my hand.

"It's perfect," she said, kissing my cheek. Curtain. Brava. Did you catch that, Harwell?

Rebekah's agent called the producers and negotiations went forward, which meant Broadway was now an increasing likelihood, and my life was surging. Jess had read the play, but I wanted to make the offer myself. She was living on Riverside Drive, in an anarchically disordered apartment, with her wardrobe strewn onto any available surface, and food indistinguishable from reading material.

Jess herself was always a joy, both willowy and sturdy, an ex-dancer who could chop wood. Today she'd cleared a chair for me, sweeping a flannel robe, an evening gown with the tags still attached, and a single angora mitten onto the floor, while she sat cross-legged on her bed, eating in a time-honored actress mode, which meant picking the frosting off a donut and nibbling it in micro-bits. I'd known actresses to split an M&M into halves because, "I'll save the rest for later, when I'm really hungry."

"So," I began, "*Enter Hamlet*. I want to ask you something, and you're completely allowed to say no, but if you do, I'll cut your throat and then mine. But here goes: I'm pretty sure your mom is going to play Sarah Bernhardt. How would you like to be Maggie?"

I'd expected whoops of exultation, but Jess was more withdrawn. After that party, I'd been surprised that Jess and Rebekah hadn't filed restraining orders against each other, or at least stopped speaking, but this hadn't been the case. As Farrell had explained, "When you watched Rebekah pull that gun, and when you found out that Jess had been sleeping with Rebekah's boyfriend, you were shocked, because you're a nice boy from New Jersey. But that was far from their first time going at each other, and Rebekah had intended to enthrall the room, while Jess was staking out her own turf and making Rebekah pay attention. We're in New York, on the Upper West Side, and this is how people behave."

"Nate," Jess said, moistening a fingertip to scoop a single hot-pink sprinkle from her donut, "you know I love you and I love the play and I love the part, and of course I'd kill to do it. And I'm so grateful. But I'd just like you to think about something. My mom is a great actress, and she does her best as a mother, within a certain limited range, and I do love her forever. But before we jump into this, just know: it may not be easy. And it's your play and I don't want it ruined."

Jess, like other children of unbalanced, Oscar-winning parents, was savvy, as to warning signs, hiding places, and interventions. These kids have often raised themselves, even amid opulence. They've memorized the phone numbers of private physicians, psychiatrists, masseurs, and pharmacists, before they can tie their shoes (and they are expert, by necessity, at forging signatures and telling overwrought production assistants that "Mom's still got the flu, but says she'll be back on set by tomorrow, Thursday at the latest").

"Jess," I said, with the reckless aplomb of a first-time playwright hijacking the world to his single-minded ambition, "if you do my play, with your mom, it won't just be a dream come true. It will be the very best shot this play can have, because you're both so talented. And just between you and me, and I haven't done this deliberately, but you and your mom may very well have inspired this play. And Farrell always told me that luck and fate are unstable commodities that can't be ignored. You have to lasso them, and hang on for dear life. So I'm prepared for anything. Are you?"

She grinned, with a wicked acceptance of whatever lay in store. This buoyant, why-the-fuck-not spirit is the essence of theater. It's a world without even a minimal safety net; the theater attracts the already crazy, and converts everyone else.

"I can't wait!" yelled Jess, and the whooping began, as I plucked a comb from my glass of orange juice.

Toward the end of our first week of rehearsals, I got a midnight call. "My darling," said Rebekah, mildly slurring her words, "I'm not getting what I need, and I'm not sure if it's the script or Jess or Jonathan, but please, help me out. I need to feel . . . I want to feel . . . as if Sarah is trying to excavate her own life, warts and all, and teach Maggie, and heal the world. I want the audience to feel as if Sarah lives in every one of them, and holds their blood-weary hearts in her hands, and . . . and tosses those hearts back, freshly replenished and beating with love. Do you know what I'm saying?"

Farrell's voice told me, "You're talking to a madwoman. You will never win. Don't try to reason with her, not without a switchblade. She's not listening anyway. Just keep saying yes. And I don't know what 'blood-weary' means either."

"Yes, Rebekah," I swore, "I'll have new pages tomorrow."

During the second week, romance brewed. The actor playing Laertes, Hamlet's buddy, had been cast with Scott Baltimore, a minor TV star from a show called *Harbor Island*, a heavy-breathing, teen-oriented nighttime soap. Scott was cheerful and cooperative; he was an actor because he was so good-looking everyone had always told him he should be an actor. He was twenty-two and he'd caught Rebekah's eye.

I got back early from a lunch break and hit the communal restroom. There were heaving moans originating from a stall, but before I could make a quick exit, Scott stepped out, his shirt open, saying, "Hey, some privacy next time, okay?" He adjusted his fan-worthy hair in the mirror, gave himself a studly once-over, waggled his eyebrows at me, and sauntered out, as Rebekah left the stall, buttoning her blouse. She looked happier than she had in days, rubbed my shoulder, and as she opened the door to the hallway, instructed me, "Tell Jess."

I didn't tell anyone, especially not Jess, but I reasoned that whatever or whoever was reinforcing a more even-keeled Rebekah, I was good with it.

The next day there was a bravura tantrum during Rebekah's costume fitting, as recounted by Jackson: "I presented three racks of possibilities, so Rebekah could find out what she likes. I want her to be completely comfortable, and I've shown her all of my Bernhardt background, we've got a wall of photos and sketches and swatches. Bernhardt's real Hamlet costume was a bit stodgy, with a fur-trimmed tunic and these ballooning leg o' mutton sleeves, plus a full cape and tights. So I adapted it, to be more, let's be frank, slimming, but when Rebekah tried it on, oh my Lord. She began yowling that she looked like a convertible sofa and a pile of unfumigated old hotel drapes and that Sarah would never be caught dead in, and I'm quoting, 'this revolting lump of steaming dogshit.' And she was standing right in front of the pictures of Sarah in exactly that outfit, only worse, but I didn't think it would be constructive to point that out. Then she grabbed a pair of shears and started hacking at the sleeves."

"So what did you do?" I asked, mesmerized but so glad I hadn't been there.

"I let her do whatever she wanted, so she'd be part of the process. This isn't really about me, or the costume, it's about how Rebekah feels about herself, and my job is to support that."

As always, I was so impressed with Jackson, and not only his meticulous craftsmanship but his warmth and insight about Rebekah. "I'm here to serve the artist," he concluded, and I could hear Farrell finish Jackson's thought: "Even if she's out of her mind."

I was awakened the next morning at 7 a.m. by a call from Florence. "Schnookie," she told me. "Ve have a situation. Webekah has quit."

I started choking, and wondered if, through his minions, Harwell had provoked this. The producers begged and badgered Rebekah's agent, and after uncommunicative hours Rebekah accepted a meeting, with Jonathan and me, at her apartment. We steeled ourselves in the elevator as I mentioned, "I was here once for a party, and Rebekah pulled a gun."

Rebekah had assumed a fetal position in the depths of her couch, cocooned in at least four shawls and cradling a cup of herbal tea.

"Boys," she said, "I'm so sorry, about all of this. You deserve so much better, but I'm just not up to this. But thank you for coming."

If she was playing passive, I'd go for aggressive. I'd Farrell her.

"Rebekah," I said, "whatever happens, I have to say something. Working with you, as you brought this character to such rich and hilarious and deeply moving life, well, it's been a thrill and a privilege."

"What do you need?" asked Jonathan. "How can we help you?"

Rebekah took a protracted, moody sip of tea and did her gazing thing, at an oil portrait of herself, idealized in a blotch of pastels, over the mantel.

"I don't know," she said. "I just don't think it's a match. And I'm not blaming either of you, not entirely."

She spoke for just under an hour without taking a breath. She went over the "quagmires" of her first two marriages; the moral contortion of being invited to the Reagan White House (she'd gone, but worn an Amnesty International pin on the lapel of her St. Laurent tuxedo); Nancy Reagan's lack of "any real pizzazz"; why Bernhardt was overrated because she'd never had to please studio executives; why this "Meryl Streep person" was "talented, I've heard"; why she'd almost had Jess aborted but was "so glad I didn't"; the curse of receiving an Oscar, a Tony, and an Emmy at such a young age and having "nowhere to go"; her idea of Jess being padded to appear "not really overweight, but more real"; why she'd had no interest in playing Lois Lane in that last Superman movie, even if she'd never been "officially" offered the role; how someday she'd like to "take a run" at Blanche DuBois in *Streetcar* "once I'm the right age" (in the script, Blanche is thirty); how much she loved her new yoga instructor because he'd "reawakened entire intermediate zones of my torso"; and then, out of nowhere, she looked directly at me and said, "You miss him, don't you?"

"Rebekah?"

"That boy, from my party. The beauty. I've asked Jess about him, over the years, and she's told me that you're apart. And that he married that odd girl in the plain white dress. But every time I see you during rehearsals, oh, you're wonderfully attentive, but I can tell—you're a million miles away."

She wasn't wrong, and I was floored. For all her self-involvement, Rebekah was attuned to human emotion. She collected fragments of rage and yearning, like a Stanislavski-trained pack rat.

"I'm sorry if I ever seem distracted," I admitted. "It's a difficult situation, but I shouldn't drag it around with me."

"No," Rebekah said, a light returning to her eyes. "It's glorious. I'll use it! Oh, my dear Nate, this is just what I've been searching for, something or someone to dedicate my performance to! A tribute to Sarah herself would be too easy, too formulaic. What was that boy's name? Farrow?"

"Farrell."

"This show, the flame of my performance—they're for Farrell. I'll bring him to you."

I was almost offended, at Rebekah co-opting my life, at her claiming a deeply personal separation as her own, but why not? I had to stop myself from believing in her too fully, from imagining that there was a supernatural element to her skill set, and that when Bernhardt entered, in a superbly lit haze, holding for entrance applause, Farrell would stand beside her.

"All I can say," Rebekah declared, revitalized and ushering us out, "is that I'll try. I'll do the best I can. See you tomorrow!"

Technical rehearsals brought us into the theater itself, a smaller, lovingly refurbished, one-hundred-year-old Broadway house. At 8:30 a.m. on Monday I stood a few yards from the marquee, where the signage had just gone up: "REBEKAH TANNER in *Enter Hamlet*, by Nate Reminger." And beneath the other credits, in a box, "And Introducing Jess Janeway" (Jess had sagely clung to her father's last name, despite Rebekah's huffing that the Barrymores and the Kennedys "matched").

This was a cinematic moment. I was a young enough, untried playwright, with a show indisputably on Broadway. There were already full-page ads in the *New York Times*; Farrell and his father must've seen them. I should have wallowed in this milestone, or at least permitted myself a few seconds of memoir-ready tingle. But I was rattled, with premonitions more acute than any expected jitters, and despite Rebekah's best efforts, Farrell wasn't here. And part of me was glad. Where was this coming from?

On opening night I went by my parents' hotel room. "We are so proud of you," said my mom, who'd lost ten pounds and bought an expensive new dress, which was sleek if more glitzy than her usual, understated style and purchased at a Manhattan boutique; she was anticipating red carpet grandeur.

"We were already proud of you," said my dad, who'd broken out a rarely worn tuxedo, "but I keep telling everyone at work, my son has a show opening on Broadway! We're just bursting!"

I hugged them and worked to quiet the anacondas chomping away at my intestines, because my parents deserved better. I wanted to be what they were describing, a talented offspring buffing the Reminger legacy, but—no, I couldn't think even five minutes ahead, or I'd be done for, I'd be heading for a tall-enough building or the electrified third rail of the subway tracks.

The theater was packed with a spiffy, mostly invited audience, friends and relatives of everyone listed in the program. The pressure was unsparing, for the show to be a hit, for everyone's gamble on me to pay off. Only Jackson had practical-minded solace, dragging me into a corner of the basement wardrobe room and telling me, "I know what this is. I've been here before, although I'm lucky, because I'm off to the side. But this is your play and you've worked hard and you wish you could disappear, or have it be tomorrow, or die during the curtain call so at least you'd get sympathy reviews. Well, tough shit—it's your opening night, and you don't have to enjoy it, but you're here."

I hugged him with a navy buddy's camaraderie, as if we'd just received dual, drunken tattoos, reading "Broadway Forever."

"And they're with us in spirit," he added, "Farrell and Sally."

The show went well, with a frenzied quality caused by such a vocally cooperative crowd. I didn't catch a word, cocooned in dread and thoughts of Farrell, and how if he was present and holding my clammy hand, I'd be both thankful and even more sickened, because he'd be someone else, the very best someone else, whom I'd disappoint. The audience stood and cheered, and bouquets were presented to Rebekah and Jess, who clutched each other warmly for the TV crews jamming the aisles, while adjusting their faces to optimum angles. Jonathan and I were trooped onstage, and I felt honored and targeted.

The opening night party was its own hyperventilating behemoth, held at Tavern on the Green in Central Park, in a series of glass-walled dining rooms lined with buffets and jammed with audience members and hangers-on there for the free lobster roll. The trees, visible through so much glass, had been wrapped with white twinkle lights, for a holiday-in-hell effect. My parents, along with fourteen family members, occupied my table, rising for star sightings and vowing the show would run for years. These were wonderful people, taking a boisterous Broadway holiday, and I'd never want to let them down, as I turned into a head-bobbing, lipstick-kiss-covered zombie. Ariadne, dapper in a tux, her hair sharply trimmed and glossy, was seated with Jackson at Jess's table. She pulled me into a gruff hug and barked, "It was fine!" Sally had sent her handwritten regrets and a textbook, unstudied arrangement of white tea roses loosely tied with a pale blue ribbon.

Assistants were dispatched to Midtown newsstands, to collect the next day's papers. There's a pause on every opening night, when the air changes. If the gods grin, and the notices sparkle, a producer will silence the mob and read the raves aloud, as the crowd glows, congratulating themselves on picking a winner.

This wasn't the case, not tonight. My peripheral vision told me that whispered, forceful conversations were underway, and producers were leaving for conferences in side rooms. An assistant tapped Jonathan and me on our shoulders, ushering us into a smaller, unused dining area, as if we were low-level thugs being shanghaied at gunpoint to face a displeased godfather, but instead newspapers, far more lethal enemies, had been opened on tables.

The *Times* began well, hailing the play as hilarious and "at times, fresh." Everything scudded downhill from there, as the words branded themselves into my memory: "hackneyed," "trite," "tiresome," "wasted promise." Rebekah was lavishly adored, as "our indefatigable Ms. Tanner," and Jess was anointed "a bright new star," for which I was glad, since I'd talked her into this. One of the other papers was effusive, and the rest were tepid at best, relying far too much on words like "tepid." The TV reviews, from sneering middle-aged men in heavily dandruffed blazers, were worse. Thirty seconds of local airtime brought out the smarmy lizard in these moonlighting junior college English professors.

I'd never been reviewed before, let alone publicly flayed. My guts had been hollow for hours; this was more like being swamped by an invisible, centrifugal blast, leaving me upright but sapped, and unable to move. I wasn't angry or defensive, and I'd braced myself with foreboding, but none of this mattered. Because I agreed with the verdicts.

I had to get out of there. I was dimly aware of voices, pledging that there were enough decent "money" quotes for an ad campaign, and that the critics were insufferable snobs, and that no one was sorry they'd backed my play. But the mood was indisputable. The ship wasn't going down—it had settled onto the ocean floor.

There's nothing sadder than my mom's hopeful face, silently asking if I'd seen the reviews. I couldn't surgarcoat anything, leaning in to whisper, "They're terrible," and receiving a hug. My mom may have taken the reviews harder than I did, not out of shame, but from wanting to shelter her cub from those snarling newsprint hacks. I couldn't explain to her, "But Mom, they were right," because she'd only hug me tighter and whisper, "Shut up."

I made my rounds hastily, thanking everyone and vowing to call and get together, on some inconceivable day when I could appear in public without wearing dark glasses, and under an assumed name. Jackson was invaluable. He grasped what was happening and steered me through the mob, which was thinning out quickly. Bad news defeats even a choice of baked Alaska or pecan pie à la mode. Ariadne said, "Fuck 'em all," which made me smile for a millisecond, and I thought about hiring her as a hit-person, because she'd be willing. I kissed Jess, who told me, "We'll talk," and I waved to Rebekah, who was still encircled by celebrity first-nighters, her agent (hurriedly listing film offers "now that you're available"), her publicist (confident that Rebekah's marketability remained "in the clear"), and Scott Baltimore, who gave me an inexplicable thumbs-up.

I didn't blame Rebekah for anything. I understood her more intimately. She'd been fed through this particular grinder many times before, and while the world, and the critics, had most often extolled her, she'd internalized that with each play or movie or, God forbid, TV series, the odds were awful. Her madness, I saw, was an effective barrier, against the customary accolades, the blistering pans on the horizon, and the incoming platoons of ever-younger new actresses. She'd chosen a treacherous life, which was structured to keep her so painfully needy.

The biting Central Park air helped, but not enough, and Jackson shoved us into a cab and dropped me at my building, patting my hand and swearing, "Oh my darling, don't worry—there are starving people all over the world, and for tonight you're allowed to be happy about that."

As I trudged up the five flights, I pictured those malnourished masses, in scraps of muddy burlap, clasping their emaciated infants to their bony sternums, and reading those children the *Times* review aloud.

I fell back onto the bed, my mind imploding with everything and nothing. Aside from that morning with Mr. Covington, I'd never been this defeated and limp and eviscerated. There was nothing to clutch at, no spindly, leafless branch of hope or brief but undeniable glimmer of sunlight. I was resoundingly and royally fucked, and it was my own fault, because I'd believed in—what? The inspiration of a trick's rent-controlled one-bedroom? In wielding my Broadway debut to defeat Harwell, who could now gloat over the sorry outcome? In myself? Yes, this is self-pity, when the tanker truck pulls up to the curb and the driver checks his clipboard, reporting, "And we've got eight thousand more gallons of this primo-grade stuff on the way."

I heard it. A sandpaper-y noise from the hall. Was it my neighbor, an elderly drunk who rarely forsook his precarious archives of old *Life* magazines and moldy, stacked takeout containers? Was it the most inept burglar, about to be so wrenchingly disgruntled, at my owning nothing of value, most especially my future? Was it, God willing, a drug-crazed killer with a machete, whom I could welcome by muttering, with justifiable irritation, "What took you so long?"

I listened. There was whistling:

I never knew what I needed
Until one day you were there . . .

I opened the door.

"What's new?" asked Farrell.

NIGHTTOWN

17

We didn't embrace, not yet. I was too shell-shocked. Farrell walked me to the bed and sat beside me.

"How bad?" he asked.

"The worst."

"I know. I saw the *Times*, the *Daily News* and the *Post*."

I winced, but I was gratified at not having to chronicle my evening, or wait morosely as Farrell skimmed the reviews. It began to sink in, that he was actually here. Was this Rebekah's uncanny doing? Had she manifested him through her performance, or simply tracked him down?

"What . . . ," I said, not ready to touch him. "What are you doing here?"

"You had a show open tonight on Broadway."

"But—what about your father?"

"I'm dealing with him, I'll tell you about it later. And I'm so sorry about the Waldorf; I was in Wichita mode. But tonight is about you. I saw the show."

"What? When? How?"

"I flew in today. I stood in the back tonight. I saw you, but you were surrounded, and I didn't want to interrupt the gang worship."

"So—you saw the play? What did you think?"

I'd done it again. I'd breached a primary commandment. I'd asked a question I never wanted the answer to. Except I did. Because it was Farrell.

"It's not great," he said. "But anyone with half a brain can tell that you're funny and talented. It's a first step, a maiden effort. A promissory note, an IOU to the audience. To yourself."

Everything he'd said was fair and charitable. Honest but uplifting. But it wasn't enough. I craved something else, something larger, some credo for the rest of my pitiable life, but I had no idea what such words might be. Farrell did.

"Here's what's going on. We finally have something in common. Since birth, I've been given far too much, for only the most random reasons. Pure privilege, a blank check, and the keys to a Porsche, and then the keys to a Ferrari, once I'd forgotten where I'd left the Porsche. I did as I pleased. Until I met you. Wait, don't say anything, I'm not blaming you. I'm grateful. Because when we were together, my happiness reached the most absurd dimensions, but was still unmerited. And when my father showed up, I knew: kindergarten was over. I had to think matters through. Life is either something that happens to you, and knocks you flat, or something you confront and study and edit. You make every effort to do better. To be better. So that's what I've been doing. I've been earning you."

"Farrell?"

"And now it's your turn. You're still, for all intents and purposes, a child, and you've been handed a show on Broadway. Almost no one gets that. You've undoubtedly labored over it, and done your limited best, and you've planted your tiny ragged flag on West 45th Street, in a jewel box of a theater. You can call yourself a playwright."

"A failed playwright. The show may close tomorrow."

"Boo fucking hoo. You've done it. And just like me, you've been slapped, hard. Something which was absolutely necessary, for both of us. This is where we start."

"Start what?"

"Getting back to work. Setting our course. There's so much to analyze and so many details are still up in the air. But first I need something."

We kissed, not with the voracious passion of long-separated lovers, but as if we were sealing a contract, although I wasn't sure of the specifics, or of what we'd be building together. Farrell hadn't told me anything, about Sally or his family or why, just by being with each other, we weren't attracting every sort of combustible trouble.

"And next," said Farrell, "I need something else. And no, I'm not talking about sex, not yet, although you will be receiving the fuck of your life, a fuck that will make you forget the word 'insipid' ever existed."

"I'm going to kill you."

"Afterwards. But first I'm prescribing—tonight. Remove your decent-but-woefully-expected opening night off-the-rack Armani suit and put on as little clothing as you dare. Because we're going out."

I surrendered control. I stripped off my cigarette-smoke-and-debacle-scented party wear, and tugged on my most shamelessly threadbare and low-slung jeans, a white T-shirt, and Adidas. I was that gay. I was all gay. I was going out with the hottest man I'd ever known, at a loss as to where we were headed, which was the roadmap for our relationship. Farrell was in white Levi's and a white oxford-cloth shirt, without a belt. Easy access. We deposited my graduation Timex, Farrell's Cartier tank watch, and his emerald ring on my dresser. I had my keys and some cash. We left, without any further physical contact. Tonight was about delayed and then constant gratification. Fuck *Enter Hamlet*. Fuck Harwell Covington. And especially fuck that Channel Five critic with the comb-over, the stiff polyester Father's Day necktie, and the five rubbery chins. Fuck everything and everyone. Farrell and I were going to be gay in New York, which on that night in cultural history not only mattered, it ruled.

"Wait," I said, as Farrell hailed us a cab, which stopped like a shot. Among Farrell's superpowers was what he called cab magnetism. He would half raise his arm to signal for a ride, when three cabs would triangulate, vying for his favors.

"What about Sally?" I asked. "Does she know you're here? Is she okay with this? With us?"

"This was her idea, or at least my coming here was. You'll be seeing her soon enough. She's been extraordinary. She once came into my room at 2 a.m., unable to sleep, because the new matte cream paint on our entryway walls was a half shade off from the eggshell enamel on the wainscoting. She told me, 'I can't live like this.' "

I looked forward to a reunion.

There was a roiling, fractious mob outside the velvet-roped entrance to Studio 54 as Farrell and I stepped from our cab on Eighth Avenue, to avoid the cross-street gridlock. Rabid clubgoers were working every hand flutter, lip moistening, and quadrant of exposed skin, straining to provoke assent from the emotionless, blond-quiffed doorperson as he idly scanned the night sky over their heads, for more appealing extraterrestrial guests. I'd been to 54, as the knowing called it (last month's extinct cognoscenti were still using "Studio"). I'd sometimes been ushered in, but other nights not, without any rationale I could fathom. As I went to ask Farrell if this was his first time at this already legendary nightspot, he'd traveled farther down the block, standing indifferently across the street from the club, as the doorman waved him inside; and Farrell took my hand and we squirmed through the less fortunate, who were muttering "Hey!" and trying to ascertain who or what we knew.

The velvet rope, hooked to stanchions, was crucial to the club's hyper-charged aura. On one hand, the practice was repulsive snobbery, elitism at its nasty worst, but there was a hitch: entrance wasn't based solely on *Vogue*-centric, camera-ready perfection, obvious affluence, or dearly held fame (anything from Grammy winners to tabloid murderers out on bail). The club had pioneered in one respect: originality counted. Youth was an asset. Less conventional sexuality was a plus. The club boasted a more adventurous sizzle, prizing the biggest names, the biggest dicks, and the most out-there drag, all tossed onto the dance floor together.

The space had begun, in the 1920s, as a legitimate theater, and had been empty for years and reinvented as a TV studio in the fifties. Farrell and I passed through the darkened lobby, where the tarnished mirrors reflected only glints of clubgoers' larger diamonds and glitter-dusted bodies already responding to the music. A tunnellike hallway was lit with blue-tinted landing-strip pin lights, embedded along the floor, as revelers were launched into the arena.

"Have you been here before?" I asked Farrell.

"Never. But it's rather good."

We stood where the theater's orchestra seating had been replaced with gray industrial carpeting and neon-lit bars, manned by shirtless hunks, mostly aspiring models or actors, in the most butt-hugging, skimpiest track shorts, many on roller skates, whom Farrell dubbed, "Sex elves. Nice touch."

We sat on a carpeted ledge, a few yards from the dance floor, to observe. The place was crowded, but not overly so (another luxury). We took in a Swedish supermodel's swirling yards of stick-straight platinum hair; a couple's expert undulating, somewhere between choreography and anal sex; Liza Minnelli, swinging her oversize Halston scarf, a cigarette, and a tambourine; a muscle god in a jockstrap and a Native American headdress (in a pre-aware era, such headgear was an accessory). At other clubs, dancers wanted to be enveloped in anonymous, smoky darkness, but not here. Studio 54 was a spectacle, where stars went to be seen, and where the merely fabulous made their bid for stardom.

"Come on," said Farrell, heading for the dance floor and claiming a spot toward the back; we were just getting started. As the lights strobed, and poles rigged with neon and mirrors descended from above, rotating inches from our heads, and cannons shot silvery confetti into the air, and the dancers howled with pleasure, I took a real look at Farrell, as he danced. He was shedding not just his shirt, exposing a wifebeater (as they were known in those insensitive times), but years of regimented family gatherings, coded conversations, and Wichita gamesmanship. I didn't know what was going on in his life, but whatever it was, he had to dance, his eyes shut, his arms in the air, inhaling the music and shouting along with the crowd, sending adoration to the DJ.

As for me, I was suspended between my Broadway angst, which was receding, any who-the-fuck-knows thoughts of the future, and my sheer, devouring gratitude at being with Farrell. He puts his hands on my hips and we moved together, borrowing rhythms from the dancers beside us, letting the disorienting lasers, the visibly throbbing speakers, and the shaking dance floor have their way with us, as we both ignored

Baryshnikov dancing with Bianca Jagger. At Studio 54, celebrities were gilded croutons, emblems of the evening's success, whose presence was snubbed and scrupulously noted, for tomorrow's phone gossip. Photos from inside the club were rare and curated, as part of the global tease.

Farrell took me by the waist and up the stairs to the theater's balcony, to the carpeted platforms strewn with oversize Ultrasuede pillows (Ultrasuede being the only designer-approved synthetic). We reclined; the lighting was a vampiric dusk, and there were scattered couples and threesomes, engaged in sex and drugs, along with the zonked napping caused by both.

"It's comfy up here," said Farrell. "It's like a nursery for junkies."

His hand was unbuttoning my jeans, and he slid onto his knees. I'd never had sex in public before, and while no one was paying attention to us, this was new. As Farrell lowered my underwear (yes, by Calvin Klein, who was dancing downstairs) and took my cock in his mouth, I put my hands in his hair and decided, This is so much better than getting called "uninspired" in the *Post*.

Once Farrell was beside me, and after a kiss (as a thank-you-very-much following his blowjob), he said, "My father died yesterday."

At this altitude, the music was muffled, so I'd heard every word. "He died? How? Of what? Farrell . . ."

"Stop. You're the first person who knows, outside the immediate Manson family."

"Farrell?"

Should I hug him or feign grief or congratulate him?

"He had a massive heart attack two days ago. In a hotel room with his second-string mistress. Of course he didn't want to be taken to a hospital, but the poor woman panicked, and dug a phone number out of my father's wallet, for an executive assistant, who called my mother. Who took the reins. Harwell lingered for a day, but the doctors alerted us that there'd been extensive damage to almost every internal organ, especially because of the delay in treatment, which was my father's own fault."

"Did you . . ."

"Did I get to see him, before he died? Yes. My brothers and I were granted two minutes each, as my mother was parked in a corner, fingering her rosary and doing her crossword. I have no idea what was going through her mind, and she still hasn't said anything. But I was brought in last and I sat by the bed. I had zero expectations, or any microscopic desire, for a bout of last-gasp father-son bonding or a miraculous cure. And you're the only one I'll tell this to, but of course I'd staged this scene a thousand times, although I was usually standing over him with a heavy candlestick and hatching an alibi. But these final countdowns, they're never what you expect. He looked smaller and wizened, with an oxygen tube up his nose. I considered taking his hand, but, I don't know, I couldn't fake even an iota of tenderness, and in some perverse way, I didn't want to insult his meanness. Which was his greatest accomplishment. Does that make any sense?"

It did.

"And he made a harrumphing noise, just a shadow of his usual contemptuous snort. And he said . . . he said, 'I've almost been proud of you.'"

This is why I don't envy the rich. Because while the less wealthy, or even the destitute, can curse their children with words or lovelessness, with rich people the money's always there as well, like an accountant with a green plastic visor, reading ticker tape in a corner.

"So I said to him, 'And I almost love you.' Which made my mother glance up from her puzzle, like a nervous tic. And I got out of there. He died a few hours later. Sally's been helping my mother, to ward off my brothers' wives, who'd cart off the silverware if they thought the coast was clear. But God bless Sally, because the first thing she said to me was 'You should be with Nate. Go.'"

On the dance floor, Rebekah had sailed in with an entourage, including Jess. As Farrell had said, nothing is ever what you expect.

I didn't want to press Farrell for more details, not yet. Tonight's purpose was clear. We were both crossing a rickety rope bridge, high above a gorge, but we'd only ventured a few steps out.

"Come on," Farrell said. "Downtown."

The cab brought us to a barren stretch of King Street, not quite the Village and a hike to SoHo. I knew where we were: a warehouse that, on certain nights, became a club called the Paradise Garage, which was revered with far greater emotion than Studio 54. I suspected that since his marriage, Farrell had been compiling a list of New York City destinations. There was a line outside, but not for culling the herd; this was about weeding out the violent or the bigoted, anyone who'd do harm.

The club's interior was capacious and unadorned, for a friendlier vibe, like a block party or backyard cookout that happened to draw thousands of strangers. Farrell and I toured spaces ordinarily parked with cars and delivery trucks, with one area redesignated and Astroturfed for hanging out and conversation, while another had tables laden with baskets of fresh fruit—bananas, oranges, and mangos—and tin washtubs with ice and bottles of juice. Denizens were high on every conceivable substance, but the snacks were Mom's wholesome staples.

The club's true décor and matchless achievement was the crowd. To this day, I've never been anywhere as naturally diverse, loving, and sexual. There were tribes of teenagers, many rejected by their families, who usually hung out at the piers, and aspiring models fresh from Omaha and Czechoslovakia, and department store makeup artists, and firefighters from the Bronx. Every color, body contour, and gender mélange was represented. I don't know how this happened, but an easy, unforced, glistening utopia had formed, as if everyone's best self had left the message: "Meet me at the Garage, 3 a.m."

Like everyone else, Farrell and I danced even as we jostled to the largest and most open zone, where the crowd became a single, joyously mutating organism, a pulsing mass of waving hands, shaking butts, and the most amazing dancers I'd ever seen, people able to touch the floor with the back of their head, spin like a dervish, and then freeze and leap seven feet into the air, and couples who read each other's body as if it were written in Braille. It was the kind of place where everyone had to gleefully accept that they'd soon be drenched in everyone else's sweat. The music was staggeringly great, the DJ mixing classics with songs no one had heard until that night, because the Garage was where the shrewdest record companies dropped their new 12-inch singles, from their most rapidly ascending artists. The best music was ratified by the fringes, the excluded, who fought bigotry and a plunging economy with the most surefire intuition for hits.

As Farrell and I danced, at the center of this fabulous delirium, Farrell removed his wifebeater. Maybe incited by me, or from refusing to succumb to Midwestern poundage, he'd been working out. His ordinarily etched body had been mouthwateringly honed, and dancing only emphasized every abdominal and tricep and those pelvic ridges called cum gutters. "Jesus Christ," I told him. "Maybe you got married, but your body didn't."

"Now you," he said, reaching for the hem of my T-shirt and yanking it over my head. This was a gay rite of passage, a pectoral bar mitzvah: the first time a guy takes his shirt off at a club. It's separate from a beach or a bedroom, obliging a more elevated confidence. I was a certified gym rat, and I could itemize my body parts in the bathroom mirror, but I hadn't crossed the line to flaunting myself, or acting as if it was foolish to remain clothed in such a tropical environment. There was unaccustomed air on my chest and stomach, as Farrell pulled me against him, our sticky flesh grinding together, from lips to crotch. This was a declaration of gay body consciousness, which could turn problematic (Are my calves too skinny? Do steroids really cause hair loss and shrink your balls? Is it worth it?), and gay body celebration, with a fuck-you vanity, an admittance that yes, I spend two hours a day in a crypt-like basement gym with rusted equipment, and here's why.

As Farrell and I let loose, after years of uncertainty and distance, I saw Ariadne, dancing on a high plywood box, in a corner of the dance floor, a few yards behind Farrell, except she wasn't just dancing, in a black T-shirt and black stovepipe jeans, she was executing an intricate yet spontaneous routine, while twirling and tossing two enormous pieces of silk, fluid square yards, one printed with rainbow stripes and the other a more abstract fireworks tie-dye. I'd seen other people do this at clubs, but I didn't know Ariadne had enlisted, or how she'd gotten so good at it, as if she were a nimble traffic cop coached by Balanchine. When Farrell and

I danced our way over, Ariadne greeted us with a hard-at-work grimace, but minutes later she hunted us down and we opted for a break at a meatpacking district diner.

The place was on an eerily deserted block, otherwise the turf of hookers and drug dealers, with the occupants of slow-moving vehicles rolling down their windows to conduct business. The brightly lit diner was an oasis for late-night felons, garbagemen, subway conductors, and other city employees just getting off their shifts; and the city's floating population of hard-core dancers. We took a booth, with Ariadne carrying canvas pouches housing her meticulously folded flags, which she also called silks or rags.

"When did you start, what exactly is it called—flagging?" asked Farrell, once we'd ordered lemonades and a shared platter of fries.

"I was going out with an older butch," Ariadne explained, "who was really a better friend, but she got me into it. There's a whole underground of Flaggots, who go to clubs and also perform at pride events. I'm on the parade committee so people have been teaching me."

"You're really amazing," I said, which pleased her into dropping her perennial scorn a demi-notch. It occurred to me that flagging for hours at a time was an excellent deployment of Ariadne's amphetamine-fueled energy, and a cardiovascular exercise that was keeping her tightly muscled and whippet-thin.

"Tell me," she asked Farrell, "what the fuck are you doing here?"

Farrell described his father's death, still examining it, as Ariadne listened attentively, because this was a sufficiently serious topic.

"So what are you going to do?" she said. "And is the fatwa lifted? Can you guys see each other?"

Farrell slumped in his chair; his upheaval was so recent. "I don't know," he said. "But I'm counting on it. I haven't really talked to my brothers or my mother, because they've been cloistered with their attorneys. I have a call in to mine, but I haven't heard back yet. I still . . . I'm not sure he's dead. He'd controlled everyone's lives for so long, there may well be some end-of-life protocol that's kicked in, so his head will get freeze-dried like Walt Disney's and be toted around in a bowling bag to board meetings."

"Are you glad he's dead?" asked Ariadne, not unkindly; she was respecting Farrell by not being polite.

"I . . . yes, of course. Which is a Godawful thing to say about anyone, but he was an irredeemable person. Over these past few years he'd schedule regular sessions, as if he was my parole officer, to oversee my marriage. Which he was delighted about, but he wasn't stupid. He once said that if my getting married had been a financial ploy, to undermine the corporation, I'd regret it. And he'd been making noises about grandchildren, not because he'd pat them absentmindedly on the head or even learn their names, but because he was collecting evidence of my allegiance to the cause."

"What about your brothers?" I asked. "Weren't they closer to him?"

"In a way. Meaning, because even though heterosexual men aren't supposed to form attachments to anything except money, beer, and lawnmowers, they pleased my father by marrying the most Caucasian women they could persuade, then they reproduced compulsively and worked for the corporation, mostly by spying on other high-level execs and writing up infractions and any tremors of mutiny or, God forbid, and I really shouldn't say this, because it may cause him to return in a pillar of fire, but the things my father feared and hated the most were . . ."

"Gay people?" I suggested.

"Audits?" added Ariadne.

Farrell dropped his voice to a sub-whisper, so Ariadne and I leaned forward.

"Unions."

"But Farrell," I said, "what if this is an opportunity, to redefine everything? Your dealings with what's left of your family, who may also be feeling liberated? And the scope of the corporation?"

"Nate," he said, "you're basing everything you've just said on *The Wizard of Oz*, and even more on that climactic scene in *The Wiz*, when after Evillene, the wicked witch, dies, and all the factory workers sing 'Brand New Day' and launch into cartwheels."

I was mortally wounded, because he was correct. I'd also been recalling the corporate hoedown finale of *How to Succeed in Business*, where the executives break into a production number as our hero belts "Brotherhood of Man." It's hard for me not to frame all world events through a musical-comedy lens. It's my particular strain of gayness, coursing through my veins and tinting my brain with Technicolor.

"But are you in any way okay?" asked Ariadne. "Or are you just covering?"

"Stop asking," Farrell said sharply, and even Ariadne flinched.

We'd been treating Harwell's death as a boldly declared holiday, but Farrell was hard to read. His life had been irretrievably upended, potentially for the better, and he was reeling. I wasn't sure what shape his adjustment would take, or how I could help him. After gazing out the diner's plate-glass window at an off-duty cop taking a cigarette break with a woman in a fake-fur bomber jacket and a flesh-colored leotard, Farrell stated, "I know what I'd like to do next."

On the street, before Ariadne returned to the Garage, she handed me and Farrell bright yellow capsules, with the advisory, "It's 4 a.m., so if you need to keep going, these will help."

"What are they?" I asked.

"Mostly speed with the tiniest bit of acid and maybe some coke," said Ariadne, as if she were recommending a light dessert wine.

Farrell had kept a bottle of water, so after Ariadne was gone, he downed his pill, commenting, "We don't want to be rude." I hesitated, because as a committed control freak, I rarely did drugs. In New Jersey I'd witnessed vacant-eyed classmates topple over during homeroom or plow their families' Datsuns into telephone poles, so I hadn't been tempted. But tonight was a special occasion. I was still wired, from Farrell's reappearance, the explosive news about Harwell, and my opening night fiasco. The evening's theme was fuck everything, so I borrowed Farrell's bottle and gulped the pill.

"These are probably one-tenth the strength of whatever my mother's on," Farrell remarked.

Farrell guided us to a doorway a few blocks away, on an even grimier stretch of cobblestones without streetlights. There was a line of men, being grunted at by a doorperson, a beefy, unshaven stud, shirtless under his sagging biker's jacket, with his enormous cock outlined by paper-thin denim. His buzz cut was partially obscured by a black leather topman's cap, and he clenched the remains of a cigar in a corner of his mouth. The leather scene in New York was flourishing, but often with what were yawned at as Leather Barbies, marketing analysts and insurance reps who flirted with S&M, accenting their wardrobes with, say, a studded vest or rawhide cuff. I'd met one guy whose arms had been inked from wrist to shoulder with split-tongued demons and tumbling dice, which he shrouded with the long sleeves of a Saks Fifth Avenue dress shirt and a white lab coat for his day job as a Westchester pediatrician.

The guy at the door wasn't a carefully stubbled dilettante or fair-weather sadist. He was a surly Hell's Angel who liked dick, and God knows what else. He was Cerberus, guarding not the gates of hell, but The Hole, the city's most notorious and frequently raided gay sex club. I'd never been, as I suspected there weren't mixed drinks or a jukebox with every version of "Tomorrow" from *Annie*, including Vegas lounge acts and the Norwegian edition.

"Farrell," I asked, as we took our places on the silent line, "are you sure about this?"

"Lose your shirt," Farrell replied, calm but intent. This was where we'd been headed all evening. We hung our shirts from the rear waistbands of our jeans, as the door daddy gave us a bored once-over, searching for an excuse to send such smooth-skinned suburban debutantes home. But Farrell's face and body were impossible to discredit, and his cool demeanor defeated the biker, who shrugged us inside.

The Hole had been shut down more than once, so to stave off further prosecutions it was operating as a bogus private club, and was undoubtedly a front for laundering mob money. To preserve the club's legal status, another beer-swilling thug sat behind a card table in a cramped vestibule, invoking a $10 "membership fee" and coercing everyone into signing a guest book. Most guys had written names like John Smith, Dick Johnson, and Cam Shaft, but Farrell and I logged in as Meryl Streep and Sigourney Weaver, which, Farrell noted, "will be especially effective if the guest book is subpoenaed."

We descended a steep, narrow, brick-walled stair in total darkness, reaching a warren of dank, cement-floored chambers minimally lit by red bulbs. There wasn't music exactly, but a throbbing hum, a muffled electronic metronome. In the first room men, most in heavy leather, shuffled around, as if idling in some purgatorial government agency, or packing a subway platform. A hand cupped my ass, while another rubbed my chest, and a stranger's lips brushed my neck. I caught Farrell's eye as he was being similarly molested, and he indicated another doorway. He took my hand, and we gauntleted past more curious fingers, as I thought, Now I know how a car feels going through a car wash.

The next room was more open, with various pursuits available. A naked man was roped to an X-shaped wooden apparatus, his arms stretched over his head and his legs splayed; his face was covered by a zippered black leather hood, and he was groaning despite the ball gag in his mouth, as another guy knelt and blew him.

Another bottom, in the tattered remnants of his underwear, was trussed up on a set of chains and pulleys, being swung between at least four men who were twisting their willing victim's nipple clamps and inserting the handle of a whip up his ass.

"Sorority hazing," Farrell murmured to me fondly, "remember?"

I was distanced and aroused. These groups were playacting and not inflicting any unwanted pain, but there was an undeniable turn-on, as well-built men lived out shared fantasies, and dared each other to go further. I didn't participate, but Farrell and I lingered, as he ran his hand along my spine, making me shiver. No one was talking, aside from a muttered "Take it, bitch" or "Harder," and I could hear the crowd breathing, like a single snuffling beast. There were three porcelain troughs, like bathtubs, set into the floor, each hosting a naked man lying on his back, one of them handcuffed, the second with multiple piercings, including a graduated row of rings along his cock, and the third trough held someone whose wrists and ankles had been duct-taped, and five men, one wearing only leather chaps, were pissing on him. Despite what reminded me of a leather sleep mask, I recognized the guy getting greedily peed on: he was Florence Gruber's ordinarily perky and helpful assistant, who spelled his name Thom. He was writhing and opening his mouth to receive more urine, as I thought to myself, Well, some people relax by scarfing potato chips on their couch while watching infomercials, and maybe this was less taxing than taking messages for Florence. I wasn't repulsed by the sight of Thom being degraded, but I wasn't attracted either; I try to decode fetishes even if I'd never partake, like playing Pac-Man or touch football.

Having passed by these exhibits, Farrell and I entered a final chamber, which was devoted less to torment and more to hard-core sex. There were mattresses on the floor, where men were fucking, often in groups, while someone else was bent over a metal table, wearing only motorcycle boots and getting fisted, with a can of Crisco at the ready (the label guaranteeing a flakier pie crust). Small vials of poppers, and amyl nitrate–soaked bandanas were being handed around, and the acrid aroma was pervasive. Poppers simulated having a perpetual heart attack, but gave me a headache.

Farrell and I stood before an exceptionally good-looking pair of guys, with one fucking the other from behind. I couldn't discern if they were a longtime couple or hadn't been formally introduced. They might've been soloists from the Joffrey, or models whose granite jawlines promoted manly aftershaves and four-wheel-drive pickup trucks, or a sous chef and a podiatrist. Gay New York practices a physical snobbery, but also a sexual equality. Hot is hot, no matter what borough or bus route it hails from (and of course, construction workers, mail carriers, and plumbers are common porn roles; the dream is a swarthy slab of beefcake who can also fix your air conditioner). The couple at The Hole were getting off, on each other and on being so flagrantly exposed, and Farrell's hand was inside my jeans, fingering my ass, which made me moan. He turned me toward him and my shoulder blades were against the wall and Farrell's tongue was down my throat, and our pants were open.

"No," said Farrell, stepping away, and pushing me toward a leather sling, hanging from chains looped to an industrial hook embedded in the ceiling. Farrell slipped off his shoes and pants and, naked, hoisted himself into the sling, securing his feet in leather straps, his legs spread wide. His eyes glassy but not unaware, he said, "Fuck me."

Whatever drug I'd taken had kicked in, sharpening the atmosphere, as if everything in view, especially Farrell's body, was glowing with an unearthly but hypnotic fluorescence, like film being manipulated during the development process. I shoved my jeans to my ankles and stepped between Farrell's legs, as someone tossed me a communal tube of lubricant. As I fucked Farrell, men gathered around, a few stroking Farrell's body but not interfering; the group was more like a team of enthusiastic observers, or a pit crew, willing the action. Two of these bystanders started making out with each other, and I was shocked and pleased, because what Farrell and I were doing was having a powerful effect, and I tried not to think about the *Daily News* critic remarking, "Ho-hum effort by novice playwright."

I locked eyes with Farrell, his arms raised over his head, clutching the chains of the sling, as he shoved himself onto my cock. He was doing exactly what his father had hated most: he was enjoying himself, in public, with another man. And beyond that, Farrell was energetically disgracing the Covington name, and using our fuck to defy convention, expectations, and that morning when Mr. Covington had forbidden us from being together, and threatened my life. If this recalled a Black Mass, it was also an exorcism, an expunging of guilt and sin. The men around us may have been similarly motivated, to repudiate small-town upbringings, numbing day jobs, and hectoring, shaming voices. I loved this about New York: the salesguy spritzing you with cologne in an aisle at Bloomingdale's might have been trussed up the night before, or dressed as a state trooper with mirrored aviators, mock-arresting a French horn player from the Philharmonic.

The Hole was close enough for Farrell and me to stagger back to my apartment. Farrell had lost his wifebeater, or it had been nicked by a stranger as a souvenir, but his oxford-cloth shirt was knotted around his waist, as if we were loping home from an intramural soccer match on a playing field at Groton or Yale. My T-shirt was looped around my neck, advertising my walk of shame. It was past dawn, and on every corner I saw other men and women, all equally fucked out or danced out or both, blinking into the morning and saluting the city, by lifting a cardboard cup from a Greek coffee shop toward the harsh sunlight.

Farrell and I capsized onto my bed, our limbs flung across each other. As we drifted off, Farrell kissed my cheek and asked, "Will you come with me to my father's funeral? In Wichita?"

Through my fog of drowsiness and confusion and the dwindling residue of Ariadne's yellow capsule I said, "When?"

"Tomorrow."

18

The producers increased their investment in *Enter Hamlet*, to give the play a continued run. I was appreciative and embarrassed, as Farrell scolded, "The show isn't just about you. It's giving everyone jobs and health insurance. And if people read the ads, with the judiciously selected quotes, they'll think the play's a hit. So shut the fuck up."

He was right, but my physical presence was no longer a factor, and a trip to Wichita was vital, for me to support Farrell, get out of town, and conduct a shamefully overdue snoop into Farrell's geographical and family background. I'd be helming an archaeological expedition, delving into Farrell's origins.

We flew out on a Covington Industries corporate jet, which wasn't as glamorously luxe as it sounded. I was counting on staterooms and an open bar with a mini dance floor, but it was a standard jet with rows of grudgingly larger seats. It took off from a smaller airport, at a time of Farrell's choosing. A stouthearted cadre of Covington executives was also onboard, in duplicate dark suits, grasping Farrell's forearm and gruffly repeating, "We're so sorry for your loss."

"Do you know them?" I asked Farrell, once we were in the air.

"Mostly. But they worked for my father, so they're a surveillance squad. Anything I did was summarized and transmitted. I'm never sure if they're tyrannized or junior versions of my father, jousting for scraps."

Another exec, his brow convincingly furrowed, stopped by and murmured, "Sorry for your loss. He was a great man."

As the exec trotted past, Farrell said to me, "He was a very great man, as I mentioned last night WHILE YOU WERE FUCKING ME IN THAT SLING."

Change was definitely on Farrell's agenda. "So what's the schedule?" I asked.

"The funeral's this afternoon, which will be polite, but tomorrow's the family sit-down, with lawyers, which will be a cannibal feast. I'd like you to be there—is that okay?"

"Of course, whatever you need. Have you heard anything else?"

"Not yet. I'm in this fugue state. I could be repressing everything, and I'll sob over the casket, or reach inside and perch him on my knee as a ventriloquist's dummy—'Hi, everybody! I'm Harwell Covington, who wants my money?'"

"Farrell!"

"What?"

"I don't know, I mean, you're in a very weird place, so maybe you shouldn't make any quick decisions."

"We'll see."

He fell asleep on my shoulder. We hadn't gotten much rest, and I was tempted to lean into the aisle and tell the execs, "Long night, watching people getting peed on. We've all been there."

Sally met us at the Wichita airport. I hadn't seen her since that day in Boston, before her wedding, but she was unchanged, with an asterisk: she was visibly richer.

Her simple navy dress was of a weightier shantung, her spectator pumps were kidskin, and her heirloom pearls had put forth a second strand.

"Hello, Broadway playwright," she said, as we embraced.

"Hello, Wichita homemaker," I replied.

"Have you been taking care of our boy?" she asked.

"He has," said Farrell. "What do we know?"

Sally drove us in her navy-blue Mercedes. The costly vehicle suited her; she handled the car like a pro. "Your mother's still in seclusion," she told Farrell, in the front seat beside her. "I went by, but she was praying." Without looking at me she said, "Be quiet."

"I didn't say anything! And Jews pray, too, you know. For better reviews."

"Wainwright was put in charge of choosing the casket, and he and Lindsay made up the guest list. He'll also be speaking. You and Bolt are off the hook, because your mother wants Father Densmore to run things. There may be Latin."

"There may be a demonic possession," said Farrell.

"Bolt drafted the obituary that was sent to the national newspapers, and *Time* and *Newsweek* are doing more extensive stories. *60 Minutes* has reached out for a 'Passing of a Titan' piece. There are hideous jungles of floral tributes, along with handwritten notes from the President and Mrs. Reagan, most members of Congress, across the aisle, and the CEOs of General Motors, Ford, IBM, and dozens more, I can show you. He's being treated as a cross between Thomas Edison, Churchill, and John D. Rockefeller, with a sprinkling of *Citizen Kane*. It's quite something."

Farrell stayed silent. "I'll stall the press about a personal statement, but maybe we should prepare a couple of paragraphs, for a general perspective."

"Absolutely," said Farrell. "How about 'A Loathsome Bastard Slaloms Into Hell'? Or 'America's Third Richest Man Dies by Popular Demand'?"

"Both good," said Sally.

"I'll fiddle with it," said Farrell. "Nate's going to help me."

It hadn't occurred to me, but of course—my currently savaged writing skills might be applicable. I rolled down the window. I'd only traveled through the Midwest as a child, on an educational cross-country road trip with my family. I'd wiled away most of that odyssey flipping through comic books in the back of our Chevy station wagon with my brother, as my mom yelled, "Look out the window! It's America!" I faintly remembered the Grand Canyon; rest stop gift shops that sold miniature license plates from each state; and gnawing the head of a milk chocolate bunny from Wisconsin, the dairy state. I might've passed through Kansas, but so far, everything was flat, with the not-that-tall buildings rising like cutouts from a pop-up book. I was a rabid New York chauvinist, downgrading every other city to a rough draft or an also-ran, a minor metropolis that furiously envied New York. Only later in life did I concede: there are residents who adore Des Moines or Racine, and such locales have their own vital cultural scenes and breathtaking vistas. But today this was Mars, with grazing cattle.

"Sally, before we head to our place and get dressed, I want to show Nate my parents' house," said Farrell.

"We've only got an hour," warned Sally, "but I think your mother's at the hairdresser's."

"I want Nate to have context," said Farrell.

We approached what I at first took for a municipal building, a city hall or central post office. It occupied a full block in an obviously well-to-do suburb. It was more fortress than castle, of a deep-red Victorian brick, with rounded towerlike structures at the corners. It didn't seem to have windows. With perfunctory landscaping, the building existed to loom and intimidate, and to dwarf any homes nearby. There were no porches or awnings, no exterior welcome or grace note.

"Covington Hall," said Farrell, "the century's first maximum security private residence."

Sally activated an iron gate, leading to an underground garage, and we took an elevator, which Farrell said was bulletproofed and under video observation, to the main floor.

The civic, austere, embalmed quality held. There was paneling and columns and mantelpieces, in a judicial dark oak. Any wallcoverings were in deep green or burgundy, with muted patterns, and the high, narrow slits that passed for windows had heavy velvet drapes. It was a house deliberately without sunlight, most likely to preserve monolithic privacy. Mr. Covington hadn't wanted the sun to intrude, or illuminate his nefarious deeds.

"This is where I grew up," said Farrell, "although my brothers and I were restricted to our quarters in the upper regions."

He marched over to a large sofa, like an Oldsmobile covered in a stiff brownish horsehair, without any indentations, as if no one had ever sat down. Farrell did. He bounced a few inches.

"It's strange," he said. "I thought an alarm would go off."

I was given an abbreviated tour, but there was a sameness to the conference room and dining room and library; everything was in place, virtuous and stodgy. It wasn't like Great-Aunt Mirielle's Gothic Revival daydream. This was a house that was lived in, but only in the most purposeful areas. Covington Hall was grand, costly, and depressing, and had most likely smelled like a dead man's house for decades. The property was a monument to Harwell Covington, and now it was his tomb.

"Let's go," said Farrell, "before we start to fossilize."

Sally and Farrell's home, ten blocks away, was the opposite, thanks to the couple's harmonious taste, although Sally had taken the lead, as part of their arrangement. It had hospitable stone porches, nestled among pine trees, Japanese maples, and flower beds cunningly gauged to bloom throughout the year. There were gables, shutters, and a pale blue front door with a fanlight and a stained glass panel of a sailboat beneath a full moon.

The interior was Sally with money: gleaming floors, luscious white woodwork, just the right carpets, and furniture in wicker and blond wood, with cushions in cheerful mattress-ticking stripes and not-too-explosive prints of daisies. There were blue-and-white delft tiles around a central fireplace, and brass lamps with white linen shades.

"It's so lovely," I said. "I almost believe it."

"Almost," said Sally, studying her handiwork. "It's kind of my sketchbook."

Sally and Farrell had separate bedrooms. "Which isn't suspicious," Farrell told me, "because my parents have separate wings. I was surprised they were on the same continent."

Farrell and I got dressed in dutifully dark suits; he wasn't jittery but at odds. I didn't assuage him, because today wasn't a speed bump or sidebar. Farrell's life, and whatever peace he could make with his father, were in the offing.

Sally, in her flawless black sheath and small, veiled velvet hat, all designed and shipped by Jackson, outclassed Farrell and me by miles. She made mourning chic.

The church was a cathedral, less filigreed than St. Patrick's on Fifth Avenue, but close enough. Cathedrals are permanent stage sets, or clerical LSD trips, designed to silence ecumenical doubts and conceal crimes. My family's New Jersey temple, which we rarely attended, was blandly modern, all honey-toned wood and free-form brass lighting fixtures, like an airport lounge in a midsize Swedish city. As always, I related to organized religion only in terms of theatricality; the ethical history of such institutions becomes far too depressing.

Farrell had asked me to sit next to him, down front, with his family, but I'd resisted. I wanted Farrell to pace himself in disruption. There was so much at stake, and my presence shouldn't serve as a detonator, not yet.

As I took my place in a corner of a rear pew, beside some of the execs from the jet, I caught sight of the back of Mrs. Covington's sternly coiffed and veiled head, anchoring a row of other Covingtons, the wives and children blond and compliant.

Sally was beside Farrell, although she rotated her head a quarter of an inch, for my benefit.

There was a colorless hymn, and then the equally colorless Father Densmore spoke of Harwell Covington, "Not merely as a man of great accomplishment, but even more, a man of humble yet distinguished faith." Farrell's head vibrated, as Father Densmore plowed on: "Harwell's worldly success was unparalleled, as was his generosity, to this parish and its members. He was a man of secular achievements, but, if I may be so bold, to everyone here at All Souls, he was our homegrown saint."

Was that steam gushing from Farrell's ears?

Father Densmore praised Mr. Covington's bankrolling a refurbishment of the rectory, where Father Densmore lived, and his underwriting of a food pantry and a reading room for sacred texts, most likely at the insistence of Farrell's devout mother. None of this, I was sure, had entailed any major infusions of cash. But Mr. Covington had broken or bent most of the Ten Commandments, so maybe he'd tacked on a minor investment in salvation, just in case.

Wainwright, Farrell's thirty-four-year-old brother, stood beside the closed coffin and cleared his throat. As I'd glimpsed at the Waldorf, Wainwright was an aging jock, his quarterback physique solidifying into a country club golfer's heft. He barely resembled Farrell, but that was more a function of personality.

"My father was a fine man," he began, something you'd say in a paid eulogy about a stranger. "He was a devoted husband to my mother, Ingrid, and a proud dad to his three boys."

Steady, Farrell, I thought, you can handle this.

"My dad . . . ," Wainwright went on, but he faltered, his voice more genuinely woebegone. "My dad didn't take us to ballgames or play catch in the yard, and he wasn't there at graduations and christenings. He'd inherited a corporation in crisis, and he'd devoted himself, twenty-four hours a day, to consolidation, restructuring, and growth. His success was, and will always be, a great American example. And all my life I wanted to tell him that I loved him, and could be there at his side, serving his vision. He wasn't big on birthday presents, or new bikes, or spur-of-the-moment ice cream. And sometimes . . . well, he could let you know, when you weren't up to snuff. And that was . . . not my favorite time to be around him. But he believed in his country, and its greatness. And he did his best. Not just for me and our family, but for people around the world, who might like a new dishwasher or a mid-price sedan, or just someone to look up to, someone who saw the bigger picture and got the job done. I'm sorry, I think my dad would want me to pipe down and get back to work. And I will, Dad, we all will, first thing Monday morning. And while you won't be there, as long as Covington Industries survives, your spirit will get to the office before any of us."

Wainwright's speech was suitable for a shareholders' statement, but had also been moving. Life couldn't have been easy for any of the Covington sons, and Wainwright had expressed a choking grief, rather than recrimination. I still hated Mr. Covington, but I didn't hate Wainwright, not yet.

I rode to the cemetery with Sally and Farrell, but Farrell wouldn't talk about the service: "The level of hypocrisy, and so many of the hats, I just . . . I can't. Later."

I stood a few, proper yards away from the Covingtons and the other mourners, as Father Densmore said a prayer and the coffin was lowered into a grave beside Mr. Covington's parents and siblings, in the long shadow of a twelve-foot-high granite obelisk bearing the Covington Industries logo, because why waste prime real estate. At least the family hadn't engraved the company's slogans, "The Best to You from Covington" and, as voice-overed in the TV ads while a frustrated housewife eyed the delivery of a neighbor's refrigerator, with a built-in ice maker, "Covet a Covington."

Wainwright put his arm around his mother's shoulders to little effect. Farrell stood with Sally, her hand steadying him. I wondered if the woman Mr. Covington had been with in that hotel room was positioned even farther out than me, or a representative cohort of his mistresses, or if they'd been intimidated or paid off. I'd only attended funerals for distant relatives, so the ceremony was a curiosity; but with the rich, a funeral is always just a beginning.

That night, Farrell sat on the edge of the bed, as I asked, "Is your mother okay? I couldn't tell."

"I never can," he replied. "We'll see what she says tomorrow."

"Was it rough for you, the whole funeral?"

He didn't say anything for a long time. Had my question been dopey or even offensive?

"I'm not sure what I was waiting for," Farrell finally said. "He couldn't be someone else, and I mean, sure, he was a product of his time and the Covington horror, which would be a fabulous name for a drive-in movie fright flick. And I could rummage through his psyche and ask his girlfriends if he'd ever been warm, or lighthearted. I can hold him at arm's length, as a case study. But mostly I stared at the coffin thinking, You son of a bitch. And swearing I'd never be anything like him."

I still hadn't told Farrell about his portrait, and what had become of it. Did he need to know, and hate his father even more? I decided to at least delay the information. As I watched Farrell's profile, even in distress, I saw the portrait come to life, restored, which was enough for now.

I put my arms around Farrell, something which even his mistresses would never have done with Harwell.

"We could steal a pair of your father's wing tips," I suggested, "and burn them."

"Not unless he was wearing them."

The family summit was held at 11 a.m. the next day, in the main conference room at Covington Hall. Ingrid and her sons were seated around a large mahogany table.

Farrell and I sat together, at his request. Franklin Marsters, the corporation's lead attorney, stood at one end of the table, white-haired and diligent in a three-piece gray suit, with rimless eyeglasses welded to his face. There were yellow legal pads on the table before each family member, along with fountain pens and crystal carafes of water; lemon wedges would have been a disdained frippery. Backup lawyers sat along the walls, their attaché cases open on their laps. Maybe these lawyers would be called up, to replace a first-string lawyer injured during the scrimmage. Sally and the other wives were stationed a few doors down, at a breakfast buffet.

It felt like a merger was looming, or the annexation of a conquered foreign territory. Farrell squeezed my knee under the table. I was the valet in a frock coat who hands Lord Whomever his dueling pistol.

"Let's begin," said Franklin, hefting a four-inch-thick bound document. "First I'll reiterate my profound sorrow at the passing of a wonderful man, whom I had the pleasure of working with for over forty years."

Profound? Wonderful? Pleasure?

"Harwell Covington's Last Will and Testament was created ten years ago, and its contents are familiar to Mr. Covington's family members and their representatives. In that draft, Mr. Covington's estate was to be distributed to his beloved wife, Ingrid, in the amount of 50 percent of all assets, with the remaining 50 percent to be divided equally among his sons, with the stipulation they remain in the employ of Covington Industries, with graduated annual payments over a fifty-year period, with possible extensions."

He didn't list any charitable bequests or gifts to Harwell's staff, or his mistresses.

"But six months ago, Mr. Covington amended the original document with a significant and witnessed codicil, which I will read."

Farrell's posture shifted. Had he been briefed on this codicil?

"'The distribution of assets shall remain intact,'" Franklin read, in a sonorous voice tinged with the smugness of someone who knew what was coming, "'except with respect to my son Farrell Covington.'"

Wainwright and Bolt sat up straight, like ass-kissing front-row schoolboys, as Mrs. Covington contemplated Farrell, with an unblinking repose. Her face was a pale echo of his, lightly powdered and emotionless, the green eyes more gray. Her hair wasn't any particular shade but had been back-combed and sprayed into a disciplined helmet, like an icy cliff in the Antarctic. Very Margaret Thatcher's disappointed second cousin.

"'As Farrell knows,'" Franklin continued reading, "'he'd been prohibited from making even the most infinitesimal contact with Nathaniel Reminger, for well-considered reasons. Yet he did exactly that, at the Boston apartment of Sally Mayhew, who would become Farrell's wife. I took no action at the time, with little desire to condemn Farrell out of hand. I subsequently learned of numerous additional bids to communicate with Reminger.'"

What was he talking about? A disconnected phone call, late at night? Intercepted mail? The Waldorf, where Farrell and I hadn't really spoken?

Franklin went on: "'Farrell must not and will not dishonor his family and endanger our corporate reputation. From this causation, I wholly and in every respect disinherit him, and suspend him, for all future time, from any role in Covington Industries. I do this from agonizing sadness and severe disappointment, and after extended and informed deliberation with Farrell's mother.'"

That ice-blooded fuckhead. Lobbing grenades from beyond the grave. No, not grenades—nuclear warheads.

"Farrell," said Mrs. Covington. I'd never heard her speak. Her voice was birdlike yet punitive, a belligerent sparrow. "This wasn't a decision made in haste."

Which made it worse.

"While you were at Yale, your father told me, against his better judgment, about . . . your proclivities, and I questioned everything. Were your defects my doing? Had I neglected you in some critical way, or failed to stress more acceptable practices?"

She wasn't only high-minded, but stricken. Rebekah would make a tasty meal of this role. But even Rebekah, at her tousle-tossing hammiest, wouldn't have dared Ingrid's delicate hand, reaching despairingly toward her pestilent offspring.

"But ultimately, and after long consultation with Father Densmore, I concluded: I had no part in this. No blame. But I could implore your father, to step in."

I'll bet she did. Harwell had cited Ingrid's influence, but she'd been the mastermind, the weaponized plutonium behind the tyrant's New Haven fusillade.

"I recommended that, for your own good, we cut you off, financially and otherwise. But your father was convinced that you'd respond, to not only an ultimatum, but to articulate guidance, to clarity. And your marriage gave us such hope, that you'd turned a corner, and were well on your way to rejoining our family. And that someday, you might know Jesus Christ with an unshakeable faith."

I wished Jesus were there, to insist, "This wasn't my idea."

"But when your father produced irrefutable evidence, that your marriage was not just a sham, but a vicious mockery of all we hold dear, you left us no choice. You broke our hearts."

She was the sobbing martyr, the Mom Who Tried Her Best and Then Some. The Christian on a Mission. Our Lady of the Tearstained Codicil.

"I pray that, at some juncture in the near future, you'll disgust even yourself, and seek whatever professional help, or spiritual counsel, is available. But you must come to that on your own. And this family can't subsidize your sickness."

Farrell's breathing was even. Why wasn't he vaulting across the table, or setting the house on fire?

"I'm not asking for your sympathy, Farrell. We're past that. And I've reconciled myself to reality. I have two fine sons, and one unfortunate and blasphemous error."

Everyone in the room, even the majority who were siding with Ingrid, gasped at the extent of her cruelty, but made no objection. Father Densmore was rueful and saddened yet saw no other way, an attitude he'd rehearsed in the mirror, right down to the drooping eyebrows, the wagging chin, and the kindly half smile.

There was a vibrating stillness. Today was a high-noon gunfight, or a well-mapped ambush. Ingrid had swaggered into the corral, pistols blazing, with high-priced lawyers, God, and self-righteous superiority in tow. She was ostensibly a grieving widow, but she'd been polishing this script for years.

"Was this codicil common knowledge?" Farrell asked, without raising his voice. "Bolt? Wain?"

Wainwright sputtered, but didn't deny anything. Bolt, who was thirty-nine, leaned back in his chair, marking his legal pad with a pen, not doodling but making one slash after another, as if crossing items off a list.

"Dad took me into his confidence," said Bolt. "And Farrell, I bet that right this second, you hate him. But you've brought this on yourself. Dad tried so hard to help you, he had his staff confidentially research doctors and drugs, he put himself on the line. And you laughed at him, at our family. You've acted so damn full of yourself, as if we're dimwitted Wichita yokels and you're some fancy-ass homo dancing around New York City. With your little . . . I don't even know what to call him, with this silly faggot you've dared to bring here, as if he has any place at this table. You rub our noses in it, in your filth and your lack of respect, for every opportunity Dad gave you. And we're all still being way too polite, so Farrell, I'll make this clear. Here's what Dad, and this codicil, and everyone in this room is saying to you, and to your repulsive little buddy: fuck you."

"Bolt!" said Ingrid, not alarmed by what he'd said, but at his profanity.

"Sorry, Mom," said Bolt. "But someone had to say it."

Bolt called his parents Mom and Dad, as if the Covingtons were a jolly American clan, with Pop in a "Kiss the Cook" chef's toque at the patio grill, passing paper plates of burgers and hot dogs to his strapping lads and "better half" wife, bearing a platter of soft drinks in Dixie cups.

"Farrell?" asked Franklin. "Is this document clear? Are there any questions?"

"None," said Farrell, strangely unflustered. "But my attorney, Devin Llewellyn, has some remarks."

A younger man, seated along the wall, stood up. He was well over six feet tall, with tortoiseshell glasses, a gray suit patterned in an extravagant, for this crowd, windowpane check, and tasseled shoes. He was also the only Black person in the room, and most likely the neighborhood and the county. His legal pad was covered with notes, and he stepped forward.

"My client, Farrell Covington," said Devin, "has in his possession the following materials: video and audio recordings along with signed affidavits from fourteen women, the youngest, at the time of the events in question, sixteen years of age, willing to testify under oath about sexual relationships, some lasting years, with Harwell Covington. We also have authenticated copies of personal and corporate bank statements, of monies paid to many of these women, to purchase their silence. Harwell Covington coerced two of these women into terminating pregnancies, and paid for the procedures. Jean?"

His associate, an Asian woman in her twenties, activated a projector, sending images onto a previously unused screen on the wall beside Franklin. There were grainy but eminently recognizable shots of Harwell entering hotels and restaurants with one woman after another, some of them far younger than his sons.

"In addition," Devin continued, "we have sworn statements from an Edward 'Eddie' Corso and a Ted Warbowski, both currently serving life sentences, on other charges, in federal penitentiaries, attesting to Harwell Covington hiring them to menace Covington Industry employees, and in three instances, to murder these employees or their family members."

There were mug shots of these criminals on the screen, both believably homicidal. "Neither Mr. Corso nor Mr. Warbowski harbor any expectation of reducing their prison terms or securing improved circumstances. Both have said they will testify, again under oath, simply in order to 'get that Covington bastard.'"

A shot of Harwell having a backroom dinner with Corso and Warbowski, not people he'd normally socialize with.

"We have also been given access to findings from federal investigations, with proposed charges of tax fraud, theft of intellectual property, and copyright violations by Harwell Covington, along with the existence of questionable offshore accounts opened in the name of Ingrid Covington, which Mrs. Covington may not be cognizant of. Or perhaps she is. A fact which could be determined under cross-examination before a grand jury."

Shots of a series of forms, with Ingrid's signature.

"All of these materials have been kept secure, along with multiple duplicates. The originals have been repeatedly examined by teams of forensic experts, and judged credible. Because while Harwell Covington is deceased, Covington Industries, and his wife and adult children, are liable for his misdeeds and could suffer enormous financial consequences, if these files were to be made public. The reputation and companies of Covington Industries would also be subject to extensive and quite likely irreparable damage."

Ingrid's lips had been thin and parched, but within the past minutes they'd disappeared entirely. She was otherwise implacable.

"On behalf of Farrell Covington, I've been authorized to propose the following: if Farrell is returned to his position on the board of Covington Industries, with full voting rights, and if his inheritance is not only restored but made equal to that of his brothers, combined, he might be inclined to keep the aforementioned materials in private hands. If not, said materials will be released in full, to the *New York Times*, the *Chicago Tribune*, the *Los Angeles Times*, the *Wall Street Journal*, and all broadcast networks."

"You wouldn't!" Bolt shouted. "And no one will believe any of it! Not coming from some little fairy!"

"Some little Covington," Devin corrected, "with direct knowledge of his father's crimes. And if you'd prefer to have your own experts evaluate these documents, photographs, and recordings, they'll be made readily available. To you and to prosecutors in Washington."

Bolt shut up.

"On a separate front," said Devin, "and at Farrell's direction, I've compiled an inventory of Covington-owned properties that will be consigned to his name, including homes on Park Avenue in Manhattan, the Champs-Élysées in Paris, and Eaton Square in London. Farrell will no longer be employed by Covington Industries, and his inheritance will be transferred immediately and in full, rather than allotted piecemeal over time. All further expenditures and investments by Covington Industries will come under Farrell's review and be subject to his approval or veto. Mr. Marsters, are there any questions?"

Franklin, now ashen, had been studying a concise summary of everything Devin had touched on, copies of which Jean had distributed to everyone in the room, even me. I couldn't wait to show mine to Ariadne, Jess, and Jackson. Ingrid was staring at her copy, most likely assuring herself of a conspiracy between her gay son, his Jewish lover, and his Black and Asian lawyers. This lineup was undoubtedly what filled her mind whenever she heard the words "New York City."

"I . . . I'm sure that there will be many questions," Franklin said, "once our legal team has been able to comb through these obviously preposterous and radically unfounded charges and demands. Young man," he said to Farrell, "you're not getting away with this."

"May I comment?" Farrell asked Devin, who assented.

"Everyone," Farrell said, standing and placing his hands on the table, "Devin's the best there is, and everything he's said has been assiduously researched and is 100 percent accurate. And more than likely, no surprise to anyone in this room. Mother, I do hope these chronicles won't affect your weekly bridge game, or cause you to develop a facial expression or an inner life. Bolt and Wainwright, we've done you a service, in cataloguing Father's transgressions, as a model for your own, a kind of degenerate to-do list for sticking on the fridge beside your children's crayon drawings and your subpoenas. And dear Father Densmore, I apologize for not slipping these documents to you sooner, to punch up your eulogy, which lacked a certain—how to put it—colorful authenticity. Those telling, that's-our-Harwell details that really bring a tribute to vivid life. And Mr. Marsters, might I suggest, as to your no doubt massive response: save your breath, your blood pressure capsules, and the overtime of your staff. Because we're not messing around."

Farrell leaned down and kissed me, and told the room, "Harwell Covington. Husband. Father. Capitalist. Adulterer. Murderer. Bigot. Proud American. Honorable Christian. Rest in fucking peace, you malignant reptile."

Later that night, at a local steakhouse, after Farrell and I had recounted the morning's meeting to Sally, for the third time, I said, "It was incredible. So Hercule Poirot. But Farrell, when did you start coming up with this?"

"After Sally and I got married, because my father kept being paranoid. And Devin's firm had sued Covington Industries on a pollution case, where factory runoff had caused a cancer spike in a small town in Michigan. Devin had fought for years, but Harwell had settled out of court, for nowhere near enough money, and the complaint was sealed. Which meant Devin had a score to settle. We used my father's playbook against him. The best private investigators. Discreet lawsuits to reopen closed criminal cases. Devin chased down disgruntled ex-employees, a lot of them outside the country, and got them to go on the record. We took our time and verified and re-verified. I didn't think my father was going to die, but a confrontation was inevitable, so I had to be ready."

"But, Sally," I asked, "did you have any idea? What Farrell was up to?"

"I had an inkling," she said, taking a sip of champagne, "but not about everything. It was better if I didn't, so I could be cordial around the Covingtons."

"Sally was busy," said Farrell, "scoping out every local charity and cultural institution, and figuring out how and where we could do the most good."

"I didn't want to give Farrell's money to some vaguely titled Genteel Assistance organization that would spend everything on salaries. We've been working directly with homeless shelters and hospitals and schools in low-income areas. And Farrell convinced his father that the Covington Fund for the Arts was a superb tax write-off."

"So, Farrell," I said, "have you heard anything back, from Devin? Or Franklin Marsters?"

After we'd left the meeting, Farrell had lobbied for fresh air, exercise, and chocolate. We'd gone for a run and dropped by an overly cute restored ice cream parlor in our sweats. I kept marveling and congratulating Farrell on his coup, but he wouldn't go near any of it, until he'd received an official response to his proposal.

"Yes," said Farrell, at the steakhouse, trying not to cheer or tip over the table. "Devin says that Marsters denied everything, and blathered about how they could sue me for slander and have me tied up in court for decades, and even get me thrown in jail, but that for the sake of expediency, and to respect Ingrid's feelings at this difficult time . . ."

The three of us mouthed the words "Oh my fucking God . . ."

"The remaining Covingtons are consenting to my terms, with exceptions. I'm on the board and I'm getting the money, but all documents will be confidential, and I can still be out-voted on corporate financial outlays. So I'll be back in Wichita at least twice a year to tussle with my adorable brothers and the crumbling Roman aqueduct that gave birth to us. Which I can deal with. And we'll begin compensating the families of the people Harwell had killed, even if it's tough to connect all the dots and get him declared criminally responsible. But otherwise . . ."

He lifted the white tablecloth and knocked on the restaurant's oak table three times.

"It's done."

After years, Farrell had prevailed. It was tricky to position him as an underdog, but he'd been battling a corporate Goliath, a bastion of billion-dollar arrogance. And the gay guy, whom the Covingtons had ostracized and demeaned, the descendant of Great-Aunt Mirielle, had won.

"So Farrell," I said, "you're free."

"No, better," he replied. "I'm rich."

As Sally and I pelted him with dinner rolls, he went on. "I haven't even begun to think about what this means, because I don't want to jinx it. But I do have a very important question. Sally, you've been astonishing. You came to Wichita with your eyes open, and minimal jewelry. And of course, the money belongs to both of us. Unless I decide to go full Covington and have you eliminated. But Sally, or as I like to think of you, our own Mrs. Covington, what do you want to do? About any of this? All of this? Name it."

It was like we'd pulled a bank job, or looted Tiffany's, and had dumped the cash and the estate jewelry onto a motel bed and were rolling around in it, awaiting police sirens.

"I've been thinking," Sally said, "and I've made some plans. And both of you are going to laugh at me, just howl like idiots, so by all means, get it out of your systems."

Farrell and I obligingly emitted hyena-like yelps.

"Are you done?" asked Sally. "Because here goes. I've had an interesting spell, as a Wichita Lady Bountiful. I've made the rounds, and we've opened a Covington women's health center, and sent a few graduating classes of underprivileged kids to college. But it's not enough. And Farrell, you and I should get divorced, although I'm in no rush."

"And I like having such a responsible wife," said Farrell, "which may also become useful for contractual reasons, in case I'm incapacitated or unable to choose just the right cashmere turtleneck for a court appearance."

"And I imagine," said Sally, "that you and Nate will want to be together, somewhere far from here. And I've been a touch underemployed. Vestigial. Half-hearted. So I've signed up for at least a year in Calcutta. Where I'll be volunteering with Mother Teresa at her orphanage and hospice."

Farrell and I were dumbstruck. With anyone else, this would have come off as a punchline, or a do-goody whim, to be swiftly abandoned by morning. But for Sally, it rang true.

"But Sally," said Farrell, "are you aware that, in Calcutta, almost none of the better boutiques stock lemon verbena hand cream?"

"Which I'll stockpile," said Sally. "But it's past time I tested myself, and everything I tell myself I believe in. I'll be dealing with disease and primitive sanitation and the poorest of the poor, but there's something to keep in mind: I've never seen anything half as elegant as the saris worn by Mother Teresa and the nuns in her order. Pure white, with a cobalt stripe at the hem. As Jackson told me, those saris are positively Grecian. And once I'm wearing one, I'll be ready for anything. With an extra-dry martini afterwards."

"When do you leave?" asked Farrell.

"Two days from now," Sally said. "I went through the application process and I've had my immunizations and I've got a bed in a sort of dormitory, at least to start. I'm scared out of my skin but I can't wait."

"Sally," I said, "you're going to be great, and we expect constant updates, from Mother Sally. And we should tell Father Densmore about this, because he's been doing such fine work among the wretched zillionaires of Kansas."

"I'll keep that in mind," said Sally, as Farrell lifted his glass of champagne for a toast.

"To Sally," he said. "Calcutta's gain."

A little after 1 a.m., I woke to find Farrell gone, and I fretted that his family had kidnapped him, or he'd left on a pilgrimage like Sally's, and that either way, I'd been abandoned. But there was a window and I saw him alone in the backyard, in the moonlight.

I padded downstairs barefoot and we sat on a garden bench. The backyard was ample and inviting, but not overly manicured, just grass and trees and a small pond, rippling with the moon's reflection.

"For so long, for so much of my life," said Farrell, "I've been letting my father dictate the rules and the prizes and how the game is played. But I've trounced him. At least for today. Answered prayers."

"You don't have to pick a next step right now. You can savor this. Or at least, I don't know, be satisfied."

"And I am. But let me ask you about something. Because I'm in freefall."

"I'm right here."

"For the first time since college," said Farrell, "we can be together."

Our hands found each other. For that instant of Kansas moonlight, we were tentatively optimistic and, I wouldn't call it afraid, but—we were almost adults, a state colored by a sense of how fragile and temporary any victory can be. I remembered what Farrell had said about getting slapped and being better. And my family had a tradition of obsessive-compulsive superstition. When something decent happened, a windfall or my play being optioned, my mom would say "*kina hora*" and mime spitting on the ground, by repeating "poo poo poo," to confuse the evil eye, the tribulation that lurks behind any Jewish accomplishment.

"*Kina hora*, Farrell," I told him. "Poo poo poo."

"Or as we say in Wichita, my darling—here we fucking go."

HOLLYWOOD

19

Two days later we brought Sally to the airport, with her ivory canvas luggage and wearing a straw hat with a pale blue ribbon and a sprig of tiny blue silk periwinkles.

"You already look destitute," Farrell told her, and she waved from the gate, like Eloise off on the first commercial flight to Jupiter.

Farrell and I took the Covington jet back to New York. The executives on board had heard rumors regarding their leadership, but were apprehensive about asking direct questions.

As we were about to disembark, Farrell told his former coworkers, "You're all gay now."

Farrell slept at my place, but spent his days uptown, at his freshly inherited Park Avenue address, the full top floor of a distinguished building where the co-op board had rejected pop stars and mere millionaires for being trashy and cash-poor.

Harwell had purchased the five-bedroom apartment decades before, but only for brief business trips, as he'd hated New York City, because of course he did. New York was the sworn enemy of Harwell Covington, because it can't be subdued or reprimanded or told what to do, not for long. And even on the Upper East Side, Harwell might encounter undesirables, like his son.

"But I don't mind the neighborhood," Farrell told me, "because it's convenient to the Metropolitan Museum and Central Park, and the building has storage rooms on a lower floor, for bassinets and out-of-season clothing and gold bars, in case there's a recession. I don't think it's my ultimate New York apartment, but I'm going to see what I can do with it. It's my Calcutta."

Collecting and restoring homes had been one of Farrell's goals, the way other people amass baseball cards or ceramic thimbles painted with every state bird. This urge wasn't my own, but I trusted Farrell's acumen. When he showed me around the place a week later, demolition was underway. The square footage was immense, with an entrance gallery running the length of the apartment, connecting to rooms painted a dusty Wedgwood blue or sage green, the literal shade of old money. The apartment looked like what it was: an impersonal way station or a glorified five-star hotel suite from a faded era.

"I'm gutting it," said Farrell, clutching a cardboard tube of rolled-up blueprints and coughing from the dust as a construction crew sledge-hammered walls and dragged bathroom fixtures to a freight elevator. "But I can't stay here while the work's being done, and if I keep bunking with you, in that firetrap, we'll become a headline in the *Post*: Gay Couple Found Dead After Feud Over Folding Chair. So should I rent some interim place? Maybe Chelsea, where so many homosexuals seem to be gravitating? Because there are five gyms, three leather bars, and a halfway decent florist?"

"But first," I said, "there's something that's long overdue. I've met your parents, so you're going to meet mine."

Farrell was entranced. This was a milestone we'd overlooked while events had intervened. I'd been awkward about bringing Farrell to New Jersey: Was it safer for my hometown to hover as an exotic anecdote, a Narnia with piles of burning truck tires, and what if my mother and father didn't get Farrell, or they clicked like wildfire and knocked me out of the loop? But after experiencing Wichita, I'd risk it.

The next day, my dad picked us up at the train station in New Brunswick, in our Chevy, which Farrell treated as a golden chariot. "I love your car," he told my dad, "but why does that light on the dash-board keep blinking?"

"It's been like that for years," said my dad, "no one knows what it's for. But Farrell, it's so great to finally meet you. After all these years."

I hadn't told my parents everything, just that Farrell had a troubled family history but he'd landed on his feet. They were so excited about getting to know, as my mom exuberantly called him, "your wonderful gay boyfriend," that they hadn't asked for a three-volume biography. Yet.

"It's charming," said Farrell, as we pulled into the driveway of our suburban tract home. I wasn't ashamed of it, but it matched the homes on either side. Drunken commuters had been known to lurch into the wrong house.

"Farrell! Get over here!" said my mom, loitering outside the open front door, because she couldn't wait.

"Mrs. Reminger!" said Farrell, as my mom admonished him, "It's He-lene!"

I didn't see Farrell for the next hour, because my mom, after walking him through the house, asked his opinion on her new set of dishes from a Vermont pottery ("They're perfect! Durable yet evocative!") and then sequestered the two of them in our TV room. Later, when I asked Far-rell what she'd been after, he said, "Anything I would tell her. She's says you're so secretive. You'd never told her I was a nationally ranked square dancer."

I was about to push for an unvarnished account of my mom's cross-examination, except, blessed by a rare jolt of common sense, I didn't. That night, over dinner, my mom said to Farrell, "Nate told us not to bring this up, so I'll just say that we're sorry about your dad's passing."

I'd terrorized them about Harwell's death being off-limits, and I was about to make a button-your-lip gesture, as a prelude to a hanging-myself-with-a-rope gesture.

"Even if your dad was . . . ," my mom kept going, and then to my dad, "Pete, what was the word Nate used?"

"A maggot-brained pterodactyl regurgitated from the bowels of the underworld?" Farrell suggested.

"That's it!" said my dad, which settled matters. As hall-of-fame Jewish liberals, with a shelf of Woody Guthrie folk albums, along with PBS mugs, tote bags, and refrigerator magnets, my parents had never warmed to Harwell's isolationist, Klan-friendly Republicanism.

"Farrell," said my mom, "you've been out there in Kansas for so long. Are you back for good?"

"I hope so," said Farrell, as my mom concluded, "If you boys move in together, I can give you my old dishes."

"We were concerned," said my dad, "that Nate was going to end up an old maid."

"It happens," said Farrell, as I kicked him under the table.

"We want to see your place in New York," said my mom, as Farrell and I stacked our Saran- and foil-wrapped leftovers, plus the sealed Tupperware bowl of oatmeal raisin cookies, which, my dad had said, "are your colon's best friend."

"You must come by, the minute it's viewable," said Farrell, "and you'll stay over, as my guests."

My mom was so pleased by this she dug her fingers into my dad's forearm, making sure he was pleased as well.

"I can't tell you how much I've loved finally meeting both of you," Farrell said, during the extended hugs and aggressive bestowal of an Entenmann's coffee cake "for tomorrow."

"We approve," my dad told me, pointing at Farrell. "He's great."

"There was a time," said my mom, "when we thought you'd broken Nate's heart. But we're so glad everything's worked out."

"So are we," said Farrell, kissing my cheek, causing the Reminger family, myself included, to kvell helplessly.

"You have nothing to complain about," Farrell told me, on the train home, "your family is nirvana."

"And I know the house is small," I said, "but my mom has some nice things."

"And the way you put that proves the most fundamental fact of the cosmos."

"What?"

"That you are your mom."

After slapping him, I leaned against Farrell's shoulder, as it had been a long day. But I'd advanced another square in my board game of maturity. My boyfriend had met my family. We were officially announced, like a royal couple facing the cameras at a press event.

"But my contractor's extended the renovation another month, just for the kitchen," said Farrell. "So I'm meeting with a broker tomorrow, to see what's out there."

"Or," I said, because I had news, "you can come with me to LA."

Months earlier, before *Enter Hamlet* had opened, Florence had sent me on exploratory meetings with movie producers, because, as she'd groused, "You haf to make money. Your income must double each year or at least exist. Or I vill send you to television."

Harry Nailsback had a proven track record with mid-range features, meaning prominent roles for women, no superheroes, and a ceiling on profits. At his office in Midtown I was interviewed by a recently hired junior executive named Brett Starber. Brett was younger than me. After an impatient Long Island childhood he'd skipped college to burrow deep into show business, working as a casting assistant and a gopher in a Broadway publicist's office. At eight years old he'd sent Mike Nichols a letter critiquing Nichols's work on a Neil Simon play and angling for an internship (Nichols had asked Brett to hold off until he could cross the street by himself).

Brett was tall, with a rabbinical beard and spectacles, and while he was overweight, his height and manic intensity telegraphed brute strength and unstoppable self-reliance. Even then he was the most inquisitive and driven human being I'd ever met, unstintingly ravenous to absorb information, X-ray every play or movie for structural secrets, and connive to meet and manipulate whatever talent had blipped on his all-consuming radar.

"I'm Brett," he'd said, almost shaking my hand but already on the move, "can I get you anything? Water? Soda?" He didn't linger for a response, so I ran after him into an editing room. "Look at this," he said, pulling up monitor footage from a film-in-progress. "It's so hot."

The fragment of a scene was from a torrid, ill-omened teen romance between a ballerina and a motorcycle-riding Golden Gloves boxer from Queens. They'd broken into a community center after hours and stripped off for a swim and sex. Brett had been accurate: the nudity went farther than expected, meaning pubic hair but not full-frontal. The actress was blank and blond, but the guy had promise, with a hard-bodied, credibly blue-collar smolder.

"Right here," said Brett, "you can almost see his dick."

We'd bonded, as only two gay, Jewish New York show business addicts can, over *goyishe* flesh. While graphic porn was available, movie star skin was more taboo and elusive.

Brett hired me to write treatments for ideas we'd brainstorm. These treatments were at most three pages, devoted to a brisk storyline and descriptions of characters composed entirely in terms of the stars who might play them ("Nick's a Stallone-style lug, with a two-fisted heart of gold"). Treatments would also link everything to previous hits ("It's *Star Wars* meets *Saturday Night Fever*, for a dance contest that can halt a meteor shower blasting right for Australia"). Brett and I were educating ourselves, but he outpaced me in every respect, tutoring me on story beats, comic set pieces, sequel potential, and the dictum that "a star will only sign on if a script has at least three separate scenes that prove he's a star." He wasn't after crap, but he was voraciously restless to make things happen. Every second without a blockbuster, or at least a project on the boil, was a lifetime wasted.

Farrell and I had dinner with Brett, and afterward Farrell said, "Brett's either going to rule the world or kill everyone on the planet and then ask, 'What? They were so slow.'"

I'd spitballed an idea for a rowdy comedy set in Atlantic City and a New Jersey convent, in which a nun, at a charity casino night, is revealed to have unholy gambling prowess, and via a gangster's manipulation, she swaps places for a week with his showgirl honey, an uncanny lookalike. It was "The Princess and the Pimp," or as I titled it, *Habit Forming*.

The script had been sparked by Farrell's family and their unswerving allegiance to the Catholic Church. I'd craft a commercial comedy in which sequins, spike heels, and blackjack would complicate our nun's piety. Of course, my treatment didn't stress this subversion, only the what-would-Jesus-do high jinks of a nun's potential romance with a Travolta-style mob hit man. Brett loved the idea, set up a phone pitch, and within days *Habit Forming* had been optioned by Clarion Studios, a major player. I'd submitted a few preliminary drafts, and Clarion wanted to fly me out for at least a month, for meetings and further revisions.

Farrell was game, because neither of us had spent any meaningful time in California. At first, as we took the freeway from the LA airport, I was crushed. With its car culture, strip malls, and lack of street life, the sprawling arbitrariness reminded me of suburban New Jersey. "It's Piscataway with sunshine," I told Farrell, who was behind the wheel of the convertible we'd rented.

"Just wait," he counseled, "the whole point of California is knowing where to look."

After an hour, we glided into the circular drive of the house Farrell had sublet, on the beach in Santa Monica. It was a well-maintained relic of 1930s golden age divinity, a French Normandy cottage with a de rigueur tennis court and swimming pool, glass doors opening onto a terrace, and across the sand, the Pacific Ocean. I was entering Farrell's latest dream, hesitantly sampling the enticing unreality.

"Do you know where we are?" he asked. I didn't, so he unreeled background data: "This is where they lived, for almost ten years. Cary Grant and Randolph Scott. When I was talking to brokers, I was amazed it was still here."

From his carry-on he reverently removed a copy of a movie magazine from 1932, preserved in a plastic sleeve. There was a photo spread, of the two handsomest men who've ever lived, cavorting in the gayest way imaginable, in what had once been the home of silent movie queen Norma Talmadge and, later, Howard Hughes. There were pictures of Cary and Randolph in the briefest, most clinging white satin swim trunks, working out together with barbells, swimming side by side like carefree dolphins, breakfasting in matching terry-cloth robes, and wiling away an evening at home reading, with Cary lolling on a couch and Randolph in a close-at-hand armchair. Their mutual pleasure couldn't be more obvious, and good Lord, they were in great shape (Cary had begun as an acrobat, while Randolph had played every high school sport).

"But how did they get away with this?" I asked, sitting beside Farrell on Cary's couch.

"It was called hiding in plain sight," Farrell said. "Back then, there was an unspoken agreement with the press, never to ask about gay stuff, and this place was called Bachelor Hall. They were 'roommates,' even though both of them were already playing leads and making plenty of money. They'd occasionally go on studio-arranged dates with starlets, and years later both of them got married, repeatedly, but look at these pictures. I mean, swoon. Beyond swoon. Swoonsturbation."

The house was haunted by the spirit of gay movie idol bliss. "But can we afford this?" I asked.

"I can," said Farrell, "especially now. And if you want to kick in your per diem, that's fine, but you don't have to."

I was torn. My housing allowance, from the studio, was meager, while Farrell had made a sizeable dent in the Covington Industries bank balance. My living off Farrell's largesse was—unethical? immoral? lucky?

"Stop being you," Farrell advised. "It's only for a month. And Cary and Randolph want us to be here. It's a gay safe house."

I gave in, without even a token struggle. The gay karma was too potent. That night, as we made love in the master suite, Farrell mused, "Do you think they're watching us?"

My mental porn clip, of Cary and Randolph fucking beside us, was a spectral aphrodisiac, and the four of us got busy, redefining screwball comedy.

The next day Farrell drove me onto the Clarion lot, through the iconic, ironwork gateway that had been featured in many Hollywood-set films. I was the latest recruit in an anguished, well-compensated field corps of East Coast writers whoring themselves in Tinseltown, or I hoped I was. I liked my idea for *Habit Forming*, but as with *Enter Hamlet*, I was a novice, unsure how the system operated.

"Have fun at work," Farrell said, off to scout the estates of Beverly Hills.

I spent the morning at the studio, in meetings with the Clarion team. I remembered everyone's name but would trip on their titles, which were modified by the words "executive," "deputy," "associate," "junior," and "chief." Brett had quit his Manhattan job after being hired as a full-fledged associate something-or-other at Clarion. It was a major and rapid promotion. Brett had rented a house in the Hills, wherever that was, and I was floored when I saw him. In the month since our last session in New York, he'd lost almost fifty pounds. He was near-skeletal and I worried he'd been ill. Should I question his drastic alteration, or compliment him?

"It's because LA is his next move," Farrell speculated, when I told him about Brett's transformation. "He wants to fit in. I bet he thinks that if he isn't thin, they'll call him a fat boy and dismiss him, and he'd never stand for that. He's working every angle. Leaving nothing to chance."

Farrell's instincts were solid, and at a series of lunches Brett only ate potato skins, and when I alluded to this, he admitted, "I have a doctor back in New York who gave me this diet." He was so fixated on success that every technique became a mania. He might starve himself to the top and then vanish entirely, becoming, with the pluck of a harp string, the Invisible Executive Producer.

The meeting kicked off with the most strenuous enthusiasm. Ron, a member of the Clarion squad, told me "We are crazy insane demented for *Habit Forming*." "It's so-and-so's total passion project," said Lance, name-checking Clarion's president. "We can't wait to get started," said Bruce, rubbing his hands together, like a cartoon bunny with a napkin tucked into his collar. Nicole, the lone female in the room, added, "We're fast-tracking it." The guys wore undetectable variations on costly, draped navy-blue suits from fashion-forward Japanese designers, over white open-necked shirts. Nicole adapted the look via a limp, steel-gray silk pantsuit. It was as if primary colors, or any colors, had been banned. As with many organizations, a uniform had evolved, to eliminate panic over excessive individuality or choosing the day's outfit. Not standing out made an employee less of a target, in an industry propelled by scape-goating.

I admired a photo of the studio's Fourth of July softball game, on a shelf in Ron's office, and he said, "That was such a great day," but when I asked him to identify the players, it turned out that a majority had already been fired.

"They're mostly good guys," Brett told me later, with regards to the Clarion crowd, "but they're all terrified of losing their jobs, which they will, sooner rather than later. Just pay attention to Bruce, who's the alpha. Nobody will ever have an opinion, not a real one, until they've heard from Bruce."

"It's so weird," I told Farrell that afternoon, back at our house, or Cary and Randolph's house. "Everyone's being nothing but nice, but they'd tell an inner tube it was a genius."

"It's only your first day," said Farrell, "and Brett has your back. Come with me."

Farrell had turned on the air-conditioning and opened the doors to the sand. "It's the ultimate LA gesture," he said, "wasting electricity and exploiting nature at the same time."

The beach was deserted, because everyone was either in meetings, at their acupuncturist, or browsing for more shapeless Japanese navy-blue silk outfits on Rodeo Drive.

Farrell waded a few feet into the ocean, barefoot, with his shirt completely unbuttoned and the cuffs of his white pants rolled up. He shut his eyes and tossed his head back, truly relaxing for the first time since Wichita. Jackson had once said there's a period in everyone's life when they reach the peak of their beauty: "Even if they're hideously grotesque, there's a week, or a year, when their skin clears up and they find the right haircut and they look the best they ever will. With average-looking people, there's a window of real improvement, when they've worked on their body, and their facial features start to make sense, and they shine, although it passes, and they revert back to their everyday, less attractive selves. It doesn't have anything to do with age; some people will never surpass their three-year-old gorgeousness, and others will turn distinguished and brooding and godlike, overnight, at seventy-eight. But with the epically beautiful, with the immortals like Farrell, whenever it happens, you can't even be near them. It's too much, they're shooting rays of beauty from every pore. And that's when you understand the phrase 'classical beauty,' and you get why Michelangelo captured whichever little Italian laborer it was, who posed for the *David*, at just the right time. Because if Michelangelo had waited, he'd have missed it. The window. The dazzle."

Farrell had scaled that pinnacle. He'd always been stunning, and most likely always would be, but there'd been a shift. He was no longer burdened by his father's crippling imperatives. He'd fought his way clear, and while I'd been at the studio he'd traversed LA with the top down and become not tan, with that beach-bunny, orange-peel, baby-oiled sameness, but—burnished. His hair was its traditional tumble, but more golden. California had made all this possible, because California thrives on shameless beauty. I began to cry, maybe because time was passing.

"What's wrong?" Farrell asked.

"Nothing. All good."

A guy stood a few yards off, gaping at Farrell, which people did. This voyeur wore a square-cut bathing suit, a denim shirt, sunglasses, and a jaunty canvas hat. Natives dressed for the beach in LA. After a few seconds he was gone.

The next morning I was peppered with questions regarding our heroine, Sister Bertram: "Why does she have a man's name?" "Can she take off her, what's that head thing called, her wimple, and have, like, gorgeous hair that she doesn't even know she has?" "Do the nuns take showers together, like in a locker room?" "When she prays, would it be fun if she started out by saying, 'Hey there, God,' and instead of saying, 'Amen,' she said, 'Catch ya later'?" "If a nun gets horny, does she maybe forget the words to a hymn?" "When Sister Bertram gambles, what if she gets turned on?"

In answering these questions, a smattering of which had merit, I wavered between wanting to scream, "Did you really just ask that?" and a knee-jerk desire to please.

Brett told me later: "Just nod and look like you're listening and ig-nore 90 percent of what they're saying. But always stay focused, because there's an immutable law of the universe: sometimes even a moron can have a good idea." Brett's two even younger assistants were juggling plas-tic oblong walkie-talkie-like devices, and Brett was interrupting his guid-ance to talk into these handheld gadgets. I'd never seen such a thing; "They're wireless phones," Brett explained. "Everyone's getting them, so you can make calls from everywhere."

I couldn't accept this. I was like a crochety farmer, doubting them dadgum horseless carriages, or an erudite professor, snorting that tele-vision, "the idiot box," would never last. When an assistant loaned me one senseless contraption and Brett called me on the other, I was as-tounded, and spoke very loudly and clearly, as if Brett were Alexander Graham Bell. I wouldn't own such a suspect gizmo for years, but it struck me: anything that would enable Brett Starber to conduct busi-ness from, say, the peak of Mount Kilimanjaro or while sitting on the toilet was a hazardous advance. It would take only a hairsbreadth more science before Brett could teleport into my dreams, red-faced and howling for more pages, although in fact this had already happened, more than once.

The second assistant stuck a Post-it onto my sleeve. Farrell and I had been invited to a party that night, at the Brentwood home of an agency overlord, whom I'd never met. Like so many recently built LA show-places, this wasn't technically a house, but a stack of glass rooms and pavilions, cantilevered on a hillside overlooking the city.

It was a multimillion-dollar architectural folly that would buckle into shards and splinters, from an earthquake or a deal gone sour. The grounds were populated by a predominantly male guest list, subdivided between the momentarily powerful and the ambitiously nubile.

Farrell and I sipped Evians on a ledge jutting outside a bedroom above this humming flesh bazaar. Brett appeared, in an oversize, untucked striped linen shirt and Bermuda shorts, his concession to ease, which didn't suit him. Brett didn't belong in the wild, where he couldn't slam a door with the push of a button under his desktop, launch coffee mugs at walls, or make outer office personnel tremble, vomit into wastebaskets, and book economy flights back to their Iowa hometowns, where nobody roared obscenities at them for not leaving their squalid apartments before dawn to refill a Scotch Tape dispenser.

"Do you know these people?" I asked him.

"Most of them. The peppy guys in T-shirts and spotless white sneakers are development types, and the older men with hair plugs and blazers are either studio heads or agency honchos. The cute guys in Speedos are actors, and let's use that term loosely, and the naked guys in the pool are hookers."

"But why were we invited?" Farrell asked.

"Word gets out," said Brett, as the man I'd seen on the beach approached us, toting a white wine.

"Hey, Eric," said Brett. "Have you met Nate and Farrell?"

"Not technically," said Eric, who only had eyes for Farrell, because I was a brunette and a writer; if I were a woman, as far as Eric was concerned I wouldn't have existed.

"Eric Nordstadt," he said, "welcome to my house. Farrell, who represents you?"

Brett, without a second's hesitation, answered, "I'm Farrell's manager."

"Yes," Farrell confirmed, "since forever."

"Have I seen you in anything?" asked Eric.

"He's mostly done theater, back in New York," said Brett, confident Eric would interpret the word "theater" as "something I've vaguely heard of that never makes any real money." Brett reeled Eric in: "Clarion brought him out here to talk about a part in the project I'm doing with Nate."

"Hmmm," said Eric, still only to Farrell, "we should talk. Brett has my information. You guys get down there and mingle. There's a sushi bar and a make-your-own-mai-tai setup. Go for it."

An assistant, at a prearranged signal, alerted Eric to an international call, a housekeeper drowning, or a weeping client locked in a guest bathroom, and he wandered off.

"What was that about?" I asked Brett.

"A new face in town," said Brett. "Farrell's already causing conversation."

This was a gay twist on the time-honored Hollywood discovery story. It happens in every gay feeding ground, from Fire Island to Mykonos. Each season someone indisputably and extraordinarily desirable pops up, a world-class commodity, on the deck of a magnate's yacht, a bar stool at the latest orgasmically reviewed Swedish/Catalan fusion restaurant, or jackhammering concrete at a Midtown demolition site, and even if no one knows this stunner's name, he's sanctified as the Face of the Season, and topics will include "Who's Had Him," "What Does He Like to Do in Bed," "Is He for Hire, for How Much," and "Is He Already Over." Sometimes this instant Apollo will be a Broadway chorus boy fresh from Akron (the guy every gay man in the audience notices), or a Brazilian soccer player, or a gas station attendant who's hitched a ride. But somehow, so quickly, the phones are swamped, the hubbub triggered by only "the guy with the eyelashes."

Farrell had been stashed away, at Amherst and in Wichita, so he was an ingénue. "Do you want to act?" Brett asked him. "Or, more precisely, do you want to be in movies?"

"I have no idea," said Farrell.

Later, as we sat on our terrace, I vacillated. Farrell had been held captive by his family's machinations, and tonight, after less than a week in LA, he was fielding interest. Maybe those early college days would be our only uninterrupted span together. Maybe he was already gone, again.

"If that Eric person gets in touch," I asked, "will you take the meeting?"

"He already has," said Farrell, "there was a message on our machine."

"And?"

"And I'll talk to him, just to see what it's about. It can't hurt. And I've got the time." My face must've betrayed me, because he added, "And this weekend we're driving up the coast, just you and me. I booked a room in Big Sur. Don't you love how I said 'Big Sur' as if we've been here for years?"

The trip was pure coastal stream-of-consciousness. With the top down, our hair pleasantly windswept, and the radio alternating between Donna Summer and Linda Ronstadt—a gay man's sex goddess and just-jilted best friend, respectively—California was at its most rapturously languid, meaning unhurried, scenic, and without judgment. It's a place where everyone can be spiritually blond. And I discarded exactly that simplistic East Coast sarcasm, as I waved to the freckled girl in the Jeep passing beside us, in her fringed suede vest and round iridescent purple-lensed sunglasses.

The bedroom of our rambling, cedar-shingled hotel had a skylight, and the windows were open to the pine and salt-air breeze. The chill called for the softest cotton blanket, and as I lay in Farrell's arms with my head on his chest, I predicted the frozen waste from a passing jetliner crashing through the skylight and fracturing our skulls, a freak tsunami flooding the room, or my being awakened by a middle-of-the-night phone call concerning a family member's health.

"It's okay to like this," said Farrell, kissing my hair. "We've both been through some shit, which means nothing, but don't cross your arms and deny the granola."

"I'm not."

"Say it, right now. The California state motto. And make me believe it. Say you're happy."

"I can't. The Cossacks will stampede our village and burn our humble dwellings. They'll slaughter our oxen."

"Say it."

"We're New Yorkers. If we say we're happy, the subway will stop between stations for five hours, a manhole cover will explode, and the sanitation workers will go on strike. And we'll picket with them."

"Nate, I'm rich. Which isn't any ultimate protection, but it's a buffer. And you're working, as a writer, which is a step in the right direction. And I love you. And I'm saying that to your face instead of calling you at 2 a.m. from Kansas last year and wanting to say it so badly but hanging up."

"Was that you?"

"Who else? I just—I had to hear your voice. But if we'd talked, my father would've found out, which he did, or I'd have missed you so much that I'd have lost hope, which I almost did."

"Okay, here goes . . . and if God's listening, I'm a hostage and I'm being forced to read this as part of a ransom video . . . but . . . I love you so much, and I'm happy."

We waited, for a whiff of brimstone or a villainous chortle, but neither happened. It was just us. "But for how long, *bubbeleh*?" snarked my ancestral trepidation. Jews are the people who import anxiety to paradise (that's why they started the movie business). Before the serpent tempted Adam and Eve, Adam's cousin Bernie had nagged them about serpent insurance, wearing at least a hat and applying sunblock with zinc oxide. Even my gayness had failed me at Eric Nordstadt's party; it was as if I hadn't converted my homosexuality into Los Angeles currency.

My next meeting, after I'd delivered new scenes, went combative. Said Ron, "Why is Mother Superior so mean to Sister Bertram? Why can't they be buddies?" Added Lance, "And what if Gina's not a showgirl? What if she's a stripper? Strippers are hot." Alpha Bruce, unfurling his wrath, declared, "I think we need to start from page one and rethink everything. Nate, we love your work but you've got to go deeper. Have you done any research?"

I'd done reams of research, on Catholic dogma, gambling addiction, and the mob's role in Atlantic City corruption. Bits of this had proved helpful, but whenever I'd present any background information to the team, they'd tilt their heads like unsure cocker spaniels, and Bruce would decree, for example, that the fact of many lesbians opting for convent life as a refuge was "not a direction we need to go in." I expressed my frustration to Brett, who devised a countermeasure. I'd spend a weekend at a convent outside Carmel and narrate my expedition, which might invigorate the team, or as Brett said, "At least get them to shut the fuck up for a few seconds."

Farrell, meanwhile, had his meeting with Eric Nordstadt, which he replayed to me with his feet in my lap on Cary and Randolph's couch: "It was interesting. Eric works for an agency called International Corrosive Manipulation or Paranormal Artistic Ergonomics . . ."

"Incorporated Creative Partners," I corrected, "and Eric's their top agent and one of the founders."

"Right, and they've just moved into this building that they commissioned from a prize-winning Icelandic architect, and it's very pretty, and correct me if I'm wrong, but don't all modern buildings in LA look temporary? As if they're the packing crates that the next set of impersonal modern buildings will be shipped in?"

"Yes. Brett says the ICP building went fifty-eight million dollars over budget and the foundation is still cracked."

"And everyone was lovely. I think even if you get arrested for slaughtering a busload of orphans in LA, the first thing the officer will do, before reading you your rights, is ask if you'd like flat or sparkling."

"And then the judge will ask if any of the orphans were hot."

"Of course. And Eric's sitting behind this empty slab of glass the size of North Dakota . . ."

"Brett has a rule, about how clutter is counterproductive. So he only touches any piece of paper once. And honchos like Eric don't have books because they pay underlings to read books for them and summarize the books' movie potential in a two-sentence memo, and they don't have photos of their spouses and kids because of ongoing litigation."

"Got it. So it's just me and Eric and a huge framed rendering of the building we're sitting in, and he asks if I've ever acted before and I say no, and he says that's actually great because it means I haven't developed any bad habits. Plus he loves discovering raw talent."

"Only in LA is having no experience considered a plus. Because if you haven't been attached to a bomb, you're way ahead."

"Then this other guy, a middle-aged Welshman named Drake Kenterly comes in . . ."

"Who's major, because his last three rom-coms have made over a billion dollars . . ."

"And he's studying me from different perspectives, and framing me with his hands, and he and Eric tell me about their newest project, about a working-class secretary from Staten Island who's mistaken for a hooker and goes along with it to get a better job, because the hooker was hired by the CEO of the company where she works. It's called . . ."

"*Love for Sale*," we said together, because everyone at Clarion was buzzing about this script, which had been tinkered with over an eight-year span by at least twelve writers, and had, under studio edicts, evolved from a dark indictment of American consumerism into what the press releases called "a heart-touching soufflé for anyone who's ever been in love, or wants to be."

"And they want me to read for the role of Julian Morebrooke, the CEO, who's an Ivy League hotshot. It's because they're spending most of the budget on the female star, so they'd like to, as Drake put it, 'find someone brand-spankin'-new' for Julian.' Someone who'd be cheaper."

"And what did you tell them?"

"I told them I'd be happy to take the script home and then give it a shot. I mean, why not?"

I thought about all the actors back East, driving cabs on fourteen-hour shifts and proofreading in law offices at midnight and waiting tables for a subminimum wage, who'd kill for a single line in a studio movie, because it would qualify them for health insurance with their union. Farrell hadn't been handed the starring role in an A-list movie, not yet, but he was being considered, on the basis of his looks.

I'd never been jealous of Farrell's beauty, because what would be the point? I was just smart enough to fixate on my own physical flaws, and leave his perfection alone. Beauty, as Jackson had once said, "is a gift to us all. I think of beautiful people as precious artworks that can steal your credit cards. And we can comfort ourselves by remembering that it's so much harder for gorgeous people to age."

I hadn't resented Farrell's money, because he was so unstintingly generous and because his family's wealth had caused so much bullying and grief. Farrell had undergone doorman-holding-the-umbrella-over-your-head, handmade-shoe-trees, limousined hardship, but I wondered: Did I begrudge him his luck? Was Farrell currently in the right place at the right time with the right face? Wasn't he always? Did he attract luck?

"I'll never get the part," he insisted. "I'm not an actor, and I'll embarrass myself excruciatingly, and Eric and Drake will scramble to thank me for coming in as they hustle me out the door and refuse to validate my parking let alone my humanity."

But what would happen if I became a movie star's spouse, or "friend," or plus-one, that damning shorthand for the guest of the person who's actually been invited to the party. Hollywood problems are the most divorced from reality, which explains cocaine overdoses in saunas, pet therapists who treat "the whole animal," third nose jobs, and people introducing their pool boys as "aquatic consultants." Hollywood problems are why everyone out there is so have-a-fulfilling-day cheerful, right before their body is pulled from what's left of the leased Maserati.

20

That weekend I took a bus to the Our Lady of Mount Carmel Abbey, because while Bruce had signed off on the trip, there were budgetary restrictions, and the bus conveniently stopped at the gates of the abbey. This was an overnight, and with my knapsack and Adidas, I was my own Maria von Trapp, a conflicted little Jewish foundling tossed from a Greyhound in the general direction of Catholic redemption.

As I hiked up the curving gravel drive, the abbey revealed itself as resembling a sumptuously refurbished hacienda-style villa in Beverly Hills, with sweeping views, an orchard of fruit trees, a working vineyard, and a tranquil courtyard fountain. All it lacked was an oak-planked *Last Supper*–style outdoor table, groaning with just-picked grapes spilling from a woven cornucopia, a thickly crusted loaf of home-baked bread, brimming goblets, and an earthenware jug abundant with sunflowers. As I got closer, this exact table was visible beneath a pergola, being minutely tended to by a film crew shooting a TV commercial for the best-selling Little Sisters of Mount Carmel cabernet. As an assistant with a headset kept me at bay, so I wouldn't ruin the take, a woman trotted up on horseback and asked, "Are you Nate? I'm Mother Gregory."

She dismounted, and I walked beside her as she led her steed into a corral. She was in her fifties, wearing a wimple, jeans, and a down-filled vest, or Convent Casual.

"I know what you're thinking," Mother Gregory said, "and we're not always this glamorous. People think we receive money from the Church or the Vatican, but it's not true. The abbey is self-supporting, so the vine-yard pays the bills."

I'd been expecting a more stereotypical hardliner, a beady-eyed des-pot slamming my wrists with a ruler, but Mother Gregory was jovial and plainspoken. She brought me to an adobe guesthouse where I'd be sleep-ing. "There's a shared bathroom," she said, "but you're our only visitor right now. Feel free to poke around, but please respect the sisters' privacy. We're a cloistered order, and many of us observe a vow of silence. And you're doing research for some sort of film project, I believe?"

I couldn't bring myself to admit the truth, that I was being battered by studio execs over a sex comedy that wouldn't get papal approval. So I said, "Yes, it's a movie that's still in an early stage of development. It's about a journey of faith."

Thank God Jews don't have Hell, or I would've just booked a flaming first class ticket.

I spent the afternoon dropping by the simple chapel, where the nuns prayed every three hours; a barn with cows, pigs, and chickens; an elabo-rate, hand-carved nativity scene displayed year-round in a shed; and the abbey gift shop, my natural destination, as I prefer the retail aspects of all major religions.

The sisters, as far as I could tell, were hardworking, uncomplaining, and elderly. Mother Gregory may have been the youngest. My research had covered this decline: many convents were being abandoned or sold, as the nuns died of old age, without younger disciples to care for them and take their places. Mount Carmel was being inventive, with lines of handmade beeswax candles, calendars with daily inspirations, and CDs of chants and hymns, my favorite being *Music of the Martyrs*, which I bought as a Chanukah gift for my mom.

I had a hushed dinner with the sisters in a dining hall, where they paid no attention to me, intent on their simple meal and, I assumed, schemes for tunneling into town after lights-out. Farrell's presence would've caused more of a stir; his incipient stardom was bothering me more than I'd anticipated. He was paging through a sought-after script while I was breaking cracked-wheat bread and sipping a thin broth with women who never gave beauty or money or Hollywood a second thought. As the sisters filed out, Mother Gregory tapped me on my shoulder and took me into her office, which, with its battered desk and dented filing cabinets, had seen better days.

"Have you got what you came for?" Mother Gregory asked.

"I'm not sure," I said, being reasonably honest, given my location. "The abbey is beautiful and the sisters are really dedicated."

"And what were you were expecting? Beetle-browed monsters, or chirping novices?"

Both.

"Mother Gregory, may I ask you something? Are you happy?"

I hadn't intended to pursue this, but Mother Gregory was a spiritual figure so I'd blurted out a layman's idiocy. I was treating her like a fortune-telling marionette in a glass booth on a carnival midway, a turbaned wizard that knows all and tells all.

"Oh, Mr. Reminger. Why do people, especially young people, always ask me that?"

"Because people like me have two fantasies of religious life," I replied. "I think of this place as either a prison work farm for women who don't like wearing makeup, or as a Shangri-La, some secluded village where the nuns are three thousand years old and possess mystical secrets of contentment and eternal life."

"You're gay, right?" she asked, smiling.

"Yeah, but I'm just visiting, so is it okay if after I fall asleep the nuns don't grab me and beat me with branches in the name of saving my immortal soul?"

"Sorry. Too late."

I was almost sure she was joking.

"Mr. Reminger," she said, "Nate. I know plenty of gay people. But maybe you're not really gay, or gay enough, because then you'd know who I am."

"Mother Gregory?"

She held her hands around her face, hiding her wimple: "Karyn Barstow."

Oh my God. Literally.

"You dimly remember, don't you?" she said. "Or you saw that mention last year in *People* magazine. Yes, I was Karyn, and I costarred with Bobby Darin in *Love Goes to College*, and with Troy Donahue in *Corporal Mindy*, and opposite Elvis in *Reno Romance*."

Of course. She'd been a button-nosed starlet in snug angora sweaters, swingy poodle skirts, and saddle shoes, virginal but perky, courted by every pop idol from thirty years ago. She'd forsaken show business right after her twenty-fourth birthday and entered a convent, an unlikely switch marveled at by fan magazines and parochial school faculty alike. Every so often she'd give brief, noncommittal interviews reaffirming her decision, and after his death, she'd called Elvis "a good-hearted but searching young fellow."

"So you don't hate me," I asked, "because I'm gay Hollywood trash?"

"No. Although that was going to be the title of my next film. That's why I retired."

"Why?" I asked, sure she'd been asked this a thousand times and would wearily unspool a boilerplate answer. But I was curious: "Why did you leave?"

"Because . . . I suppose because I was where you may be now. Being flown places, being wined and dined, meeting famous people and the people who work much harder behind the scenes to keep them famous. The waterfalls of money. The hotel suites with five dozen roses from the studio brass and complimentary buckets of champagne on ice. All that delicious fuss."

"Well, I'm just a writer."

"I'm so sorry. Biblically, screenwriters are ranked below the lame, the halt, and the blind. Because even Jesus couldn't help them."

She was charming me, so I granted, "I know what you mean about Hollywood. It's very exciting and confusing, and I think Hollywood likes it that way. To keep everyone hyped up and hopeful and second-guessing every move."

"Yes. I was seventeen when I got there, fresh from a Junior Chamber of Commerce talent contest in Turtle Head, Kentucky. I hopped off the bus just in time for the last gasp of the contract players. They fixed my teeth, my accent, and put me in a waist cincher that dislocated my ribs. But I loved it, every flashbulb and phony interview and premiere in a strapless gown. It was everything I'd listed under 'someday' in the pink leatherette diary that I hid under my mattress. And everyone was so nice to me, even Elvis. He called me his little sister, and said I should let him know if anyone bothered me. But I could tell, he was taking the same diet pills I was. From his eyes. What a sweet, sad wreck of a man."

"So was that why you left? Was he a cautionary tale?"

"No. Because there were far worse cases, girls hooked on anything you might imagine, sleeping with anyone who claimed to be a producer's nephew, and there were photographers who kept reminding me that Marilyn Monroe had posed for a nude calendar. But I'd laugh. I was from Kentucky. My mama drank grain alcohol, and my daddy staggered home once a year, at Christmas, because there might be something under the tree worth selling. I could take care of myself."

"So?"

"So one day, when I was twenty-three, I looked at the stack of scripts in my dressing room, with the titles written in marker along the sides. And most of those titles contained the word 'honeymoon,' 'Paris,' 'debutante,' or 'girls.' That's what I was being sent. But if I pined to be taken seriously, and refine my craft, I could fly to New York, enroll at the Actors Studio, and get patted on my pretty little head for playing, what's her name, Masha, in an all-star *Three Sisters*. Or I could get married, because I'd had plenty of prospects. A Texas rancher. The head of an airline. Sinatra, but he might've been kidding, or soused. Those were my retirement plans. But I believed in something: Our Lord Jesus Christ. And look at you, trying not to twitch and hightail it out the door."

"No! I don't not believe in God," I insisted.

"Control your wild enthusiasm and unshakeable certainty."

"It's just . . ." I hesitated. "I don't like what some people do, especially to their kids, in the name of God."

"Agreed," said Mother Gregory. "But Nate, we're not talking about you, not yet. I don't need you to give yourself to Jesus, and he might not be interested."

"Hey!"

"Calm down." She was toying with me and entertaining herself. I didn't think Mother Gregory had much opportunity for conversations like this, with gay Jewish screenwriters. I was her porn.

"So I sat myself down," she continued, "and I asked myself, what did I really want? In a perfect world, which could never exist. But if you don't start there, with your most dearly held dreams, why bother with anything? I was ruthless. From the farthest back I could remember I'd had my heart set on being a star. On being chosen. With my face on an Interstate turnpike billboard and a supermarket checkout magazine cover and twenty feet high on the screen of the Turtle Head Pantages movie theater, five shows a day. And I'd done it. But that dream was very different from becoming an actress. Acting was a means to an end. Mission accomplished."

I applied this to myself: How badly did I want to be a writer? What did I have to say, that no one else could? Was I capable of saying it with any real skill? What if writing was just a way to wriggle out of getting a real job, and committing to a day-to-day routine? Was writing an adolescent postponement, an eternal gym excuse? "Nate can't grow up, he's typing"?

And if I was a committed writer, shouldn't I be hunched over my twelve-hundred-page manuscript in my New York hovel, or in an unheated cabin upstate, scraping by through teaching assistantships and dribs of grant money, living on rice cakes as I tortured myself over a masterwork, preferably set among migrant workers or ennui-stricken heterosexuals, instead of seeking Hollywood guidance from Mother Malibu?

"So what about marriage?" Mother Gregory asked herself. "I'll be honest with you, as I was with myself. I barely thought about it. I wasn't a virgin, which isn't any of your business, but sex and weddings and raising a family, oh, I admire all of it, I can appreciate the satisfactions, but not for me. When I saw myself, at my most fulfilled, I was alone, or with a small group of like-minded people, living quietly and being of service. And that image, that goal, truly excited me. It felt forbidden and out of reach and absurd. But if I didn't risk everything, I wouldn't just be griev-ously unhappy, I'd be wasting God's effort in putting me on this earth. So when you asked me if I was happy, there's your answer. Happiness is beside the point. I'm being of use."

Case closed. I had to become a nun. Or Mother Gregory should win at least a Golden Globe, for everything she'd delineated. She was Sally in a few decades, Sally slopping the hogs in her pearls and teaching inner-city kids to plant tomatoes in a vacant lot, maybe while singing a catchy anthem of weeding-and-watering uplift. No, I was training myself, to steer away from musical-comedy translations of suffering and renewal. Mother Gregory wasn't about to gaze trenchantly out her window at the Interstate and warble "Climb Ev'ry Mountain." Unless I begged her to.

"So Nate," she said, leaning back, like a poker player either bluffing or with the hand of a lifetime, "is that your attitude, towards writing? How much does it matter to you?"

"On my best days, it's my life. But I'm scared, that I'm not up to it. That I just like the end product, having written. My name on the mar-quee. But when that happened, it was terrible. Because I'd thrown myself into it, with so little result."

"How old are you?"

"Twenty-eight. Old."

"Over the hill. If I'd realized you were so decrepit, I would've taken you out to our pasture and shot you, as a mercy killing. Nate, I have no idea if you're a writer. But your not knowing, and doubting yourself, that's all to the good. It means you have something to prove. And are you in love?"

"Yes."

"Have you got a picture?"

I opened my wallet, removing the strip of black-and-white arcade shots of Farrell and me, making faces and smooching in a boardwalk photo booth.

"Hubba hubba," said Mother Gregory. "He's very nice-looking."

"Not that you aren't," I repeated with her.

"That is something I envy," said Mother Gregory. "I don't know if I miss it, because I've never really been in love. Except for, you know . . ."

She tilted her chin toward heaven.

"But don't feel smug, or sorry for me," she added. "Because God is the finest boyfriend you'll ever come across. He's always there, he listens, and he doesn't interrupt. And he's never asked me to lose weight or dye my hair. But still, the two of you, in these pictures, you're captivated by each other. What's it like, being in love?"

"I can't say, because I'm in the middle of it. We'd been apart, but now—we're together and I'm not sure what that means. Dreaming about him, for years, that was easy. I'd ask you for advice, but can you pray for gay men?"

"I can pray for you to try and change and be miserable for the rest of your life, like so many gay men I met in Hollywood. Such a misguided shame. But if you ever tell anyone I said that, I'll ask God to smite your balls off."

"*Mother Greg!*"

"I'm sorry, this is the one thing I miss, from the old days. Talking to boys like you. My makeup artist. The backup dancers. Roddy McDowall."

"You knew Roddy McDowall? Did you ever meet Cary Grant or Randolph Scott?"

"Excuse me, I'm not that old. And yes, I did. But I'm not here to gossip about anyone but the apostles, and please don't ask me about Matthew, I wasn't there. But Nate, you're in my prayers. Because you took a bus, to talk to a nun. And because I'm a sinner. As far as I know, I'm the only nun who gets to vote for the Oscars. I've kept up my Academy membership."

A feat that made me recall Sally's vow, to become the first saint on the best-dressed list. I trusted people of faith, as long as they didn't spurn fashion, and were willing to arm-wrestle over who should win Best Supporting Actress, and then take the fight outside, blacking the eye of anyone who downplayed Candice Bergen's chances or called Meryl "a long-shot neophyte."

"Anything else I can help you with?" Mother Gregory asked, standing up. "My child?"

"You're only saying 'my child' because it's making me giddy," I said. "Because of how many times I've seen *The Sound of Music* and *The Trouble with Angels* movies, with Hayley Mills sneaking out for a cigarette at her parochial school."

"*The Trouble with Angels*," Mother Gregory decreed, "is the reason I became a nun."

"What about Debbie Reynolds?" I asked.

Mother Gregory turned to stone. I'd overstepped. Debbie had played the acoustic guitar–strumming heroine of *The Singing Nun*, a movie based on the real-life tale of a sister with a hit single. But Debbie, as a spunky, rosy-cheeked up-and-comer, had undoubtedly been Karyn Barstow's competition. Debbie was a nun too far. I swiftly changed the subject.

"Just one last thing—I love Farrell so much, he's the guy in the photos."

Mother Gregory touched her heart and placed the back of her hand against her forehead, melting.

"Shut up," I said. "You're a nun. But if I ever lost him I . . . I don't know what I'd do. Or if time would stop, or if I'd gain so much weight that I'd explode, you know, suicide by Sara Lee frosted brownies. And I don't just mean if he died, because there are other ways for love to . . . become secondary. Or negotiable. Especially out here. How do I not think about that?"

"You can't not think about it. It's impossible. It's like not thinking about God, even if you don't believe in Him. Nobody thinks about God more than atheists. But if you really love this guy, either we should perform a musical number at a sock hop right this second, where the dancers form a huge heart . . ."

"And we wear cheerleader uniforms with Cupid embroidered on them . . ."

"Okay, you're gay. But you have to be grateful, no matter what happens, that you and . . ."

"Farrell . . ."

"Really gay. You should give thanks that you and Farrell found each other in the first place. Because your love for each other, for however long it endures, that's God. So don't piss God off."

I thought about this, when I took an earlier bus back to Santa Monica the next day, and walked in on Farrell in bed with another man.

21

Farrell was fucking Bobby Heffernan, who played a crusading district attorney on *Legalese*, a much-awarded, high-minded series about young lawyers in Los Angeles, defending clients, as the ads trumpeted, "from pro bono storefronts to the very halls of power!" Bobby's character was a roguish, womanizing bachelor, thirty-ish with two marriages behind him. Bobby was audience catnip, with his often shirtless, rippling torso clad in gigolo-grade Italian suits.

There'd been rumors about Bobby, which he'd strenuously contested, and he'd broken off a year-long engagement to a female sitcom star, both of them tearfully confessing, to every media outlet, that they'd love the other person forever "as a dear friend" and they'd like privacy to heal. And here he was, his legs over Farrell's shoulders, his hands knotted to the bedposts with neckties. Farrell saw me and didn't say anything, as a flummoxed Bobby tried to ascertain what was going on, whether I had a camera, and if he could phone his publicist while immobilized.

Farrell, not taking his eyes off me, lifted the sheet, inviting me to participate. What was this? Was Farrell bored with me, had our sex life gone stale, was Bobby Heffernan (undoubtedly) more attractive, more of a novelty, and more famous than me? Was this the quantum effect of Los Angeles on any relationship, no matter how loving and forsworn?

Could Mother Gregory FedEx an instructive psalm targeted to cheating at the beach?

On the other hand—Farrell and I hadn't been monogamous. We'd been separated for too long. I didn't know who'd been available to him in Wichita or on business trips, and he hadn't grilled me about tricks in New York. We'd performed for the crowd at The Hole, but this was more intimate. We'd never brought up three-ways, but they'd never been condemned.

Was I ready for this? To share Farrell, at least physically? To expand our repertoire? How conventional was I? Or was LA redefining my perspective on fidelity and pleasure, or was "redefining my perspective" agentspeak for starring in a spaghetti western or a straight-to-video Godzilla installment? I was getting a hard-on, from catching these two great-looking men going at it, and from one of them having been the first major male star to expose his naked ass during prime time, as well as right here. I could act the outraged spouse, or coolly depart without a word (to test whether Farrell would run after me), or ask Bobby if he really made more money per episode than anyone else on his show (the LA response). But before reaching any conscious verdict, I was kicking off my shoes and unbuttoning my shirt.

As a lesser point of this triangle, I might've been ignored or relegated to a sideline coaching role, but this wasn't the case. Farrell and Bobby, with their head start, vied for my services, and Bobby, of course, liked recruiting a new fan. Three-ways become a mathematical equation, and Farrell and I teamed up, to drive Bobby out of his mind. Sex with a celebrity contains an element of erotic vengeance, as if the unknown players are overturning the star (and yes, we did). There was a sexual relay slant as well, with each of us taking a breather and then diving back in, as if obeying blasts from a referee's whistle. The only thing lacking was the greater and more lasting emotional melding I had with Farrell. Bobby Heffernan was more of a lark or an appetizer, and an experiment. There wasn't much going on behind his eyes, beyond a headliner's voracious zeal to be adored and a puppy-dogish gusto for constant stimulation, augmented by an occasional cry of "Man, that's good!" as if the three of us were buddies in a Super Bowl beer commercial.

"Okay," said Farrell, after Bobby had kissed us both, taken a call from his manager, and retrieved his Lamborghini (last year's network bonus), an hour later. Farrell hadn't let me say anything yet, but poured us glasses of wine, even though we rarely drank. The bottle of sauvignon blanc had been nestled in a gift basket from Clarion, with a card addressed to a different screenwriter.

"Yes?" I said, awaiting Farrell's—what? Explanation? Apology? Studio notes?

"I was going over the script and freaking out about auditioning," he began. "And you weren't here to slap me, so I went to the gym to distract myself. And Bobby was in the locker room and he came over and asked if I was an actor. And I said that maybe I was, and I told him about the audition and he offered to read the scenes with me and give me pointers. So we came back here and . . ."

"You got the part," I said, dryly, from a questionable moral high ground.

"Is this the worst thing I could've done?" asked Farrell, not accusingly or with any guilt. "When he kissed me, I almost shoved him away, but I didn't. He wasn't you, but in the strangest way, because he's famous, it didn't seem like cheating. More like—getting an autograph. Or taking a meeting. Is that the most pathetic excuse of all time?"

I looked at the ceiling. I looked at Farrell and said, "I can't believe I'm saying this, but no, it's not. I didn't resist either. We were star-fucking. It's like we were sneaking into Bobby's house and criticizing his furniture placement, and how different it looked in *Architectural Digest*."

"The hand-tooled Moroccan leather footstool," said Farrell.

"That non-ironic driftwood coffee table," I recalled.

"Are we turning into the biggest Hollywood sluts?" Farrell asked. "I mean, is this how we're going to start tipping hot gourmet supermarket delivery guys?"

"No," I said. "I mean, not unless we haven't been to the cash machine. Do you want to do this again, with Bobby?"

"Not really, although he asked. It's more like, this was the answer to the question would we fuck Bobby Heffernan? And we both said yes."

"But you said it first," I pointed out.

"Okay," Farrell asked, putting down his wine, "how much do you hate me?"

I reflected on this. Was today a no-going-back upheaval? Would any subsequent sex be considered post–Bobby Heffernan? Were we marked or lessened by this?

"If I hadn't taken that earlier bus," I asked, "would you have told me about it?"

"I'm not sure. We've had a sort of unspoken agreement about this stuff," Farrell said. "At least while we were apart. And I don't regret it, but I don't have any inexpressible longing to do it again. It's like arugula. Exotic, but I'll pass. Oh my God, am I being a repulsive creep, by comparing our sex life to a salad ingredient?"

"Yes," I said, laughing. I grabbed Farrell's neck and kissed him, and then asked, "Was that better? Than Bobby Heffernan's work in that very special episode where he found out his character's brother was gay, after the brother got arrested in a raid on a bathhouse? And at first Bobby was disgusted, but then he accepted his brother for who he was and represented him at trial and got the case tossed out on a technicality? Am I a better kisser than that?"

Farrell wavered before answering, causing me to howl, "Excuse me?"

"I was thinking it over," he said. "That was a very moving and important episode." We hopped in the home's outdoor shower together, scrubbing off Bobby Heffernan. There was a residual tentativeness, the wobble from continuing to define ourselves, as a couple and otherwise. California was everywhere, caressing each impulse and forgiving any lapse. California wanted us to be happy, without restrictions or sorrow. I was getting used to blaming and thanking California.

That night, when Farrell reached for me, I thought, If I was a neglected wife on a soap opera, my shoulder would flinch, or I'd feign being asleep. But I wasn't a neglected wife, and if I was being honest, I was even more turned on, because between Bobby, Cary, Randolph, and Mother Gregory, my life was hitting a gay stratosphere. This might be amoral self-deception or genuine exploration, but above all else, it was a next chapter. After so many years, Farrell and I were still getting to know each other.

In the morning I read through Farrell's audition scenes with him and only said, "A little more Bobby Heffernan" once. Farrell was good; while not a trained actor, he didn't oversell his personal charm and it came across. Sometimes the most magnetic human beings are irredeemably wooden on camera, but Farrell relaxed. He didn't plead for approval, which, as an audience member, made me watch him, and might make for romantic-comedy bliss.

He was also believably masculine, but not a pig. A trace of ambivalence has made many leading men exceptionally desirable; women find them intriguingly diffident. This was Cary Grant's calling card. He was a frazzled, sputtering hunk who relished his female costars, but at an elusive arm's length, until a final, often ambiguously wisecracking clinch. Even thoroughly straight stars, like Hugh Grant and Peter O'Toole, have taken advantage of this dichotomy, as beautiful men up for sparring with Julia Roberts or Audrey (and Katharine) Hepburn.

"Was that in any way okay?" Farrell asked, after a third time through.

"That was great," I said. "When you concentrate on the girl, it really cooks."

"Did you buy me as straight?" he wondered.

"Yes," I said, "you're the greatest actor who's ever lived." I ducked as the script sailed past my head.

I adjusted my own movie over the next few days, with my sojourn at Mount Carmel as a resource. To honor Mother Gregory and her history, I made her comic counterpart less cartoonish, with a long-ago fondness for slot machines. But I was unsteady. My initial concept for the script had been buried, beneath an avalanche of contradictory memos.

"I get what you mean," said Brett, after I expressed this vexation. "You're in development hell."

"What's that?"

"It's how studio people keep their jobs," he explained. "As long as they're giving notes, they can report back on how well everything is going, to uphold the in-house delusion of some imaginary blockbuster in progress."

"So what should I do?"

"I'm not sure," said Brett, who, unlike his compatriots, could concede a momentary insecurity. Brett would bluster and lie seamlessly to maneuver actors, directors, and extra shooting days into place, but he was after the most accomplished product. He was programming himself for success, but despite hated concessions, success on his own terms.

Farrell auditioned for Eric and Drake, who were sufficiently pleased to bring him back the next week, for what was called a "chemistry read," with his potential costar, an instantly and globally recognizable name. She was America's sweetheart, which meant her hairstyle was slavishly copied and skewered; her broken engagements were deconstructed on the op-ed pages, as indicators of the country's soulless rot; and she couldn't sneak away from the ten-acre Bel-Air estate she'd designated her "zen sanctuary" without being swarmed by shouting paparazzi, weeping fans, and glassy-eyed stalkers with pickaxes and chloroform in the trunks of their cars.

"She couldn't have been nicer," Farrell said. "She gushed all over me, called herself a mess, and only took two calls while we were talking. She made such an effort to be a person, although I yearned to tell her, 'Darling, it's fine, but you're not.'"

"How did the reading go?" I asked.

"Good, I think. Everyone laughed, and she hugged me and gave Eric and Drake a meaningful look, as her assistant was racing in with a thermos of herbal tea, a baggie of vitamin supplements, and an already lit cigarette. So we'll see."

My next meeting at Clarion was equally lauded. My latest draft was met with everything but confetti, Roman candles, and balloons. The huzzahs included "Great job, you!" "Huge leap forward!" "It's like a totally different script!" "I got chills!" I wasn't sure if my work had improved, or if I'd succumbed to the group's worst and conceivably most commercial instincts, or if anyone on the team had actually read the pages. Brett gave me a "Let them be them" stare as the conversation leapt to casting.

Our leading actress should own the most dizzying comic chops, since she'd be playing both a frowzy, cantankerous, but ultimately marshmallow-hearted showgirl along with the most sheltered and chaste young nun. As

I brought up an ideal contender, Lance asked incisively, "But is she fuck-able? Because if we want any guys to come see this movie, they're gonna have to want to fuck her." There was general consensus on this, from a roomful of men who were either gay or not likely to grace any Most Fuck-able lists themselves, unless comb-overs and nose hairs became erogenous zones. Nicole, who was suffering from Stockholm Syndrome, said, "But isn't it more important that she's funny?"

The guys were puzzled by this, so Nicole let it go. Our list expanded, with fuckability the foremost factor; debits included "Nah, she's like, twenty-eight," "I would fuck her, but only if I was seriously out of it," and "She used to be totally fuckable, but now she's borderline, I don't know what it is. Maybe it's because she's English."

I accentuated talent, but was quickly rebuffed. Studio casting sessions are like bar fights for guys who get pedicures and yowl at their private chefs. ("I can't taste the cilantro, Zach! We've talked about this!") Brett bided his time, at last proposing an up-and-coming Black actress who was breezily funny and whom audiences adored. But the racial aspect befuddled the team.

"I love her," said Lance, "but would the guy have to be Black, too?"

"He could be," said Brett, "but he doesn't have to be."

"But if we go interracial," said Ron, "we need to be careful about the South. So could we keep Sister Bertram and Danny platonic? You know, they really like each other, but as buddies?"

"But the star's also playing Gina," I said. "Who's been living with Danny for years."

"As buddies," Ron repeated.

The round table swung between a Klan book club, an earnest NAACP meeting with only white people attending, and a frat house history of race in America. "If they're both Black," said Lance, "they can kiss but then we might be accused of over-sexualizing Black people."

"What if Danny's Black and Gina's white," postulated Ron, "or would that upset Republicans who, like it or not, sometimes buy tickets?"

"What if we don't worry it to death?" asked Nicole, in the voice of someone resigned to the fact that no one was listening.

"Guys, guys, guys," said Bruce, glowing as if he'd glimpsed the face of God in his Diet Coke at just the right table in the Polo Lounge of the Beverly Hills Hotel. "I've got it. Oh man, it's perfect. What if . . . what if . . . we cast Gina and Sister Bertram Black, but we say she's Latin?"

There was a silence, the sort that reverberates after a boss challenges his staff to be honest about his fragile new mustache. Seconds later applause kicked in, as Lance pounded Bruce on the back shouting, "You're the man!" and then whistled through his fingers, Nicole concentrated on the next payment on her trendily vintage Mustang, and Brett semaphored me, "I will deal with this."

After that session I cursed myself for not speaking up and condemning the flurry of offhand slurs. But this was LA, where outrage was for suckers and eggheaded East Coasters who drove Hyundais and clipped coupons to buy generic cornflakes. Where the only insult was cratering ticket sales on an opening weekend. It's not that New Yorkers, let alone the fly-over denizens, were models of equality and refinement. It came down to twinges of remorse. In LA, no one made anyone else feel bad, let alone stained, over their social misconduct. In New York, if a Wall Street partner dated a girl his daughter's age, it was on the sly. In LA, a studio chief would either flaunt the young lady at a museum opening, taking full credit for her augmented breasts, or he'd marry her. There was an honesty to LA, where there was no such thing as a furtive lust, but there was a metallic aftertaste.

"I have no idea what's going on," I told Farrell, back in Santa Monica. "I think they liked the rewrite, half of them are racist beyond words and the other half are some weird ultra-liberal/ignorant hybrid, and Brett is doing his damnedest to get the movie made, he says that's the bottom line, for both of us, at this stage of our careers. I'm sorry, I'm yammering, so how was your day? Did you hear anything?"

Farrell had been quiet, and I worried that he'd been rejected and I'd been insensitive and self-absorbed, the perfect name for an LA law firm.

"Right before you got here," he said, "I talked to Brett. Eric called him, because he thinks Brett's my manager. I got it."

"You got it?"

"Yup. They offered me the part, contingent on a meeting."

"Oh my God!" I yelled, "This is amazing! Farrell! You're going to be a movie star!"

He stood, dazed and thoughtful and not quite internalizing anything, as I hugged him.

"How do you feel?"

"I'm not sure. I mean, I never expected this. It just fell into my lap. Which makes me suspicious as hell. But on the other hand, why not? Although the words 'why not' have justified every great crime, world war, and terrible new crossbred short-haired cat in recorded history."

"Farrell," I said, taking him by the shoulders, "this is the American dream. To alienate your entire family, send your wonderful but fraudulent wife to India, have an incredibly hot boyfriend, and become a movie star!"

"Wait," he said. "I also get a boyfriend?"

I made the only logical move, hustling him out to the terrace and shoving him, fully clothed, into the pool, where I jumped in as well.

"So I guess this is happening," he said, as we surfaced and held each other, bobbing like jubilant corks.

"I should be jealous," I told him, "but I'm not. Maybe because you've somehow become an actor without being needy. I didn't say that! I love actors! No, maybe this is happening to make up for all those years in Wichita. Because your mother will see the name Farrell Covington in lights, or at least in plastic letters, at the Wichita Cineplex and she won't know what to do. Everyone will congratulate her, and Father Densmore will see the movie twelve times and jerk off to your picture in *People* magazine. You deserve this."

"I don't," he said, and this wasn't false modesty. "I know what real actors put up with for even a walk-on. And look at Jess, dealing with her mom. But before you got here I thought about it. I absorbed the improbability. The Hollywood anarchy. And I decided, as with everything else in our lives, let's see where this goes."

"Excuse me," I said, pulling myself up onto the edge of the pool, "are you saying that getting the lead in an A-list studio movie is a stepping stone? To what? Will you run for Senate? Or train for the pole vault? Except hold on, there's one thing that's forbidden, because I will smother you in your sleep with a pillow."

"What?"

"You can't make an album, just because you're a movie star."

His eyes lit up. "Fuck you," he told me, dragging me back into the water.

We had dinner at the house, because Farrell said we owed it to Cary and Randolph. "Maybe that's why this is happening," he said, over the double-chocolate brownies from a local bakery. "Both our movies. Maybe Cary and Randolph lent a hand."

"But if you're going to be a movie star, maybe you don't need a second brownie."

I only said this because, yes, of course I was jealous, but only in terms of the most standard, I'll-never-be-a-movie-star pouting. Denying Farrell dessert would be my revenge, a screenwriter's dagger. And of course, writers are indefatigable snobs. We can be furious at or exasperated by actors, who mangle our words, and at directors, who steal credit for our genius, and at critics, for carping. But bone-deep envy is sacred. It's reserved for other writers. Farrell would always be better-looking than me and richer and more in demand, the whole of which I'd file under "Life as We Know It," but if he ever wrote so much as a paragraph or scrawled an idea for a one-act on a cocktail napkin, his body would never be found.

"We don't start shooting for three months," Farrell sniffed. "And Eric has a fitness shaman he goes to, out in some canyon, who gives him holistic colonics."

"You mean enemas?" I said. Bruce had been bragging about his colonics to Nicole, but I'd erased any of the more queasy-making images.

"We are leading the most preposterous lives," Farrell said, and I couldn't contradict him. We were fortunate and out of place and imperiled, meaning, we were in LA, with its shifting tectonic plates, unnaturally serene climate, and entertainment industry. It's Vegas with far worse odds, but at least for that night, we'd stacked our chips.

"But you said something about a meeting," I recalled. "Isn't Brett doing your deal?"

"I think so," said Farrell. "I'm not sure why, but they've asked for you to be there, too."

Eric and Drake were awaiting us in Eric's office the next morning, and we all had water.

"So how about Farrell?" Eric asked me. "Can you stand it?"

"He's going to be wonderful," I said.

"The discovery of the year," agreed Drake. "The decade."

"We put him on tape for the studio bigwigs," Eric went on, "and they are over the moon. And Farrell, once this hits the trades, you can expect other offers, a landslide. So please remember, we got here first."

"And I'm so grateful," said Farrell. He hadn't made his peace with this; he was thrown and less verbal than usual. Or was he test-driving a protective humility, for future magazine profiles?

"So," said Eric, leaning against his desk and downing the latest electrolyte-infused water with real papaya extract. "There's just one thing, and I hate even having to bring this up, and believe me, it's totally not my idea, I'm just the messenger, but the studio wonks insist, and they have a job to do. So we should talk about your, let's call it, your lifestyle."

"My lifestyle?" asked Farrell.

"Both of you," added Drake.

"The publicity and marketing people are all over this," said Eric. "And they're crazy excited, because Farrell's not just a great new face, he's got a compelling backstory. Farrell, you're from one of America's most distinguished families, although you've lost your dad, and I'm so sorry about that, but it keeps you relatable, right? Because sooner or later, everyone loses their dad."

I was sure Eric was about to add "Yay!" but he held back.

"And you're married to Sally," Eric continued. "Who does so many good things to help . . . people in need, and we love that. So far, so fabulous. So . . ."

His glance traveled from Farrell to me and back again. There was a weightlessness to Eric; he was reed-thin and bright-eyed, like a painted toy soldier or a mass-produced Pinocchio with bendable limbs. He seemed about to jump onto his desk and nibble an acorn.

"So the two of you are together," he said, "and personally, I love that, I mean, I wish I could meet the right guy, but with the agency moving into our new flagship space, who has time? But here's my thought: The agency and the studio are investing in Farrell. As a property. There will be many millions of dollars spent on a huge summer movie, top-lining America's sweetheart, and she's going to fall in love with this incredibly hot new guy. Which means we need the world to fall in love with that guy. And, okay, I know this sucks, but the world isn't ready to fall in love with a gay guy. It's a betrayal. It makes our leading lady come off like a fool. And yes, I hope and I pray that someday, there will be such a thing as an openly gay movie star, but we're not there yet. Are you following?"

"I think we are," said Farrell, undisturbed.

"Yay! Because here's what we're after. You guys are at the Cary Grant place, which is to die for, oh my God, I love that house, although the kitchen is a total gut, and the pool could stand an upgrade, but you can't stay there. Because, think about it, Cary and Randolph both got married, a lot. Tony Perkins got married. Rock Hudson got married. Bobby Heffernan's been engaged, twice. So we'd like you to, let's just say, cool it. No public appearances together, not without women. No more all-male pool parties. No dance clubs. And even in New York, separate addresses. The world will be watching, through binoculars, and cameras with zoom lenses, especially once our movie opens, and especially if it's as ginormous as we think it's going to be. And nothing should interfere with that, or fuck with what is, let's be honest here, Farrell's big break. So all we're asking for is—a smidgen of caution. Farrell, you can't mention Nate in interviews. If someone brings up his name, you can say, 'He's a screenwriter, isn't he?' Because you're a happily married man. And Nate, don't worry, because we haven't forgotten you."

Of course they hadn't.

"Because I'm hearing great things about *Habit Forming*, and you're with Florence Gruber in New York, I love Florence, what a character, but if you really want to write movies, big ones, the kind every writer wet-dreams of, you should think about our agency. Because we have access and clout, and we do packages, teaming big-name directors with up-and-comers like yourself. So we'll take you on as a client. Done."

He was pleased with himself, every loose end merrily snipped. He'd delivered variations on this speech before. Probably most agents with gay clients had. And Drake was here to underscore the creative perspective. I'd once written a play with a gay theme, and sent Florence an early draft. She's as liberal as they come, but even she'd asked me, "Haf you considered vat this play might do? To your pwospects?" Which was precisely Eric's coaxing show business argument. If there was pushback, he'd haul out the heavy artillery, meaning phrases like "in the real world," "I can give you examples of far more talented people who've destroyed their entire careers," and "I don't make the rules."

"Farrell," said Eric, "that was a ton of bricks, except it really isn't. It's a lifestyle adjustment, to achieve a larger and fabulous goal."

"And Eric," said Farrell, with a gleam in his eye, a gleam I'd seen before and looked forward to. "Eric, if I say no, if I'm not willing to . . . adjust my lifestyle, would that be an insurmountable problem?"

"I'm afraid it would be," said Eric.

"You will be astonishing in this film," Drake assured Farrell, raising his palms, already blown away. "And I'm not gay, but I am from Wales, so I know a few things about being an outsider. But this isn't even an accommodation, let alone a defeat. It's a method, a time-honored tradition. Because that's what Hollywood's about, isn't it? Creating romantic illusions? And we'd never want to shatter or distort those illusions."

"I understand completely," said Farrell, which made Eric and Drake exchange a savvy nod. "I've told some enormous lies; in fact, I've lived them. And they work, to a certain extent. They're effective."

"Exactly," said Eric, as I glanced at his doll-size feet, which were vibrating with how well this was going. Where did he buy such miniature Gucci loafers? Was there children's sizing?

"But then those lies become toxic," said Farrell. "So when it comes to disguising my life, and excising the man I love, and tossing whatever microscopic shreds of decency I've managed to retain into the Pacific, or the pool at your next, even more expensive and architecturally unstable home, here's my answer."

He stood up, fully himself again, reclaiming his customary esprit, and said, "Not today."

He set his bottle of water onto Eric's desk and held out his hand to me, which I took. We executed a brief dance step, a modified foxtrot, he dipped me, and we tangoed out of Eric's office. In the hall Farrell's first words were "Thank God I'm rich."

We sat in the convertible, in the parking lot, as the impact of what Farrell had just done, with my collusion, made itself known.

"Are you sure about this?" I asked. "Because that was very brave and well staged and I'll remember every second of it for the rest of my life, but is that really what you'd like to do? Give up everything? Becoming a movie star?"

"What makes you think," Farrell replied, "that I consider that everything?"

This was one of those distancings, when Farrell's privilege and even selfishness separated us. Yes, I was reflecting a popular trope, of movie stardom as an ultimate jackpot, a Valhalla of fame and money without effort. No one ever really wants to be a movie star, as a profession of memorizing lines and daily rehearsal, with catatonic days and stifling nights of hanging around for lighting adjustments, last-minute script consultations, and luring your totteringly cross-addicted costar from her acting coach/ crystal meth supplier and her trailer. Folks don't categorize being a movie star, or a rock star, as a job, but as an exit, and a glory-drenched elevation, from their unfulfilling workplaces and disappointing paychecks. Becoming a movie star is a synonym for, if not happiness, at least cutting the line at Disney World.

But for Farrell, saying no to Eric, even from the finest intentions, imposed little economic or even psychological hardship. Because Farrell, as a result of wealth and physical attributes, was already a star. And sometimes I served as his audience, his spellbound fan, and I was being reminded of that.

"I'm sorry," Farrell said. "I spoke for both of us, which I had no right to do. You could become a client of Eric's agency. So should I get my high-minded ass back in there, and claim some momentary aneurysm, and renegotiate?"

"No. Never. I would hate you. I'd hate me."

"And perhaps the most depressing facet, of this morass," Farrell said, "is that Eric's gay. I mean, I presumed Drake wouldn't have a clue, about what was going on."

"Hold on," I said. "He is Welsh."

"But Eric is really . . ." Farrell searched for the words. "I'm trying not to despise him, because he wanted all this to work out and he's not wrong, about any of it. But he was still doing his agency's bidding. And smearing a chipper, we're-all-in-this-together, fighting-the-good-fight smiley face on things."

As we drove back to the beach, I brooded: How was Eric going to spin this, to his industry cronies? Would he tell the truth and repeat what Farrell had said, or imply that negotiations had disintegrated because Farrell wasn't right for the part? And how might this affect my career? I was out to my parents, and I thought of myself as being out to the world, but when I'd been interviewed, before *Enter Hamlet* opened, I'd never dropped a word about being gay, because no one had asked. Being gay was an open secret, a subject for smutty off-the-record innuendo and coded provisos. I was political, but aside from straggling through a few gay pride parades, and living in New York, and being equipped to compare productions of *Mame* (the original Angela Lansbury sensation versus the less sizzling Angela Lansbury revival), and sucking cock, how gay was I? I hadn't even recognized Karyn Barstow, not right away.

Sprawled in Cary and Randolph's living room, Farrell wasn't just reconciled to the morning's outcome, but jaunty, as if he'd been pardoned by the governor.

"You really didn't want it, did you?" I asked him.

"No. But I didn't not want it. It's just—it felt like I'd polished off an especially colossal ice cream sundae, and then someone asked if I'd like another, with chocolate sauce and sprinkles. Which might make me vomit, but still—more ice cream!"

The phone rang. It was Brett. "Hey," he said, and whenever he opened a call with "hey," he was about to either wheedle for a favor, present painful news, or craft an especially accomplished lie. In LA, these are often the same thing.

"I talked to Bruce," he said, "and here it is: You've delivered two drafts and a polish, which is what your contract called for. And they're not renewing it."

There it was again: that hollowness, that vision of a stick figure, plummeting through my stomach swinging a hatchet and cackling mindlessly. That harrowing descent into failure, that drowning on dry land, choking on my own inadequacy.

I wasn't talented enough or experienced enough or anything whatsoever, and I never would be. I was replaceable. I'd been essentially fired, only, because this was Hollywood, the word was outlawed. In Hollywood being dead made you "unavailable." Having cancer was "taking some time for myself." Getting fired was not being renewed.

"Why?" I asked, and Brett was straightforward.

"Because they're all dicks," he said. "And because you've been flailing, which isn't your fault. Because they keep asking you to do things you don't want to do. And because when studio people get nervous, they fire the least powerful person in the room."

"But it's my movie," I said. "It was my idea."

"Of course, and contractually, if they make the movie, you'll still get a cut of the profits. And I told them, that even if we get some other writers to punch up the script, we should seriously think about bringing you back. Which they were up for. Which means nothing."

"Okay."

"Talk to Florence. Tell her what happened. She's got a lawyer, right?"

"I think so."

"And Nate, I'm so sorry about this. It's truly fucked up."

He'd stood up for me, but the movie was his project as well. He had his own contract and a still uncertain career. I couldn't hate Brett, but this was, at heart, a Hollywood relationship, meaning, as with Eric Nord-stadt, the food chain was carnivorous. And I was festering to lash out at someone.

"And Brett," I said, "you'll be getting a call, from Eric Nordstadt, who's going to be pissed. Because Farrell turned it down. The rom-com."

"What? Why?"

I took a fleeting satisfaction in knowing something Brett didn't know. Nothing could knock him off-balance, but I had. I'd acquired the most valuable plunder in Brett's, or anyone else's, Hollywood, even beyond money or status: information.

"Eric asked Farrell to basically stop being gay. To never be seen with me and to only talk about his marriage. They want a straight movie star and Farrell said no."

"Whoa. Man."

Brett was staggered but computing. Brett was gay, but like me, he worked in a behind-the-scenes capacity, which was far less burdened. Fewer people care, because audience members jabber through the cred-its. My relatives asked, "So you write the words?" While Brett's aunt Syl-via had queried, "So, producing—do you go to an office?" But Brett was soaking up the Hollywood manual and eclipsing every fellow student. He wanted, even more than Harwell Covington, to win, and as with Harwell, Farrell's noncompliance baffled him, unless he could interpret it as a strategy toward greater leverage. Brett also resented anyone else in charge, and often sought to eviscerate such people, so Farrell's insolence might tickle him.

And unlike Harwell, Brett had higher motives. Both men crushed their enemies, but Brett had heroes (including Carol Channing: he was a fellow show queen, another humanizing factor. When Brett obsessed over theater, he became, not a calculating kingpin-in-training, but a besotted fan).

"Give Farrell my best," Brett said. "And I'll be in touch with you. We'll talk."

This was how Brett stepped away from every conversation, with an enticement, a door left ajar. All the angles.

"Was that Brett?" Farrell asked. I'd taken the call in our bedroom.

"Yup. And I'm pretty sure—no, that's not true, it's a fact. I've been fired."

Farrell took this in, and said, "Thank fucking God."

"Why?"

"Because those people, at Clarion, they were driving you mad. They're idiots, and you were listening to them. You were being paid to listen to them. I loved the script, your script, your original script. But if you keep trying to please them, you'll slit your throat."

I slumped onto the couch beside Farrell and he put his arm around me. "We're both such irretrievable losers," he said.

"You're not. You made a choice."

"Which everyone out here will think was the most gargantuan mistake of my life. And you've made a choice as well. You're choosing sanity. Because we can't stay here."

Cary and Randolph's home was sunny and theatrical, a well-appointed backdrop for a 1930s romp. Cary and Randolph had carved out a life for themselves, together, until greater forces, and their own ambition, had intervened. That was the Hollywood trade-off. Pleasure interrupted. High-wire adulation. Everything at a price, which almost everyone is willing to pay. Because the houses are so nice.

We made arrangements to fly back to New York, because, aside from everything else, we had a memorial to attend. Terrence Whitby, our classmate from Yale and my fellow cater-waiter, had died, after an illness lasting less than two weeks. He was our age.

THE
LIMITS
OF STYLE

22

Terry Whitby had been the first Black member of Yale's most prestigious a cappella singing group, the Whiffenpoofs, thanks to his miraculous tenor voice and a long-delayed, work-in-progress minimization of the group's bigotry (women were still prohibited). Racism was an everyday factor. Terry had told me that when the Whiffs, as they were known, had toured the South, in certain cities he'd be housed with a local Black family, for safety, while the other guys had reservations at a hotel. Terry might've been the first openly gay Whiff as well, but that was a tougher call.

Gossip, via Jackson, whispered that the Elizabethan Club, an on-campus literary appreciation society housed in a small clapboard building, with a vault containing original Shakespearean folios, had been founded in the 1920s by Cole Porter, after Cole's boyfriend had been rejected by a similar organization.

Terry and I had done plays and musicals at school, and traded shifts and inside information about our coworkers at so many banquets and galas. ("That one looks like a lumberjack," he'd once divulged, "but in the sack, I swear to God, he just wanted to be spanked. I finally told him, 'I know you've been a very bad boy but I'm exhausted.'") Terry was haughty and elegant. There'd been rumors of an extended fling with a much older, esteemed American composer and conductor. The last I'd heard, Terry was living with an age-appropriate boyfriend in Chelsea and overseeing the composer/conductor's archive. Terry also did a club act, of standards and R&B. In a less raucous era, he might've been an in-demand entertainer, at the Carlyle or the Rainbow Room. Terry's handsome, preppy bearing had a retro quality. He'd once appeared in a Ralph Lauren ad with a yellow Shetland sweater draped over his shoulders (this was after Ralph had begun integrating his campaigns).

The memorial was held, appropriately enough, in the great room of the Yale Club in Midtown. Terry's fellow Whiffenpoofs had reunited, in white tie, facing the room in a semicircle, with a space left between an alto and a bass, for the departed Terry. Six years after graduation, their harmonies could still enchant, even if some of their formal wear had to be let out.

"I love hearing them," Jess whispered to me. "I know they're a remnant of the worst cultural imperialism, but they sound divine."

"But what did Terry die of?" asked Farrell—we'd heard accounts of a rare cancer or a lung infection.

"I talked to his boyfriend," said Ariadne. "He said it was bird flu."

"Bird flu?" I asked. It sounded like an exotic fever a ruined belle would perish from in a Tennessee Williams play, or what an American heiress abroad might succumb to, after a chilly midnight in the Colosseum, in Henry James.

"No one's ever heard of it," Ariadne said. "I asked Jake Tiernan over there, he's a resident at Mount Sinai, and he says it's mostly been found in sparrows and hawks, and that no one ever dies of it."

"Look at Andrew," Jackson said, about Terry's private-school-tutor boyfriend, across the room. "I told him how sorry I was, but I didn't want to pry. He said it was completely unexpected, and that Terry was only correctly diagnosed the day before he died."

"Jesus," I said. Andrew was standing with Terry's straight identical twin brother, who'd become an eerie tribute, as if Terry were taking a final bow. Andrew seemed frail, which wouldn't be unexpected after such a bewildering loss, but he coughed several times. Later he told me,

"I'm not sure if I have what Terry had, but my doctor put me on antibiotics, so he says I'll be fine."

The Whiffs closed with a medley of what had been Terry's solos, delivering a final, wistful "Someone to Watch Over Me."

Farrell took my hand, as I was blinded with tears, because Terry had died so young, and because the memorial was exactly what he would've wanted, a Gershwin-blessed cocktail bash with an attractive Ivy League guest list.

A week later, Andrew died at St. Vincent's Hospital, a few blocks from my apartment.

"Did you see it?" asked Ariadne, when we'd all gathered the next day at Charlie's, a theater district hangout. *Enter Hamlet* had stumbled along for another month and closed, but I was still officially a Broadway playwright. The play hadn't been a notorious flop, with a framed poster on the restaurant's wall of shame, so I was compartmentalizing, and my friends were respecting that. As Farrell had told me, "Get over yourself."

"See what?" asked Jess.

"Of course I saw it," said Jackson, "and I've doubled my potassium supplements."

"See what?" Jess demanded.

"The article in the *Times*," Farrell told her, "what are they calling it? GRID or something?"

"Which stands for Gay-Related Immune Deficiency," said Ariadne. "There've been one hundred and thirty-eight cases and sixty-eight deaths so far. I bet that's what Terry had."

"I'm not following," said Jess.

"It's some sort of disease," I said. "The doctors don't know almost anything about it except that it's targeting gay men, especially in New York."

"It's like when everyone started wearing those see-through plastic belts," said Jackson. "I'm sorry! I shouldn't be joking! But I wanted to tell every gay man, 'Take off that belt. You're not a twelve-year-old girl at a mall.'"

"And they don't know what it is?" asked Jess. "How do you get it?"

"They don't know," said Farrell.

"Although the article talked about gay guys being promiscuous," said Ariadne.

"Gay guys?" I said, in mock disbelief.

"Promiscuous?" echoed Farrell, with even more incomprehension.

The restaurant was packed with actors, directors, and every breed of theater rat, along with in-the-know theatergoers, peering around for cast members from the shows they'd just seen. It was an atmosphere I loved, fizzing with confidentially exchanged scuttlebutt and gushingly over-the-top compliments, as a mutual support remedy for the chronically unemployed. The waitstaff was recruited from out-of-work chorus boys and girls (as they were still called, for a gum-snapping 1940s zest). Every so often, at the lofty mâitre d's discretion, this talented crew plopped down their trays and burst into a musical selection from a currently running hit; tonight's treat was the opening number from *The Best Little Whorehouse in Texas*, executed with verve, flapping aprons, and a choreographed twirling of dish towels.

The effect was unexpected, stirring, and met with a hearty ovation from everyone in the place. It also changed the subject.

Farrell was making progress on his Park Avenue renovation, but sleeping at my place. That night in bed, I asked him, "Should we be worried about that thing in the *Times*?"

"I don't know. I don't think so. It was upsetting, but it seems contained, like a cluster. And I get suspicious when they talk about targeting gay men."

I agreed because I wanted to agree.

Marcus Randall died three months later. He was a universal crush, a Byronic actor who looked morosely irresistible in his trademark black turtlenecks. Everyone, of every gender, wanted Marcus, and he'd behold his devotees with rueful pity, as if confessing, "I'm sorry to be so moodily captivating, but it's out of my control."

Marcus had advanced from playing murderous, scarred off-Broadway delinquents, to pocket watch–wearing, top-hatted gentlemen in Shaw revivals at Lincoln Center, to prominent, often nominated roles in quirky film festival hits. His art tormented him. He'd once told Farrell and me, over drinks, that, "I have no idea if I'm talented or not, I feel like this despicable fraud. Some nights I can barely step onstage, because I'd like to refund the audience's money. I'm a mediocre pretender, fooling everyone."

"Marcus," said Farrell, "when you say things like that, you really should be holding a skull and standing on a turret, with the wind and rain in your hair."

"I would adore that," Marcus admitted.

Marcus didn't mind being chided, as long as the conversation circled around him, so we delved into his bisexual renown.

"Do you like having sex with men and women equally?" I asked.

"I don't mean to. I don't want to. But they wait there, at the stage door, in the late evening chill, with these beseeching eyes. And they ask what it feels like to be me, and sometimes having sex is the only way to end such a painful line of questioning."

"Marcus," said Farrell, "do you ever lounge on a park bench with a book of Yeats by your side, lowering your head an essential two inches so your bangs will flop onto your forehead just so?"

Marcus gave us his profile and murmured, "At times."

Everyone predicted stardom for Marcus, which he was worthy of, but he developed purplish lesions over his neck and half of his face, and moved back to his family's home in Massachusetts for treatment, and died the day after he got there, of pneumonia. He was thrity-two.

That July, Farrell and I were invited for a weekend at a sprawling beachfront home on Fire Island, by an older couple, who arrayed their lavish, glass-walled summer place with younger guests, not so much lecherously as to unveil their latest raw silk batik fabrics from Thailand; their import business had paid for the house and an Upper East Side brownstone. I'd been to Fire Island before. A year out of college, utterly broke, I'd dance all night at the Pavilion—the central club—with Ariadne, and pass out on the beach. One August, while Farrell was in Wichita, I took a quarter share at a party house, which meant two weekends in a claustrophobic, cedar-paneled, windowless room with bunk beds. It had been like sleeping in a humidor with three strangers and their damp towels.

But the sacrifice had paid off. The air on Fire Island is intoxicating, an almost visible ribbon of sex and indolence. I'd never been able to write during my time there, as the ambience dictates only leisure. It's an oasis and a hive; I'd once been lent someone's shack for a weekend, and awoken to find porn stars splashing in a neighboring pool, taking a dip between filming hard-core scenes. The island overwhelms and frightens some newcomers, through untrammeled gayness. But the primitive luxury and languid raunch had ravished me. Unlike LA, Fire Island isn't a company town masquerading as Sodom. It's a bauble, what God made on the eighth day, just for Himself and His lazily erotic angels.

This was Farrell's first visit, so I did my due diligence: we took the Long Island Railroad to Sayville; then a boisterous, disco-blasting van to the dock; then a packed ferry to the island itself. Farrell and I found seats on the open, uppermost deck, with the salt spray in our faces. "This is invigorating," said Farrell, as we neared the harbor, "it's like how gay men first came to America."

As we disembarked, a crowd in Speedos and sarongs rushed to fling themselves onto their friends. This ritual lacked only a young Judy Garland, in MGM's *The Harvey Girls*, trilling a jubilant "On the Atchison, Topeka and the Sante Fe" as her train chugged into a small, turn-of-the-century Arizona train station. But there were also three guys manning a card table, handing out Xeroxed fliers with information about what had been labeled the gay plague, the fliers advocating "safer sexual practices." Some partygoers shunned these offerings, and a few grabbed a flier, crumpled it, and shoved it into a garbage bin. Farrell took a flier and said, "This is interesting. It's like landing on a tropical isle but being asked to wear a hazmat suit."

The house was half a mile off, by boardwalk, as we pulled our belongings in a red wagon. A man ambled toward us, naked except for Ray-Bans and a Betty Boop tattoo on his hipbone, dangling in one hand, alongside his cock, a menthol cigarette and a whiskey sour in a plastic cup. "The cigarette is a tribute to his divorced mom," Farrell decided.

Cars are banned in the Pines (the Island's most upscale community), and the larger homes are wondrous, implausible boxes with multiple guest rooms and gourmet kitchens. They're a gay man's equivalent of Barbie's Dreamhouse, constructed only for play. I told Farrell, "This whole place is a barrier island, and every twenty-five years a hurricane levels every square inch." I'd once seen a hunk, surveying the damage after a storm, during which beachfront fiberglass swimming pools had been washed out to sea, drifting through the surf like immense conch shells. The hunk had crouched at the top of a flight of wooden steps, which now led to nothing. He'd remarked, to the debris, "Don't mess with Miss Ocean."

"Hello, sweetheart," Farrell said, as a deer wobbled toward him, licking his hand. The deer population had undergone a breeding spree, well fed off leftover brie and scallops, from alfresco bacchanals on the dunes. This deer and Farrell commiserated; they belonged on the cover of a children's book about vacationing wildlife.

That night, after a feast, but preceding a nap, drug-taking, and the 2 a.m. march to the disco, Farrell and I lounged with our hosts' other guests, on white canvas–upholstered sofas, stacked with cushions, with a view of the waves. Fire Island is one of the few spots where New Yorkers can scan the stars in the clearest night sky, as a design element, like our host's lineup of costly, citrus-scented Rigaud candles.

"So what about this?" asked a guest, brandishing the flier. "Should we be panicking? Or even worse, thinking about the Hamptons?"

"I've heard that only bottoms get it," said someone else.

"And that porn stars and hookers are immune," said his buddy.

"A guy at my gym was sick," added our second host, "but he's back and he seems okay."

"I won't stop having sex," vowed Chad, in a taut gray T-shirt that read "Property of UCLA Swim Team." This was the height of a craze for workout and military gear, with the dream of resembling a gymnast or Navy Seal, in hopes of attracting one. Every gay man on the island was in faded gray, a camouflage print, or anything marked "Lifeguard" (even on guys who couldn't swim).

"We're all going to get it," said Farrell, not threateningly but not backing off. "And we're all going to die."

Everyone stared at him. "I said that," he amended, "because it's what we're all thinking. And I wanted to hear what it sounded like out loud."

At sometime after 5 a.m., Farrell and I, shirtless and dripping with sweat, took a much needed break on a balcony outside the Pavilion, leaning on the railing overlooking the bay, where decent-sized yachts were moored and rich older widows and their interior designers could be seen through the windows—portholes?—playing backgammon, kept awake by the booming music from the club.

"Farrell," I asked, "do you really think we're going to get sick?"

He put his arm around my shoulders and said, "No. I won't allow it."

I wanted to believe him, but like every gay man in New York, San Francisco, and Los Angeles, along with other gay capitals around the world, I was experiencing a constant, jagged pulse of fear and anxiety, from both the known, meaning hospitalized friends, and the unknowable.

In 1985, Farrell and I turned thirty, a few months apart. Brett had been hiring me for rewrites on other movies, and Farrell had finished his renovation and begun to bankroll fledgling organizations dedicated to battling what was now the AIDS crisis (for Acquired Immune Deficiency Syndrome). The global deaths and infections were in the hundreds of thousands, met by deliberate government disinterest.

Reagan wouldn't mention the plague, despite wife Nancy's gay pals, one of whom, Jackson opined, had retaliated by designing her a humiliating pair of spangled black velvet evening knickers.

Farrell and I no longer went dancing, but not from our advanced ages; in gay New York, thirty was both doddering and sophomore year. We were like so many people, hunkering down, subsisting on unverifiable medical rumors and escalating rage at the world's indifference, because the disease was affecting primarily gay men, drug addicts, and people in Africa, or, as Farrell put it, collectively, "the help." We settled on a mutual, solitary birthday celebration on Park Avenue.

Farrell had eliminated walls and fustiness, not for a faux-loft cliché, but as an expanse of austere, imaginative comfort, a touch reminiscent of his New Haven townhouse. His father had sold the Hockney, but Farrell had bought it back, and it held pride of place in the central living area, like a hunting trophy, or a window into gay happiness. There's something sun-drenched and uncompromising about Hockney's work: he depicts life at its most shimmering and evanescent, as a dream that can't last, except, radiantly, on canvas. I treasured Hockney's pictures as defiantly gay, as if he couldn't be bothered with prejudice, or transcended it, which is rare.

. In the style of the moment, Farrell had installed low, black leather seating, recessed lighting, and a stark, modern, white marble slab of a fireplace. Farrell wasn't a decorator or an architect, but more of a movie director whose medium was his own surroundings. When I'd stay over, I'd feel politically guilty, undeniably poor, and suitably impressed, in equal measure, but mostly, because the apartment was such a potent expression of Farrell's taste, I'd value his satisfaction in using his family's money to catalyze a home they'd never understand and might even hate.

On our birthday night, we indulged in coconut cake and champagne. As a couple, we'd set a rhythm and never strayed, because we were scared of the virus, but more due to our steady pleasure in each other. We'd been together, intermittently, for over ten years. "Do you still love me?" I asked, shattering that cardinal commandment, of never asking a question where the answer might devastate me.

"Are you asking me that," Farrell replied, "because you still want to be here, or because you don't want to die alone, or because of the heated marble floor in our bathroom and the perfectly calibrated water pressure in the shower?"

"Are those different things?"

"Do you still love me?" Farrell asked.

"Yes. It's the only thing I know."

I was being dramatic, or at least theatrical, but I didn't care. Our relationship was intuitive and eccentric, and that may have been the key to its survival. We'd been aggressively undermined by Harwell, separated for years, and almost swept away in the Los Angeles undertow. We were improvising; this was the exhilaration and the necessity inherent in gay coupledom. I liked never being quite sure of where Farrell and I might awake, and what we'd be wearing.

But our singular equation had never accounted for illness, let alone death. Farrell and I finished our birthday cake in silence, thanks to a potentially uninvited guest: AIDS had become a hideous given. Were we both infected? There wasn't a reliable test. This was life during wartime, with disfigurement and loss on everyone's calendar, along with inventive memorials, daily hospital visits, demonstrations at City Hall, and 2 a.m. phone calls from people seeking reassurance about chronic nosebleeds. So many friends were already gone, but I couldn't bear to cross out their entries in my address book. Their names and phone numbers were a scribbled legacy. If this was a gay plague, it demanded a gay response. As Jackson liked to say, paying homage to any really effective red dress, "It's a fuck-you with flair."

I returned Farrell's gaze. "When I said no to Eric Nordstadt," he told me, "here's what was happening: I'd lost you once, to my father's machinations, and I won't let that happen again."

"But . . ."

"Of course. And it's not that we won't obsess over what's going on, but we can resist. We've had enemies before."

"But, Farrell . . ."

"I'll only say this once, so I hope you've reached a sufficient echelon of maturity."

"What?"

"I love you more than I love my vintage Murano glass table lamps, with the subtle gold flecks."

"You don't mean that."

He took my hand. I was so lucky to have found Farrell, and to keep finding him. He was my first line of defense, against my own whining insecurities, the world's hatefulness, and the ever-encroaching shadows devouring men like us.

We made love, both tempting death and spurning it. Farrell getting fucked in that sling had been directed, in part, at his father. Now, as Farrell fucked me, I was determined not to see the skull beneath his handsome face, or have my moans become sobs. We were Nate and Farrell, and being gay, and in love, and having sex, wasn't a solution to anything, but it was the life raft we clung to, as the waves broke over our heads. Best of all, I could spite my rivals, those imperious Italian lamps on the bedside tables. "He's mine," I told them, as they sneered. "For now."

That year, Rock Hudson died of AIDS, although this wasn't officially announced. But his polite truck driver good looks and silky, tell-me-where-it-hurts voice had been ravaged, as witnessed by fans of *Dynasty*, the hit series about a conniving ultra-wealthy family, or as Farrell had called them, "the Covingtons with sequined shoulder pads." Gay men had long known that Hudson was a fellow traveler and suspected his illness, but the tabloids were sniping about his kissing a costar onscreen, even after Doris Day had defended and embraced Rock publicly. We loved Doris, although, as Jackson noted, "We've always loved Doris."

"I wonder how Eric Nordstadt feels about Rock," Farrell asked. Certain stars, especially Elizabeth Taylor and Madonna, were rallying to the cause, but they were often alone in their outspoken efforts. As Brett told me, "No one's ever sick in Hollywood—they'd rather have people think it's botched plastic surgery." He added that Eric Nordstadt had died, although his obituary cited leukemia, at thirty-eight. This wasn't necessarily a lie. People were dying not specifically of AIDS, but of the illnesses their compromised, skeletal bodies could no longer ward off.

Eric's death dissolved any residual bad feelings. He'd been deeply conflicted, but he didn't deserve to vanish, and Brett said that during his last months, Eric had used his Hollywood contacts to raise money for research. Eric's ashes had been tossed into the surf of his beloved Santa Monica beach. I pictured Cary and Randolph blessing his memory and cursing the plague. The rising toll among young, recently healthy men was, shockingly, no longer shocking. Only the public response could horrify.

AIDS, many evangelists were thundering, was God's punishment, and I questioned what Mother Gregory would make of this. I doubted she'd approve. The God I believed in, my personal deity, spent His time making things, which felt intrinsically gay, as if humanity were a crafts project reliant on pipe cleaners, glue, and brightly colored jumbo yarn, as if God were present in Jackson's resplendent costume sketches, stapled with crêpe georgette swatches and braided gold trim. Or was God a triple threat, a heavenly hyphenate, a writer-director-designer in one? And yet, while God had the taste to invent gay people, he'd fashioned their doom, and that was when I sensibly stopped thinking about God.

But gayness remained a central fact of my life, encompassing Farrell, New York, and the theater, everything that defined me. Gayness was under the most ferocious attack, and I wasn't sure where to enlist, how to arm myself, or who was in charge of our side.

A year later, at 11:12 on a Tuesday night, Farrell and I were watching the news in bed at his place. Farrell was wearing gym shorts, and I noticed a small dark red, almost black mark or bruise, on his shin. Before I could say anything, without turning away from the television, Farrell said, "Yes it is."

23

Farrell had been to his doctor on Madison Avenue. He imparted this, his eyes on the Channel 7 *Eyewitness News* gay weatherman predicting an unseasonably warm November.

I couldn't talk. I'd foreseen this happening to Farrell or to me or to both of us, but my reasoned anticipation wasn't swaddling me in any way. The worst outcomes unreeled through my brain in a hyperspeed blur, of agony, antiseptic hallways, ravaged emaciation, a gasping death, and an inadequate, unfinishable eulogy. I shut my eyes and snapped them open, as a means of stopping the tape, and existing only for this second, for this nightmarish yet commonplace hurdle, for this offhand announcement of Farrell's diagnosis.

"Were you going to tell me?" I asked.

"I just did."

"So you were tested?"

Testing had become possible, a punishing innovation, since any treatments were feeble at best.

"Yes. They took blood."

"And?"

"I'm positive. And progressing."

He shut off the TV and turned to me, saying, "I'm going to deal with this. But there's one thing I'd like you to do, and that's get tested yourself. Dr. Jarvis can do it."

"Okay."

I got out of bed and went into the bathroom. I didn't have to pee, so I walked right back out.

"I agree, I should get tested. On one condition."

"What?"

"That you let me come to the doctor with you, and be a part of this."

"No. Absolutely not."

I should have respected Farrell's decision and his privacy, for the sake of his dignity and mental health. But we were spoiling for an unbridled, completely inappropriate, all-bets-are-off fight, because I had a million things to say, which of course I shouldn't, but fuck it.

"Farrell?"

"Yes?"

"I want to be there. I want to go through this with you. I can't go crazy worrying about what you're not telling me."

"Too bad. This is my illness."

"What if I have it, too?"

"Then you can make your own choices."

I strode into the bathroom and out again, like some crazed figure on a cuckoo clock, chiming every fifteen seconds.

"Why? Why can't I come with you? Why don't you trust me?"

"Because I love you dearly, and you mean well, but you can't handle this. I'm barely handling it. And before you answer, maybe you should make another bathroom circuit."

I almost did, but went scorched earth, billowing mushroom cloud instead: "You don't think I can handle this? Fuck you!"

Maddeningly calm, Farrell said, "Darling, the worst things you've dealt with are bad reviews, studio executives, and standing next to me. But this is somewhat more dire. And you're not equipped."

I'd never been so ballistically aggrieved, like a cartoon rabbit whose head had burst into flames, shot into outer space, and whooshed back to earth. Farrell was partially right, in that I don't express anger well. My voice squeaks, my eyes bulge, and my gestures tend toward jazz hands, or what Farrell called "neo-Fosse shimmy mitts."

"Excuse me?" I squealed. "EXCUSE ME? First of all, as for my standing next to you, there was one time, and I've never told you this, to spare your precious monumental ego, but we were on Fire Island and a bartender told me I should dump you and he gave me his number and said brunettes are a billion times hotter and that he really liked my nose! And as for the rest of it, I don't care if I can't handle it! Because I'm going to handle it! Because you're the love of my life and if that doesn't mean anything, then just FUCK YOU!"

My rage was free-floating, blasting at AIDS, the Almighty, and the Reagan administration, but especially at a denunciation Farrell had previously slung at me, his go-to, cheap-shot attack: my status as an emotional lightweight, a tragedy tourist, a coddled baby chick unprepared to "handle" raw life on the open prairie, or in an emergency room.

"Would you care to hit me?" Farrell inquired. "In your baroque Jewish running-away-from-home-by-sitting-in-the-basement-with-your-Barbie-doll-in-a-shopping-bag, theater-boy fashion? With the bloodcurdling violence of someone who's owned more than one cheap mirrored music box with a rotating plastic ballerina?"

Why had I ever told him any of that? Or let my mother make copies of the photos? Or asked him to win me another identical music box at a carnival ring-toss game?

"Yes I would like to hit you! And I'm going to! I'm going to hit you because you're being such an unbelievably spoiled, snotty rich white boy, I-have-AIDS-so-I'm-special ASSHOLE!"

As Farrell stayed on the bed, serenely observing me, I hoisted one of his prized vintage Italian glass lamps over my head, swearing, "I'll do it! I mean it!"

"You wouldn't dare," said Farrell, his voice trembling.

"Yes I would! And I will! And let's just remember, this lamp is one of a pair! And if I smash it, you'll never find another. You'll be left with ONE LAMP! Nobody wants ONE LAMP!"

"Give me that!" Farrell shouted, moving toward me.

"No! Not unless you let me come with you and be a part of this! Otherwise this lamp is over! And you know that malachite box on the coffee table in the living room? Out the window! And the Hockney?"

"Fuck you, Nate, I'm serious! These are my things and you have no right!"

"Well, you are my thing and I have every right! So you'd better fucking choose!"

I savagely aimed the lamp at the door frame. The collision would be catastrophic. Farrell was out of bed, lunging for the lamp as I held it farther out of reach. "DON'T!" he yelled, in a strangled screech I'd never from heard him, the supplicant keen of a mother begging a lawless warlord for her infant's life.

"So I go with you?" I said, pretending to lose my grip on the hostage lamp, then catching it.

"Fine!" said Farrell, twitching with helpless, indignant ire. "Give it to me." I moved slowly, because we'd reached a volatile tipping point. I deposited the lamp in his arms. He cradled it and spoke to it, in a furious croon, telling the lamp, with regard to me, "I hate him so much."

Farrell returned the lamp gently to the bedside table. Both the shade and the base would require months of therapy to feel safe, as the rugs chortled.

"You said I can come with you," I reiterated. "And I know where that lamp lives."

Farrell regarded me from a million miles away, rooted in the land of the sick, the HIV-positive, the statistic in the *Newsweek* article. It dawned on me, and I'd been boneheaded not to identify this sooner, but Farrell wasn't frightened of having AIDS or even of dying. More than any of this, he loathed being pitied. By mauling his lamp, I'd drafted our policy statement. We would be ourselves, and not the wan, brave, heartrendingly stooped terminal patient and the stalwart nurse taking his elbow in the weak autumn light of Central Park. We might very well become those people, but we'd add quotation marks and better scarves.

Farrell opened his arms and I held on to him, as our breathing

synched and we silently mapped out the clichés and vowed to never
utter them.

"If you ever touch my lamp again," Farrell hissed in my ear, "I will give
you AIDS."

Being rich supplied Farrell with quality healthcare. Dr. Jarvis had been
in the forefront of AIDS triage, and he'd been appointed as the head of an
infectious disease unit at Lenox Hill Hospital. He was gay, in his forties,
and had lost over a thousand patients to the disease. "He's a hardnose,"
Farrell warned me.

I had my blood drawn, but the test results would take a week. I bar-
gained with God: Would Jesus like house seats? I name-dropped Sally,
as if her good works reflected well on me. I prayed that I'd die before
Farrell (while imagining the pictorial depth of his grief). I disputed the
test's reliability, and went for stretches of forgetting I'd taken it, until I'd
walk past the building of a dead friend, count the windows across the
third story to his (former) apartment, and be extradited to Hell. For gay
men, getting tested had become another spin of the New York roulette
wheel, like riding the subway late at night or eating anything from a
falafel cart. But in not yet knowing I was unscathed, in the limbo of the
unsure.

On the day my results were due, Farrell said that after his test, he'd
asked Dr. Jarvis to hold up two envelopes and let Farrell point to one,
but Dr. Jarvis had rebuffed him. If I was positive, Dr. Jarvis's nurse would
schedule a consultation, but instead, Dr. Jarvis called me himself: "You're
lucky. You're negative."

I asked how this was possible and Dr. Jarvis said, "We still have no
idea, of who's more vulnerable or even the incubation period. But you
can seroconvert, so you and Farrell will need to be vigilant, and use condoms and maybe just cool it as much as you can."

When I told Farrell my status, he said, "Thank God," hugged me, and
added, "So every time we've had sex, you didn't really mean it."

I was thankful and relieved, of course, but numb. How had I es-
caped? Was there any larger meaning? I felt the same as I had a day
earlier, or a lifetime earlier, yet disconnected, as if the results had been

switched or I'd rigged the lottery. Mostly I remembered Mother Gregory's credo about being of service. I wasn't sure, aside from my dedication to Farrell, and my admiration for Sally, what form my becoming useful might take.

That night, Farrell stuck to his side of the bed, as if an unbreachable wall had gone up. I wouldn't force myself on him, as proof of my heedless valor, and Dr. Jarvis had cautioned us. We were both wide awake. But every night couldn't become sero-discordant melodrama or a shuddering crime scene. I put my hand on Farrell's shoulder and left it there. I turned my body toward his. We spooned, like Amish elders during an unheated January, or a gay couple in AIDS-era Manhattan. Once again, we redrew our relationship. God willing, we had time, to sort out what we'd be comfortable with. For tonight, even tentative physical contact was a necessity. We were still us; and as with Harwell's odiousness or the lure of potential movie stardom or the calculus of three-ways, we'd take nothing for granted.

We couldn't pretend nothing had changed. I was grateful that we'd come of age during those years of limitless freedom, of reaching for each other, or sometimes another man, without terror. AIDS wasn't a punishment, but it was a demarcation. A scraped knee, a shared towel, or a kiss was no longer without consequences. As Dr. Jarvis said, transmission was a minefield. Was the man I loved a time bomb? Was I a traitor? Were we being buried alive, by microbes and fate, which was a more operatic, and therefore gay, word for death? Only civilians asked these questions.

Aside from the lesion on his leg, Farrell's health was steady, and Dr. Jarvis told us that rates of progression varied. He said that Farrell should continue working out, eating well, and avoiding stress (he joined in the laughter after this third tip). As we walked home from an appointment a few weeks later, Farrell said, "It's like being told you'll be executed, someday. So clear your schedule and keep in touch."

I wrote, submerging myself in plot and dialogue and then surfacing and trying not to scream. I compelled myself not to hover over Farrell and surreptitiously inspect his body for fresh marks of illness. I wouldn't treat him as a patient. Farrell began researching restoration-worthy historical properties around the world. We attended meetings of ACT UP, the activist group that demanded the fast-tracking of experimental drug trials and funding from the city and federal governments. The group convened every week and sometimes more in the gay community center on 13th Street, a converted schoolhouse. Our first session was in a large, open, crowded room, with members jammed onto bleachers, like a jabbering, ferociously agitated pep rally. I saw lawyers with document-packed briefcases, who loosened their rep ties an eighth of an inch because they'd become guerilla fighters; club kids from the Paradise Garage in neon patent leather hot pants and shredded black T-shirts with the motto "Silence=Death" in Pepto-Bismol pink; leather guys from The Hole in painstakingly frayed, sleeveless, open, plaid flannel shirts, their brass nipple rings glinting; chorus boys from Charlie's in their rehearsal sweats; drag queens in full regalia, committed to both the cause and their fans; transgender schoolteachers and Upper West Side shrinks and lesbian accountants in their suits and no-nonsense blouses; every conceivable gay New York citizen, many the more frivolous types, the party planners and window display queens who were rarely thought of as militant, but who fought harder than anyone.

Ariadne was running the meeting as a facilitator. Her wired rancor suited frontline politics. She quieted the room by saying, "Shut the fuck up," in her measured, commanding voice, but obeyed Robert's Rules of Order, which meant that everyone who'd signed up on her clipboard was allotted a three-minute opportunity to speak, about anything, and did.

"Seth Bromstein," said Ariadne, with dread, as Seth and five other Young Socialists swarmed the microphone. This group was notorious for attending every meeting of any organization in town, from Virginia Woolf centennials to Parents Without Partners, and hogging the agenda.

"We must obliterate every vestige of the capitalist patriarchy!" shouted Seth, as people began to boo, not out of disagreement but because they'd seen Seth before. "We must disrupt the economic supply chain and fertilize all people with the rich, dark soil of community leadership!"

"Thank you, Seth," said Ariadne, grabbing the mic. Her glare sent Seth and his minions scuttling. "We've got a report from the events committee. Todd and Sarah?"

Two ACT UP regulars took the stage and everyone refocused. "We're planning a zap for sometime next month in North Carolina," said Todd, a deceptively harmless-looking guy in a limp button-down, a nose stud, and fatigues.

"We're making a huge condom," said Sarah, equally dweeby in overalls, pigtails, and a thermal underwear shirt. "We're going to drape it over Jesse Helms's house."

This drew raucous cheers, since Helms was a viciously anti-gay senator who'd proposed to halt any funding for AIDS, a disease he'd called "the wages of homosexual sin."

After asking for volunteers, this pair passed the mic to Dr. Jarvis, in his white lab coat. The speakers were divided between firebrands and tireless but frantic professionals. Dr. Jarvis was a proponent of reason and methodical results, but the plague, and the country's resistant power structure, were thwarting him. "This is about money," he said, straining to harness his yearslong frustration, "for, at a bare minimum, twenty more beds. The hospitals are overflowing and people are dying in the emergency rooms, so anyone with access to funding, and lots of it, please, please contact me."

As we walked back to my place, Farrell asked, "I'm not sure we'd be especially helpful in North Carolina, are you?"

"Maybe not. The people on that committee know what they're doing."

Farrell had donated hundreds of thousands of dollars to GMHC, amfAR, and Dr. Jarvis's programs, but he was searching to do more. The next day, as we rode in his Park Avenue elevator, he gave Gretchen Carlisle-Watson, the wife of a billionaire hedge fund monster, his most cordial, yacht marina smile: "We're neighbors, and I've been meaning to ask your opinion of the Christmas decorations in the lobby. Too gaudy or not? Farrell Covington."

When Farrell first spoke, Gretchen had visibly retreated, anticipating, as most atrociously wealthy people do, that Farrell was an opportunist and might have a gun, or even worse, bad breath from fast food. But upon hearing his last name, she all but cannonballed into his lap. "I'm not sure about the tinsel," she confided. "It's a bit down-market, wouldn't you agree?"

"Thank you for saying that," said a sympathetic Farrell. Within a week, Gretchen and two of her even more well-to-do brunch cronies had met with Dr. Jarvis, who took them around the AIDS ward at Lenox Hill. Shaken, Gretchen emerged as an incipient crusader, speaking before the city council, shielding her Dior with an apron as she dished up hot meals at a food delivery service for homebound AIDS patients, and hosting an April in Paris–themed fundraiser at the Plaza. In the next Village Halloween parade, more than one marcher copied Gretchen's trademark, shellacked, Mozart-like bouffant, as an homage to a selfless socialite.

Around that time, Farrell developed a hacking cough. He suppressed it, contending there was residual dust from the renovation, but this was madness.

"Make an appointment with Jarvis," I instructed, like a hallway-patrolling vice principal. I hated lecturing Farrell, so I met up with Ariadne for guidance, at a coffeeshop near the gay center.

"I'm being an asshole," I said. "And Farrell's not in denial, but he's not taking care of himself. He thinks he can snub the disease, or put it on hold."

"And you're his mother and his nurse and his parole officer," said Ariadne, who'd fed and bathed countless sick friends, cajoled their dismissive insurance companies, notified their estranged families in Omaha or Missouri, and spoken at their memorials.

"Yes," I said. "But how do I do this? How do I help him?"

"First of all, you can't," said Ariadne, jittery from not smoking. She had been weaning herself from substances, cutting back on the pills, and obeying every self-help gimmick. Throughout the day, she'd number each cigarette along its length with a Bic pen, as a deterrent. One afternoon I'd checked, and her cigarette read 128. But she was dealing with ignorant pharmaceutical reps and an uncooperative mayor, so she had to stay clearheaded.

"So I can't help Farrell?" I said.

"He's sick. No one can. He's got Jarvis, right, who's the best. But there's still nothing out there."

"So do I just . . . watch him die?"

"Maybe. Probably. But you don't have to give up, and you sure as fuck don't have to walk around like he's already gone. Most of the guys I know, even three hours before they died, they begged the people around them to act normally and not like pallbearers. Don't lie, or get too cheery and idiotic, but this is Farrell: ask him what he needs. But if he gets really sick, tell him to go fuck himself and call 911. You get a vote."

"Thank you," I said. "Please go have a cigarette."

She'd begun digging in her backpack, commenting, "Did you know Alan Bensimmons? The stage manager? When he was in St. Vincent's, he weighed about ten pounds, but he'd push his IV pole through the halls, chain-smoking, and daring a nurse to order him to stop. One finally did and he asked, 'Why? Is it going to kill me?' "

"And?"

"And he died a week later. But not from smoking!"

We laughed because we had to, and because Alan Bensimmons had been a world-renowned bitch, so good for him for not toning himself down. There should be an eternal row of bronze cigarette butts atop his tombstone, to honor him.

That night Farrell's cough had lessened, but he had night sweats, and the sheets were soaked before midnight. Chills kicked in at 1 a.m., with uncontrollable shivering, despite layers of blankets. "I'm so sorry," he said, through chattering teeth. "I'm having a reaction to Diane Sawyer's lime-green sheath on *60 Minutes*."

I called Dr. Jarvis, who said I should monitor Farrell closely, but that he was better off at home, for the interim. He said hospitals were rife with opportunistic infections. There were no safe havens. During the day, Farrell would page listlessly through glossy, oversize magazines about Swedish royals and Belgian outbuildings, stare distantly at aerobics shows on local channels, and sip Gatorade and eat Saltines, but he had trouble swallowing, which, as he pointed out, "has never been an issue before."

I sat beside him, brought extra bedding, and loaded saturated items into the washing machine. His weight was dropping, and the lesions covered his leg below the knee and had crept onto his torso. One afternoon I caught him speaking condescendingly to an armchair: "I know I'm sick. But you're a reproduction."

Farrell may have been hallucinating, but it was a fine line. He'd have hours of calm and lucidity, when he'd ask about Jackson and Jess, who'd pledged to visit but been refused. "No," Farrell had told me, definitively. "Not like this. I mean, even at death's door I still have bone structure, but I smell."

He did, from sweating and vomiting into a plastic bucket and chronic diarrhea. I'd rotate five pairs of sweatpants and a mountain of T-shirts, so Farrell would always have something clean to change into. Two housekeepers had come and gone, the first after a day, because she hadn't "expected the situation," and the second after a few hours, although she'd sworn she would pray for Farrell, crossing herself. While I wasn't fond of shit and stench and ceaseless laundry, I maintained a caregiver's tunnel vision, doing what had to be done, from minute to minute, in a beautiful apartment. Farrell's illness had become an extreme piece of performance art, against a backdrop of brass-trimmed zebrawood bookshelves and Japanese ceramics.

We both slept intermittently, until one night I dozed off and woke at 4 a.m. without Farrell beside me. I ran into the bathroom. He was on the floor, in a river of God only knew what, having a seizure, his limbs clenching and his eyes rolled back. I called 911 and then Dr. Jarvis, waking but not surprising him, and he said he'd meet us at the emergency room.

As the paramedics were lifting him onto a gurney, Farrell regained consciousness, so I told him, "We're going to the hospital," and he nodded, as an oxygen mask was clamped to his face. I rode with Farrell in the ambulance, clutching his hand and telling him useful, useless information, about Dr. Jarvis being on his way and how, since it was before dawn, the emergency room wouldn't be crowded.

This wasn't the case. Every vinyl-upholstered chair was taken, mostly by AIDS patients. There was a familiarity to the scene. Farrell and I had sat with friends in emergency rooms all over town, and we'd memorized each hospital's floor plan, versed in which color-coded linoleum stripe led to the radiology department or the cafeteria. The patients in the emergency room ranged from the ambulatory to the guys with unshaven, sunken faces, swamped by their shapeless clothes, their canes leaning against their twig-like legs. Farrell had once remarked that these rooms were like "World War I field hospitals, with all the bandaged, shellshocked, exhausted young men, or that footage of concentration camp survivors, greeting their liberators with vacant disbelief."

I'd brought Farrell's paperwork and insurance cards and reminded myself not to hate the person behind the admitting desk, who was just doing her job, with grudging precision and a faulty Sharpie. "Jarvis?" Farrell mumbled, on the gurney, and I assured him, "Any second now." Farrell vomited greenish-black bile onto his chin, neck, and T-shirt, and as I mopped his face with a wad of Kleenex, he smiled with a deranged glee and said, "The limits of style."

Dr. Jarvis rushed in. Doctors are superheroes, welcome during any crisis. Farrell had another, more lurching seizure, coughing a geyser of blood. Dr. Jarvis shoved the gurney through a set of double doors, as nurses ran alongside. Over his shoulder, Dr. Jarvis barked, "Wait here!" So I did.

Ariadne got there within minutes, and then Jess and Jackson. It was now almost 7 a.m. We huddled together in a waiting area on a higher floor. Farrell had been in the ICU, and a nurse had said we couldn't see him, but Dr. Jarvis would be out shortly to speak with us.

"Did he fall in the bathroom?" Jess asked. "Could he have fractures?"

"I don't know," I said. "I don't think so."

"I just saw Robbie Narris in the hall," said Jackson. "He works at Barneys, as a personal shopper? They've got him on an experimental protocol, with some new drug combination, but he can't tell if it's working, but it's not not working. And he told me that Joan Collins was in the store and bought her boyfriend ten Hermès cashmere sweaters, in black, turquoise, and blueberry."

"The only reason I like cashmere," said Ariadne, "is that it doesn't fucking itch."

"And Nate," said Jess, "my mom sends her best and says she'd love to drop by. So if you'd like someone to stroll in, touch Farrell's face with a fingertip, and faint, I'll give her a call."

I was only half listening but appreciative of any bid at lightening the mood. During a previous emergency room visit, Farrell had said, "If you have to be sick, it's much better to be sick in New York. Because the medical care is as good as it gets and the gunshot victims are wearing platform shoes."

Dr. Jarvis appeared, in scrubs with his mask around his neck. "As far as we can tell," he said, "Farrell's had a series of strokes, due to multiple infections which came out of nowhere. He's unconscious but I don't think he's in pain. We've got him on oxygen and IV fluids."

"Is there a prognosis?" asked Jess, who quickly rephrased, "I'm sorry, I did a guest shot on a medical show so I say things like that."

"We're observing him," said Dr. Jarvis, "and hoping he comes out of it. The next twenty-four hours are critical. We don't know if there was any oxygen cutoff, or neural or motor impairment."

Translated, this meant Farrell being paralyzed or unable to speak, or suffering brain damage. I was glad for the jargon, as a bulwark against projecting a disabled, mute Farrell tilted in a wheelchair. Everything was up for grabs and panic was a luxury. Information was a lifeline.

"Can I see him?" I asked, and Dr. Jarvis said, "Yes, but don't expect much. Nate, you go in first, and if they'd like, your friends can come by in an hour or so."

There was a yellow sign on the door to Farrell's room, with a skull and crossbones, warning about contagion and mandating that visitors wear protective gear. In the beginning years of the plague, some nurses wouldn't touch AIDS patients, and their meals would be left on trays outside their doors, even if the patients were immobilized. There was a twenty-six-year-old mail carrier who lived in Bayonne but worked out at my gym, who'd been abandoned at a hospital for over a day; he lapsed into dementia and jumped off the roof.

These urban horror stories had become less common, but AIDS patients were pariahs. I was supplied with surgical gloves and a gown to wear over my clothes, but I didn't don the shower cap–like bonnet or the surgical mask so Farrell could recognize me. His eyes were shut and his breathing labored. His face had relaxed, not into sleep but a slackness, the absence of personality. Farrell was battling the medical equipment that engulfed him, for ownership of his soul, but the equipment was winning.

I moved a chair to his bedside and took his hand, not too tightly, to avoid bruising. "Hey," I said softly, as if we were honeymooning and recovering from jet lag in our hotel. I had no idea if he could hear me, but I told him, "You're at Lenox Hill and Dr. Jarvis says you're doing better. Jess and Ariadne and Jackson are outside and we'll see them later. I'm right here and I'm not going anywhere. And if you're faking, I will slap you so hard."

No response. There were tubes in his nose, his chest rising and falling. My mind darted, between banishing any thoughts whatsoever, to keep tragedy at bay, and knee-jerk practical concerns, about locating the call button for the nurse, and unpacking the duffel bag I'd brought, with clothes and reading material for Farrell. But here we were, at what was conceivably the end of the world. Which was an overly turgid, soap opera phrase, but that's what AIDS was: the grimmest theatrics, a distraught spouse at a bedside, praying for the writing staff to cobble together, if not a happy ending, at least a twist along the way.

As always, I wanted my love for Farrell to leap any barrier, to shelter both of us from every variety of harm. But this was a children's book affirmation, a song lyric gone stale. Despite Farrell's straightforwardness about being sick, we'd never had any direct conversations about death. We had friends who'd outlined their memorials, with guest lists and DJs and cabaret artists ("I want Patti LuPone to sing an *Evita* medley, inserting my name"). We were superstitious, because that's all we had, so we wouldn't allow death any excess real estate. Death was too greedy.

Aridane had told me that sometimes, to rid myself of an obsession, I should dive right into it, embracing the worst possible scenario. This resembled that bizarre diet advice about overeating your favorite food, box upon bag of, say, chocolate-chip cookies, until they literally sickened you and lost their dominion.

What if Farrell died? What would I do? I could kill myself, to bypass even an hour of life without him. But I'd gone years without Farrell's presence, surely I could manage again. Except our time apart hadn't been final, a widowhood. For a second I wished Farrell had signed on for that rom-com and become a movie star, as if that might've rerouted him from ending up here, his eyelids fluttering slightly, making me question if this was a positive sign or his spirit exiting his body.

I was watching myself, like an astral Greek chorus bickering. "Are you going for it? The Oscar-worthy heartbroken-anger-through-tears monologue? Have you sunk that low?"

To which I replied, "Fuck you. Yes I have."

"Farrell," I said, "if you can hear me, you'll hate this, because I'm telling you what to do. You don't have to stop moving towards the light or any of that horseshit. Just get better. Come back to me. Please, please, please. Do it."

I started to sob, heaving, unable to control anything. I didn't want Farrell to sense I was crying, because it might seem like I'd given up, but I also could hear him insinuating, "You're just like millions of bereft young women all over the world, who can't believe Valentino's gone."

Hearing his voice, conjuring his flippancy, made me smile. Farrell was the opposite of grief. He wouldn't die. He couldn't. As Farrell would put it, "It's so not me."

I didn't leave the hospital for three days, and while Farrell didn't improve, his condition didn't worsen. Dr. Jarvis told me, "His body may be trying to repair itself, or shutting down bit by bit. I'm going to authorize some tests, which might be helpful but more likely will reveal nothing. But they'll last a few hours, so you should take a break, and maybe run home and grab a shower. He'll be here when you get back."

I did as I was told, lifting my face into the spray from the shower, as if I could rinse off reality. I changed my clothes, and Jackson, who'd come with me, had already hailed us a cab. "He's going to be fine," Jackson said. "I've made him a card."

Jackson was acclaimed for his handmade cards. As with his sketches and portraits, he'd fold the most costly vellum, and then drip holiday messages in India ink across saturated watercolors of Valentine's Day hearts or sequined birthday seahorses or dancing snowmen with rhinestone eyes. After a spritz of spray glue, he'd accent everything with clear glitter and brightly dyed feathers. These cards required vacuuming, and recipients collected them. Jackson showed me a jumbo card with Farrell's name in dizzying scrollwork, Scotch-taped with Polaroids of Farrell and me from one of Jackson's Chelsea tea parties. Jackson's cards decorated hospital rooms throughout the city, like gilded Russian religious icons.

When we got back to Farrell's room, Jess was seated in a corner, and Ingrid Covington was standing at Farrell's bedside. His condition was unchanged, which surprised me. His mother's reappearance should either have been jolting him back to life or killing him.

"Mr. Reminger," said Ingrid.

"What are you doing here?"

She looked the same, as I assumed she had since birth, in a severe gray wool coat over a white turtleneck, as if she might be asked to perform delicate surgery on a Mercedes. If she'd been issued any protective clothing, she'd refused to wear it.

"Hello, Mrs. Covington," said Jackson, with a stunned civility. "We met at Farrell's wedding."

Ingrid glanced at Jackson as if he were a chambermaid who'd wandered into a forbidden parlor and would be fired, by a higher-ranking chambermaid. She addressed me: "Farrell is my son. And yes, he and I have been at odds, but I've always hoped this could be resolved. Our family has, of course, been keeping abreast of Farrell's activities."

Bolt entered, bringing his mother a paper cup of tea, and Wainwright trailed him. "There's no point in arguing about any of this," said Bolt. "Or in my emphasizing the result of Farrell's lifestyle."

That word. That cheesy abuse of two wonderful things, life and style. Curdled into the ugliest condemnation.

"These are Farrell's brothers, Bolt and Wainwright," I told Jess.

"We met at Farrell's wedding," said Jackson, as Bolt and Wainwright regarded him blankly.

"Are those really your names?" asked Jess.

"Yes," said Ingrid. "And young lady, may I have your chair?"

While I didn't want her to, Jess instantly stood, and Bolt moved the chair next to the bed and Ingrid sat. Wainwright asked, "Mother, can I get you anything else?"

"Not just yet," she said. "I would like to speak with Mr. Reminger, alone."

"We'll be right outside," said Jackson, on his way out, as Jess mouthed "Oh my God" to me and followed him.

"So will we," said Bolt, as he left, and Wainwright said, "Hi," to me and strode after him. That "hi" was unexpected.

I wondered if Ingrid would ask Farrell to leave, too, but no: Farrell was exactly where she wanted him, silent and unable to move or resist.

"Mr. Reminger," she began, "Nate, if I may. We met under the worst conceivable circumstances."

I wasn't about to argue, so she continued: "When I realized that Farrell's marriage was a sham, and saw you seated so proudly beside him, I behaved abominably. I struck back. I don't expect you to understand any of this, and I have no right to ask for your sympathy, but . . . my own marriage was never easy. Harwell was controlling and cold and unreachable. So I'd retreated, into the church and into myself. Where nothing could wound or besmirch me. Or so I thought."

Was she being honest? Or manipulative? I'd listen, but with the most extreme skepticism. What she'd done to Farrell was indelible and I remembered every word she'd said, to his face.

"And I don't blame Farrell, not a bit, for how he reacted. How he cut himself off, from a family that had treated him so poorly, for so long. But over these past years, I've had time to—reconsider my actions. While Harwell was still alive, I couldn't be anything but his self-righteous, scorned wife, rigid with piety. I hated everyone and everything, and most especially myself. I hope and pray you don't know what that's like, and never will."

She sighed, and put her hand on Farrell's. She was studying him, with—regret? curiosity? some brief, less embittered memory of his childhood?

She kissed his hand. This display, of a basic physical affection, was radically unlike her. She wasn't faking, either the gesture or her tear-filled eyes. I wasn't moved, but I was increasingly drawn in.

"My poor boy," she told Farrell, and then, to me, "When I was told how ill he was, I knew you'd be standing by him. And yes, I've been jealous, of your relationship. Your love. Which is opposite in every way from my own experience."

She looked right at me, with an openness I never would've predicted. Was I being an unforgiving jerk?

"Mrs. Covington . . ."

"Ingrid, if you'd like. The world is changing. You and Farrell, and so many men much like you, along with your female counterparts, are leading satisfying and happy lives. Even during this repulsive plague. I've had Covington Industries donate five million dollars to this hospital."

Oh my God. On one hand, five million meant little to her; it was petty cash, Harwell's monthly hush money. But the Ingrid I'd met in Wichita would never have done this. Was she proving something? To Farrell and to me? To herself?

"Thank you," I said. "I'm sure that will help."

"And I've spoken with Dr. Jarvis, and he's not optimistic about Farrell's condition. Which breaks my heart. Because more than anything, I'd hate that my last moments with Farrell, with my son, will be spent here, in a hospital room. I was originally seeking, somehow, to reach out to him, and at least initiate a reconnection. But now . . ."

"He might get better. Some people do. The chances are terrible, but I'm not giving up. And neither is Dr. Jarvis."

"Of course not. But meanwhile, in Wichita, we have what may very well be this country's finest hospital, with a specialty in viral infections. I've spoken to the head of the department and asked him to review Farrell's case. And I've hired a medical transport, to fly Farrell to Wichita later today."

What?

"It's abrupt, but he'll receive the finest possible care, and the staff won't be as tragically overburdened as they are here. Where their case-load is so unthinkable. I've given this so much thought, as have Farrell's brothers, and this is the only recourse. And of course, you're more than welcome to come with us, and stay as long as you'd like."

"No."

"Nate, please, I'm sorry to spring this on you, at such a terrible junc-ture, but we must prioritize what's best for Farrell. As I'm sure you'll agree."

"No. I'm sorry, maybe you mean well, but Farrell hated Wichita. That's not what he'd want. Dr. Jarvis is on top of every new treatment, and he's devoted himself to people just like Farrell. Farrell loves him. And Farrell's a New Yorker and so am I. And we're not leaving."

"I'm listening. Except, Nate, and I'd hoped I wouldn't need to bring this up, but it's not your choice. When it comes to Farrell, you have no legal standing. The courts don't recognize an official boyfriend. I'm Far-rell's next of kin. I'm his mother. I've met with our attorneys, and Bolt will confirm this, but I have legal jurisdiction over Farrell's care. Bolt will be happy to explain this to—who was Farrell's person? A Mr. Longstead?"

"Llewelyn. Farrell's lawyer is Devin Llewelyn."

"Who'll admit precedent. Nate, please don't make this difficult. Let's use this moment to do what's best for someone we both love deeply. Albeit in very different ways."

The "different ways" was what I'd been anticipating. The condescen-sion. The genteel Covington Industries disdain.

"No. I'm not letting this happen. Farrell's staying right here."

I was so outraged I'd scarcely acknowledged Farrell's presence. He was still out of it, which meant I was speaking on his behalf. Was I being spite-fully indignant? Was Ingrid right? Could Farrell receive better, or more comprehensive, medical services in Wichita?

I saw it. Farrell, should a miracle occur, waking up in Kansas, with his family around him. The family that had done everything it could to belittle Farrell, to strongarm and destroy him. He'd be home, in a grisly horror movie reboot of Dorothy returning from Oz. And if Farrell died, his family would still be in charge, which was all they'd ever sought. They didn't want Farrell; they were maneuvering to bring a Covington back into the fold and back in line. And maybe, if they could have him ruled incapacitated, they could assume his power of attorney.

"You're not doing this. If—when—Farrell wakes up, he can make his own decisions, about whether he'd even want to speak to you. But he's staying right here."

Ingrid rose and said, with what she thought was a generous-hearted smile, "It's just not your call."

"No it's not," said a voice, at the doorway. "It's mine."

Sally was standing there, in the white sari with blue stripes at the hem, of Mother Teresa's missionary order. Her blond hair peeked out from her white veil, which, being Sally, she'd arranged as a becoming snood, or the gracefully draped cowl of a forties movie star poised atop the mirrored staircase of a soundstage nightclub. She must've traveled for days, but her sari was brilliantly white and creaseless. She was beatific, having achieved her goal: she was the first saint on the best-dressed list.

"Sally?" said Ingrid, incredulously. "What are you wearing?"

"Sally works with Mother Teresa in Calcutta," I said, as I yearned for Farrell to wake up, not just to regain his health, but because he'd adore this contest of Christians.

"Hello, Ingrid," said Sally. "And Nate." She hugged me and an unhuggable Ingrid. Then Sally went to Farrell's bedside and kissed his forehead. For a guy in a coma, Farrell was getting plenty of action.

"Jackson left an emergency message," she told us. "He's the only person who has the number. He explained about Farrell."

Sally had mailed an occasional postcard, usually with an inspirational quote and a sketch of a child's face, a bell tower, or a dragonfly. Farrell and I had concluded that she was either digging in at Mother Teresa's mission or teaching everyone in India to make potpourri in tiny delft porcelain bowls as hostess gifts.

"We've had so many AIDS patients at our clinic," she said. "And a handful have improved. So I've been praying for Farrell, and I'd love to confer with his doctor, and maybe set up some sort of medical information sharing with Mother T."

"Do you really call her Mother T?" I asked. "Like Mr. T?"

I was struggling to reconcile Mother Teresa with the gruff, multiple-gold-chain-sporting, Mohawked star of the wrestling circuit and a top-rated TV action show.

"I do," said Sally. "At first she didn't quite approve, but now she's rather taken with it."

"Sally," said Ingrid. "I'm glad you're here, especially if you've had experience with patient care. Because we're flying Farrell to Wichita."

"No, you're not," I insisted.

"Well," said Sally, gracious as ever. "I'm still married to Farrell, which makes me his legal and medical proxy. And Ingrid, I think it's marvelous that you've come here, and that you're reaching out. But Farrell needs to be with Nate, in New York. With the very ill, especially with so few treatment options, the presence of loved ones can make all the difference. Mother T says that people know when they're loved. It's the basis for everything she's accomplished."

"That may be all well and good," Ingrid sputtered. "And I admire your . . . dedication, but I love my son, in my way, as do his brothers. He belongs with us."

Sally went to Ingrid, and took her hand, telling her, in a sweet but I-know-Jesus-personally tone, "No. He's not going anywhere. I've got the legal high ground, so don't even try. But I'm sure Nate can coordinate visits, as many as you'd like, for you and your boys. Because isn't that what you've been after, Ingrid? More time with Farrell?"

I was about to weep and applaud and take back any doubts I'd ever had about Sally's frosty patrician faith. Ingrid had gone from ice to granite, as she'd been bested: it's hard to argue with a woman who's been bathing the mortally ill in the slums of Calcutta, or with Sally's undimmed radiance.

Ingrid percolated for a threat or insult or exit line, but again, Sally was as close as I could conceive to Glinda descending in that glimmering bubble to liberate the Munchkins. *Wizard of Oz* references can be tiresomely gay, and I'm not bashing Ingrid as the Wicked Witch of Wichita, or calling Bolt and Wainwright her flying monkeys. But under a suitable amount of stress, like Farrell lying unconscious in a hospital bed, I was justified. Gay men are coded as "friends of Dorothy," but Ingrid was definitely a foe of Dorothy. I'll stop.

Ingrid stalked out, grabbing her cup of tea, as if we might usurp that as well.

Sally turned to me, in an elegant swirl of hand-loomed white cotton, and asked, "No bullshit, Nate, how are you?"

24

Jackson brought in an extra chair and left Sally and me alone with Farrell. She and I sat with our knees touching and I fell apart, describing Farrell's advancing illness and his stubbornness and my caring for him. She was exactly the right confessor, because she was familiar with the players and she'd had firsthand experience with AIDS patients, lending her the widest, even global perspective. Sally prayed with, or over, Farrell, which didn't bother me. Ordinarily I resisted displays of religious zeal, but Sally's love and belief were the real thing, especially because while she might condemn aluminum Christmas trees ("Why not decorate a microwave oven?") and unmade beds ("I can't look at them"), she didn't proselytize.

"You're doing everything you can," she told me, "and it's never enough. But even before I got Jackson's message, I had a premonition I should be here, and not just to get rid of Ingrid. I've missed you and Farrell and the gang."

There was a knock, and Wainwright entered, as I steeled myself for another round. "Nate?" he said. "And Sally? I wanted to say how sorry I am, for whatever my mom just put you through. She cooked up the whole thing with Bolt, and I tried to talk them out of it, but, well, you've met them."

"Oh, sweetie," said Sally, "you've always had potential. Can you get yourself out of there? I don't mean Wichita, which is lovely, but Covington Industries. Can we help?"

"I don't know," he said, trapped but squirming, a Houdini in a corporate straitjacket. Farrell had dismissed him as a born follower, but maybe Farrell had set an example.

"You can come by whenever you like," I said.

"Thank you. Mom and Bolt are flying back, but I'll try to get out here more often. It's . . . tricky."

"I remember," said Sally, and Bolt, from the hallway, called Wainwright's name and he was gone.

Farrell stayed unconscious for two more days, and Dr. Jarvis debated putting him on a ventilator to help him breathe, although I'd gathered, from the deaths of friends, that this was a final, ineffective feint, as few patients were successfully weaned from this device. As Dr. Jarvis held off, Sally and the others would rotate visits, along with my parents. Over the past years they'd been driving into town, for shows and dinners with Farrell and me, and they'd not only bonded with him, but formed a militia against me. My mom would say, "Well, Farrell and I think your hair has gotten too long" or "It's not just my opinion. Farrell says your hang-ups about Piscataway are ridiculous."

Along with their love for Farrell, my parents were fixated on my own health, and while I'd told them I'd tested negative, they scoured the increasingly featured articles in the *Times*, and the son of my mom's best friend had died recently. He'd been a gifted musician, in his thirties, but his cause of death was blurred. AIDS was receiving more fanfare, but the stigma was everywhere. Farrell occasionally introduced himself by saying, "Hi, I'm Farrell AIDS and I have Covington."

My parents had met Dr. Jarvis, whom they cross-examined and trusted. As I told him, "You're like a rabbit's foot for Jews."

"They think gentile doctors drink," he confided. "I had to force my dad to stop introducing me as 'My son, the gay Jewish doctor.'" As my folks sat by Farrell's bedside, my mom would reflexively pat his arm. This reminded me of how she'd place her forefinger on the dashboard if she thought my dad was driving too fast; my mom's anxiety expressed itself through mystical hand magic. Her touch could heal speeding Chevrolets and comatose AIDS patients.

"He's going to be fine," my mom told me, opening her purse to leave a roll of Lifesavers, as an amulet, on the tray table parked beside Farrell's bed.

"Listen to your mother," said my dad.

As they left the hospital room, they both hugged me and were careful to add a "See you soon" to Farrell, as my mom kissed her fingertips and touched them to Farrell's sheet-shrouded feet. If my mom had been Jesus, she wouldn't have merely bestowed loaves and fishes, but napkins and silverware.

I made so many deals, not so much with God as with the universe. I had no idea what to barter for Farrell's return to, if not health, at least consciousness. I promised to assign any future royalties to the hospital, and I vowed to join Sally in Calcutta. I was willing to surrender my own life, which was such small change, and I could hear the universe smirk, "Don't you own any beachfront property?"

Jackson had attached his glittering card to the wall opposite Farrell's bed, at eye level, amid a collage of pages sliced from fashion and interior design magazines. The wall was a mood board, of unusual or au courant faces; a stage-filling *Turandot* finale; a row of Hertfordshire thatched roof cottages; a sketch of a Schiaparelli opera cape from the thirties, embroidered with an eyeball and a lobster; a ballerina in mid jeté; gingham ribbon samples; a square of a toile depicting a Marie Antoinette picnic; tear sheets Jackson had found in a photographer's garbage, of dissolute clubgoers; formal portraits of heroes like Martha Graham, Eleanor Roosevelt, and Jean Cocteau; and naked gay porn stars, whom Jackson had decoupaged into the Nantucket interiors of a Ralph Lauren catalogue.

I never left Farrell's room, applying more deodorant and apologizing to everyone. Despite the flow of guests and medical personnel, much of the time Farrell and I were alone. I shut off the wall-mounted TV, since I couldn't concentrate and Farrell, as far as I knew, wasn't interested. I catnapped. I'd jerk awake, checking that Farrell was breathing. Was this what he'd want? A life in aspic? Was I selfishly keeping him alive, like a maniac with an abducted victim in the basement? I was bored and scared and, in some strange way, more in love than ever, as if, while the world carried on outside, Farrell and I were isolated, marooned on a desert island, or in a space station adrift from its orbit.

One afternoon, thinking of Sleeping Beauty, I brushed my lips across Farrell's, intending the memory of romance to awaken him. It didn't. I blamed myself. I wasn't a handsome prince, so the curse was intact. I ransacked my mind for some modern equivalent, coming up with that massive injection they jab into the chests of overdosed heroin addicts, causing them to spasm upright. I asked Dr. Jarvis about this. I peppered him with my ludicrous theories, until he said, straightforwardly, "Nate, I know you love him. It's okay."

In the early hours of the sixth day, I was scanning Jackson's inspirational array, to ferret out which images he'd most recently added—a still of Ann-Margret behind the handlebars of a Harley? A professional rugby player yanking down a teammate's shorts on the field? As I nodded off, I heard Farrell ask, in a rasping whisper, "Is that Halston?"

My head jerked around. Farrell was peering at Jackson's wall, specifically at a *Vogue* clipping of the celebrated designer, draping an outfit on Faye Dunaway, who was withholding an opinion.

"Farrell?"

"What?"

I stood up, unsure about kissing Farrell or touching him or falling to my knees to thank higher powers. I approached him gingerly, and his eyes tracked me, as if I were wearing a tinfoil hat and carrying a cleaver.

"What . . . are you doing?" he said, barely audible.

"I . . . I . . . Are you awake?"

This was a ridiculous question, much like asking someone if they're asleep.

"Yeah . . . ," said Farrell, wary as I drew closer.

I leaned over the bed, choking back tears, as Farrell's alarm grew.

"Welcome back," I said, brushing his hair, which hadn't been trimmed in weeks, off his forehead. He twitched.

"I'm sorry!" I said. "Did that hurt?"

"No, but why . . . why are you behaving so strangely?"

"Because, okay, how much do you remember?"

"I remember . . . being wheeled through a lobby, with fluorescent lighting, and then vomiting, perhaps from the lighting, and then . . . and then . . ."

I pulled up a chair.

"You've been unconscious. But now you're not."

"How . . . how long?"

His eyes were darting, and he hadn't raised his head.

"Six days."

"No."

A nurse entered, asking, "He's awake? Is Dr. Jarvis here?"

As she ran out, I took Farrell's hand. He squeezed mine in return, which I took as medically optimistic. He coughed, not as violently as before, but I pushed gently on his shoulder to make him relax.

"I really have to pee," he whispered, and as I foraged for the plastic bedpan, Dr. Jarvis came in, stern but pleased. He'd trained himself to resist deceptively good news.

"Give us a minute?" he requested. I stepped into the hall so he could examine Farrell. The world had shifted. The perfectly ordinary hallway, clogged with blinking machinery, overworked staff members, and a shuffling patient clutching a metal walker, had become heightened, as if Farrell's awakening had returned everything to a more vibrant life, a restart, not quite a musical number in which orderlies would waltz with their mops as blood-spattered surgeons did backflips, but close enough.

Farrell hadn't made anything close to a recovery, but he'd stabilized. There weren't speech or memory issues, from the strokes, but later that day, as he swung his feet onto the floor, he wilted back onto the bed. His left leg was impaired, and physical therapy was scheduled. He could eat solid food, or as he called it, "hospital dog toys," and we took walks down the hall. Farrell leaned on a cane, with which he'd swat my knees and yell, "Again, Anastasia! Dance for His Highness!" Dr. Jarvis explained that while Farrell remained very sick, continued hospitalization risked exposing his fragile immune system to whatever germs were drifting around the ward. He was sending Farrell home, with a nurse coming by three times a week to take his blood pressure and temperature and confirm he was gaining weight.

Sally stuck around until Farrell was ready to be discharged. She was sleeping at a satellite convent that Mother Teresa incongruously ran in the West Village (I'd seen other nuns strolling past the bondage shops on Christopher Street). Sally answered Farrell's and my questions about her time in Calcutta. She was living with other expats in an open dorm, and had at first been assigned menial tasks, bringing the more experienced nuns towels and metal bowls of clean water. While the mission was technically a hospital, there weren't many doctors or supplies: "Mother T is more about comforting people and hospice care, for the poorest of the poor. She wants everyone to feel tended to."

"Do you worry?" I asked. "About not having enough training or getting sick yourself, or burning out?"

"All of the above," Sally admitted. "But the nuns are matter-of-fact, and it's not like here, where people have expectations and are used to a certain level of cleanliness and equipment. It's very basic, but I'm actually doing something. I'm looking suffering people in the eye and changing their bandages and just being there. Most of the patients have been abandoned by their families. It's heartbreaking but not necessarily depressing because we're too busy."

"Well, it agrees with you," said Farrell. "Are you sure it's not a spa?"

"And the habit," I said. "It's go-anywhere."

"Day-into-evening," said Farrell. As Sally mulled whether his blasphemy merited a slap, he murmured, "You can't hit me. I have AIDS."

Sally helped us out: "It usually takes three years for anyone to be awarded the three blue stripes on their habit, which are for poverty, chastity, and obedience."

"Like merit badges?" Farrell asked. "For things nobody wants to do?"

"They're symbolic," said Sally. "But I love them, as a finishing touch, so I asked Mother T, 'What if I just wore the stripes as a tryout? A loaner?' Well, that's not exactly what I said, I think I went especially demure and let it slip that I'd seen myself wearing the stripes in a dream. So she's humoring me."

"Is there a language barrier?" I asked.

"Sometimes. But Mother T speaks English, although she was born in Albania. She's a tough cookie and she likes being a leader."

"You mean an international pinup," Farrell said.

"Mmm," Sally said, miming zipping her lip. Mother Teresa had been criticized, for her disinterest in more extensive medical treatments and her extreme religious views, along with her basking in celebrity.

"Are you going back?" I asked.

"Tomorrow. But I'm so glad I was here. Farrell, I know you're going to do well, I'm counting on you. You mustn't disappoint Nate. Don't make me call Ingrid."

I'd given Farrell an abbreviated version of his family's invasion. He'd shut his eyes and told me, "If you'd said yes, if you'd let them drag me back to Wichita, I would never have forgiven you. I'd have hunted you down with an assault weapon. Although if I'd been awake I could've vomited on Ingrid. And then pretended to die. And then done it again."

While Farrell slept, I walked Sally down to the lobby, because I had a last foolish but ardent question. "Okay," I said, cognizant that I was accompanying a blond Calcutta nun, who was causing a stir in the waiting area and snack bar, as if she might be passing out blessings or souvenir key chains. "I'm not going to tell you how grateful I am to you, because I'd never stop. But, okay, I'm just going to say this, you may have saved Farrell's life."

Sally didn't protest. She had a devout Mary Poppins quality.

"So," I continued, "let me ask—Farrell's still quite possibly going to die, but what happened, in his room, would you ever call that—a miracle?"

I couldn't believe I was asking this, but I figured for Sally miracles were tools of the trade, like a plumber's wrench or a district attorney's ability to suddenly jab his forefinger at a defense witness.

"That's not an easy call," said Sally. "Back in the day, a person had to rack up three verified miracles to be canonized, but then the Vatican reduced it to two. Which I try not to write off as cheating, or call those

292   PAUL RUDNICK

people saint-ish. But inexplicable healings count, except Farrell hasn't been healed. But he's doing better, which at the very least buys the two of you more time. And we could attribute his recovery to Jackson's photos of Cartier brooches. Or to the fact that you love him. But of course, lots of people are loved and it doesn't change anything. No one's a special case."

"So you think it was random?"

"I didn't say that. And prayer doesn't hurt. Or Western medicine. But I will say one thing."

"Tell me."

"Farrell had never seen me, with my stripes. And I'm in my thirties but I have skin like a child's. I'm not bragging, these are just things I'd mention to the Vatican adjudicators, who certify miracles. And I whispered something to Farrell, while he was out, which may have had an effect."

"What? What did you say?"

"I told him, 'You're Farrell Covington.'"

I brought Farrell back to his place, where he walked in the door and said, "Dear God. Civilization."

He made sure to get dressed most days and sit upright on a couch and read. As he regained his strength, we'd browse at Rizzoli (for novels and coffee-table behemoths on châteaux of the Loire Valley and the great hotels of Geneva), window-shop at a cluster of Italian menswear stores on Madison Avenue, and have lunch with the salesclerks and shoppers who favored a neighborhood bistro. I didn't crowd Farrell, or cluck over him, but he tired easily, and I kept an eye out, in case he fell or had any sort of medical emergency. We designated a guest room as an office, where I set to work on a new play. I couldn't revert to my previous froth, but at the same time, I wasn't comfortable accessing heavy-duty drama. I wasn't equipped, and other writers did a far better job.

My subject was obvious: everything that was happening. Other topics would be, at best, beside the point. Farrell and I had seen Larry Kramer's *The Normal Heart*, and hadn't been able to speak for hours afterward. The play was a brutal manifesto, based on Kramer's controversial days as a founder of the Gay Men's Health Crisis, a pioneering group that ultimately kicked him out, for being such a raging, uncompromising pain in the ass. The statistics for AIDS deaths and infections had been grafitted on the walls of the set and the theater itself, and updated at each performance.

Coverage of the plague had been nonexistent, so Kramer's play wasn't just funny and gut-wrenching but invaluable testimony. Only I wasn't Larry Kramer, and I wasn't adept at the scathingly political. "So write about us," Farrell suggested, "by which I mean, me."

I speculated: Farrell was an appallingly rich, youngish white guy, who had no problem exploiting his good looks, cash flow, or magisterial sense of style. A studio executive would dispose of him as "unrelatable," "niche," or "too New York." Brett had been appointed the head of production at yet another studio. He and I had talked about gay stories and he'd expressed interest, but held back. He had to answer to a CEO and a board of directors.

I indulged in a few pages of realism, a by-the-book retelling of what Farrell, and so many others, were contending with. This documentary lens came across as stilted and dry, and in no way a reflection of Farrell's valor, or the darkest humor that was rescuing so many gay men from an all-consuming misery. Ariadne and I had a mutual theatrical fanship for the work of Charles Ludlam, who'd died, in May of 1987. We'd caught every season of Ludlam's Ridiculous Theatrical Company at off-Broadway venues, and these shows had not only leavened my mooning over Farrell while he was in Kansas, they were a source of helplessly dirty laughter, frequently naked actors, and the most uncommon lunacy.

Critics would bat around the term "camp," both in tribute and sometimes to belittle Ludlam as an ephemeral gay spoofmeister. I began to loathe the word, because it could devalue a sensibility I held dear, the soul of New York gaydom, the outlaw commentary on not merely heterosexual lockstep dreariness, but the ineffable madness of life itself.

Camille was a Ludlam masterwork. He played the iconic French courtesan in a bouncing, sausage-curled wig, which made no secret of his mustache, and a frilly, low-cut pink satin gown, exposing his chest hair (Ludlam was surprisingly sexy, with a cabdriver's mug and an all-knowing leer). He lampooned Camille's tragic affair with a breeches-clad aristocrat, while revitalizing every cliché. His Camille was hilarious, touching, and completely his own. At a low point, financially and emotionally drained, Camille sat bereft in her shawl, braving a frigid Parisian December, as the embers died in her painted fireplace. Camille asked her devoted maid, Nanine, played exquisitely by Ludlam's real-life lover, Everett Quinton, to "throw another faggot on the fire," using the vernacular for logs. Nanine replied, "I'm so sorry, mistress, but there are no more faggots in the house." Ludlam scowled directly into the riotous, exceedingly gay audience and moaned, "No more faggots in the house?"

I stopped laboring beneath the tragic weight of the health crisis and took up Farrell's deadpan hauteur and Ludlam's nose-thumbing disrespect as my muses. I sampled everything, anatomizing the rigors of safe sex, the plague's toll on the cast of *Cats*, the overrun, understaffed clinics, and the showbizzy memorials where name entertainers were rated by mourners ("Bernadette looked incredible"). I wasn't just writing what I knew, which is a touch easy, I was writing what I loved.

I had a draft, which I gave to Farrell. After a quick read, he said, "Not yet. More. Funnier. Gayer. Filthier."

I revised and expanded. The central roles were Alex and Winston, a couple clawing their way through contemporary New York. The play splintered into a kaleidoscope of scenes, set in rent-controlled studio apartments and pricey boutiques and at pride parades, where the marchers included an actual group, the United Fistfuckers of America, which sponsored an annual Christmas Toy Drive. The characters were interior designers, personal trainers, and cater-waiters, the gay New York underground that fuels the city. These weren't idealized, acceptable gay role models, but the people I knew, who transcended stereotypes and were proudly butch or femme or free-range sluts. Certain AIDS presentations, especially well-intended movies-of-the-week, became hushed and dignified, with cheerless guys in crewneck sweaters and khakis, retreating to their autumnal New England hometowns to expire ("Mom, I have something to tell you"), but that wasn't my New York.

Once Farrell approved, the play went to Florence, who was pleased and aghast. "It's vewy good," she concluded, "and it vill end your caweer." She submitted the script to every not-for-profit off-Broadway theater that specialized in new work, and it was violently rejected everywhere. The responses ranged from silence to curt letters saying, "I simply can't find this funny" and "I enjoyed having a look but our subscribers would never stand for this." Over the course of a year and then another, with Farrell's ceaseless cheerleading, I wouldn't put the play aside, as an untenable experiment or an unwanted stepchild. The play attracted a director, a skillful newcomer who told me, "Everything that upsets me about this play is what makes it work."

Farrell was hospitalized again, for a blood transfusion, to combat his anemia and plummeting T-cell count, with some minor improvement. A week later he grabbed the doorjamb of my office to steady himself, telling me, "Call Jarvis. There are black spots in both my eyes and they're getting bigger." In the cab Farrell said, "I can't see anything," and I yelled at the driver to run red lights, drive on the sidewalk, anything to get us to the hospital faster. Even Farrell's bathroom collapse hadn't been this frightening.

Farrell had shingles, which could endanger his sight indefinitely. Dr. Jarvis had him immediately hooked to a near-toxic IV drip of antibiotics, as a last-ditch gamble at salvaging a remnant of Farrell's vision. As I sat beside him in his latest hospital room, Farrell said, "No. This is it. I'm not doing this."

"Jarvis says the treatment can be effective," I said. "And he's got you on the highest dosage."

I couldn't chirp that everything would be dandy or statistically favorable. Farrell wasn't a toddler or an idiot.

"If this doesn't work," he said, "I'm done."

"Jarvis saw your blood work, he says your T cells are better . . ."

"Fuck you. Fuck Jarvis."

Farrell's eyes were sweeping back and forth, searching for even an iota of light. He went on: "I've hoarded the pills and no, you don't have to be there. But I can't live without seeing things, without cobalt blue and

Jackson's scarlet tissue paper and macaw yellow. Without faces. Without art. After all this shit, I'm not going to feel your mouth to see if you're smiling, or trip over the furniture and be a good sport. I'm not making the best of it. No more."

He was serious and well prepared. There was a baggie bulging with pills, knotted with a twister tie, at the back of a linen closet shelf. Farrell had shrugged off psychotherapy ("Too many ergonomic desk chairs and hanging plants in macramé slings"), so I thought about summoning Sally, but even her boundless compassion would be futile. Farrell was immovable, about the life he'd choose to live, or end. I couldn't forbid his independence, even if I wanted to.

Farrell was a creature of irreverent opinions and epic taste but also unshakeable convictions, which had ignited the showdowns with his parents and Eric Nordstadt. After a late dinner at Charlie's, we'd once been confronted on the subway by a naked schizophrenic with a baseball bat, and Farrell had told him, "Put that down and cut back on the carbs." Farrell knew himself, and took full advantage of every resource to bend the planet to his elegant will. Life was fucking with Farrell, and he wouldn't stand for it. "I know there are many blind people who lead productive, fulfilling lives," he told me, "and appear in TV commercials striding through airports with their German shepherds, and climbing Everest and water-skiing, or at least that's what people tell them they're doing. That's not for me." Sight, along with conversation, were Farrell's primary senses. He lived through his eyes, which transmitted joy and judgment. "If I'm blind," he said, "how can I criticize anyone's down-filled coat, which I know keeps them toasty, but also makes them resemble an inflatable air mattress for when the grandkids visit."

If I shut my eyes, I could simulate blindness, but not this. His earlier cataclysm had left Farrell in a coma, but he'd roused himself, relatively intact. This was an assault, a theft, a blight that would make Farrell not merely dependent on others, which he'd hate, but only nominally himself. Other, maybe braver or more open-minded and equipped people could withstand this, and adapt, but not Farrell. He was too strict. He'd swallowed pills before, in Wichita, as a dress rehearsal, as a younger, lonelier man's halfhearted quest for oblivion. He'd been unmoored, but this wasn't drama. This would be a considered conclusion, and in a way, an act of self-preservation.

I'd raised the upper region of the hospital bed partway, so Farrell was sitting up, tethered to the IV. On that first day, I brought him orange juice and snacks, which only exacerbated the situation, when I asked, "Do you want me to hold up the juice so you can take a sip? There's a straw."

"Just leave it."

"I'm putting the carton on the tray in front of you," I said. "To your right."

"Thank you," Farrell replied curtly. He reached for the carton and knocked it onto the bed, the juice spilling.

"Hold on," I said. "I'll get a paper towel."

As the juice soaked into the sheets, Farrell said, quietly, "Thank you."

I wasn't watching Farrell go blind: he was blind. I read aloud to him, from a *People* magazine interview with an implacably moronic starlet: "Lara says that someday she'd like to play a scientist, because 'I've always been interested in why things happen on Earth.'"

Farrell grunted, so I asked, "Should we try TV?"

Farrell fumbled for the wall-mounted TV's remote control, which was buried beside the mattress. I went to help him, but he grabbed my hand and wrote something on my palm with a fingertip. Lacking options, I played along: "What did you write, Helen?"

In a garbled voice, Farrell said, "I wrote 'Can I read your sweater?'"

Against all my better judgment I laughed. We kept the TV on as background noise, as a reassurance that Farrell's hearing was operational. "Are you sitting there prissing your lips sympathetically?" he asked, that afternoon.

"I'm having sex with Jarvis."

"Ah. I thought it was *The Golden Girls*."

Jarvis had told us that the antibiotics could kick in at any time, or partially, or never. Every few hours he'd stop in to gauge Farrell's condition, moving his hand in front of Farrell's face, but Farrell didn't respond.

As we waited, before I could even ask the question, Farrell would say, "No. Still nothing."

At midnight on the second day, when I came back from the bathroom, Farrell was twisting his head from side to side, like a predatory hawk. His face scoped toward me, and he asked, "Did you sleep on your hair?"

"Farrell?"

"It's all flat on one side. And I can see the poster about washing your hands, and a nurse wearing either a Christmas sweater or a bloodstained tablecloth."

"So . . ."

"Yes. It's coming back. While you were in the bathroom. A witch appeared and offered me my sight, in exchange for our firstborn child."

"Done," I agreed.

"And your shearling-lined leather coat from the Barneys warehouse sale."

"Which doesn't belong to you. Sorry."

When I hugged him, there was an unspoken wave of exhausted deliverance, from a storm passing, or the careening pickup truck with the drunk driver, missing us by inches.

After another day of antibiotics, Farrell had only mildly diminished vision in a quadrant of his left eye. As he explained, "It's fine, because I'll just have the people I hate stay to my left, so they'll no longer exist." Once he was home, if he disapproved of, for example, a Harris Tweed vest I'd bought, he'd pretend to be blind, groping the vest and screaming, "Is it a burlap bag, or a dying pine tree, or just a sad non-Equity caroler from a dinner theater production of A Christmas Carol? Let me feel you, to see if you're also wearing buckled shoes and a polyester velvet top hat."

I smacked him, but I was too shaken for byplay. I couldn't integrate Farrell's blindness into our story. It was too raw, like some vicious tease, of more cataclysms ahead. I couldn't file it away, until Farrell goaded me to insert this particular hideousness into my play. "Go for the cheapest poor-little-Nell pathos," he recommended. "Have my character go blind and have sex with a floor lamp."

I didn't do this, but I did have the main couple separate, at the end of Act I, because Alex couldn't deal with Winston's illness. Alex was then mugged in the subway and as he lay bleeding on the cement he sang a few bars of "I Never":

I'm sad and I'm scared
Someone stop me from falling
Before I'm far too far gone
Why can't you see that this just isn't me
It's a trap, it's a dream, it's a con

Maybe I couldn't sing, but Alex could.

25

Ben, my director, and I held a series of readings, to assess the play's ongoing revisions and jump-start a production, by inviting artistic directors and literary managers and anyone else we could coerce. While the play, which was now titled *I Dare You*, seemed strong (unless Ben and I were kidding ourselves), there were no offers.

As a last stand, Florence stuffed a dog-eared Xerox of the script into a manila envelope and marched to the Annex, a dilapidated, hundred-seat, neglected theater housed on the ground floor of a tenement building a few blocks from her office. She told Ryan Detski, who constituted practically the entire staff, that she'd sit outside his office and refuse to leave until he'd read the play.

Rather than prod Florence's Teutonic bile, Ryan sequestered himself and, an hour later, told Florence, "I think I'll regret this, but I'll do it."

Ben and I were ecstatic, at finally landing an offer, even from a theater with a nonexistent profile. Farrell congratulated us, saying, "That's what you want. Someone who gets it."

We posted a casting notice, to no avail. Agents all over town were steering their clients as far away from the play as possible, for its tone and, most especially, its flagrantly and unashamedly gay content. *I Dare You* wasn't a tremulous, sexless coming-out saga, or the "universal" tale of a comfy Midwestern couple whose blameless teenage daughter accidentally contracts AIDS at a blood bank. The play was being rebuked as "a comedy about AIDS." Every actor we asked to audition was stridently warned that even reading for a part would be suspect. Straight actors had played gay roles in the past, onstage (usually in English plays) and in movies (as tragicomic, doomed queens) to acclaim and awards, but most often as a stunt, and they'd be scrupulous about effusively thanking their wives, kids, and Jesus in their bios.

A very few actors, many of them gay, came in, enabling us to discover some not only beginning but wonderfully reckless talent, along with veteran performers who didn't give a shit what anyone thought. AIDS had killed countless theater people, so closeted paranoia verged on the obscene. I'd written an assortment of female roles to be played by a single actress, and Jess stepped up, telling me, "Whatever you need." Once we were cast, Farrell had only one question: "I'm sure the group is talented, but are they gorgeous?" As far as I was concerned, they were both.

Rehearsals were arduous. I rewrote continually; this was material based on a community I cherished, so I fine-tuned every syllable. According to lunch-break gossip, the cast would place bets on which scenes I'd cut. Ben was a lesson in nurturing but unerring leadership. If an exchange wasn't working, he'd ask, "So what do we think about that?" and suggest alternatives without sighing ostentatiously and declaring, "Man, that scene really sucks"—even when it did. Some directors are only comfortable with manipulation and obedience, draping their cardigans across their shoulders and berating unpaid assistants—"Jesus, Kelly, where's my fucking espresso?" Ben was the opposite. He wasn't dictatorial, but committed to strengthening the play. A great director is an alchemy of a supportive parent and an experienced teacher, with an artist's eye. At twenty-eight, Ben was an unassuming marvel.

He and I became a worshipful audience. Our cast had already spurned the world's advice, so they were all-in, uproarious and moving and devoted to each other. There was a scene where Alex sought the advice of a horny gay priest in the pews of St. Patrick's, and the actors were rattled, and holding back. It became clear that both guys had been raised in Catholic households. Ben told the actors, with tenderness, "Okay, if you play this scene, you'll just have to accept something: you're both going to Hell." This was the most helpful absolution. The actors grinned and the scene took flight. I'd itemize each day's trials and breakthroughs to Farrell, who had the kindest and most patient response to my prattle: he listened. He later enumerated, "A playwright's spouse must memorize the following phrases: 'Much better,' 'It's really coming along,' 'You made me laugh,' 'You made me sob,' and 'Shakespeare was a hack.'"

Our dress rehearsal was a deadening slog, lasting untold hours, as lighting instruments caught fire, costumes snagged and ripped, and our budget turntable, intended to foster rapid scene shifts, groaned to a halt, like some ancient expiring triceratops. "This is why we have dress rehearsals," murmured Jackson, who was designing the show for free.

"And valium," Farrell added.

"We'll have fun," Jess predicted. "My mom keeps calling it 'your little gay sex play.'"

Our first preview took place on New Year's Eve. I sat on a bench in the back row, in between Ben and Farrell. My parents, who'd harassed me into attending, were two rows ahead of us. People at first previews are most often ghouls, slavering to spread the unholy word of an incipient mega-flop.

Tonight wasn't *Enter Hamlet*, and not just because the stage was an eighth the size. My mood wasn't disconcerted but yearning, because I had so much more on the line. The Clarion studio team would be perplexed at my caring so passionately about such an uncommercial, orphaned vehicle staged in a godforsaken space, so many blocks and light-years from Broadway, let alone Hollywood. But *I Dare You* was mine, and Ben's, and Farrell's.

The play opened with the city having sex, or trying to, as the entire cast, in disparate locations, coped with faulty condoms and hair mousse mistaken for lube and deducing that their anonymous partners were their second cousins, all in the age of AIDS. There was a mass disconcerted pause, a collective intake of breath, as the audience arbitrated whether they could laugh, and then, with decisive abandon, they went right ahead.

The first laugh, at a first preview of a new play, isn't just a birth or a verdict. It's a sign from God, far beyond the miracle of Fatima or the parting of the Red Sea. It's the Almighty in a good mood, as if He's had a long day but congratulates Himself: "My humans are funny."

Farrell clutched my hand as Ben whispered notes to his intern, an NYU theater student. The play proceeded, through scenes of AIDS tests, Star Wars–themed, red-ribboned fundraisers, and overtly salacious gym workouts. The audience's laughter didn't cease, until Winston was diagnosed as HIV-positive. There was a stillness, because the show could obviously no longer function as a comedy, but a few beats later, when a chorus boy entered, in feline costume from his Cats matinee, and demonstrated twitching his tail, the crowd was roaring again. The chorus cat was HIV-positive, too, because that's the world everyone in that theater, and in New York City, was living in.

The real test was my mom's shoulders. She'd defend her fond memories of Enter Hamlet, because the play had been inoffensive and comprehensible to our relatives. I Dare You was something else. My parents had read the script, and while they were officially receptive, their trepidation quotient mirrored my own. I was aching for the play to be funny, while my mom was afraid audience members would become grievously offended, troop en masse to my apartment building, drag me into the street, and assassinate me. And then, their torches and pitchforks raised high, they'd howl, "So where's the playwright's mother, or is she too ashamed to show her face and who could blame her?"

As the evening kicked off, my mom's shoulders had hunched in the vicinity of her ears, especially during a scene in a masturbation club. But once the crowd's affection was sustained, her body relaxed, as if being massaged.

During Act II, things continued to go well, with apprehensive exceptions. I'd introduced Mother Teresa as a character, since she'd occasionally visited the city. Toward the play's emotional apex, as Alex sat in a hospital waiting area, with Winston in a coma, Mother T glided onstage and asked what was wrong. Alex said, "My boyfriend has AIDS and I think he's dying." Mother T took a heartsick pause and remarked, "Oh no, oh dear. Is he—attractive?" Alex replied, "Yes. Very." Mother T shook her head ruefully and commiserated, "That's the worst, isn't it?"

Jess, in her striped habit, played this knife's-edge comedy impeccably, and in rehearsal, Ben and I had been convulsed. But tonight's audience was invested in Alex and Winston, and in so many guys like them, so they weren't willing to laugh. I heard Ben giving a note, and before the next performance I'd recalibrate the lines. "Well, I think it's funny," Farrell whispered to me.

Luckily, the play's final scene was a moonlit, potential reunion between Alex and Winston, with just the right trade-off of punchlines and hardship. I couldn't justify a hats-in-the-air, every-problem-solved finale. No one, especially not me, would buy it. Farrell's life expectancy was still an open question. New York was a city without answers and only the most precarious reserves of hope. So when Alex asked Winston why they should still be together, in the face of such doom-ridden certainties, Winston replied, "I dare you."

As the lights ebbed on their kiss, the audience sighed, with a hard-won, speculative pleasure, and greeted the cast with furious and loving applause. Florence Gruber stomped her feet and my dad whistled, as Farrell kissed my cheek. This was only a first preview, before a friendly crowd, but, as Ben told me, "It might be really good!"

When we got back to Farrell's place, he sat me down and asked, "All right, do you understand the difference, between this play and *Enter Hamlet*?"

"Um . . . this play is better?"

"No. This play is you. This play matters. And I'm sure some people will hate it, or find it distasteful, or whatever, but that's all to the good. Because you don't have to care. This is a play that uses the best of you, and has a reason to exist. I was eavesdropping at intermission, in the men's room, and one guy said, 'This play is like someone tapped my phone,' and another queen said, 'This is my life.' But the best thing was their friend, who said, 'Thank God it's funny.'"

I stood and paced. Because while I still couldn't boast of any literary grandeur, I wasn't embarrassed by my work, mortified at my own failings. This was a first. And of course, most obviously, this play was gay. Beyond gay. Irreparably gay. Unapologetically gay. It wasn't a naughty peek at Manhattan's gay subculture for a mainstream theatergoer's perusal. I wasn't spurning the heterosexual audience, but I wasn't courting it either. I wasn't hedging my bets. I'd put aside every professional tremor, and my own lingering yen to be admired, even by people whose politics I despised. My work had aligned with my life. I'd stirred components of musical theater, Ludlam, and screwball romance, the gay bibles. I'd met Farrell. I'd taken off my shirt at a gay dance club. I'd fucked in Cary Grant and Randolph Scott's bed.

And I'd written an unabashedly gay play, something I should've been doing all along. But *Enter Hamlet* and *Habit Forming* had value; I'd been learning to write. To become worthy of my material, of the lives that deserved the best I could come up with. The lives I was lucky to know. And the lives that had been lost.

Was this partisan theater, a merely topical signpost of identity posturing? Didn't the classic, most unfettered pieces, the touchstones like *Private Lives*, *The Importance of Being Earnest*, and *Our Town*, exist on another, more far-reaching plane entirely? And wasn't lasting artistry a value superior to momentary protest? Maybe, but the authors of those plays were gay men, restricted from any portrayal of their own histories. I was, at the very least, paying tribute through progress and hoping they'd approve or, even better, laugh from their celestial seats in the orchestra.

In short, after so much whimpering, ineptitude, and sometimes lucrative detours, I was, as Mother Gregory would say, who I should be. And in my own off-Broadway downtown shoestring manner, I was being of use.

Farrell put his arms around me and whispered in my ear, "I know. Mazel tov."

He said this with a porcelain teaspoon of lockjaw, tipping into a recorded translation. Farrell was a Connecticut bride greeting her Wall Street hubby: "Shalom, Branston!"

He sat back down.

"Are you okay?" I asked.

"I'm fine. It's just—I'm so happy for you, and you should be so proud. But of course, I've fallen behind."

"What do you mean?"

"I'm not feeling sorry for myself, or I'm trying not to, but you've pulled ahead. You've applied yourself. And I haven't done anything."

"Farrell . . ."

"Yes, I know, I've been using my family's money to do some good, but for all these years, in Kansas and LA and back here, it's been a time-out. A revving up. Cooling my heels. And fine, I'm sick, but that shouldn't be an excuse. If anything, it's a spur, a time clock. I need to start—doing what I've been put here to do."

"Which is?"

"You'll see. I don't want to tell you about it, because then I'll feel like some loser wannabe, squawking about my pathetic pipe dreams. So once I've got things underway, I'll show you."

"Farrell, I think you know this, but my play, which is far from being finished, let alone anywhere near decent, I couldn't have written a word of it, not without you."

"I know. You're welcome. Thank God I have AIDS."

"This is why you have money. Because otherwise, when you say things like that, people would punch you. And they'd be right."

Farrell grinned. It was the first time in months, if not years, that he'd uncaged his complete, willfully satanic, you-know-you-love-me smile. He was pale and haggard, and limped, and had to gain weight, but as with the greatest beauties, he could rally his magic, he could rotate the dial, and the years and hospitalizations and family warfare fell away, and he was Farrell at maximum wattage.

That night we had an awkward, limited, but satisfying version of sex, as if we were both wearing plaster casts on several limbs, and we fell asleep, not as a lingering patient and already grieving partner, but as a couple, as us. This reprieve would most likely be fleeting, which informed everything: grown-ups appreciate the present, and treat the future as a wild card, as a Jewish horoscope foretelling, "Don't ask."

The night before the play opened, with the script frozen and the production polished, I sat in the back row with Ben and Farrell, and started crying, like a jerk.

"What?" asked Farrell.

"It's just . . . and I know this is dumb, and it doesn't mean it's good, but I really like this play. I think it's working. So if people hate it, I'm going to be . . ."

By "people," I meant the critics, and I didn't finish my thought because Farrell and Ben repeated the traditional opening night mottos, about how reviews don't matter and who cares what other people think. Everyone cares, especially the people who sniff that they never read reviews; quiz them, and those people will quote full paragraphs. There's an anecdote, centered on a Pulitzer-winning playwright, on the opening night of a subsequent dud. The playwright sits on the curb, downing a stiff drink, as the cast's dainty ingénue kneels and tells her, "Remember what we said, all of us, after the dress rehearsal? About how we're so proud of what we've created, and how we've become a family? So that whatever happened next didn't matter?"

"Of course," the playwright answered, adding, "We lied."

Later, after the show, when the theater had emptied out, Ben's intern trotted in with the next day's *New York Times*. From a distance, he frowned and gave a thumbs-down, and my heart thudded onto the floor, among the discarded Playbills and incipient careers. Then the assistant smiled, because the review was a rave.

26

I Dare You became an improbable success. I bathed in that most prized
subcategory of happiness, relief. I was gratified not just for myself but
for Ben, our cast, and the Annex, all of whom had taken an impetuous
chance on a radically unproven play. The actors had been told they'd
never work again, but now casting directors flocked to performances,
dangling film work and TV pilots. Audience members left notes at the
box office; a mixed couple, meaning one guy who was HIV-positive
and another who wasn't, had seen the play on their first date. Another
man, with full-blown AIDS, thanked everyone involved because the play
hadn't depressed him. The performances sold out, with repeat customers, who'd recite their favorite lines along with the characters.

The play moved to a larger theater for a commercial run. I was interviewed ("How is a comedy about AIDS possible?"), photographed
("Do you have a good side?"), and invited to conferences and town halls
on AIDS (which had engendered greater sympathy once Princess Diana
had been photographed holding an AIDS-afflicted child). There was a
feature in *New York* magazine, with photos of Farrell and me. His HIV
status, coupled with his last name and green eyes, lent us a narrative
sparkle. There was now something called the internet, where gay men
could bicker over "What is that incredibly hot Farrell guy doing with that

playwright creep?" I was wounded, until Farrell said, "But you're doing so much, for playwright creeps everywhere." My mom preened, when, while we were buying her an end table at a furniture outlet, the gay sales-guy recognized me. Although on our way out, she groused, "Why didn't he give you an extra discount?"

Farrell and I were in *People* magazine, as an offbeat couple on the rise. AIDS had a single virtue: it turned a long overdue spotlight on gay lives, meaning, most often, white gay male lives. Black and female gay people were admonished to wait their turn, with the transgender community shunned. Other racial minorities didn't even chart. Did I feel guilty about this? Yes, but never enough. Success can kick-start generosity, but public-ity lotions the ego. *I Dare You* surfed a wave of gay theater and sitcoms and novels, although not movies, not yet. Studio economics stalked a mass au-dience, which the gatekeepers still doubted was ready. A cultural dam had broken, although journalists asked Farrell and me if they could refer to us as "openly gay." Sometimes, to tick off his family, Farrell would respond, "Nate's openly gay, but I'm much more extreme. I'm Farrell Covington Industries gay."

My limited fame caused an upset in our relationship. Farrell loved that I was being lauded, for a play he'd inspired, but for the first time, we were occasionally equal. One night in bed, he asked, "Am I your arm candy? Do people think I'm a paid escort? Are you the writer and I'm just some cheap airheaded trinket?"

"Absolutely," I replied and he glowed, kissed me, and said, "Thank you."

I asked why he was thanking me, and he said, "Because anyone can be a writer."

The most crucial prerequisite for any couple's longevity is to have both partners unequivocally accept, as a baseline, that the person they love is insane and has no morals.

Farrell postponed his confidential plans, whatever they might be, and gave me a year. The play was produced everywhere, especially gay every-where, so we were hosted in San Francisco, Chicago, and Paris. While I was happy for the play's reach, the London version was dodgy, with the actors swishing up a storm, and Farrell suggested, "Tell them they don't have to act gay. They're already English." In Japan, there proved to be a wide audience for gay material starring Japanese celebrities, as long as the stories weren't set in Japan. Denial contorts itself. In each city, I'd be contacted by the sometimes-closeted gay correspondent from the local TV station or newspaper. While this system has been dubbed the Gay Mafia, it was also a vital network of people touching base with their tribe. Promotion made for unexpected pairings. As I was about to somberly chat with the host of an ultra–left wing radio broadcast in California, she intoned, "Later today we'll be speaking with visionary author Alice Walker about female genital mutilation. But next up is Nate Reminger, author of *I Dare You*."

Farrell and I had fun, as he rated every actor playing Winston, from "not half-bad" to "I forgive him." I was even more in Farrell's debt, since he'd see the play over and over again, the tiresome price of fucking a playwright. My delayed success was more richly appreciated, as *I Dare You* was the first piece I didn't want to apologize for. There was backlash, from pundits who'd yowl things like "Why are the characters all lisping, shrieking queens? Is this a gay minstrel show?" These watchdogs often proved to be lisping, shrieking queens themselves. The most tiresome were the manly fellows, who viewed their gayness as an inconvenience, and would predict the welcome demise of "gay culture" in the wake of assimilation. Farrell and I had watched an effortfully macho gay spokesperson declaiming the need for "masculine gay heroes," causing Farrell to comment, "Darling, that is too true."

Our year crested with a protest in Washington, officially titled "A March for Lesbian, Gay, and Bi Representation and Freedom," calling for expanded AIDS research and the dismantling of prejudice. The ACT UP influence had been incalculable, as drug trials were being fast-tracked and treatments were made available on an as-needed basis. We ran into Jackson and Ariadne in front of the White House; everyone had shown up, over one million gay people from around the world. While past marches had been well attended, AIDS and pent-up, overspilling anger had multiplied the crowds. There was not merely an urgency but an absolute, no-excuses conviction. You had to go.

The day was balmy, with the cloudless, sunlit bustle of a politically substantial street fair, with the rallying cry "We're here, we're queer, and we're buying commemorative T-shirts, rainbow everything, and Harvey Milk bobbleheads." There were speakers and earnest musical acts, and we saw one lesbian, in dungeon-grade leather, with her submissive partner on a chain-link leash that was clipped to the partner's pierced labia, through the open fly of her jeans; "I love that couple," Farrell observed, "but I worry about them crossing a busy intersection." Farrell and I held hands, which we didn't always do. There was a safety to the lawns and parade grounds, and physical affirmations were everywhere. The police presence was sizeable but benign. As Ariadne said, "Gay people are so fucking nice. Working security at a pride march is the easiest job in the world." The officers would dance with the marchers, who applauded the porn iconography of a man or woman in uniform. "Whenever I see someone with a badge," said Jackson, "I wonder, are you real or a stripper at a bachelorette party?"

The AIDS quilt was spread across several acres, with thousands of denim, felt, and corduroy panels, stitched with the names of people who'd died, with personal artifacts attached. There were yearbook pages, well-loved teddy bears, graduation tassels, and pot holders. As Jackson said, "It's what the world would look like if I was in charge."

Farrell and I chanced upon a square for Terrence Whitby, the first person we knew who'd died. Farrell left me a few yards behind, as a separation. Through their illness, Farrell was linked to Terrence in a way I wasn't. There were marchers sobbing, both infected and well, or not yet visibly sick. Farrell put his arm around my waist. The quilt wasn't just a memorial but a statement of fact. All these people, stretching as far as the eye could see, were gone. The quilt was an assertively gay response to the most unthinkable obliteration. "You have to promise me," Farrell said, "that if I get a square, you'll use real fur, just to confuse the animal rights people."

"You're not getting a square," I told him.

"Why not?" Farrell challenged me.

"Because you're not," I said, because we were crying.

"All this lovely fabric," said Jackson. "I'm ignoring the double knit."

"That's what killed them," said Farrell.

I raised my hands, as if I was a mom giving up on her I-can't-take-you-anywhere offspring.

"Look at you," said Ariadne, whose eyes were damp as well, and she never cried. "What a bunch of cocksuckers."

"Thank you," Jackson, Farrell, I, and at least twenty nearby strangers answered. That night, for the first time in ages, Farrell and I danced.

We were in the lobby of some grand government building. With temporary lighting on a ceiling grid, and an eighteen-foot-high bronze statue of Lincoln towering over a portable DJ booth, it made for a shadowy, distinguished club, as if the Supreme Court had opened an after-hours disco. There were plenty of dancers, swallowed by the scale of the room. The music was pumping and well chosen, and Farrell's limp was in retreat, so we fell into a more languorous take on our old rhythms, circling each other and moving in close for the slow, bass-heavy, sleazy songs. Ariadne flagged atop scaffolding, tossing her best rainbow silks, like an industrious, irate angel. Sometime after midnight Farrell motioned me outside, as he took a seat atop a wide limestone balustrade, with the floodlit Washington Monument as a backdrop.

"I'm going to tell you something," he said.

"Uh-oh."

"No, it's good. I spoke with Jarvis last week, while you were doing press. He's putting me on a new protocol, a drug cocktail, which has been getting amazing, if preliminary, results in a limited trial."

"That's great!"

"Maybe. We'll see. Although I'm so pleased they're calling it a cocktail, as if each dose will arrive with a paper parasol and a lime wedge. But my health is acceptable, even without it, so I have to commence with the rest of my life. I'm leaving New York on Wednesday. I won't tell you exactly where I'm headed, but you'll always have a number, and I'll call you every week."

Farrell had been secretive, and active on his desktop computer, so I'd foreseen an announcement. But this was, not a blow, but another leave-taking, only we were older, and mortality was everywhere. Farrell eyed me, gauging my resilience. I was a home-front spouse, as my soldier slung his pack over his shoulder and set out for points unknown, carrying encrypted documents.

"And you can't be more specific because . . ."

"Because I need to discover if I can do this by myself. If you tagged along, you'd be rah-rah and you'd bake, or buy, cookies and ask a million questions, which I'd love you for, but that wouldn't be helpful, not just yet. And you should write a new play, to prove this last one wasn't a fluke, and I don't want to hang around and correct your grammar and circle the bad jokes in red and get in your way."

"Farrell . . ."

"You'll see. That's the most I can say. And I'll do my level best not to die. Jarvis is forwarding the prescriptions. But if the drugs don't take, if my arms fall off, trust me, I'll be in touch, which is an unfortunate phrase since I won't have hands. But being sick—that can't be who I am, or all I am. Even if, thanks to your play, I'm swoon city. Teenagers everywhere have posters of me on their bedroom walls, signed 'AIDS! Luv ya, Farrell!' "

From his tone, and from our years together, and from loving him, I didn't argue. Our lives had been atypical. As Ariadne had once told me, "You can't worry about what anything fucking looks like from the outside, or how you're supposed to behave. Everyone's not domestic or cuddly or settled. Not even straight people." Her words were universally applicable. If conservatives argued that gay liberation had resulted in AIDS, they were assigning a hardened logic where none existed. Viruses, and the world, mutated, without tidy warning labels or directions from the manufacturer. But Farrell and I had never been conventional, and that's why we'd lasted. We couldn't stop now.

"Okay," I told him. "But I'm going to have breakdowns every second and tell everyone you've abandoned me, and in my next play Winston will abuse Alex unspeakably."

"And make Alex drink his bathwater and call himself a worthless little pigboy."

"And there's my title. *A Worthless Little Pigboy* by Nate Reminger."

"I'll be there on opening night. And you're coming to mine."

I had no grasp of where he was headed or for how long, but I trusted him, because he was Farrell and I had no choice. It was getting cold, and Washington, while scenic, has a foreboding quality, like a city of militantly landscaped federal mausoleums.

But the dance music picked up, as if the DJ were subverting the architecture, and enlivening the darkness.

Farrell jumped down from the balustrade and put his arms around me, for body warmth and reassurance. He took my face in his hands and kissed me. When Farrell was first diagnosed, kissing had become, like so much else, a decision. Open-mouthed? Saliva? What about a transfer of blood? But not kissing had been untenable, as a repudiation of romance. Two men kissing was also Farrell's middle finger to his family. That night's kiss was a salute to our nation's capital, and a pledge of allegiance, that Farrell would stay well and, if necessary, wiggle his armless torso for assistance, and that someday, when he chose to, he'd command me to be by his side.

FARRELL

27

Farrell was keeping his apartment open, so for our first week apart I meandered through the rooms as if hunting for clues to his whereabouts, and I'd sleep in our bed because it smelled like him. I didn't want to act as if he'd died, so while fiddling with a new play, I took a meeting with Brett, who was operating as the most feared and significant independent producer in Hollywood, with deals all over town. He flew me out to LA, because with Brett, especially in his forcefully achieved supremacy, everyone came to him.

Brett had rented a suite of offices that, like his homes, was spotlessly glacial and impersonal, as if an FBI task force had just moved on. He wasn't interested in his surroundings, and this kept the world guessing. His desktop was vacant, except for an embedded screen that rolled incoming calls, to be taken, postponed, or deleted forever. He was casual and friendly, which meant he wanted something. Despite his best efforts at imperial obscurity, Brett was transparent. He was a brainiac child mainlining Diet Coke, making fifteen new deals during his nightly half hour of sleep.

I'd rewritten *Habit Forming* a few more times, and a slew of other writers had revised the previous writers' revisions. The movie had been made under duress, with Brett steamrolling the filming forward, greased with guile and death threats. But the star and the story were appealing, the budget was low, and the movie was a smash, as ribald family fare, a clean dirty joke with nuns leapfrogging through a casino, wimples flying. My original idea and sly intent had been corrupted, but thanks to Florence's negotiating tactics, I had a piece of the profits. Audiences were flocking, and as with *Enter Hamlet*, I was torn. Farrell had suggested an ideal approach: we never saw the movie. That way I wouldn't fulminate, and I could chalk the experience up to a nicely compensated learning curve. And *I Dare You* had centered me, in staking claim to a voice and a subject, so my angst was tempered. But trying to integrate my passion and my income was—a fool's errand? The most inconsequential discrepancy? An East Coast artiste's pampered politics?

"How's Farrell?" Brett asked. We'd never touched on the *Habit Forming* outcome. Hollywood runs on judicious amnesia.

"He's good, I think. He's getting stronger and he's off on an adventure."

In my ignorance of what Farrell was up to, I could tantalize Brett. Every second with Brett was a chess match, and he was the enigmatic Soviet prodigy.

"So I have an idea," he said, the intimate portion of our session concluded. If I'd told Brett that Farrell had been hanged for treason, or was being held hostage by a South American drug cartel, he'd have switched to a cursory, mildly interested tone, then jackknifed back to whatever was gnawing at him.

"Let's do something gay," he said. Could this be forward motion? Or a means of co-opting and monetizing a liberation movement? As Brett would undoubtedly say, with a don't-waste-my-time grimace, why not both?

"This came from the guy who cuts my hair," he said, which couldn't have been a lengthy conversation, since Brett didn't have that much hair. "He told me about how he'd been sleeping with this pretty powerful mobster, not a godfather but close. The mobster was older but silver-fox sexy, and married, for decades, to a mafia princess. Only he dumps my haircutter, and the wife, because he's smitten with a twenty-one-year-old rich girl who's a professional equestrienne."

He sat back.

"And?"

"And that's what I've got. It's just a germ, a jumping-off point, but I think there's something there. You in?"

After the most diminutive speck of resistance, I asked, "Can I think about it?"

From my Hollywood turf wars, I'd absorbed very little, except this: the indisputable, if perishable, power of maybe.

"Of course. Take your time. Overnight."

As I lay on my hotel bed, I was succumbing to Brett's innocently depraved wiles for two reasons. First, while *I Dare You* was a success, theater, except for long-running musicals, was never an overweening source of funds, and as Florence would remind me, "You'd better make some money, schnookie." Secondly, I was falling in love with Brett's idea, God damn him. Our haircutter would ally himself with the discarded mob wife, to wreak a creative comeuppance on our mobster. Maybe at his gaudy, bling-festooned, heavily fortified Catskills wedding to the horse jumper. Maybe the mob approved of this upwardly genteel match, so the gay guy and the spurned, aging princess could take the syndicate down. I was already roughing out a treatment, hyping a pitch.

The idea attracted me because it was a gay story without tears. It was an unexpected comedy about a gay underdog. So many gay plotlines revolve around a traumatic coming out, with an evangelical dad intoning, "I have no son!" Or they depict a clandestine gay romance that spirals into someone being savagely murdered by a snaggle-toothed redneck bigot and his crowbar-wielding pals. With *I Dare You*, I'd lent the gay characters authority and knowingness; they were in charge. With Brett's idea, I could have our hero, whom I'd named Marco, be underestimated and kicked to the curb, but emerge exuberantly victorious and uninjured. I'd call it *Crime Family*, which Brett loved.

This was the core of Brett's diabolical magnetism: nothing felt as good as making him happy. It was like making Stalin smile. When someone that strong-minded, with exalted keys to repeated success, favors you, there's an undeniable, if questionably healthy, high. Brett combined near-faultless gut instincts with an enviable track record. This was a potent seduction. And I might imbue a studio product with the gay oomph of *I Dare You*. Of course, I pined to tell Farrell, and have him cock an eyebrow and recall Brett's insidious effect on me. But Farrell and I were doing the same thing: plunging into the deep end.

I avoided LA, fine-tuning the script on Park Avenue. Farrell called me at least once a week. His T cells were decent, but whatever he was working on fluctuated. He'd be exultant and then, during our next conversation, dogged and abrupt. There were no details, but I hazarded Russia, Australia, or some tiny, remote island I'd never heard of. I almost didn't want a definitive geography, for suspense and to head off site-specific tension about medical care in, say, Patagonia. I clued Farrell in about *Crime Family*, and while hesitant, he concluded, "Why not? Just don't let Brett drive you mad. Or drive at all, because he'll be on the phone the whole time and he'll try to fire a stoplight."

This was my secret dread: that I'd die beside someone more illustrious. There was an airline, which I'd flown on the studio dime, called MGM Grand, which catered to stars, with staterooms and flight attendants costumed like members of a cruise ship musical revue. My phobia was that my flight would crash in the Rockies and the headlines would shout, "World Mourns Meg Ryan and Others!"

I handed in a draft and met with a cadre of executives at the estimable Landmark Pictures, a subsidiary of at least two corporate megaliths. This crew was far less antagonizing than the Clarion sharks, maybe because Brett had them cornered. But when the script verged on the consummately gay, someone would wrinkle their nose and carp, "Repetitive?" This occurred three times, until I told the group that I was born repetitive, and the complaint ceased. This is how change happens. By speaking up, with Brett Starber glowering in the corner, taking a call.

The process was surprisingly smooth, again, due to Brett's gathering clout. During stressful standoffs, or even flurries of disagreement with the budgeting staff, his face would redden and his head would visibly, throbbingly expand, as he spewed shrapnel at some hapless studio accountant: "So tell me, are you a fucking delusional idiot or a brain-dead moron? Which is it, because I want to send your parents a gift basket. Get out of my sight, you fucking manure pit." He'd deliver these thoughts in what I can only call a serene howl, as if catching up with his nana in the nursing home over the phone, while choking an anonymous passerby to death with his bare hands, just to keep in practice.

Brett's turbulence could be disturbing yet efficient, another timeless Hollywood recipe. Brett's movies were being made, and that ratcheted his legend. He could juggle millions of dollars and even more egos, production snafus, and Oscar campaigns, and this pressure may have manifested itself in his outbursts, as a release valve. He once told me, "I don't get ulcers, I give them." As our director, he hired an agreeable, straight comedy veteran. Brett wasn't backpedaling into tameness, but wisely cushioning risky material with professional savvy. Casting mirrored the resistance on I Dare You. Brett and I met with a roster of bankable, thirty-ish names, all allegedly, in agentspeak, "killer crazy" to play Marco.

Chad Stanton said, "I'd die for this, it's just what I've been looking for," but bowed out due to "scheduling conflicts" with his next action movie. Dax Dressler begged, "I'd do this for free," until being waylaid by a script where he'd rescue his family from alien invaders. Trad Nester almost bit, his deal had practically closed, until, citing "exhaustion," he departed, to spend quality time with his border collie.

Stars chase their fans' unstinting adoration, which playing a gay role could disrupt, unlike, for example, enacting a corpse-nibbling serial killer. "This is bullshit," said Brett, picking up his latest phone, which still wasn't on the market, and waking the manager of Billy Dender, a supremely talented New York theater actor who'd be perfect as Marco. "Make this happen!" Brett bellowed at the manager. "Today!" It happened. For Silvio, the mobster, Brett went with Hank Bessinger, a craggy, name-brand commodity in a long-running detective series, who cut his price for a big-screen credit. His disgruntled wife would be none other than Rebekah Tanner.

I recounted this to Farrell, who was entertained by Brett's howitzer schmooze, but commented, "Brett's a leftie version of my father. Which is how he gets the job done." I asked Farrell if he thought Brett would ever actually have anyone murdered, and he thought about it and answered, "Probably not. Because it's no fun to yell at a corpse." I agreed but wondered, was it possible to make movies without bullying? There were other, less volatile producers. But Brett was not only fiendishly gifted, he satisfied everyone's darkest, private urges: What if I wasn't nice?

I updated Farrell on our friends. Jackson had won a second Tony Award (for his mouthwatering 1920s art deco frocks in a hit musical revival), Jess was doing a deconstructed *Love's Labour's Lost*, set in a bankrupt coal-mining town, while Ariadne had enrolled in a graduate program for social work. I'd even heard from Wainwright Covington, who'd called to ask after Farrell's health.

"Wainwright?" asked Farrell.

"He was sweet," I said, "so I told him you were okay, but then his wife started yelling that one of their kids was graduating in five minutes, so we couldn't talk."

"Interesting," said Farrell, which gave me an opening to ask, "Are you okay?" There was a pause and he said, "Soon-ish," and hung up.

Shooting on *Crime Family* took place on locations and soundstages throughout the tristate area, so I was occupied, yet able to sleep in my own bed, or Farrell's. Even Rebekah flourished. At our first read-through, she'd clutched me and burbled, "Oh, Nate, we always have such a good time together!" But she was delicious onscreen, believably lacquered and dismayed and ultimately lethal, as Medea in jangly earrings and zebra-striped stretch pants. And she was, shockingly, playing her age.

During our last week, a teamster took me aside. His tasks included driving stars to the set and guaranteeing that union strictures and salaries were observed at all times. He had the silver-sideburned, leathery-tanned grit of a TV western star, and he told me, "You know something? Years ago, I was a cop. I was working undercover that night at Stonewall, when those drag queens started throwing bottles. I didn't know what the hell was going on, but my girlfriend explained it once I got home, and I thought, Holy crap, I'm on the wrong side here. I quit a few months later, not because I was such a good guy, but I needed to figure things out. So I wanted to tell you—I like this movie."

He wasn't soliciting my gay-certified forgiveness, or flaunting his re-born sensitivity. He was connecting through personal experience. The moment felt scripted, as if we were talking heads in a documentary, and Farrell later commented, "It's superb, as long as you didn't hug."

A rough cut of *Crime Family* was screened before a focus group in a cineplex at a Pennsylvania shopping center. Brett, the director, and I sat a few rows back, as a hired group leader canvassed audience members, handpicked for a demographic mix, on their reactions. "I loved it!" gushed a self-described stay-at-home mom, "Even if it was gay!" "I got kinda queasy," admitted a teenage guy in a basketball jersey, "when the two dudes were makin' out, but then it was sorta funny." "It's not a quality artwork," opined a middle school guidance counselor who'd identified himself as a "long-time film buff and scholar." He added, as if issuing an edict as the host of his own PBS half hour, "but it was enjoyable, to a certain extent."

The movie opened to reviews that were both positive and snippy. As gay acceptance entered the water supply, many critics cheered a feel-good, gay-positive romp, while the more high-minded and ostentatiously liberal cohort preferred something harsher and more rabble-rousing. "*Crime Family* is a shiny candy-box treat," the *National Review* allowed, "but where was the acrimony, scarring the wounded soul of America's sexual orientation civil war?"

Almost more than *I Dare You*, I valued *Crime Family* as a political grenade, for a central reason: it made money. The studios had rejected gay-themed projects, citing not bigotry but finances. *Crime Family* was profitable. In addition, the movie featured a prolonged, romantic, same-sex kiss. This caused near rioting in many small towns, but as Brett told the studio, "Nobody died, and the same kids who threw popcorn at the screen told their buddies to go see the movie."

My life had come full circle. I was making America gay, off-Broadway and at the mall. Harwell's most dire foreboding, and Eric Nordstadt's quandary, were inching toward not merely acceptance but endorsement (with its own negatives of dilution and ho-hum blandness). But while Farrell might be amused, he wasn't here. My career, while satisfying, was half the equation, what I busied myself with while anticipating Farrell's revelation. At last, another year later, the phone rang, and Farrell said, "Monday, 9 a.m., Teterboro. Get on the plane." As I rushed to ask what I should pack and how long I'd be away, let alone my destination, he hung up. Farrell was renewing our history. I was off on another first date, with a great-looking, conceivably unhinged cipher, my irresistible question mark.

I'd been denied even a flight number, but the cab deposited me at a smaller private airport, beside a Covington Industries jet. The plane was eerily empty, a ghost flight, as if the passengers had been raptured, or black-leather-gloved henchmen were about to burst from the restrooms and pistol-whip me. Maybe Farrell was organ harvesting. As I nodded off, I thought, This could be a *Flying Dutchman* setup, and I'd be circling the globe for centuries without respite.

The flight attendant was evasive, but let drop that we were traveling to France. "Paris?" I asked, but she declined to be more specific, "at Mr. Covington's request." Stepping off the plane, I was in the Loire Valley, wherever that was, and there was a car. The driver was as tight-lipped as the flight attendant.

We drove through the most verdant countryside, like a richly colored mural on the plaster wall of a theme restaurant. There were few structures, only rivers and farmland with islands of ancient, gnarled oaks, neatly composed vineyards, and disinterested flocks of sheep. Had Farrell engineered this? Had he commissioned the Gallic landscape of an American tourist's Chablis-tasting, beret-friendly vacation dreams?

The car turned off the main road, onto a white-pebbled drive between two high, limestone pillars, topped with urns tumbling with ivy. Another mile, and there was—a lake? a boundless moat? a private ocean? A swan crossed the otherwise placid surface as we reached a kind of bridge or arched stone approach, and there, girded by water but perched on something between an ambitious hill and an amateur mountain, was not a château or an estate, but an honest-to-God, what-is-Farrell-thinking, Jesus-fucking-Christ it's a castle.

There was a round, soaring, Rapunzel-esque tower, set into a high, rambling parade of whitewashed stone walls, ramparts, crenellations, and randomly shaped windows, all of this looming larger and more imposingly as the car drew closer. This was Cinderella's goal, if she'd been less ditzy and had requisitioned lodgings for everyone in the kingdom. It was otherworldly but ominous, designed for awe and defense. As I left the car, I stumbled because the castle seemed sentient, as if a buttress might swoop down, pluck me by the collar, and fling me into the water.

My eyes weren't equipped. There was a chained drawbridge, and monumental iron grillwork, called a portcullis, with thick iron teeth, which began to rise via an internal winch, revealing a pair of oak doors with hinges based on, and the size of, dragon wings. One of these doors swung open, and there was Farrell in a white T-shirt, jeans, and bare feet.

"You made it," he said.

"Farrell?"

He vanished into his castle, as I kept to the center of the drawbridge, so I wouldn't teeter and drown. After the doors there was darkness, or the absence of the afternoon's bright sunshine, so my vision adjusted.

I walked forward, into not just a great hall or grand parlor, but an interior world. The arched limestone ceilings curved into columns the size of grain silos, bestriding a staircase wide enough for twenty hussars on horseback. There was a fireplace suitable for roasting an oil tanker. The slate floors reached into velvet-curtained nooks, an Arthurian dining rotunda and sitting areas guarded by suits of armor with lances, beneath five-tiered wooden chandeliers and banners embroidered with coats of arms in heavy golden thread, thick as rope. Hands covered my eyes, spun me, and there was Farrell, inches away, blocking all that gloriously unnecessary masonry. We hadn't seen each other in over two years, and he grabbed my neck and kissed me, not making up for lost time but continuing our story, and sweeping me into another dimension. He stepped back, his arms wide, as if bringing the castle to life with his hands, as an illusionist's chicanery, and yes, just like in Disney's *Beauty and the Beast*, I did expect a candelabra, a grandfather's clock, and a harpsichord to begin gavotting and belting a showstopper.

"Oh my sweet fucking Jesus," I said, "what have you done?"

"It's the Castle LeSorde. It was built in 1127 and burned down twice. I came across it ages ago, but it's taken me years of hassling with the

French government to get the transfer of title approved. The same family owned it for twelve generations, until they died out and the place was abandoned for almost a hundred years. It had been plucked clean by thieves and scavengers, so when I got here, two years ago, it was just a shell, with a tree growing out of the staircase and everything frosted with bird poop."

"So how have you managed to do this? It looks like Louis the whatever just stepped out for an execution."

"I got all my ducks in a row, because the property's on the Historical Register. Which means every decision I made, from a pattern choice for an encaustic floor tile to the placement of a hammered-brass door handle, had to be vetted. Except for the kitchens and bathrooms, I couldn't use any materials unavailable when the castle was first built."

"But how did you figure it all out?"

"You'll see."

He climbed the grand staircase, his leg healed, maybe from exactly this exercise. We passed supplemental, fully restored spaces before winding up in a large, square, open room, the beams stenciled. Sagging shelving lined every wall, from floor to ceiling, dangerously packed with books of every size, bulging portfolios, and document boxes labeled with stickers. There was a sturdy, vast oak center table, stacked with more books, many of them decaying into wisps of parchment and dried leather, along with cardboard cylinders for rolled maps and elevations. There were neat piles of at least twenty fully expanded looseleaf notebooks, beside every sort of writing, measuring, and magnifying utensil.

"This is the library and my command center," said Farrell. "I've got twelve full-time assistants, researching and faxing. They've been here since the beginning. I had to do this right."

"But the construction alone, not to mention the finishes and the furniture . . ."

"I hired an army, working around the clock, and I paid them properly. I tracked down artisans from Sicily and Romania and Poland, the great-great-grandchildren of men who'd taught them how to match inlaid marble and mix plaster from scratch and duplicate stained glass,

especially a true ruby red. They were fantastic and loved the opportunity to show what they could do. I had local officials and architectural committees over my shoulder every step of the way, but you see
those notebooks? My two main assistants, who you'll meet, Adrienne
and Daniel, we mapped everything out, with contingencies and added
days, added months, for unexpected hiccups. We updated and disguised
the heating system and even installed air-conditioning in certain rooms,
with the vents hidden through trompe l'oeil brushstrokes. I had it all in
my head before the first day, so I could be clear and appreciative. I only
fired one guy, and that was because he threw a hammer at his brother.
But we got it done."

Farrell wasn't fielding questions, so I bobbed in his wake, back downstairs and through another set of doors that could crush extended families, out onto a raised stone terrace overlooking what in America we'd call
the castle's backyard, if a backyard could encompass gardens that at first
I mistook for a special effect, some projected, three-dimensional vision,
based on an aristocrat's seventeenth-century sketch, of an idea too costly
and impractical to have ever been realized.

"It's split into parterres, of course," said Farrell, steadying himself on
a railing of carved wooden spindles and heavy iron, which became delicate, like a scrupulously rendered vine. "The boxwoods were here but
savagely overgrown, and we unearthed a box of sepia photographs in a
groundskeeper's cottage, from when things were still being looked after.
The plantings themselves are designed sequentially, so we always have
color. Right now we've got sunflowers and twenty-eight varieties of roses
and an Austrian wisteria that we've been growing from cuttings donated
by a horticultural society in Vienna."

Farrell forced himself to stop, because while I loved the passionate
velocity and nuance of everything he was saying, I couldn't catch every
word, because the gardens were walloping my senses. The fanatically
manicured hedges were frolicsome, outlining circles within squares, and
squares within the circles, for an Escher-like conundrum. Other topi-
aries had been pruned into pyramids and spheres, squired by life-size
topiary bears and giraffes. There were tiled canals tracing the garden's

exquisite geometry, with a waterfall spilling from an artfully natural rise. Fountains gushed beside reflecting pools, and I turned away, flabbergasted by so much effort and prowess.

"Are you okay?" Farrell asked.

"Yeah, but I'd better sit down."

Concerned, Farrell took me back into that central chamber, perching beside me on a deeply tufted, moss-green velvet couch, trimmed with row after row of jewel-encrusted ribbon, which I knew would make Jackson weep, the way I was doing. I was overcome.

"Nate? What's wrong?"

"Nothing. It's just, Farrell—I can't take this in. Everything you've done. It's, I want to say extraordinary or incredible or every one of those dumb, fancy words, but I'd sound like a tour guide."

"So—you get it?"

Farrell was unsure and proud simultaneously; vulnerable and lacking in defensive irony. Farrell and I had been honest with each other before, about how much we cared for each other, and the obstacles we'd feared, and the people and diseases and dense, flourless desserts we hated. But this was Farrell pushing himself and calculating whether the chances he'd taken and the money he'd spent, and the ideas he'd had about himself, if any of this had value. If the life he wanted was worth wanting.

"I get it," I told him. "No one else would do this, and yes, you could've spent the money irrigating a barren desert village, although I'm sure you've done that, too. But this place, and even more, your belief in why it matters, it's destroying me. In the best possible way. I'm so proud of you. For being out of your mind."

Farrell's smile began as a difficult-to-contain impulse, expanded into a glee he'd been denying himself, and marauded into fuck-everything joy. Just a few years back, Farrell's beauty had been almost extinguished beneath a near-death pallor, as his Hollywood-appraised bone structure had gone skeletal. We were both forty-one years old, but I saw the hopeful child Farrell had once been, the clamorous, blushing freshman I'd met all those years ago, and today a still devastatingly handsome man, weathered from hard work and the sun. If there was a signature Farrell Covington cologne, his face, as it appeared right this second, would outsell Chanel, as every guy yearned to at least smell like Farrell, and every woman purchased an extra bottle, for Farrell's photo on the box.

"I love you," he said.

"Because I like your castle?"

"No. Because of course you like my castle. Look at it. I love you because you've waited for over two years, and you haven't complained, and you've trusted me."

"And I have to ask this—what does Jarvis say?"

"I talk to Jarvis all the time. He's adjusted the cocktail, which was developed by a team in Paris, so I have immediate access to every advance. I still get tired and my stomach annoys me, and no one's been on this stuff for that long, but so far it's working."

"And what happens now?" I gestured to, well, everything around us, to the three-foot-thick walls, and the barrel-like tubs of indoor orange trees I'd only just caught sight of, and the carpets that must've been hand-loomed to such regal dimensions.

"We get to live here, for as long as we like. And once we're gone, it gets donated to France, with an endowment for staffing and upkeep. And yes, there's a tax break. But Nate, I'm so glad you're here, and that you understand this, and that you're not having me committed or tranquilized or escorted back to the States under armed guard. Because I'm only getting started."

That night we didn't have sex, because we couldn't stop chattering about the castle, our friends, and the trajectories of our separate lives. We were older, so sex became a subset of getting reacquainted and reattuned to each other's wayward habits. We were shy and mesmerized as our mutual rediscovery commenced. This had become our tradition, until later the next day we embarked on our physical reintroduction as well, noting a reduction in stamina and some shifting flesh.

"You're still too skinny," I said.

"You're not," Farrell said, to make me yelp and declare that I'd only added muscle, which was bordering on true.

As we lay in one of the castle's most opulent beds, overlooking the gardens, lit at night by torches, I ruminated over what Farrell had meant, about his future and ours and if they'd intertwine.

"I need to watch your movie," he told me, his head on my shoulder, "so I hope you've brought a cassette, since I've got a ye olde VCR." I'd packed three copies, because as my mom would say, "you never know."

"Farrell," I said. "How is this going to work?"

"I've got my eye on a place in Ireland, outside of Galway," he said. "Very stately and bleak, in the middle of nowhere. Fifty-eight rooms, a working dairy, and it's done time as a reform school and a hotel. A rumor of multiple murders and ornery ghosts. That's next."

"And how long are we here?"

"In this house or on earth?"

"Both."

"The answer to those questions, as you well know, is let's see what happens and make it up as we go along. Which isn't a choice because we don't have a choice. We've turned into who we are."

We stayed for a month. I met Farrell's staff, many of whom would be continuing with him on his next project. They were devoted to Farrell. Like me, they were drawn to a calamitous personality, and the exploits ahead. Farrell and I picnicked, swam in what faded, hand-drawn blueprints referred to as the lagoon surrounding the castle, and even rode horses to survey Farrell's work from a ridge. I'd never been on horseback before and I was scared shitless. I'm not big on leisure activities that can toss me into a ditch. But Farrell persisted, my steed was gentle, and Farrell said my next play should be called *Galloping Jews*.

Farrell came back to New York with me, to see everyone and witness the city's overhaul, as Times Square became less squalid and more ordinary, a tidied-up family attraction. "It's sort of anywhere," Farrell commented, "with a Cinnabon where that porn shop used to be, the one with the huge neon sign that said 'ANAL.'" He commended the dutifully restored Broadway theaters, bankrolled by Disney, "because only a global corporation, or me, can afford to get the glazed ceramic cornices just right." But his restlessness was obvious, and one morning he kissed me and said, "See you in Ireland."

Over the next twenty years, there was the Galway manor house, a Kentucky train depot (with a siding for sleeper and dining cars), an art nouveau apartment building in Barcelona, a Marrakech compound (with strutting peacocks and monkeys that shat on guests from palm trees), a Venezuelan abbey (which Farrell cautiously had deconsecrated), palaces in Luxembourg, Edinburgh, and Egypt, and a smattering of cozier antiquities, that Farrell termed "appetizers." Each home, or nearly eradicated ruin, would be researched, reconstructed, opened to the public, and loved. Rich people love differently, because so much is available to them: baseball teams, recreational submarines, private consultations with Nobel Prize winners. Farrell's marvels weren't our children, or a hobbyist's follies. They were his movies, his plays, and his astonishingly vivid dreams. He emptied his family's coffers to enrich the world, to let schoolkids, tour groups, and most of all, incipient Farrell Covingtons revel in not merely what they could never afford, but the knowledge that these buildings, these living encyclopedias of style, these flights of a romantic imagination, could be real, or even better, approachably surreal. Farrell was Hans Christian Andersen with five Andalusian bricklayers on retainer, or Walt Disney without the off-putting, zealously wholesome poured-resin sheen.

I was more of a workhorse, churning out scripts and screenplays, some meaningful, one or two of quality, and others that didn't quite work or didn't work at all, or served as rough drafts for an improved effort the next time out. I placed gay characters in biblical times, art galleries, and the White House, to prove they belonged. Mere gayness wasn't enough. I was energized by gay perspectives on the largest topics of faith, death, and having sex in department store dressing rooms while simultaneously considering an in-between-seasons waxed cotton blouson that's awfully close to something you already own.

I was born to love Farrell and to appreciate him, and to have his eccentric quest for beauty bewitch and exasperate me, since I'd forget toothbrushes, razors, and underwear at salvaged edifices around the world. "Duplicate camel's hair bathrobes," Farrell would remind me, "are the meaning of life."

There was a year when Farrell was about to fly home, for the latest of Jess's weddings (her third, but this one more sure-footed, since he wasn't an actor). I'd seen Farrell a month before in Scotland, but I couldn't wait to have him with me. Our days in New York were a gift of intimate history. I'd rented a bigger place, still in the Village, on the top floor of a converted women's prison (Farrell had applauded this heritage). Jackson called me—everyone had cellphones—in a state of jabbering distress, over a live broadcast on every TV network. I took my phone up to the roof, where as I calmed Jackson, I saw a jetliner plow into the North Tower of one of the World Trade Center skyscrapers.

I wasn't aware, not yet, that the critical flights on 9/11 were domestic. Farrell was in the air. It took me an anguished fifteen hours before we could speak, although by then I'd confirmed: his flight had been grounded in London. But like the world, I became obstinate about any loved one leaving my sight. Once Jess's wedding had been rescheduled and Farrell was present, we launched into one of our more irrational-but-not-really, what-is-wrong-with-you clashes, as I screamed at Farrell to stay in New York permanently.

"I can't do that and you know it," he said. "So please don't take your international terrorist panic attack out on me."

He was right but I was entitled to yelp, "I don't care! Fuck you! Just fuck you!" until I slammed a few doors and took an agitated walk along a riverside pathway, joined by neighbors doing the same thing, with the still visible plume of black smoke from Ground Zero not that many blocks away. As with AIDS, the destruction became a particular insult to New York, with the plume a nihilistic downtown counterpart to the Statue of Liberty. I hugged Farrell when I got back to the apartment: "But you're still a total asshole for ever getting on a plane."

I accustomed myself to Farrell's highly focused but unpredictable globetrotting. We both took lovers but never for extended periods, because our devotion to each other was a given. The men I slept with were often wonderful people, but they could discern, sometimes after a single night together, that I wasn't what anyone would judge emotionally available. I was like someone on a limited diet or a doctor on call. Farrell and I would never belong to anyone but each other. Sometimes, because I'm a dithering cartoon chipmunk from New Jersey, I'd vacillate over Farrell's love equaling my own, so I'd phone him, or have dinner with him in Oslo, and luxuriate in him scolding me or punishing me with silence for a few hours, or rolling his eyes and asking, "Don't you ever get tired of being you?"

As we passed sixty, Farrell's fatigue increased, not so much physically but as an impatience with the liturgy of research and repair that he'd lived for. On Park Avenue he told me that he'd scouted a place where we might, as he said, "put our feet up."

"Where?" I asked. "Please don't say Antarctica or North Dakota."

"Italy. Ravello. The Amalfi Coast."

The house wasn't as grand or derelict as his logbook of architectural rescues. It was a villa, built in the 1930s by the daughter of Baron Grimthorpe and christened La Rondinaia, meaning The Swallows Nest. It had subsequently been owned by the novelist, essayist, and WASPish talk show perennial Gore Vidal, who'd lived there for decades with his partner Howard Austen, an advertising copywriter and stage manager he'd met at the Everard Baths in 1950. Vidal had happened upon the place during a postwar excursion, via jeep, with buddy Tennessee Williams. Gore and Howard were gone, and the house had changed hands more than once, but was back on the market. Farrell told me, "It wouldn't be much work, just nips and tucks, but it's the first place where the second I laid eyes on it, I thought: us."

Thanks to a technology I was dubiously adept at, I could write anywhere. The home's legacy was formidable and a bonus, much like our rental of the Cary Grant/Randolph Scott address. Vidal had written a pioneering gay novel, published in 1948, titled The City and the Pillar, which had depicted gay lives sympathetically. He'd also, during a much-publicized political debate, called the right-wing overlord William F. Buckley a "crypto-Nazi," to which Buckley retorted by sniping at Vidal as "a queer." Farrell and I were becoming guardians of gay history as real estate.

Farrell took a few months alone to inspect and tinker. I joined him in April; he didn't send the Covington jet, because there was no element of surprise. Farrell met me at the airport, and as we neared Ravello in his alarmingly rattletrap Italian sportscar, I melted with a literary and sheerly visual rush. The whitewashed stone house clung precariously to a cliff-side, with graduated levels of rooms, a zigzagging outer stairway to the beach, and a tucked-away swimming pool. It was sinfully comfortable and larger than it first appeared, at five thousand square feet, with views of the sea from almost every room. Like all of Farrell's prizes, it was both a house and a movie location, where a couple could live, and perhaps throttle each other, or survive an apocalypse, or grow old.

Farrell would be handsome till he died, but he knew what he'd once looked like and he missed it, as a wistful parent pines after a favorite child who's moved out of state. Photographers had doted on Farrell, who'd leaned pensively against a sequoia, lounged in an Acapulco hammock, and shed his clothing for moody black-and-white studies. These pictures appeared in monographs, private collections, and gallery shows, where Farrell would loiter near his twenty-three-year-old self, pleased at being recognizable. I'd catch him tightening his jawline in the bathroom mirror, or positioning his fingertips to simulate a face-lift. "Should I have something done?" he asked, and I replied, "Everything. Remove enough skin to make me a younger boyfriend."

"You'll never understand what it's like," he sighed, "to worry about disappointing people. I envy you." Then he laughed, which benefits anyone's looks, and told his reflection, "All I need is a flattering sunset and a Rebekah Tanner scarf."

"And a vodka tonic," I suggested.

"No," Farrell said firmly, "we're not an aging, bitterly feuding alcoholic gay couple, except maybe on Scrabble nights. But here's my thought, so everyone will look better: let's keep a woven Navaho basket right by the front door, and ask everyone to deposit their eyeglasses."

Farrell and I had eight years at La Rondinaia. It was as if we'd waited for the right house to become a settled couple, which was a prerogative we'd never gotten around to. We'd had the townhouse in New Haven, our sojourn in LA, and commuting between Park Avenue and the Village. But we'd never spent an extended stretch in the same place, waking up together, filling the morning with creaking limbs, the international edition of the *New York Times*, and being recognized as that nice, and sometimes querulous, older gay couple by local shopkeepers and bakers and the staffs of restaurants. We remained vain, but carried canvas tote bags and layered our sweaters against a chill, able to waste pleasant hours without conversation, or gab amiably about idiot senatorial candidates, beloved Almodóvar films, and our digestion. After Farrell's years of illness, this was a blessed time-out.

His drug regimen continued. He'd been lucky and his luck hadn't abated. There were others like him, who'd eluded the plague's last rites. Farrell said he could spot his fellow survivors on the street: "We're cult members, or people who inexplicably crawled out of the rubble after an earthquake. There's a living ghost thing, but also a confirmation, a secret handshake. I get the same vibe when they film those reunions of soldiers who served at Pearl Harbor." We had gym equipment in a spare bedroom, but we respected its privacy.

Our friends vacationed with us, which we encouraged, and we'd take weeks in the States, but less regularly. Farrell kept tabs on his many homes, but wasn't compelled to revisit them. He only moved forward, even if that meant replacing a rug or a lamp in one of our guest rooms, or taking a drive up the coast and the ferry to Capri, where Farrell would eyeball the more outlandish homes, and resolve, "I can't do a place on Capri. I love it, but I'm not ready for oversize Armani sunglasses, a Pucci tunic, and an ostrich-turquoise Birkin. Not yet."

I was interviewed one afternoon by a Yale senior who'd been studying in Rome on a fellowship underwritten by the Covington Foundation. Sten was nonbinary, smooth-skinned, rounded, and of Iranian and Swedish parentage. Sten told me up front that their preferred pronouns were they and them. More than gender, Sten's identity struck me as "student." Sten's thesis was on "Queer Theater and the Politics of Inclusion," so I was a historical resource. "You're extremely fortunate," Farrell told Sten, bringing them a lemonade. "Nate is like some brine-encrusted gay amphora, dredged from the bay by drunken sailors. You can learn so much."

"Is that your . . . husband?" Sten asked, once Farrell had availed himself of a chaise on a lower terrace.

I clarified that while Farrell and I had marched, signed petitions, and donated for marriage equality, we hadn't personally signed on. Maybe it was the sour example of Farrell's parents, or our nontraditional leanings, but with healthcare and financial proxies in place, we'd demurred. As Farrell had said, "The only reason to get married is to make the other person feel trapped, or as a starting gate for divorce." As for me, my superstitious impulses were strong ("superstition" was also my pet name for insecurity). Farrell should be with me by choice, and not from any legal obligation.

"I sort of get what you mean," said Sten. "Because marriage is heteronormative and a vestige of patriarchal capitalism, so maybe we should make something new."

"Maybe," I said. Sten was zealous and disapproving, but I didn't mind. At twenty-one, they were supposed to be. When I'd first contended with progressive language, and Vx., Mx., and Hir, I'd been of two minds: First, that this was a hoax to make me feel old and cranky, because over the course of my life I'd had to memorize my Social Security number, so many friends' phone numbers, which they kept changing, the spellings of Caitlins/Katelynnes, all those passwords, Farrell's countless addresses, and now this. Secondly, in my more sound and compassionate mind, I believed that people should be called what they'd like to be called. Ariadne had said, "It's a pain in the ass and fucks with sentence structure, but tough shit. Because you know what everyone's biggest problem is, since the beginning of time? People want change to be easy, and never inconvenience anyone. If you have to think for a half second, or read more carefully, it won't fucking kill you. Grow up." Or as Jackson demurred, "I'm just going to call everyone darling and see if they turn around."

"Do you think the word 'gay' is no longer relevant?" Sten continued. "And limiting, as an outdated label?"

I paused. The world altered daily and I labored to keep current. The word "queer" was versatile, in reclaiming a slur and casting the widest possible net, when even LGBTQ was only a sprinkling of the queer alphabet. I'd push for the most infinite buffet, of sexual preferences and gender pathways. But was I being baited, into a contest of semantic awareness?

"Here you go," I said. "I know why people, especially younger people, might disdain the word 'gay.' Your dad or mom was gay; you're queer. Saying you're gay feels narrow and square and over. Which it may very well be. But when I was growing up, it was a grail. I wanted to put 'gay' on my tax returns, as the answer to every question. I love being gay, or whatever we're calling it, and most likely, some next generation will sneer at you, and say 'queer' with pity. And there's one more thing, while I'm wagging my arthritic finger. Someone threw a bottle of beer at Farrell's head, because he was gay. I was told not to write about gay lives, because it would alienate the straight audience. And when AIDS demolished a generation, it was called the gay plague. Not queer, gay. So I like it."

"Okay," said Sten, who was recording me on their phone. "But sometimes people say, wouldn't it be great to have a play or a movie where the characters just happen to be queer? And that the queerness wasn't the whole point? Like a queer James Bond or a queer Superman?"

"I've heard that, but again, no one ever asks, wouldn't it be great to have a play or movie where the characters just happen to be straight? And that wasn't the whole point? Because, of course, it always is. And I'd love to see a queer James Bond dating a queer Superman, but not if their being queer means nothing. I'd want them to show up at the underground lair of an evil mastermind, poke around, and comment, 'Sectional seating and swivel chairs! No wonder people call you evil!'"

"You mean you'd want them to be campy."

"No. I'd want them to be interesting and smart and entertaining."

"Do you pay attention to any younger queer writers?"

I listed my favorites, to enhance my queer street cred, but invented a few names, to test Sten's. They nodded vigorously, saying, "I love all of them."

I felt guilty for lying to Sten, so to make amends I let them take a swing at me, asking if they'd seen I Dare You or Crime Family.

"I've read I Dare You," they parried. "It was cool. Like a period piece. And Crime Family is my mom's favorite movie."

I no longer felt guilty. But I refrained from asking Sten if their preferred pronoun was actually "bitch."

"Do you think that in the future, no one will even think about any of this, because human sexuality will be so inclusive and evolved?"

Since we had cable, Farrell and I had binge-watched the latest limited series where lithe, saucer-eyed, genderless teens swallowed substances, orgied in the stalls of club restrooms, and mooned over each other online. This show had a retro quality, from the flimsy, nipple-revealing sixties-style outfits to the strobing, disco-era, dancing-while-high cinematography. It was sweet, like so many pieces that strain to be shocking and genre-shattering. The show was already nostalgic for itself. I'd lasted through many cycles of sexual exploration, unnatural hair colors, and independent films that built to extended, silent close-ups of the central, dolefully broken character staring out to sea or across a field or from the window of a bus, but it would be elder-snobby to tell Sten, "I remember unisex. It all comes down to jumpsuits."

"Who knows about the future?" I said, choosing gay-Yoda benevolence. "But I think, as a rule, the more queerness, and the less punishment, the better."

"But do you admit that your financial and artistic success have been made possible by cisgender white male privilege?"

Sten had been saving this, as a death blow. I'd seen it coming.

"Of course. But let me ask you—how many lives are you going to get?"

"What?"

"Of course I've benefited from being a cisgender white man. But I've also worked hard, as has Farrell, who's dealt with extreme family and health issues. And in a perfect world we'd all be doctors and nurses and the rich white people would donate all their funds to worthy Indigenous causes, and then they'd listen attentively to a completely justified roll call of their ancestral sins and graciously kill themselves. But despite the undeniable and horrific history of prejudice and injustice, we each only get one go-round. And I won't apologize for enjoying mine. And remember: there are folks far worse off than you, staring daggers at your hemp shoulder bag from a crafting site that also sells scrunchies made from recycled water bottles. Both being items you bought after the first installment of your grant from the Covington Foundation cyber-arrived in your bank account."

"I was celebrating! And the money from the sale of this shoulder bag goes to support a women's collective in Kabul!"

Sten clutched their shoulder bag defensively, to deflect my lucky guess.

"I'm not criticizing you. Quite the opposite. You deserve pleasure and sponsorship and the occasional éclair. Everyone does. But there's nothing duller than morose white people awarding themselves atonement certificates. And equality isn't enhanced by huffiness."

Sten's face was quizzical and, for the first time, amused, by an old man's marzipan aphorisms. This was my favorite response, because Sten was tantalized yet not quite sure I was serious. They were in danger. Irony is a quick glide toward sophistication, and they might find themselves relishing a novel that hadn't undergone a sensitivity edit.

"Are you getting along?" Farrell asked, returning with a box of butter cookies. I'd taught him well, in the art of Jewish hosting.

"All done," said Sten. "And Mr. Covington, thank you so much for the grant from your foundation. It saved my life."

"So you owe me a thank-you note," said Farrell, "because I'll be judging you on your signature."

"He's weird," Sten muttered to me, on their way out. "But he's really good-looking. I mean, even now."

When I repeated this flattery to Farrell, I omitted the words "weird" and "even now." I'd save them for later.

That night, as we lay in bed beside each other, both wearing drugstore reading glasses and thick wool socks, Farrell asked, "Are we happy? Or happy enough?"

"Did you say 'happy enough' because you're too scared not to qualify it?"

"Yes. I don't want to attract the evil eye, or termites, or my mother."

Ingrid, out of spite, was ostensibly alive (Farrell had once theorized that she was an ancient demon, encased for eternity in "a battle-ready girdle and low-heeled pumps"). Farrell hadn't spoken to Bolt in decades (Devin Llewellyn handled Farrell's business affairs), but we received Christmas and birthday cards from Wainwright, so there was a flicker of hope, for the Covingtons of tomorrow.

"Do you ever wish we'd had kids?" I taunted him.

Farrell calmly turned his head and inquired, "Do you ever wish I'd thrown you into a cage with nineteen bawling infants, five third graders with German measles, and twelve teenagers talking about their innermost thoughts while texting and playing video games?"

"If you could go back and change anything, would you?"

"These are the most hateful questions, like when people ask, 'What would you tell your younger self?' Because there's only one acceptable answer. I would've fucked him."

"You started it. You asked if we were happy enough. Which is the title of every Jewish rom-com."

"I asked you that because I was eavesdropping on your chat with Sten, who's adorable, and I think you should write a guide to the most up-to-the-minute, Sten-approved language, called *Them's Fightin' Words*. And I also thought that, in a way, Sten's our child. Or our grandchild. And I'm so glad we're still around to see so many fascinating and exhausting cultural developments. From our Ravello roost."

"Me too. And okay, you don't have to say anything back, but do you know one of my favorite parts of our life? That I couldn't have predicted any of it. Or that we'd end up here. Which is pissing off Gore Vidal, because he still thinks it's his house. Which is fine. Everything's borrowed."

"I never thought I'd live this long," said Farrell, who was sixty-eight.

"I stopped thinking about anyone's life expectancy years ago. I'm just grateful."

"For what?"

"Are you going to make me say it?"

"Yes."

"I'm grateful that my new reading glasses are stronger, so I don't have to do that old person thing of holding my Kindle a few feet away from my face. Although having a Kindle is probably the giveaway, that I'm Jurassic."

"I'm grateful that my hair's now entirely white. Gray is so middle-ground. So half-hearted. Gray hair is the beige of old age."

"I'm grateful we no longer have to keep up with everything, and can pretend we're senile. When Sten asked me about gender Marxism and its intersectionality with climate change, I squinted sagely and said, 'Spatula.'"

"I'm grateful for our heated mattress pad. All right, it's official. I deserve my own BBC series as a retired postmistress who solves crimes in the village."

"I'm grateful for Harwell Covington."

"Why?"

"Because he's not here. And you are."

I was rewarded with a kiss and then more, but as we reminded each other, old people having sex is vital and life-affirming and to be blurred and cut away from quickly in movies.

Eight days later, I looked up from a weeks-old copy of the *New Yorker* to see Farrell on our uppermost terrace, facing the water and making a lyrical motion with his hands, as if conducting an unseen orchestra or, more likely, the symphony of fine weather, the rough-hewn ceramic jug he'd just arranged with fresh peonies, and our new roof, which had been overdue. A few minutes later I heard a noise, as if Farrell had stubbed his toe, or shooed away the feral cat that had been skulking around the neighborhood, or spied a throw pillow out of place.

When I went to find him, I peered down at his body sprawled on the lowest terrace, with his head twisted against the cliffside. I called Farrell's name and I could hear the rising dread in my voice.

As I waited for the ambulance to arrive, I wasn't sure if I should cradle Farrell or if that might increase his injuries, or if he was already gone, since he wasn't breathing or responding in any way. I thought I'd prepared myself for this moment, given Farrell's medical history, but all I felt was a shrieking, raw panic, a need to scream, Not yet, not now, you promised. The sky was still its customary cloudless blue, the bougainvillea vine was still wafting lightly in the breeze, and the feral cat was idly considering the two men who occasionally fed her scraps from their lunches. Except one of the men was . . . no, it wasn't true, I wouldn't let it be true. How could I stop this, what favor could I call in? What additional miracle could I demand? This was a mistake, a nightmare, a concussion, anything not final. Our story couldn't end here.

According to the doctor who examined the body at our local hospital, Farrell had died instantly of a broken neck. There was no evidence of foul play or suicide, which I already knew. "He was older," the doctor said, "he may have had balance problems, and his records indicate he was HIV-positive." It had become a mark of strange pride, when a gay man our age died of something other than AIDS. Dr. Jarvis spoke with the Italian authorities, confirmed the cause of death, and I scheduled a flight back to New York.

On the plane, I thought about how I'd freeze time, to the seconds before Farrell had died, so I could steady him. I had no interest in being young again and re-meeting Farrell at Yale. I wanted him back just as he was. Or I wanted to die and surprise him, in a heaven that resembled either La Rondinaia or some Bavarian hunting lodge or partially intact Greek temple Farrell had happened upon. I wanted to be anywhere but on a plane with an urn of his ashes in my luggage. He'd specified cremation because "I'll always be in demand, so I don't want some mortician's assistant having sex with my corpse. Not without a corsage and a moonlit swim."

The Park Avenue apartment was echoing and airless, as if we hadn't lived there for centuries. I wasn't demented, hallucinating Farrell doing yoga stretches or computer searches for William Morris fireplace tongs in another room, but I did envision a portal, some slash in the time/space continuum, hanging in midair, that I could squeeze through to locate him.

There were extensive obituaries in the *Times* and the *Wall Street Journal*, along with an in-depth piece on the *Vanity Fair* website describing Farrell as the Secret Covington. The family's contributions to repellently right-wing candidates and causes were covered (Ingrid was howlingly anti-abortion and pro–voter suppression), in opposition to Farrell's largesse with AIDS organizations, inner-city education, global human rights, and the arts. He'd never dissected his estrangement from his family in the press, telling me, "That isn't the idea. I don't need to spill everything. The idea is to let Ingrid worry that I might." Farrell's Wichita childhood was cited along with his educational background, at Yale and Amherst, and his stature as an architectural authority, a collector of rare homes, and the longtime partner of writer Nate Reminger. Farrell hadn't sought media attention. His wealth and upbringing had made it taboo, and his brush with rom-com stardom had nudged him press-shy. He'd appear in portraits, and in the photos accompanying my interviews, where he'd concentrate on the lighting, griping, "Why is there a shadow across my chin? I look asymmetrical."

Farrell's memorial was held at an Episcopal church a block from the apartment, not out of any religious conviction, but because Farrell had loved the building. "It's a pocket cathedral," he'd said, "like a fun-size St. Patrick's. For when I tell God we'll catch up later, once I'm not so overbooked."

The pews were full, with friends and the people Farrell had engaged to oversee the multiple districts of his life. There were diligent staff members from his foundation who'd been with Farrell for decades; seam-stresses and stonemasons from the houses he'd renovated, whom he'd kept continuously employed and who'd flown in from all over the world; students like Sten who'd received financial assistance; Farrell's research team and his dry cleaner and the eighty-nine-year-old Swiss gentleman who made his work boots. No one attended out of obligation. People had loved working with Farrell, because he remembered birthdays, favorite hand-dipped chocolates, and the names of everyone's pets. As I greeted mourners by the door, Brett appeared, alone.

Brett's own life had been torpedoed. After decades of producing increas-ingly well-thought-of films, from idiosyncratic directors, and adventurous Broadway shows, often by playwrights of color, his workplace misdeeds had caught up with him. Journalists, and most especially the internet, had been prowling for incidents of abuse, and Brett had thrown staplers at his assistants' heads, belittled them relentlessly, and sent at least one hapless twenty-three-year-old to the hospital, after Brett had forcibly closed a lap-top on his hand. Despite settlements and nondisclosure agreements, these repeated transgressions had come to light, and Brett had issued a state-ment, taking an early retirement.

Farrell's memorial was, in fact, the first time I'd seen Brett since his downfall. While I couldn't defend him, I'd known how desperately he'd pushed himself, and I remembered him as the outsider who'd lost fifty pounds, seemingly overnight, in a bid to please a savagely mercurial world. While I hadn't worked with Brett for years, I couldn't disown him. Farrell had once said, "Brett always behaves as if something awful's about to happen, and if he just works ten times harder and screams louder and punishes someone, maybe it won't."

"Hey," said Brett, aware that he might not be welcome.

"Thank you for being here," I said. "Please don't throw anything."

He smiled, painfully, and said, "Farrell was a good guy. And a total flake, which I mean as a compliment."

"Oy," I said, the only word that could begin to cover my loss and Brett's travails.

"Oy is right," said Brett, heading toward a seat in a corner. He was an outcast but not a criminal. Harwell would've considered him an amateur.

Jess and Jackson sat together down front beside other friends from school, while Ariadne, still toned and limber, flagged from the pulpit as Farrell's touchstone dance music played, songs downloaded from a span of over forty years (the minister had been bribed). Jackson had kept his word and created a second portrait of Farrell, who'd sat for him during a visit at La Rondinaia. The watercolor depicted an older but still dazzling Farrell, with a fragility, as a battered Dionysus, his green eyes still glinting with beckoning, I'm-not-done-yet mischief. This framed portrait had been placed on an easel, which rose from the hundreds of flowers Farrell had specified when he'd been hospitalized after blacking out in our bathroom: "I want daisies and bluebells, nothing funereal, no roses or lilies or, I can't even say it, carnations. Why would anyone ever want a flower with the word 'car' in it? Carnations can only be sent on Mother's Day, to make sure your mom remembers you hate her."

My parents had died five years earlier, within weeks of each other, from cancer (throat and ovarian). They'd been regulars at La Rondinaia. They'd gushed over the house, but the maze of steep stairways had rattled them. I should've heeded their apprehension. What my mom had loved most was the fact that Farrell and I were together at last, in a suitable home, "like human beings." My parents had been puzzled by Farrell's transcontinental excursions and our separations, because our relationship hadn't duplicated their own. "You're entitled to your ideas," my mom had said, "and we respect that, even if they're *meshuggenah*, which means fucking crazy." Ever since I'd come out, my mom had sworn freely at me, something I'd prized, as it meant she'd relinquished any vision of herself as an example. "Don't listen to your mother," my father had once told me, when we were alone. "Live your own lives, and keep sending us pictures of Farrell's houses, because we're doing a scrapbook."

The Remingers were represented by my brother, Max, two years my senior, although the word "senior" now applied to me and half the people in attendance. After leaving Piscataway at seventeen, Max had dabbled in motorcycles (buying, riding, rewiring, and selling them), odd jobs (minor plumbing and spackling), but mostly in shoring up a backwoods home near Albany, making a subsistence living, meeting smart, amenable women, and pursuing a bucolic life. Once, before he dropped out of high school, I'd asked him what he wanted to be and he said, without hesitation, "Retired."

Max had made a rocky peace with my parents, driving his van to New Jersey for a few hours of détente until my mom nagged him about community college and he'd take off. He and I hadn't been close, although his defiance had marked me. He'd been either switched at birth with a more circumspect Jewish child, or he was an anomaly, a resolutely free spirit. We'd speak on our birthdays, and he was interested in my career, and in Farrell, without prying or envy. We had little in common. He despised New York, and his hair and beard flowed to his waist, for a Hell's Angel/conspiracy theorist élan. Today he'd made an effort (which would've pleased our mother), wearing his sole necktie on a denim shirt beneath his denim jacket. His outfit was threadbare and stained from actual labor, rather than workwear chic.

"So, you doin' okay?" he asked me.

"So far."

"Farrell was a good dude. I liked him."

"Me too."

"Yeah, that's why I liked him. He made you happy and he didn't take any shit."

Which was exactly right, and after an awkward hug, Max doffed his grease-spotted engineer's cap and took a seat.

Gerald Whitby, who was Terrence's twin brother and the president of Farrell's foundation, spoke first, praising Farrell's generosity. "Farrell had so much money," said Gerald, "and he loved to give it away. Sometimes we had to stop him, from answering every letter with a check, because many of the requests are fraudulent. Farrell would say, 'But I love their handwriting. Anyone who knows cursive deserves something.'"

Adrienne, Farrell's longtime director of research, called Farrell "my hero. If it wasn't for him, I'd be locked in a museum toting up inventories that no one would care about. Farrell made everything so vivid. When I showed him an original charcoal drawing of the front doors at Castle LaSorde, Farrell looked at it and told me, 'I just came.'"

Sally had hit town the night before. She'd been traveling, too. In the years since Mother Teresa died, Sally had been designated the order's goodwill ambassador and go-to fundraiser, with optimal results, thanks to her fresh-scrubbed glamour, friendship with Mother T, and approachable spirituality. Today she wore a modified habit, which Jackson had designed. It was a short-sleeved white linen sheath with her cherished three blue stripes at the collar and hem. Her hair, in a long blond braid threaded with silver, caught the light, and her face, while lined, still radiated humor and devotion. With a slight swagger she told the crowd, "I'm Farrell's wife. I know. It was a perfect marriage because we almost never saw each other. But in all the ways that count, we loved each other. And Farrell loved Nate beyond all imagining. When I was having an especially trying day, I would think of Farrell and Nate together, and I'd feel better, remembering that laughter and rehabilitated Swiss chalets and some really skimpy bathing suits were out there, somewhere."

Sally kissed my cheek as I replaced her behind the podium. Amid so many faces, there they were: Ingrid, Bolt, and Wainwright. I'd had Devin Llewellyn notify them of Farrell's death, and include the time and date of the memorial, but I hadn't heard from any of them. Ingrid was smaller, a shrunken doll in her black coatdress with a stiff rounded white collar and a pearl circle pin. Bolt was bulkier, with his glower permanently affixed, while Wainwright was slimmer, with a fashionable haircut and could it be—tears in his eyes?

"I . . . I'm not sure I can . . . ," I began, not as an opening gambit but because I was unable to speak. As I raised a palm to telegraph whatever self-control I could muster, I heard Farrell commenting, "That hand thing is a nice touch. We're talking Daytime Emmy. Keep going." I took the deepest breath of my life and said, "I met Farrell when we were both eighteen, and we've never been apart, except for years at a time. It was clear, from the beginning, that we'd make our own rules and ignore them, that Farrell was more than likely psychotic, and that if he didn't love me back I would die. No one has ever made me, or everyone else here, so happy. Farrell was an event, a parade float, and a holiday. Not to mention easy on the eyes. He told me to say that. I just . . ."

I was losing it again, and clenched my fists so I'd continue.

"I just . . . There were days, when I was about to lose Farrell. Because we'd lost so many friends. And each time Farrell went into the hospital, I'd walk myself through the worst and most realistic outcome: that he wouldn't be coming home. And each time I couldn't do it. I couldn't imagine my life, or the world, without Farrell. And not just because he could drive me up the wall."

Dr. Jarvis was seated behind Jess. I'd met him at the door, and he'd been more of a mess than me, saying, "I wish I'd been there in Italy, in case there was something I could've done." I told him how grateful Farrell and I had been, for his endless ministrations, and now he was smiling at me, and giving a thumbs-up, to help me finish my speech.

"But if you loved Farrell, you loved all of him. And I did. And I always will. And I need to stop talking. Except, oh, one more thing, because Farrell would get so angry if I forgot to announce this. And when he got angry, terrible things would happen, involving Farrell begging strangers on the street to critique my shirt, honestly.

"So here goes: Farrell's great-aunt Mirielle wasn't as lucky as we were. She fell in love, and the world turned its back. There's a grand Gothic Revival house in Newport, Rhode Island, where Mirielle might've been happy, with the woman she cared about so deeply. But that house sat empty for decades, until it was sold, but rarely occupied, as a vacation place for a tech guru who decided it was too fussy. Two years ago, Farrell was able to buy the house back, for some preposterous amount. But Farrell being Farrell, that didn't matter. He had plans for that house. Which has been refurbished and will open next month as the Farrell Covington Center for LGBTQ Studies, with residencies and study materials and speakers and seminars, all overseen by the very young and capable Sten Hauser. So Farrell's work goes on. Thank you all for being here."

As the crowd applauded, Sten beamed. I'd contacted them about the job a few days after Farrell died, for a sense of ongoing Farrell-ness. I resumed my place near the church door, for tears and embraces, as people filed out.

At the best cast parties, for plays everyone cares about, the festivities can last till dawn because no one wants to leave, and break the spell. Farrell's memorial was like that, because everyone had an anecdote they wanted to relate, or needed to express disbelief at Farrell being gone, sometimes by only saying, "Fuck." Sally held my hand, which wasn't like either of us, but her support was vital, as Ingrid and her sons descended on us. "That was fine," said Bolt, not shaking my hand. "It's sad he's gone." He patted Sally on the shoulder as Ingrid and I squared off.

"So," she said, "you won."

"Yes I did. But not enough."

"What do you mean?"

"Farrell's not here."

"Ah. Of course. I can't forgive you."

"I'm not asking you to."

"But I'm glad, that you and Farrell were . . . what you were."

"Do it," I heard Farrell hiss, "ask her, 'Who are you and what have you done with Ingrid Covington?'"

"Thank you for that," I told Ingrid, although I'd been tempted to go full Farrell.

"But may I tell you something?"

"Why not?"

Ingrid's eyes glittered as she averred, "Happiness is overrated."

I loved her for this, as Farrell had paid homage to his father's meanness. The Covington iciness was an undeniable accomplishment, a fastidiously tended monument to willful repression, a granite plinth with a statue of a faceless giant refusing dessert.

"Our lawyers will be emailing you," Bolt interjected.

"I'm prepared," I said, because I was. Devin had briefed me on what to expect. Farrell had left an ironclad will. If the Covingtons sued, Devin had the damning files on Harwell in reserve. In fact, he could present them in short order, because he was two feet behind the Covingtons, smiling at me, with his husband, a high school music teacher. Farrell and I had been at their wedding.

"I'm so sorry," said Wainwright, with an unexpected hug, as Bolt escorted Ingrid to their car. "Can I call you? Would that be okay?"

"Of course."

"I just wanted to let you know, and Sally, that my kids are grown now and I'm recently divorced. I'm still working for the company, but I'd really like to assist with Farrell's foundation, in any way I can. And this is my girlfriend Emma."

Emma was younger than Wainwright (in her fifties) and I was pretty sure she was Jewish, which would be another blow for Ingrid.

"I'm so sorry for your loss," said Emma. "Wain says Farrell was terrific."

"You guys inspired me," Wainwright whispered, so Ingrid and Bolt wouldn't overhear. Then he hugged me again, kissed Sally on the cheek, and followed his family.

"Whoa," I told Sally.

"Wain's a good egg. And for a Covington, he's gone wild."

"Can you hang out? At Joe Allen?"

Joe Allen was a theater district restaurant, heir to the late, much-lamented Charlie's. I'd reserved a secluded rear table, where Sally and I joined Jess, Ariadne, and Jackson.

"Well, this sucks," said Ariadne to a general consensus.

"But there's an upside," said Jess. "With Farrell not here as a comparison, we all look better."

"Valid," I said.

"I will only comment," said Jackson, "that it was a lovely memorial and Ingrid and Bolt snubbed me, although Wainwright was shockingly nice."

"So who gets his money?" asked Ariadne, and we all expressed outrage until she said, "Oh fuck off, we're all thinking about it. I just don't want his repulsive family to get their claws on it."

"I talked to Devin," I said, "and he says the Covingtons will come at me with all they've got, but they don't have any standing. And I'm being assigned Farrell's voting rights on the Covington board."

"Even though you weren't married?" asked Ariadne.

"Farrell had everything spelled out. And no matter how much cash he spent and donated, the Covington Industries profits keep rolling in. I'll be inheriting half of Farrell's estate, with the rest going to Farrell's foundation."

I'd been lofty about never taking money from Farrell, with gaping loopholes for our homes and the transportation he'd contributed. I'd made my own living, but as he'd alerted me, "I'm leaving you a bundle, which you can spread around wherever you'd like. But please keep a decent slice in trust for clean underwear and a hairbrush. I promised your mother."

"There are bequests for each of you," I told the group at Joe Allen's. "With funds marked for Sally's personal use, and a major donation to Mother T's organization."

"But Sally's a saint," Ariadne said. "She doesn't need money."

"Of course I do," Sally chided her. "For day-old bread. And I've got my eye on a crude wooden bowl."

"I knew it!" cackled Ariadne. "You whore!"

"And I've put La Rondinaia on the market."

Everyone vociferously objected, because the villa was so beautiful, Farrell and I had been so happy there, and they were fishing for future invitations.

"I can't go back," I said. "Not after what happened to Farrell. It's enchanted, but no. There are things I couldn't get past. And I'm having the other houses signed over this year, to the various governments and historical trusts. Farrell was going to wait, but I don't want the properties to decline. This way they'll be kept up."

Rebekah wafted over, lifting her arms in supplication, like a Greek prophetess before a blazing pedestal. She was crowding ninety but clad in a style that Farrell had called "eternal actress": everything was fluid, featherweight, and a slimming black, with ropes of egg-sized amber beads and hammered-gold discs on swaying chains. Her signature haystack of hair was more or less intact and more or less hers. Her makeup was more pronounced, on loan from either the ebullient madam of a whorehouse or a turbaned storefront psychic.

"My darling!" she cried, stroking my cheek. "Poor Farrell! I was desolate when I heard! Is the memorial tomorrow?"

"It was today, Mom," said Jess amiably. "I told you. I put it on your phone."

"Oh no! I'm awful! I've let everyone down! And look at you, all of you! I remember when you were babies, we were all infants, and now . . . Time is a thief."

The well-fed gentleman she'd been dining with, who was undoubtedly wooing her for a role, was calling for the check, so Rebekah kissed me and departed, as if mysterious dark forces were yanking her backward.

"I'm so sorry," said Jess. "I'm just glad she remembered Farrell's name."

"She's . . . still Rebekah," I said.

"So where will you live?" asked Jackson.

I was about to invent an answer, but instead I looked at everyone, as Rebekah had dictated. We were shuffling toward grizzled, but when old people view their friends, they see them as they were. I wasn't fooling myself, denying the sagging eyelids, stubborn pounds, and high collars shielding crepey necks. But I knew who we'd been, so I factored that in.

We were ourselves, only closer to death. Jess had become an awarded and much-employed character actress, with a long-running stint as a by-the-book yet forgiving police chief on a classic series. Ariadne was a certified substance abuse counselor, consulting at shelters and prisons throughout the city. Jackson had five Tonys, or was it six, and he oversaw a full-floor atelier, with eight assistants to handle the touring companies, commissioned gowns, and ballets, along with the quirkier off-Broadway plays Jackson still designed for free.

Jess had a twenty-three-year-old daughter fresh out of drama school. Ariadne had cycled through relationships, some lasting years; and Jackson was also a visiting professor at the Yale Drama School and the New York Fashion Institute, and had a second home in South Carolina.

We had a shorthand, and an instinct for when to cluck over each other and when to let things go. I was sliding along that spectrum but unsure where I'd land.

"Nate?" repeated Jackson, as he slid a manila envelope across the table in my direction. "I've been meaning to give this to you."

The envelope contained an eight-by-ten photo of a group of young actors onstage, in what seemed like a somber Russian drama, complete with heavy armchairs and a samovar.

"It's a senior thesis production from the drama school," said Jackson. "Designed by one of my students. Do you recognize anything?"

I studied the photo. One of the actors was wearing my bearskin coat, which I'd donated before graduating. The coat was now over a hundred years old. It had survived Farrell.

"Sweetie, are you okay?" asked Sally.

"I was just thinking," I told her, "we're both widows."

I got back to Park Avenue after midnight and fell onto the couch, in the dark, without removing my current coat, a Burberry tweed extravagance that Farrell had lobbied for. Could my biography be told entirely through outerwear? "I love that idea," I imagined Farrell commenting. Maybe I could sit here forever, waiting up for him, like a petulant, unforgiving parent. The day had been a respite from thinking about anything except rote social behavior. I was alone in a way I'd never been since I was eighteen years old.

Since Farrell died, I'd been vigilant. I'd tiptoed around his absence, as if by never truly accepting its finality, I'd be safe, or at least permanently numb. But now everyone, my friends, the remnants of my family, and any distracting strangers, had departed. It was just me without Farrell. I tried comforting myself, by invoking gratitude for the decades we'd shared. Which was more avoidance, more meaninglessly embossed script on a drugstore sympathy card. Farrell was gone. I hadn't just loved Farrell: he'd defined me. I'd craved being worthy of him. He'd guided every decision. Even when we were battling, I'd felt so lucky. I needed Farrell's arms around me, and his delicious scorn. I hated the world.

Farrell gazing into my eyes at the Cross Campus Library. Farrell fucking me, that first night at his townhouse. Farrell materializing after the opening of *Enter Hamlet* and saving my life. Farrell in Wichita, vanquishing his family. Farrell always so many steps ahead, shaping my life, surprising me with a French castle, challenging me to do better because he believed I could, and allowing me to love him.

As Farrell had vomited on himself while being wheeled into the emergency room on a gurney, he'd said: "The limits of style." If he'd died that night, I would've granted that our shared belief in the transcendence of meticulously composed offhand gestures and a slouchy linen cardigan was small and ineffective, a very few notes in a minor key, even an insult to suffering. And there were so many people back then, and every day in human history, whose gregarious spirits and innate knack for tilting a fedora couldn't save them.

And yet. How could I keep Farrell alive, not as a crippling delusion but as, maybe, a guiding spirit—or was that the name of a canceled soap opera? The gloom was everywhere, and this would be my life, for however long it lasted, a soulless murk.

Who was I without Farrell? An afterthought? A lesser half? Or was I simply an ache, a hollowness, someone far too aware that his luck had run out, and that from now on, I'd be reduced to myself. I could feel Farrell slapping me, and jeering at my Richter-scale self-pity, but fuck him. He'd left me, so I no longer had to listen. I only had to sob, defiantly and help-lessly, on a couch where we'd napped together, where I'd nursed him, a couch he'd chosen, so it now felt not inviting and cozily familiar but alien, a relic, much like me. With Farrell beside me, I had an ally and a history, someone who knew everything about me and loved me anyway. Without him I became, for the first time, truly old. I didn't want to be here. I didn't want to be anywhere. I wondered, how do people get through this, and I knew instantly: they don't.

My eyes fell on a tin ladle, which rested on a sideboard near the Hock-ney. The ladle had been a gift from Mother Gregory, mailed to me after *I Dare You* had opened, with a note reading, "Congratulations. You're of use." And also, "Say hello to your cute boyfriend." I'd written back to thank her, and we'd emailed occasionally, mostly arguing over Oscar nominees (we'd both been staunch Judi Dench fans). She'd died eight years earlier, of natural causes, at her California convent. With so few sisters in residence, the buildings and land had subsequently been sold to a teenage pop star, who'd put in a pool and a yoga studio. I'd heard from Mother Gregory shortly before her death. She'd sent me a photo of her much younger self, sitting beside Elvis on a movie set, with the caption "Jealous?"

I sensed it. Not Farrell's presence, or Mother Gregory's, but a com-mand, an instruction, maybe from both. I switched on a few lights and slid back the door to Farrell's walk-in closet, large enough to require a municipal government and a marching band. I stood at the center, beside the mahogany island, where Farrell would coordinate outfits, adding or subtracting an overshirt or set of cuff links, assuring his accessories, "All woven leather belts are not crafts projects." Farrell's personal mastery had sworn by costly, effortless understatement, but he'd cultivated a ward-robe, a Farrell Covington collection. I touched the sleeve of one of five tuxedos, from disparate eras. I inhaled a gray cashmere crewneck, five-ply but weightless. Was this Farrell's tomb? Could I be buried in his pyramid beside these treasured garments? Or was every item a cruel reminder, of the brightest events, of Farrell turning to me, and me catching my breath, not just at how great he looked, but at his eternal optimism, the beacon of his personality, and his willingness to kiss me, right before we'd leave the apartment, because there was no one more romantic. If Farrell had a religion, beyond architecture and vocabulary, it was romance. It was his insistence on making the world gleam. It was us, or the us he'd imagined and we'd spent our lives becoming.

I considered trying something on but didn't, because I'd be lumpy and askew, since I wasn't Farrell.

Because I was alone in a soundproof chamber, I did it. I sang, in a croaking whisper, to reduce total humiliation, even in private:

> *I never thought there'd be someone*
> *Who'd make me become someone new*
> *I never thought I'd wish on a star*
> *I always assumed that I'd watch from afar*
> *I never dreamed you'd be here in my arms*
> *But you are*

I smiled, at the arch melancholy, the self-indulgence, the tattered, discount-bin album cover with my airbrushed face gazing moodily off camera, titled *Nate Reminger in a Blue Mood*. Farrell was here. Farrell would always be here. Style has no limits. Which is such a gay thing to say.

Acknowledgments

This book was written after I'd lived a good long time, and wanted to at least begin to make sense of things. And while it's entirely a work of fiction, it was inspired by many people and events, including a man I met on a train going from New York back to my hometown in New Jersey. I was a teenager interviewing at colleges, hovering between innocence and ignorance, and someone, whose name I never learned and whom I never saw again, struck up a conversation, not in any way sexual. This man offered sage advice about life and my future, and I sadly remember no specifics. What I do remember was that he was extraordinarily handsome, tan in November, and that he carried the most impressive piece of luggage I've ever seen, a most likely custom-made, discreetly gold monogrammed, unstructured dark leather bag. All of this made a curious and significant impression: he was generous-spirited, chatty with a stranger, and seemed to hail from a distant, intelligent, sophisticated world that I could only dream of. He wasn't Farrell Covington, but he possessed Farrell's confidence, humor, and, yes, style, in being utterly and magnetically himself.

In helping this book take shape and find a home, I'd like to thank my superb editor, Peter Borland, and my supremely gifted agent, Esmond Harmsworth, along with the wonderfully generous folks at Atria, including Libby McGuire, Sean deLone, Laywan Kwan, and Elizabeth Byer.

Above all, and as always, I'd like to thank my partner, John Raftis, who told me I've already dedicated too many books to him. I'm grateful for his patience, his strength, and his courage, not to mention his skills in driving, baking, gardening, and, just when I think he's going to say something annoying, saying something calming, sane, and thoughtful instead.